## SOLWAY SLEUTH-

### The First Recruit

Mystery and adventure in south west Scotland at the end of the 18th century.

With her husband in jail young Gretna Marshall, one of the Galloway travelling people, is feeling alone and vulnerable so she is delighted when she is asked to become the first recruit to the Solway Sleuth-Hounds, the Laird of Longcrags' band of private investigators. She is relieved to have found the protection of a powerful patron but all too soon she finds that the service of the Laird means danger. But with the help of the remarkable Sawney, the young lawyer of the future, stern Michael the leader of a tribe of tinklers, and Rooskie her little dog who brings his own individual talents to the pack, Gretna struggles on.

The story moves between the Solway shore, Dumfries and the notorious village of the Bridgend with its underground labyrinth of cellars, that hiding place for refugees and felons.

These were turbulent times and the Sleuth-Hounds find themselves involved with Solway smugglers, Robert Burns, the effects of the French Revolution, even the Jacobite Rebellion of 1745 although it happened fifty years earlier.

The historical background of 18th century Dumfries and Galloway has been carefully researched and there are detailed historical notes and sketch maps.

*Solway Sleuth-Hounds* is more than just an exciting story. It is also a fun way of learning history.

12 - adult

Evelyn McKinnell

The Mid Steeple, Dumfries 1790

Mary S Moffat has also written

Ghost Dog of the Solway
The Canine Cavalier
Historical Fiction for Children. A Bibliography. (Reference).

WEB SITE

**http://www.marysmoffat.co.uk/**

Mary has a very comprehensive web site which is being constantly updated.

The site gives details of her other books. There is a section about the founding of the Rooskie Press and an ongoing Rooskie Press newsletter which is updated every month.

There is also a section with photographs of the Solway coast — which forms part of the background of *Sleuth-Hounds*.

Another section gives biographical details about Mary herself.

One of her interests is dog training and there is a large dog section with pictures and information about her Papillons. There are also links to other web sites.

Also on her web site is a bibliography — *Historical Fiction for Children*. This is not just a list of books. There is a synopsis and a detailed note for every book. The Bibliography is also updated frequently.

## Acknowledgements

I would like to thank, firstly, Alex Gerrard for the proof reading and editorial advice; and especially for his patience and help over the last few years.

And then my artists.

Evelyn McKinnell for the front cover, and the frontpiece.

Halla Whittier Valentine - DeLeon for the inside pictures of Gretna with Lucy and Rooskie. And also of Lucy and Rooskie by themselves.

Christine Dickman of California for all her encouragement

And lastly Margaret Hogg of the dog class and owner of Charlie, Cavalier King Charles spaniel, for saying that my books are *a fun way to learn history.*

# SOLWAY SLEUTH-HOUNDS

## The First Recruit

by

Mary S. Moffat

http://www.marysmoffat.co.uk/

Illustrations

Cover design — River Design
Front cover illustration and frontpiece — Evelyn McKinnell
Internal illustrations – Halla Whittier Valentine - DeLeon
Photographs of Dumfries and Southerness – Mary S Moffat

Rooskie Press

First published in Great Britain in 2005 by the Rooskie Press

ISBN     0-9551477-0-0

         978-0-9551477-0-8


Printed and bound in Great Britain by Antony Rowe Ltd for the Rooskie Press



Rooskie Press,
32 Moffat Road,
Dumfries,
Scotland.
DG1 1NY
UK

# Contents

## Grandfather's Story

## Illustrations

# THE FACTS BEHIND THE STORY

## PROLOGUE

## THE SOLWAY SLEUTH-HOUNDS

I have decided that it is finally time for me to organise a permanent record of the startling events of my childhood, events in which I myself played a small part. The Solway Sleuth-Hounds – that determined band founded by my father – deserve to be remembered and now I am going to make sure that their work is not forgotten.

I was brought up on the Longcrags Estate near Dumfries in south west Scotland. Longcrags lies partly on the lower slopes of Crowfell – or, as it is sometimes called, Criffel – that hill which overlooks the western side of the Solway Firth.

My father, Gilbert Aitken, was a justice of the peace and the Laird of Longcrags. To help him in his duties he recruited his own company of investigators. He chose them carefully. All were people who could move about freely and make their enquiries where members of the rich and influential classes would only arouse suspicion and hostility. For this reason many of the Sleuth-Hounds were travelling people or tinklers who had access to their own sources of information and also had wide ranging connections.

The Sleuth-Hounds formed a pack and all the members worked together and supported each other. They all brought to the pack their individual strengths and each member made his or her special contribution.

This all began in the 1790s, a time when smugglers sailed across the Solway and landed their secret cargoes at dead of night, when Robert Burns, exciseman and poet, wrote *Tam o'*

*Shanter* and searched for contraband. It was a time when many stared uneasily over the dark water to where the French Revolution cast its shadow over the whole of Europe.

And in the recent past was the Jacobite Rebellion of 1745. Yet, although it happened over fifty years ago, the Sleuth-Hounds still found themselves caught up in its aftermath.

My father soon found that his intrepid Sleuth-Hounds worked well as a pack. But then he began to wonder if they were perhaps not *too* efficient as they began to reveal the secrets of his own family, secrets which my parents would have preferred to remain forgotten.

Anyway, enough of this. Here are the first of the Sleuth-Hounds. More recruits joined them later, as you will learn.

## GRETNA MARSHALL

Gretna Marshall was one of the Galloway tinklers and she was the first recruit. Her first case concerned an indiscretion committed by the noted poet Robert Burns, and her second involved my sister Charlotte, who was, in time, to become herself the most remarkable of the Sleuth-Hounds.

At first the arrangement seemed ideal for both Gretna and my father. Gretna's husband was in jail and she had been left alone, unprotected and vulnerable. But she now had a wealthy patron, and, as far as my father was concerned, Gretna could call upon the wide knowledge of the travelling people and go where a more conventional investigator would be unwelcome, if not actually in danger.

But things did not work out exactly as my father had planned. Gretna turned out to have a flair for her new work and she also uncovered some secrets about the Aitken family itself.

Also, she was not really a tinkler. She had run away from home and married at Gretna Green. Afterwards, to show that she was making a clean break with her old life, she changed her name to Gretna. But what was her real name and what was her story?

## ALEXANDER McBEAN

Commonly called Sawney Bean, after the leader of the legendary clan of cannibals. How he hated that nickname! How he wished people would address him as Alexander!

Sawney – the name he had to settle for – was the second of the Sleuth-Hounds.

When it all started he was only fifteen, but he was small for his age and looked more like twelve. This was a great hardship for him as he had a mature mind trapped in the body of a little boy. He worked as a clerk in the Dumfries office of Mr Gordon, Writer to the Signet, my father's agent and legal advisor. Sawney was ambitious and did not intend to be a clerk all his life. He hoped to become a law apprentice and that my father would pay for him to study at Glasgow University. But my father would not do that until Sawney grew a bit. As he was, he was far too useful to the Sleuth-Hounds. Adults are expected to have grounds for their actions but it is generally accepted that boys do all sorts of strange things for no apparent reason at all. A boy could act in a way which would be questioned in someone older. Sawney's best disguise was himself.

But as time passed I found myself increasingly asking one question? Why was Sawney so sure that my father would pay for his legal studies?

## MICHAEL MARSHALL

The leader of a band of travelling people and Gretna's brother-in-law. I gradually found out that Michael had a long time understanding with my father.

## ROOSKIE

Gretna's little dog. He used to belong to my mother but my father gave him to Gretna, and she changed his name to Rooskie because she wanted him to have a gypsy name. Rooskie is gypsy-tinkler cant for 'basket' and Gretna called him that because he was small enough to go into a tinkler's basket.

Rooskie may have been small and appealing but he turned out to be a true member of the Sleuth-Hounds in his own right.

## ISABEL AITKEN

My mother. Outwardly calm and ladylike, but this demeanour masked an astute mind and a steely determination. My father thought that the idea of the Sleuth-Hounds came from him, but he was wrong. The idea came from my mother, but it suited her to let my father believe otherwise.

It was my mother who was the true leader of the pack.

Now that I have introduced the Sleuth-Hounds it is time for some of their work. Sawney – how like a lawyer – always has the most to say but, as the Sleuth-Hounds started with Gretna, then I shall let the lady have the first word.

I hope you enjoy these records of a remarkable group of people.

As I sit here at my desk I think how lucky I am to live in such a beautiful part of the country. Behind me Criffel stands clearly etched against the sky. Below me I can see the blue waters of the Solway where Charlotte and I still often gallop along the shore and where, out in the Firth, one can hear the waves beating against the Barnhourie Sandbank – or, as my sister would prefer it – the singing of the Barnhourie mermaid.

But now over to Gretna.

Struan Aitken,
Laird of Longcrags,
Dumfries. 1840

# CHAPTER 1

## THE POWER OF PERSUASION

I looked at her carefully as she entered my cell. I had seen her type before – countless times. Quietly but expensively dressed in a dark green riding habit, a wealthy lady bringing comfort and solace to the unfortunate prisoners – or calling on the sinners to repent and praying with them.

Just another way in which the rich amuse themselves.

I was soon to find that I was quite wrong. Mrs Isabel Aitken, wife of Gilbert Aitken, Laird of Longcrags, had come, not to give help, but to ask for it.

I sat up on my bed of straw and gazed at her in amazement. She was the last person I would have expected to see in my cell.

The jailer saw what he thought was a good chance to impress an influential lady like Mrs Aitken. He was going to show her that he could control his prisoners. Suddenly I felt the toe of his boot against my ribs.

"On your feet, tink. Show some respect for this good lady here."

His kick did not hurt me. It was only a light tap. I suppose I should have been grateful for that small mercy, but I was not. It was almost as if he were saying that I was not even worth a proper kick, that he was not prepared to dirty his boots with me. No his boot did not hurt me but the venom and contempt with which he spat out the term of abuse, 'tink' really made me wince. But, cruel as his words had been, they at least lacked the coarseness, vulgarity and profanity of his usual language. Mindful of the presence of a lady the turnkey was making a determined attempt to 'speak proper.' And there are certain words a lady must never hear! While he was at it he also modified his broad Scots tongue. But his speech was all that was affected. There was no change in the hard, cruel way in which he treated his prisoners.

I made to get up but I was not quick enough for him.

"Do you hear me? Move. At once, you cur."

He turned to Mrs Aitken and said,

"You've got to be firm with her kind. I know she does not look it but this particular one can be a bit of a firebrand. But don't you worry. I can handle her. I'll see she does not give you any trouble."

I rose slowly to my feet. As I did so I glanced at Mrs Aitken and I noticed the quick look of anger and utter disgust which crossed her face. Then she got control of herself again and spoke sharply.

"Jailer, you do not need to worry about me. I well know how to get the respect which is due to me – whether from my own servants, the workers on my husband's lairdship or any visiting tinklers. I would appreciate it if you would let me deal with Mrs Marshall in my own way."

I listened to all this with great interest. This sounded promising, very promising indeed.

The jailer realised he had misjudged Mrs Aitken and had made a big mistake. He hastened to make amends.

"Very sorry, I'm sure, Mrs Aitken. I should have realised that a lady like yourself would have no trouble controlling the lower classes."

I brushed the straw from my dress. Anything to give myself time to think; time to clear my mind. A few moments ago I had been feeling particularly despondent, but now, with Mrs Aitken, hope had entered my cell. To her the visit might just be a form of diversion which had the added virtue of making her feel good, but, nevertheless, I might be able to use her appearance to my advantage. So long as I watched my runaway tongue.

I was just newly turned eighteen and feeling alone and vulnerable. Two years ago, after a quarrel with my mother, I had run away from home and married one of the Galloway tinklers. I had been so determined to make a complete break with my old life that I had even changed my name – to Gretna after Gretna Green where I had been married. At first all had gone well and we were both blissfully happy. Then my Danny had been arrested and thrown into prison. He had always dealt with the business of all relevant licenses – pedlar, wagon etc. – but there was some discrepancy and, with him in jail, it was found that I was not covered. So I too was arrested and thrown into jail, charged with being a 'vagabond.' All that morning I had lain on my pile of straw trying to work out what I could do. Surely some of the other travelling people would come to my aid? Of course they had never really accepted me. Michael, Danny's oldest brother, had always made it plain that he disapproved of his brother marrying a gadgi or house-dweller. Danny should have married one of his own kind. But even if Michael disapproved of me he could not ignore the fact that I was now his sister-in-law. Why had he not come to see me in the Mid Steeple?

It was probably because of Michael that I had been put in the Mid Steeple of Dumfries in the first place. It is not a jail as such. It is a small building with a clock tower and spire. It was planned as a meeting place for the town council, a repository for the town records — and a jail. All worked out as planned except that the town council decided to meet elsewhere and their place was taken by the justiciary court.

It was always too small for a jail and so the old one continued to be used. But the latter was in a dreadful condition and, what to the authorities was much worse, very insecure. I had probably been put in one of the few cells in the Mid Steeple because it was expected that my friends would help me to escape. But no one had come near me and I was beginning to wonder if I had any friends at all. I had been left alone with my all-too-vivid imagination for company. I knew only too well the treatment that was commonly meted out to tinklers. I could imagine the pain of a public flogging or the searing agony of a burning branding iron being pressed against my cheek. Only if I were lucky could I hope for banishment.

Of course there was one thing which I could do. Return to my own family. They would welcome back their wayward, errant daughter. But on their own terms. I would be exchanging one prison for another. No that was very much a last resort. I had chosen to marry my tinkler husband and I was proud of him, even if the rest of the world regarded him as a worthless wastrel. The thought of going back to my mother's condescending assumption that I had now realised my foolishness – that was unbearable.

But the knowledge that I did have that option would mean that I did not have to accept what Mrs Aitken had to offer me – whatever that was. Unknown to her I did have a lifeline.

I wondered why she was here, when my own family – or rather Danny's – had not come near me. Yet here she was standing in front of me, the wife of the Laird of Longcrags, a lady whom I had never even met. At that time it seemed strange to me but I have since learnt one of life's paradoxes. Very often the people who help you most are those you have least call on. But then, in my bare cell, such thoughts were far from my mind. All I wanted to know was the reason for her visit.

I had to wait for my curiosity to be satisfied.

It was evident that Mrs Aitken was not going to speak to me in front of the turnkey. She needed to get me alone. But the stupid man was too foolish to see that. He stayed and watched carefully as she glanced around the bare, stone-walled cell. A solitary creepie stool, an upturned box which acted as my table, no bed, only some straw on the floor, and one small window which did not open. She looked awkward. She was clearly jolted out of her usual comfortable existence.

The bareness of the room horrified her – and this was something which the shrewd, grasping jailer did not miss. He was obviously the kind who tried to extract every penny possible from the luckless prisoners and their friends. He cleared his throat and carefully started his campaign of extortion.

"As you see Madam, we can afford to provide only the bare necessities, but if, out of the goodness of your heart, you would like to provide some little comforts for the lass, then I am sure that can be arranged. And at a very reasonable cost." He hesitated and added, "A few blankets perhaps?"

He was trying to be respectful and deferential but without success. He sounded exactly what he was, greedy and sly. I saw that Mrs Aitken shared my opinion. We did not need to be told. We could both guess the turnkey's background — a former prisoner who had gained his freedom in return in doing a job which most people would find exceedingly distasteful. There is the common saying — a poacher turned gamekeeper. But a prisoner turned jailer is far more likely. I could see that Mrs Aitken was disgusted by the man's coarseness and obsequious manner.

But the turnkey was too dense to see this. He continued,

"She is the dainty one. Last night she was offered good wholesome beef collops and she refused to eat them. But if Madam wishes to provide something more suitable for her delicate taste then it can be organised. And at a very fair price."

Good wholesome collops he said. I thought back to the mess of fat and gristle covered in lukewarm grease. Why just looking at it had nearly made me feel sick let alone eating it.

I tried to adopt a suitably respectful attitude for Mrs Aitken's benefit. I stood with hands clasped and eyes cast down submissively. At the same time I fought back a desperate urge to scratch. The straw was rough and had irritated my skin. Moreover it was home to several nasty wee beasties who revelled in the taste of human flesh. But it was important for me to maintain my dignity and I suffered the dreadful itch.

The turnkey was still not finished.

"If Madam would like some tea I could have it sent in. And there would be only a small charge."

Mrs Aitken spoke with a quiet dignity, which made her anger all the more frightening.

"I do not like your attitude. I hope you are not trying to exploit your position and take advantage of the unfortunates who have been consigned to your care. I trust I do not need to inform you that my husband is a Justice of the Peace." She paused and then said very deliberately,

"Tea will certainly not be required. I am a busy woman and I want to speak to Mrs Marshall in private."

I looked up quickly. It seemed that I was to find out the reason for Mrs Aitken's visit at last. But I was sorry about the tea. Cold at night, the room was stuffy and airless during the day and dust from the straw hung in the air. I had not slept the night before and now my throat was dry and I had a slight tickle in my throat. I also had a slight headache. Tea would have helped but it was a small matter compared with my other problems. And I would certainly be glad to see the last of the jailer – horrible man.

But we had to wait a moment or two yet before we could get rid of the obnoxious man.

His manner changed and he became very deferential. The mention of a Justice of the Peace had obviously made him fear for his job.

"Of course, Madam. I did not realise I was keeping you. No offence meant Madam. I'll leave you to your business right now."

But Mrs Aitken was not prepared to let him off so lightly. He had tried to take advantage of her – and no one does that to Isabel Aitken. She had one last arrow of anxiety for him and she let it fly.

"One last point. I do not drink *adulterated* tea."

The jailer had been about to open the door but now he turned and said with deep emotion,

"Madam I am distraught and devastated that you could think such a thing of me. I can assure you that I deal only with true and honest merchants who would never dream of diluting their product with sand or any any other harmful substance. I have far too great a respect for … He would have continued but Mrs Aitken interrupted abruptly,

"I repeat. I am a busy woman and I wish to speak to Mrs Marshall in private."

At this the jailer removed himself quickly. Mrs Aitken shuddered as the cell door clashed shut, the key turned in the lock, and, for even greater security, a bolt was rammed home.

Obviously Mrs Aitken was not used to jails. So prison visiting was not one of her pastimes. She had really come specially to see me.

She may not have been used to jails but she still had her wits about her. There was a small grill in the middle of the door. Mrs Aitken went over to it and looked through. She was making sure that the turnkey did not have a chance to eavesdrop. Then she walked back to me.

Now for it. We were alone at last but she did not speak at once. There was an uneasy silence. She seemed to find it difficult to know what to say to me. When she finally managed to get the words out I was absolutely astounded.

"I believe you may be able to help me." A pause and then, "and my husband."

I raised my head and looked at her, puzzled. Then I dropped my gaze again and tried to give the kind of response which would be expected of me.

"How can a poor girl like me help a fine lady like you, Madam?"

I spoke quietly but I knew I still sounded remarkably well-spoken for one in my position.

Mrs Aitken tried to explain.

"Being one of the travelling people you have special gifts which could be very useful to us – and contacts. There are many who respect the name Marshall."

She may not have intended it, but something about the way she spoke rubbed me up the wrong way. She was being too polite. I felt as if she were talking down to me.

"Madam, I may bear the name of Marshall but I am no kin to Billy Marshall. And neither is my husband."

I did not really need to make that last statement. Everyone knew that Gretna Marshall was no relation to Billy Marshall and I had been told often enough that I did not need to deny it so vehemently. There had been plenty of times when it might have been to my advantage to tacitly let people think that I had some connection with Billy Marshall the legendary gypsy chief – some would say king –- who had died the previous year (1792).

Mrs Aitken struggled to continue.

"Nevertheless, you have contacts. Because of your calling you can travel freely about the country. You can go where we would not be welcome. You can ask questions and get answers."

I stiffened slightly. What did this mean? What was coming next? Was I being asked to become a spy?

I looked up quickly.

"I'll not betray my friends. Or my kin."

"I'm not asking you to," Mrs Aitken retorted at once.

"I think you can still help me without being disloyal to your friends. In return my husband can help you."

I was still looking wary. Mrs Aitken sighed to herself and finally came out with the reason for her visit.

Some articles had been stolen from her house. She wanted me to try to find them for her.

"And have the thief hanged or transported?" I flashed. "Probably someone who stole to feed their children. No. You cannot bribe me with your offers of help. I may be just a lowly tinkler but I do have some pride. And I do not betray my own kind."

Mrs Aitken ignored my outburst and spoke quietly.

"We are both more interested in getting the articles back. That is more important to us than having the thief punished."

There was silence for a moment. She must have seen the disbelief on my face because she forced herself to give a full explanation. There was one article in particular, a small, silver salver.

A few days ago the Laird had had some guests for a small dinner party. He had been very generous and over-hospitable with the wine and spirits and some of the gentlemen had drunk rather more than they should. One of the guests had a diamond stylus and had carved some verses on the silver salver. The verses were rather indiscreet and it would be inconvenient if the salver were to fall into the wrong hands. Mr Aitken was a prominent Justice of the Peace and it would not do for him to be associated with such ideas. He would not be able to deny that it was his salver because it had 'Longcrags, Dumfriesshire,' embossed on the back. If I could help to recover it, Mrs Aitken and her husband would not ask too many questions about the culprit.

Then something just came over me. I may have been living as a tinkler for over a year, but it did not alter the fact that I had been brought up as a member of a wealthier family than the Aitkens. In a sense my demure, submissive attitude before Mrs Aitken was something of an act.

I couldn't help it. I tried desperately to stifle a giggle but somehow a splutter got out. I shouldn't have done it but I said mischievously,

"Robin Burns. I thought it was usually windows he carved his verses on. So now he has graduated to silver."

Mrs Aitken spoke primly and severely.

"I did not mention any names."

"You did not need to, Madam. It can only have been Robin Burns."

Once started I found it hard to stop.

"Everyone knows about the Stirling window, Madam."

I proceeded to quote.

> ' The injured Stewart line is gone,
> A race outlandish fills their throne:
> An idiot race, to honour lost –
> Who know them best despise them most.'

The quotation finished I added,

"Then there was a dreadful fuss. Why I don't know because it was quite true, what he wrote. But he went back and broke the window because he thought these verses might make it more difficult for him to enter the Excise."

I was about to ask her just what Robin Burns had carved on the salver but, just in time, I bit back the words. That would have been going too far. Instead I lowered my head again and tried to look submissive.

I knew that Mrs Aitken was not fooled. She realised that my dutiful meekness was just a performance, and one which I found difficult to keep up.

But I was not one of Mrs Aitken's servants. My own upbringing apart, my travelling connections now meant that I did not belong to her world. I belonged to a quite different society with its own morals, beliefs, and loyalties.

Then it suddenly dawned on Mrs Aitken that she was not going about things the right way if she wanted my help. She changed tactics. First she tried to frighten me.

"Gretna, we can both help you. I do not think you realise the seriousness of your position. Do you know anything at all about the penalties for vagrancy? Can you imagine what it would be like to have your ear nailed to the wall by the common executioner, and then cut off?"

I closed my eyes tightly and winced. I had once seen a tinkler who had had an ear cut off — and I could hardly bear to look at her.

Mrs Aitken spoke very quietly.

"I see that you do actually know what I am talking about."

She remained silent for a few moments to give me time to think over what she had just said before trying another form of persuasion. She had latched onto something which I had said earlier. I had been able to quote in full the Stirling window verse. She said quietly,

"Do you admire Robert Burns as a poet?"

I answered respectfully.

"Very much, Madam."

"Do you know that he was recently cautioned by his superiors in the Excise for being indiscreet? Any more follies and he could lose his job. Would you not like to help Robert Burns if not me?"

A long pause and then,

"Tell me how you think I can help, Madam."

Mrs Aitken explained. The thief was probably one of the servants. Mr Aitken would arrange for me to be released. He would allow me to camp in the grounds of his house. I could take my basket and go to the kitchen door. The cook and the housekeeper would be told beforehand to allow the servants to speak to me. If I kept on the alert I might learn something. There was more to it than that. My camp would be near the house. No doubt some of the servants would come to me there where they could speak to me more freely. Of course all this was more likely to apply to the female servants. The plan was not so likely to succeed if the thief was one of the male servants. Then again, there could be two or three working together.

Even so, it was worth a try.

"Well, Gretna" Mrs Aitken ended softly, "Will you help me?"

I was now looking thoughtful and undecided. Mrs Aitken knew exactly how to turn my indecision to certainty.

"If you help us, then my husband can help you. And also your own husband."

That did it. Hope sprang into my eyes.

"How Madam?"

"I am sure you realise that when his case comes to trial your husband will almost certainly be condemned to death. But my husband could speak for him and plead for him and instead of being hanged he would be transported to Australia. Better still, he could even avoid being brought before the court at all. He could petition for transportation and my husband would ensure that his petition would be accepted. Then there would be no court case."

She paused and then continued, trying frantically to get through to me.

Transportation to Australia was not such a bad fate. For a few years my husband would be in a prison colony. Then he could be granted his ticket of leave when he could work as a farm servant. Or – remembering who she was speaking to– or even a pedlar or hawker. But he would still be subject to certain restrictions. Finally, he could be granted a pardon and he would be a free man in Australia, although he would not be allowed to return to Britain until the full fourteen years were up. I could go out and join him if I wanted. Mr Aitken would help me with money and travel arrangements.

I listened intently. In one way this was the miracle I had been praying for. But it was all so unfair. And I could not help saying so.

"He's innocent, Madam."

"Can you prove it, Gretna? Would you want to risk his life in a court case? Or would you rather not accept what we have to offer?"

She had me there. No I could not prove it. Not with one of the wealthiest men in south west Scotland prepared to give evidence against him. I would have to accept Mrs Aitken's offer. But there was still one thing I was doubtful about. I asked cautiously,

"What happens, Madam, if I try to find the salver but fail? Even if I do my very best?"

She did not answer directly.

"Do what you can. I am sure it will be more than you think."

I did not like that evasion, but I decided to accept it. I was being offered life for Danny and the protection of a wealthy guardian for myself. I little knew then that the security I was being promised was deceptive and rather like a Solway beach – a wide expanse of sand deceptively safe at low tide but fraught with danger when the flow tide rushes in and traps the unwary on island sandbanks. So it was to be with me in the service of the Laird of Longcrags – periods of calm followed by ones of peril and hazards. But that was all in the unknown future. At that moment, facing Mrs Aitken in my prison cell, all I could think about was Danny. Suddenly a picture flashed before my eyes – a picture of Danny with his hands tied behind his back stumbling up the steps to the scaffold.

If helping the Aitkens meant saving Danny's life then I had no choice.

I succumbed to Mrs Aitken's powers of persuasion.

I became the first of the Solway Sleuth-Hounds.

# CHAPTER 2

## SETTLING IN

I was soon to see what could be achieved by the power and influence of the gentry when combined with the forceful personality and gift for organisation of a woman like Isabel Aitken. Events now moved with a startling rapidity, with the speed of a Solway schooner scudding before the wind with the tide in her favour. Once I had made my decision Mrs Aitken did not give me a chance to change my mind. She strode over to the door and rapped loudly with her riding crop. She obviously expected the door to open at once like Aladdin's cave and when nothing happened she knocked once more. This time her crop positively thundered against the door. I heard the scurry of quick footsteps, the bolt being drawn back and the key in the lock. The door opened revealing a very flustered looking jailer. Now he was abject and silent. He had clearly learned his lesson – that Isabel Aitken was not to be trifled with.

As she was about to leave she looked back at me quickly,

"You will soon be hearing from me, Gretna."

So saying she swept through the door. Before it closed I heard her say to the jailer,

"Now, my man, I have some instructions for you — and for your good wife."

I threw myself back down on the straw and thought about the new direction my life had just taken. I had found myself a wealthy protector, which was a great relief. There was a precedent and example for this — the legendary gypsy king Billy Marshall who had enjoyed the patronage of the Earl of Selkirk.

But there were some undefined doubts gnawing at the back of my mind. I had tried to break free from my background and upbringing but it seemed that I was something of a failed rebel. The gentry still had me in their snare.

I did not have time to work out what was really bothering me because my thoughts were interrupted by the arrival of the jailer and his wife with hot water and a tub.

The turnkey left at once and his wife – a much pleasanter character than her husband – told me to call her "Effie" and then added cheerfully,

"Mrs Aitken thought you might like to get washed, dear. And she gave me these clothes for you."

Here she indicated a bundle she was carrying.

I had a good wash. It was symbolic as well as practical. I felt I was washing away all the prison associations and, I sincerely hoped, memories.

Effie undid the bundle and shook out my new clothes. Mrs Aitken had provided me with a full set of practically everything. I examined the garments and was delighted. All were good quality working women's clothes, practical and comfortable. Also bright and colourful.

First there was a linen shift and leather stays. But it was the outerwear that really charmed me. There were two lindsey woolsey petticoats, one dark green and the other red, then a leaf green bedgown, also lindsey woolsey. Very suitable for the colder autumn days which were just about to come.

Effie helped me to dress. First the underclothes and then I put on the petticoats – the red one first and the dark green one on top. As I pulled on the bedgown I wondered, as I always did, why it was called a bedgown, a long loose jacket worn over petticoats. But it was never worn in bed so why was it called a bedgown? Why worry? It was my favourite colour anyway. I tied the blue apron round my waist and then it was time for the linen cap. Gretna Green marriage or not, I was still a legally married woman and my cap showed that.

I have always refused to go barefoot and I was pleased to see that Mrs Aitken had also provided a pair of soft cowhide shoes and a pair of knitted stockings to go with them.

There was one other thing she had given me — a tartan screen. This was rather like a small plaid but it was worn either as a shawl or over the head. It was a good, warm, woollen one, which I would really appreciate in the winter days ahead. It came complete with a silver brooch to fasten it with. I did not recognise the tartan — a striking red and green — and I looked at it curiously. Knowing Mrs Aitken the tartan would no doubt have a special significance. But I would have to wait to find out what it was.

When I was ready Effie handed me a small box.

"Mrs Aitken was most insistent that I should give you this."

I opened the box. It contained a pair of earrings. An act of consideration or a token to secure our agreement?

No, more than that. The earrings contained a very special message for me. Isabel Aitken was saying,

"Keep your pretty ears, my dear – both of them."

Her gift was a very subtle warning that, if I did not agree to serve the Aitkens, then I could be in danger of suffering the barbarous treatment often meted out to the travelling people.

I turned the earrings over in my hands. They were unusual. They were simple drop earrings, made of polished horn. I examined them more closely and saw some delicate and intricate carvings of birds in flight – symbols of freedom. She was saying,

"You will soon be free Gretna – free to do exactly what I tell you."

Effie took one look and exclaimed,

"They're beautiful. Let me help you to put them on."

As she did so I thought quickly. The earrings had probably been made specially. They were made of horn so they had probably been made by a tinkler as many tinklers – like Billy Marshall himself – were horners. It would have taken time for the craftsman to finish them so Isabel Aitken had had them made before her visit. She had been very sure that I would agree to her request. She had been proved correct and I felt a sudden pang of annoyance.

I was now ready and Effie stood back and admired me before bundling up my old clothes, which, she told me, I would need later. In my new life it seemed that there would be times when I had to look respectable and times when I had to look otherwise. Then she left me.

I walked round the little cell getting used to my new clothes. I was entranced with them. The petticoats were a perfect fit, just clearing my ankles. That is the way I like them. I do not like my skirts too short. Some might feel that mid calf is a more practical length, a length which is cleaner as it keeps the skirts well clear of any mud or dirt, a length which also means that the wearer is less likely to trip over them. Be that as it may, I prefer my skirts a little longer.

But there were several things which puzzled me. How had Mrs Aitken known how to get such an exact fit? Most people do not realise just how small I am and I would not have been surprised if she had given me clothes which were far too big.

There was more to it than just the fit. She had chosen green, my favourite colour. My mother always used to dress me in blue and when I protested she would say,

"It brings out the colour of your eyes, dear."

But I had always preferred green and now Mrs Aitken had provided me with garments of my favourite hue. Was it just a coincidence? I was certain that it was not. Not with Mrs Aitken. But how and where had she learned so much about me?

I fingered my significant earrings thoughtfully. I went over to the tartan screen which I had placed on top of my bundle and examined the silver brooch closely. I had a strange feeling about it. I had seen one exactly like it before. It had been made by a tinkler from stolen spoons which he had melted down. Michael had made a special visit to Danny and myself to warn us of that particular tinkler. "He's trouble," he said. As he left us he gave us strict instructions to avoid him as we would an adder which had just crawled out of the heather.

I examined the Celtic knots on the brooch trying to find some minute differences in the pattern fiercely telling myself that it was a common motif after all. But I failed to convince myself.

What was the connection between Mrs Aitken and the travelling people?

Here my thoughts were broken by the sound of footsteps in the corridor outside. Two sets of footsteps, the heavy tread of the jailer accompanied by a lighter footfall. The door opened and I struggled to suppress a look of surprise. The jailer had brought with him a young boy who seemed to be about twelve. He was neatly dressed in dark breeches and jacket and his hair was tidily tied back. I was wondering who he was when the jailer introduced him, in words which I found absolutely amazing.

"This young gentleman is Mr Alexander MacBean. He is a clerk to Mr Gordon, Writer of Dumfries and agent to the Laird of Longcrags. Mr MacBean has an important communication for you."

I was so surprised at this little boy being described in these terms that I hardly heard the door slam shut. But once we were alone I turned my attention to Alexander. I still could not think of him as 'Mr MacBean.'

Alexander began to speak and I was in for another shock. He did not sound like a little boy. He spoke very precisely and used long words, obviously a lawyer of the future.

"I trust you are well, Mrs Marshall."

I realised that this was something of a formality but, under the circumstances, I thought it a rather silly thing to say.

"I often act as messenger for Mr Gordon and I have been asked to entrust to you these important documents. Kindly peruse them and let me know if you have any questions."

So saying he handed me a package. Mystified I opened it. To my delight I saw that it contained a wagon license and a pedlar's licence, both made out in my name. I cannot describe my relief. Now I could travel about the country freely without the worry of being arrested for vagrancy. I looked at the date and noticed that it had been signed two days ago – by Mrs Aitken's husband. So she had been very sure that I would accept her offer.

Alexander was still speaking.

"You are soon to be released. I should advise you to make your preparations."

What on earth did he mean? What preparations? All I had to do was to pick up my bundle. I said simply,

"I'm ready now."

Alexander smiled quietly.

"Please be patient, Mrs Marshall. There are legal procedures to be observed, papers to be signed. And arrangements are being made to have your wagon and pony brought here. But rest assured, I shall return shortly."

He turned to the door and prepared to knock for the jailer. Suddenly I felt that I did not want this strange boy to leave. I had derived an unexpected comfort and reassurance from his visit. Also I was curious to know more about him. I had already deduced that he was much older than he looked. He must have been to be trusted with so much responsibility. And his neat appearance and slightly pompous speech were, no doubt, to try to make himself look and sound older.

Before he could knock I said quickly,

"You are a clerk to Mr Gordon?"

He dropped his hand and turned to me,

"Yes, for the present at any rate. But I do not intend to remain a clerk. I hope to become an apprentice and go to Glasgow University to study law."

Desperate to keep him talking I said,

"So you hope to become a Writer to the Signet yourself?"

Alexander raised his chin and said firmly,

"No, not a Writer. I am going to be an advocate. And one day I shall defend unfortunates in the High Court in front of Lord Braxfield himself."

He sounded so definite, so sure of himself. But did he need to practise for the High Court all the time? I said simply,

"I wish you every success."

Suddenly he smiled and there was an almost mischievous twinkle in his eyes. When he spoke again he sounded almost normal.

"It is surprising what determination and industry can achieve. And, since you are too polite to ask, yes I am older than I look. I am actually fifteen, but, since I look like a schoolboy, you may call me Alexander. And now I really must go but I assure you I shall soon be back. And while you are waiting I am sure Effie can arrange some refreshment for you."

He knocked for the jailer who came and took him away. I little realised then just how much I was to see of Alexander in the future and how closely we were to work together in the following years.

I was most unsure of Effie's 'refreshment' but when she brought it I had a very pleasant surprise. It was the first edible food I had seen in the three days since I had been locked in the Mid Steeple. Effie brought cheese, oatcakes and an apple together with a wooden dish of tea. Remembering Mrs Aitken's earlier accusations about adulterated tea I looked at the bowl dubiously before taking a cautious sip. I was soon reassured. It was good and pure and I drank gratefully glad to have something to soothe my aching throat.

Shortly after I had finished Alexander came back for me. He picked up my bundle and I threw my screen round my shoulders. The jailer saw us along the corridor to the main door, opened it and stepped aside for us to pass through.

Scarcely able to contain my excitement I stepped out into the open air.

The main doorway of the Mid Steeple is at the first floor level and I found myself standing on a small landing at the top of an outside stairway. I paused and stood there, tightly gripping the wrought iron balustrade. There a slight breeze and I revelled in it. It seemed an eon since I had last felt the wind in my face. I took a deep breath and looked over the plain stanes.

Then I noticed my wagon and my shaggy, black and white pony Lucy, my darling Lucy. I suddenly realised what she was doing and I smiled to myself. Near her was a large handcart piled high with an enormous load of hay. Lucy had edged nearer the handcart and was helping herself – unseen by the urchins in charge of it. My clever little Lucy. Then I had a sudden thought. What on earth was I doing here? I should be with her.

I was so near liberty. I wanted to race down the stairs but I could not. Alexander had decided to be a gentleman and was walking in front of me so that if I tripped he would break my fall. So I was forced to walk slowly and sedately to freedom.

Alexander reached the foot and turned to look back at me. Suddenly a young man rushed up shouting rudely,

"Sawney Bean. Out of my way. Some of us have work to do, Sawney Bean."

He pushed past Alexander who lost his balance and fell sprawling on the ground. I just escaped the same fate by taking a firm hold on the railing as the obnoxious young man ran past. I hurried to help Alexander who had now struggled to his feet.

"I am all right," he said calmly. He looked at me and decided I needed some kind of explanation. The young man turned out to be Walter Beattie, Mr Gordon's apprentice.

Alexander explained simply.

"He's jealous of me because Mr Gordon gives me more responsibility even although I am younger than him and I am just a clerk whereas he is an apprentice. So Wattie always tries to make life difficult for me."

"He called you Sawney Bean," I said uncertainly.

"My childish nickname," said Alexander patiently and resignedly. "He knows I hate it so he uses it at every opportunity. He can never say just Sawney which I don't mind. Well not really. But with Wattie it has always to be Sawney Bean."

"Work it out," he said as I still looked puzzled. And I did. Sawney was an old Scots diminutive of Alexander. And in Dumfries it would be just too tempting to drop the 'Mac' from 'MacBean' and get just Sawney Bean.

Sawney Bean was a figure from the folklore of the area. Long ago in the dimly remembered past a family of cannibals had lived in caves on the shores of south Ayrshire and had preyed on luckless travellers. They had been discovered at last, hunted down and taken to Edinburgh where they were all put to death with much savagery and barbarity. Small wonder that Alexander hated being called Sawney Bean. But at the same time I could not help thinking that Sawney suited him. Alexander was too grand for him.

I was struck by Sawney's calmness and by the fact that he just accepted Beattie's rough treatment. Was Sawney always so placid? Did he never lose his temper? It was a long time before I learned that some people are not in a position to to do this and that giving way to natural anger is a luxury many just cannot afford.

Sawney led me over to my wagon and introduced me to the man in charge of it, one of the Laird of Longcrags' estate workers who was to escort me to the lairdship of Longcrags or Longcrags Estate. Sawney rubbed Lucy's nose and I could see that he shared my love of animals. Then, in his formal manner, he said his farewells assuring me that he was certain that we would meet again. I little thought then just how soon and in what circumstances.

I climbed into the wagon and the estate worker, whose name was Jimmy, handed me the reins. He, himself, was to ride behind me.

Now, back in my own wagon and with Lucy in front of me, all I wanted was to get out of Dumfries as quickly as possible. At that very moment I felt it would always have frightful associations for me. By leaving Dumfries I would also be leaving behind the grim memories of my loathsome imprisonment. I tugged on the reins and persuaded Lucy to leave the hay and we were off down the High Street.

We had to cross the River Nith and the most direct way was to go down one of the lanes or vennels which led to the river. The nearest was the Wee Vennel, otherwise known as the Stinking Vennel. I guided Lucy round a pen containing pigs and we were in the lane. For once I did not mind the smells of rotting rubbish, the river of sewage and the occasional dungheap. No matter how pungent they were free smells and that was all I cared about. I turned my attention to my driving.

I drove slowly and carefully down the Vennel. It seemed an age but it was probably only about five minutes before we arrived at the end of it. Before turning into the Whitesands I looked up quickly at the second floor apartment where Robin Burns had lived with his family when he first came to Dumfries. It suddenly occurred to me that it was to Burns that I actually owed my present freedom. It was thanks to his indiscretion that Isabel Aitken had sought me out. I rounded the corner onto the Whitesands, that open ground beside the River Nith, then turned right, towards the Old Bridge. This was the busy part of the Whitesands – breweries and tanneries on the land and, on the river, timber rafts. I drove cautiously taking care not to knock anyone down. I certainly was not going to risk another spell of imprisonment. I reached the Bridge at last, the Old Bridge – that familiar landmark of Dumfries, that old, narrow, sandstone, arched bridge, my path to freedom.

Then I found I could not cross immediately. There was a delay because a flock of sheep was being driven off. It was a large flock and so I had to sit and wait in an agony of frustration as they poured off the narrow bridge. I was desperate to get across. The bridge marked the end of the jurisdiction of the Dumfries magistrates and I would not feel properly free until I was on the western side of the Nith.

At last I thought the sheep were all over but it was only a gap and then a collie hustled several more on. In my impatience it almost seemed as if a whole new flock was coming through. Eventually the shepherd appeared with his other dog but I was still not able to guide Lucy onto the bridge. Behind the sheep was a long tailback of carts and wagons which had been forced to wait. The Old Bridge is too narrow for two wagons to pass safely. There are two passing places in the middle but it is better to avoid using them if possible. So I waited and fretted. I looked upstream to the half-built New Bridge and thought longingly if only it had been completed!

Eventually the last cart rolled off and I was able to drive onto the bridge. Once across we passed a few buildings and then we were on a road between fields. We had left Dumfries and its hateful memories behind us. We were now in the Stewarty of Kirkcudbright, and I really felt free at last. Now, with an open road in front of me, I urged Lucy into a trot. Behind me lay my imprisonment, in front of me liberty and a new life.

I was completely euphoric but then I thought of Lucy and slowed her down to a walk. But we still made good time. We passed through some woods and then the village of New Abbey with its corn mill and ruined Sweetheart Abbey with its romantic associations.

We were nearly there. A few miles past New Abbey we turned off the road onto a track on the right. Shortly afterwards we came to the gates of the lairdship – or estate – of Longcrags. My new life was about to begin.

We arrived late in the afternoon. Jimmy drove straight to the stable block. He pointed to a clump of trees nearby and told me I could station the wagon there. Lucy was free to use one of the paddocks. Then he left me.

I set about making myself comfortable. I unhitched Lucy and pushed the wagon into the position I wanted. That was quite easy. My wagon was not the kind of gypsy wagon seen in romantic pictures. It was just a plain, ordinary cart with a cover of waxed cloth. It was not a wooden cart either. It was made of wickerwork. Whatever anyone else may have thought this was ideal for me. The wickerwork meant it was very light, easy for Lucy to pull and for me to push into position. And if the wickerwork ever needed repairing then I could do it myself quite easily.

These were all important considerations now that I was a woman on my own. I had to be able to manage without the help of masculine muscles.

My wagon had another advantage. It was large enough for me to be able to sleep in it so I did not have to lie on the damp ground.

I checked and found that everything in my wagon was just as I had left it, but with some additions. Some food had been left for me, eggs, bread, oatmeal, cheese and some tea. I lit a fire and set about making a simple meal.

Later that evening the Laird came down to the stables. I was subsequently to find that that was his usual custom. His horses meant everything to him and he checked them every night. This was one reason why he had chosen this site for my camp. His evening visits to the stables were well known and afterwards it would be quite easy for him to come across to me and inquire about my progress without arousing any surprise or comment.

That first evening he strolled over to me and said courteously,

"I trust that you are comfortable and have everything you need."

He had spoken automatically without thinking, the way in which he would speak to a guest.

I answered him politely and thanked him for the food. He looked rather uncomfortable. Almost — and this is really unbelievable — ashamed.

"To-morrow, if you go round to the kitchen the cook will have something more for you. A pie perhaps, and some potatoes."

He then became more business-like. He told me what he had planned. Money had been stolen, money which the cook had for paying suppliers. This seemed to suggest that the thief was one of the servants. Apart from the silver salver, the only other articles missing were a pair of silver candlesticks.

If the thief was a servant then I was well placed. Giddy servant girls were always eager to see a tinkler. If I were to tell their fortunes I would find their tongues loosened and I might learn something.

"The telling of fortunes is against the law," I murmured nervously.

"So much the better. Then they will have to come to you in private. They will speak more freely then." The Laird paused and tried to sound reassuring.

"In this case, we will overlook any fortune telling."

Then back to practicalities. He told me the best time to go round to the kitchen would be mid-afternoon. His wife had quietly warned the cook to expect me. So saying he wished me good-night and turned to go. Then he had an afterthought. It was going to be a cold, frosty autumn night and stables are always warm. He came back and said,

"There are a couple of empty stalls in the stables. And plenty of straw. You can sleep there if you choose. And the pony too. It will be warmer than out here."

So saying he walked away quickly.

I watched him go thoughtfully. The Laird was a kind man. He was also very perceptive. I guessed that he realised that I was no ordinary tinkler. He himself was far more of a sleuth-hound than I would ever be. If anyone could pry out my secret it would be the Laird of Longcrags.

Not for the first time I regretted changing my name to Gretna after my marriage, my act of defiance showing that I was making a complete  break with my old life. But that might turn out to be just the fillip the Laird needed to find out my real name. At the very least Gretna Green would provide a starting point for any enquiries.

Once the Laird had left I took him at his word. I did not want to take Lucy into the stables yet. Time enough for that when the winter really set in. The paddock would do her just now. But for myself I carried some blankets across to the stables and laid them on a bed of straw and prepared for a night of unexpected luxury. I was proud of the way in which I had coped with the hardship of the last year but I must admit that I really enjoyed the comfort of that night in the Laird's stables. Next morning I awoke really refreshed to a bright, autumn day. I went back to the wagon to prepare breakfast. But first I took time to look around. I looked across to the big house.

Longcrags stood on the lower slopes of Crowfell, or Criffel as it is sometimes called. The buildings were rather unusual. Instead of being behind the big house the stables were somewhat to the side of Longcrags. The driveway from the main gates swept up to the house and then continued in a huge curve to the stables so, from where I was, I had a good view of the steps leading up to the front door. Before the house was a wide expanse of well-sythed short grass.

I looked across this lawn to the house itself. Longcrags was really just a large farmhouse which looked rather untidy as various extensions had been added from time to time. But, in its own way, it was attractive. Red and white Longcrags. Built of dark red sandstone (no doubt from the Locharbriggs quarries just north of Dumfries) it had newly painted sparkling white doors and window frames. The estate was obviously well kept and well managed. The Laird could easily have afforded to build himself a new house, a much grander one. This was what many of his neighbours among the surrounding gentry had done, but why go to unnecessary expense? The haphazard additions made the house look rather strange but at the same time it also made it look comfortable, like a person who had just exchanged stiff formal clothes for homely old garments.

I suddenly realised that all this told me quite a bit about the Laird. Ostentation and appearances clearly meant very little to him. And, what was more surprising, probably to Mrs Aitken too.

Solid and well built the house stood proudly on the hillside, hurling defiance at the frequent Solway gales. But it was worth enduring the storms for the wonderful view across the Firth.

And on my first morning at Longcrags, I could really appreciate the scene before me. Then it would have been hard to imagine the icy blasts of winter, as it was a perfect autumn morning with only a gentle breeze. Looking down, I was able to see the blue waters of the Solway and even the sails of a schooner. I looked across to Cumberland to where Skiddaw and the Cumberland fells were sharply etched against the sky — where my home had been, once, but no longer.

I stared pensively at Skiddaw for some time and then I shook myself into action.

After breakfast I sat in the wagon knitting. I wanted to build up my stock for my basket. But I had another reason for knitting. I find it relaxing. Also the rhythmic movement of the needles and the repetitive, almost automatic actions always clear my mind and help me to think, and I certainly had a lot to think about.

First of all I considered my own position. Why had I been singled out? Why me and not another traveller? Mrs Aitken must have had a reason. Of course Danny gave her a hold over me – Danny's life for my obedience. But somehow I did not believe that was the whole story. But what was? I thought back over our conversation. Mrs Aitken spoke the standard English of polite society but I had heard at once the slight Cumberland underlay. Was it possible? Did she have an inkling of my past identity?

I pondered over that question for some time and then left it. Be that as it may, my present task was to find the silver salver and I turned my thoughts to it.

What could Robin Burns have carved on it that was so dreadful? Something coarse and crude? Knowing Robin Burns that was perfectly possible. But that would not cause such consternation. It would be embarrassing for Mrs Aitken but the men would just laugh. And the Excise would not be bothered about bawdy verses. No. It must be something political or perhaps even treasonable. Something against the royal family? Or something in favour of the new republican government in France? If the verses were treasonable then Robin Burns could have far more to worry about than just losing his job. He could be arrested and imprisoned or even transported to Australia like Thomas Muir and Thomas Palmer. And what about the Laird? The verses had been carved in his house. Could this mean that he would be implicated too?

I forced myself to leave the question of the verses on the salver. That was none of my business. It was just idle curiosity on my part. My task was to find the salver itself, not discover what had been carved on it. I set about trying to puzzle out how to find it.

The Laird had made a rough plan. But so often our plans do not work out the way we intend. And so it was in this case. The Laird had brought me here in the hope that my travelling status would attract the servants as later turned out to be the case. But what he had overlooked was that I might also attract the attention of his own children. And that I myself, in turn, would be dragged into the affairs of his family.

The Laird had forgotten about Lucy. She was the kind of pony any horse lover would be drawn to. In particular children would be fascinated by her. And children often talk more freely than their elders.

I was just about to find this out.

It was the middle of the morning. Suddenly three children and a woman who looked like a governess came towards the stables. A small dog ran to and fro in front of them.

One of the children was a boy of about ten. He caught sight of Lucy in the paddock. He ran over and stood at the fence. Always curious Lucy trotted over. I went and joined them.

"Is this your pony?"

He did not wait for an answer but just prattled on.

"Can I give her an apple? I always bring apples for the horses. I'm Struan Aitken. Who are you?"

The other three had now joined us. Apart from the governess they consisted of a girl of about twelve and an older girl who might have been fifteen and who obviously considered that she was far too old for a governess.

Struan patted Lucy and then asked,

"What's her name?"

"Lucy. She is called Lucy because she was born on the shores of Luce Bay."

The younger girl took one look at Lucy and laughed.

"What a funny pony. It's too heavy and its coat is too long. My pony is clipped."

Her brother was scornful.

"This one can't be clipped. She has to live out, eejit."

It was obvious that Struan had picked up much of the speech of the grooms.

The girl was not to be silenced.

"It's such a stupid colour. Those silly black and white patches. My friends would laugh at me if they saw me on a pony like that."

Struan was about to retort when the governess silenced them.

"Stop this quarrelling at once. If you can't behave then you are all going back to the schoolroom. Now show Mrs Marshall you have some manners."

Amazing. The second time in two days that I had been treated like a human being. But the girl had to spoil it.

"You don't have to be polite to a tinkler."

The governess spoke sharply.

"That's enough, Charlotte. You have to be polite to everybody. Now back."

As the governess led her charges away the girl was still defiant.

"I'd just as soon go back to the schoolroom. Struan always spoils our walks. He always wants to come to the stables. It's boring."

Struan lingered.

"I'll be back," he hissed at me before taking to his heels and running after the others.

He was. Just after lunch. He did not come directly to me. First he had a riding lesson with the head groom in the paddock where I was able to watch him. I liked what I saw. Struan sat deep in the saddle and had good hands. He was very attentive to his instructor. When the lesson was over he went back with his pony to the stables. He was gone some time and I thought I would not see him again that afternoon but I was wrong. He suddenly came running up to me. He went to the fence, called Lucy and rubbed her nose while he babbled on.

"Did you see me ride?" he asked proudly.

"I love horses. I have been helping to groom Silver. That's my pony. Lottie, she's my sister, says that we employ grooms to do that, but Father says that if I learn all about horses now then when I am grown up I shall know whether my groom is doing his job properly or not."

He teased out Lucy's thick mane.

"My big brother, James, has a beautiful horse. I wish they would let me ride him. James was at the races last month. At Tinwald Downs. You know, just north of Dumfries. I wanted to go too but he would not take me. I'll have to go now. My tutor will be waiting for me. 'Bye."

It was nearly time for me to go round to the kitchen but first I had some hard thinking to do. The Laird was assuming that the thief was one of the servants but could it possibly be one of his own family? I would have thought Lottie capable of absolutely anything. More important was what I had just learned from Struan. He had an elder brother who had been to the September races at Tinwald Downs. Could he have placed a few bets and lost? Could he have debts to pay and was he afraid to tell his father?

It was a possibility, but how I was to follow it up I just did not know. I would have to think about it later. I shied away from the dreadful possibility that the thief may actually have been one of the Laird's family. If it was, and if I discovered the truth how on earth would I tell him?

I pushed such frightful thoughts to the back of my mind. It was now time for me to go round to the kitchen.

My investigations had not started off in the way the Laird had planned. They had begun, not with the servants but with his own children. But now it really was time for me to turn my attention to the servants.

*Lucy*

# CHAPTER 3

## AN END AND A BEGINNING

I took my basket and walked round to the back entrance. The cook had been warned to expect me and she told the servants curtly,

"You can have ten minutes and then back to your duties."

I would have expected all the servants to have crowded round me but only two did so. A third girl remained at her work scouring a pot.

One girl picked up a lavender sachet and breathed in its scent while the other girl tried on a pair of mittens. She called to the girl at the pot.

"Come and look, Annie. She's got some lovely things."

Annie just ignored her.

The girl with the lavender sachet asked, "Can you spae my fortune?"

"We are not supposed to do that nowadays," I said softly.

"We'll come ower the nicht," whispered the girl.

The cook brought a basket of her own over to me.

"There's a pastry for you. And some potatoes, " she said, looking sternly at the girls who now realised that their little interlude was over.

After that all that I could do was to go back to my camp and wait. It was late in the evening before the two servant girls came over to me. The one who had bought the lavender sachet was Meg and the other was Janet.

"Can you spae?" asked Meg anxiously.

I answered carefully.

"Sometimes. I have some small skill but I do not have the gifts of others among my people."

That was true. I was not making it up. I do not have the usual talents of the travelling people but occasionally I will have a sudden flash of enlightenment or a premonition that something is going to happen.

Meg looked disappointed. That dreamy expression, her whole manner, Meg had wanted me to tell her about her young man.

I spoke cautiously.

"You do not need my help but there is one close to you who is much troubled."

The two girls looked at each other. Then Janet said,

"Annie, the scullery maid. She's fair fashed aboot something. She's aye muttering to herself."

Meg dismissed this carelessly.

"She's simple."

"She's got much waur these last few days. There's something wrang," said the more serious Janet.

Meg suddenly looked thoughtful.

"True. And she's taken to ganging oot early o' a morn." Janet stared at her and Meg explained. The other morning she had woken early. She had got up and crossed to the window and looked out. She had seen Annie hurrying towards the back gate.

"There's nae reason why she shouldna hae an early daunder," said Janet solemnly.

Meg gave a loud laugh.

"Annie, an early daunder. Ye ken how she likes a long lie."

"She does that a'richt," said Janet quietly.

Meg pondered for a bit and then tried to give a reason for Annie's unaccustomed behaviour.

"It all began efter she started seeing Granny Simpson. I'm siccar the auld witch has pit a spell oan her."

Janet was alarmed.

"Ye shouldna say sic things. If Mrs Robertson were tae hear ye..." (Mrs Robertson was the housekeeper).

"Why fur no? It's the truth. Granny Simpson is a witch an' I dinna care whit Mrs Robertson says. Granny Simpson has pit the evil eye on Annie. Admit it. You're feart o' the auld bissom yoursel'."

Janet denied it but sounded very unconvincing.

"I don't like Mrs Simpson, it's true. And I try to avoid her whenever I can. But it's havers to say she is a witch. And Mrs Robertson tells us it is wicked to think such things."

"Well I'm telling ye, the auld wifie gars me grue. That way she has o' staring at you withoot blinkin.' And auld Will Scott always has to tak his dug by the scruff o' the neck and drag it past her gate. It will never walk by on its ain. And have you noticed, the sun never shines on her cottage."

She went on and on. Janet and I were both affected. Janet began to look more and more uncomfortable and even although I told myself not to be so stupid, I found myself becoming alarmed and even panicky.

I struggled to put an end to all this and asked them if they would like to see my pony. But this was one time that Lucy failed to work her usual charm. The girls admired her and stroked her but they were still quiet and despondent. I offered to walk back with them to the big house and they both agreed with disturbing eagerness.

I left the girls at the back door and walked slowly back to my camp, mulling over all they had told me. What had I learned? Had they given me any clues to the thief of the silver salver?

Meg was probably under the influence of a young man. Was he a good or a bad influence? Could she have stolen for him? It was possible but somehow I did not think so.

And what was I to make of all this talk of a witch? Of course I knew that there were no such creatures as witches, but it was only just over sixty years since the last witch was executed in Scotland and many superstitious country people still believed in them.

Moreover, if I were to be strictly honest, listening to Meg had made my own flesh creep.

I puzzled over the witch question and then decided that I had better concentrate on Annie and her early morning activities. I would try to follow her. That would at least make me feel I was doing something if nothing else.

Next morning, just before dawn, I crept round to the back of the house and hid myself among some bushes. I had a long wait. Gradually the sky lightened and the trees were black silhouettes before, in their turn, taking on something of their normal colour. Suddenly the kitchen door opened and Annie came out. I followed her cautiously.

Annie walked along a track behind the house. She reached a small plantation and rushed along a little path. I continued to shadow her, flitting from tree to tree and not making a sound.

Annie came to a clearing and got down on her hands and knees. As I stared in amazement she crawled round in a circle. She then rose up and stood for a moment with her arms outstretched. Finally she took a vial from a pocket under her petticoat and drank from it before turning and scuttling back the way she had come.

I returned to my wagon. I had plenty to think about. Remembering Lottie's harsh words about Lucy I decided to give her a good grooming. She badly needed it. She had been neglected while I was in jail. Moreover I would think better with a brush in my hand.

I was still brushing Lucy when the children and their governess came for their morning walk. There were only two of them. Charlotte was missing.

Struan came up to me.

"Lottie's in the schoolroom. She's in disgrace," he said gleefully.

I dropped the brush and picked up a hoof pick. This was interesting.

The little dog had followed Struan. He managed to get his tiny teeth round the hand strap of the brush and ran off with it. Struan did not chase him. He stood still and called,

"Patch. Fetch."

The dog turned, bounded back and dropped the brush at Struan's feet. Struan picked it up and gave it to me saying proudly,

"He always does what I tell him."

He then proceeded to tell me all about the dog. He was a comforter.

I looked at the little black and white dog carefully. It was just a pup and it did not have its full coat yet but I could visualise what it would look like in about a year's time. The coat was short but thick but I knew it would soon be long and luxuriant. The tail was curled tightly over the back with yet no sign of the long hair which would, in time, cascade down over the flanks. It was like a toy spaniel but smaller and lighter. It had a little face with sharp, pointed features and big, bright eyes.

A true comforter, except for one thing, instead of drooping spanielwise, the ears were pricked and erect, although that would not be so obvious once it had its fringes. Struan informed me that Lottie thought that Patch should be drowned. This brought him back to his sister again and he told me why she was in trouble.

It was her birthday and she had been very ungrateful when she had been given her presents. In particular she had been really disgusted with James's present. He had given her a book, a cheap book. Lottie had thrown it at him and said,

"I don't want it. Give it to the tinkler for her basket. That's all it's good for."

Struan suddenly realised what he had said. He stopped and looked awkward. To put him at his ease again I started to admire the little dog.

After Struan had left I sat and thought. James had given his sister a cheap birthday present and last month James had been to the races. There was no way out. I would have to mention my misgivings to the Laird.

That evening I told the Laird of Annie's strange behaviour. Then, plucking up my courage, I said tentatively,

"There's something else I should mention."

Nervously I told how James had been to the races. Could he have lost money betting? That morning he had given his sister a very cheap present.

It was all right. The Laird was not angry. It was true that James had lost money at the races but he had confessed to his father himself. The Laird had paid his debts and he was sure that his son had learnt his lesson. At least that was what he told me, although privately I still had a few doubts.

He was more interested in Annie. He frowned when I told him about Granny Simpson. There was nothing he could do at the present but he would have her watched.

Then he started to make plans. It was arranged that I should keep a special look out for her the next morning. The Laird and some of his most trusted servants would do the same.

Next morning I went directly to the clearing and hid myself there.

Eventually Annie arrived. This time she just stood and waited. After a while a woman appeared. Annie took something from beneath her skirts and offered it to the woman. Although they spoke quietly I could hear them quite easily.

"Whit's this?"

"A pair o' siller candlesticks. I couldna get ony mair siller."

"Candlesticks. Whit use are they to me? Tak them back. I asked you fur money."

Annie started to cry. At first she sobbed quietly and then she started to howl.

The woman looked around anxiously. She had to find some way of silencing her quickly before she brought some of the lairdship workers to the scene.

"Wheest. Wheest. A'richt then lass. Oot o' the goodness o' ma hert I will accept whit ye hae gied me and I shall say nae mair aboot whit ye owe me. Noo dry your een and gae in peace."

I waited until they had both gone and then made my way back. I found the Laird and told him everything.

I had done all I could. It was now up to him and he acted at once. He guessed that the woman would have been Granny Simpson. At once he wrote out a warrant for her arrest, signed it and sent for his constables. In an amazingly short time they were on their way to her cottage.

That was not all he did. He also sent a message to a neighbouring laird who was also a Justice of the Peace asking him to come over to Longcrags as soon as possible.

Then he sent for Annie and had her brought to the room he used as a kind of office. I was there too, along with Mrs Robertson, the housekeeper.

Once Annie, fidgeting nervously, was standing before him, the Laird confronted her with what she was supposed to have done and asked her if it was true. He did not expect such a violent reaction.

Wringing her hands Annie cast herself at his feet.

"Forgie me, Laird. Please forgie me," she gulped. "I had tae dae it. I didna want tae. But ma puir mither. She was deeing. An' auld Scott's dug howled a' nicht, an' ma puir mither was burning — as she will in Hell."

At this Annie broke down completely and sobbed convulsively.

The Laird was dumbfounded. This was one thing he could not deal with – a distraught, howling, wailing female.

He was about to say something but he could not get the words out. The housekeeper, however, knew exactly what to do.

"I shall fetch herself," she said decisively and made a rapid escape.

Herself, in the form of Mrs Aitken, proved difficult to find and so the Laird had to suffer Annie's snivelling a little longer. But this wait made his relief all the greater when Mrs Robertson re-entered the office with his wife, who took charge at once.

"We need something to calm the girl," she said, practical as always.

"Some wine perhaps. No tea would be better. Tell them in the kitchen, Mrs Robertson, and then come back here yourself."

She did not ask Annie any questions but she did get her to sit down. Then she just left her alone and walked over and looked out of the window. Annie's frenzied sobs subsided somewhat and by the time the tea was brought in she was merely weeping quietly. Mrs Aitken made her drink some and then started to question her carefully. She spoke in a flat, expressionless voice.

"I have been told that you may have been responsible for the theft of a pair of my candlesticks. We have always treated you fairly and, if it is true, I am sure you must have had your reasons. Now, start at the beginning and tell me the whole story."

At this Annie gave a kind of shriek.

"Forgie me, Mistress. Forgie me. It was ma puir mither. She's gaeing tae gang tae Hell..."

To my surprise Mrs Aitken put her arm round Annie's shoulders.

"Nonsense. Your mother is going to do no such thing. Now who put such a wicked idea into your head?"

"It wis auld Granny Simpson. The witch. She telt me."

"From the beginning," Mrs Aitken said gently but firmly.

Gradually Mrs Aitken began to extract the whole story from Annie. It was a dreadful tale of deception, unscrupulous trickery, extortion and the vulnerability of the superstitious country people.

To be brief, Annie lived in the servants' quarters at Longcrags but she tried to visit her mother whenever possible — which was not difficult as she lived quite near. Also, Mrs Aitken and Mrs Robertson were both sorry for the girl and made special allowances for her and gave her extra time off. Annie's widowed mother had a cottage and a small piece of land. Recently everything seemed to have gone wrong. First, the hens stopped laying and then the cow's milk dried up. After this the cat, a superb mouser, was found dead. Much worse was to follow. The bad luck did not end with the animals. It transferred itself to the family and Annie's brother broke his leg when a cart overturned.

It was at this point that Granny Simpson first visited Annie.

"Your faimly is accursed," she intoned solemnly.

"The evil eye has been pit upon ye. But I can help."

Annie refused to listen and sent her away but before she went Granny Simpson turned and said,

"There wull be waur. Ye should hae listened tae me."

A few days after this Annie's mother fell ill with a fever. Soon she was sinking fast. Now Granny Simpson became a regular visitor. Ostensibly she was trying to help by bringing nourishing broths and the like. But all the time she was working on poor Annie. She told her that that her mother was going to die, but she knew how to make sacrifices to the devil to make him do what she wanted. Annie refused to listen. Her mother's fever got worse and night after night Annie's sisters would sit by her bathing her burning brow. One night Granny Simpson came to Annie and said that her mother was experiencing some of the penalties she would soon be enduring in Hell. The fever was just a foretaste of the fires she was going to suffer for her sins. Here Annie broke off and stared at us wide-eyed.

"The cloth," she stammered. "The cloth which we used tae bathe ma mither's brow. It was steaming, as if ye had wiped the inside o' a hot oven wi' it. Ma mither was burning — as she would later in Hell."

"The power of suggestion," the Laird muttered grimly.

Mrs Robertson just shook her head. She looked absolutely furious.

Annie was starting to howl again but Mrs Aitken took hold of both her hands and said firmly,

"Just tell us what happened next."

Annie made a special effort and managed to continue. Granny Simpson told her to think about what she had said and left. No sooner had she gone than Annie heard the howls of Will Scott's dog up the lane — howls which went on and on. And, as Annie well knew, a dog howling at night was a sure portent of death. Then there was the smack of a switch three times against the shutters. Again Annie knew what this meant. Death could announce itself by a mysterious and supernatural noise. This was all too much for her and she decided to ask Granny Simpson's help after all. She rushed out of the house. When she came to the next part of the story she could hardly go on.

"The licht," she gasped. "The deid licht."

This time Mrs Aitken had quite a struggle to calm her but eventually she found out what Annie had seen. There had been a strange light above the house — the 'licht before death' which signified that someone in the house was dying.

"An' it kept oan moving. An' naebody else saw it but me."

When she saw that Annie raced to Granny Simpson. The old hag told her she had left it rather late but she would see what she could do. After some weird rituals she told Annie it was all right and she could save her mother. Annie begged the old woman's aid and the witch came to her rescue with various magic liquids, ointments, powders, and burnt offerings. Miraculously, Annie's mother recovered.

Then the sorceress said that the devil had helped her and now he must be sent away again. She told the, by now, terrified Annie that she could send the devil away but Annie would have to pay her for what she needed.

Annie had stolen the money and the candlesticks but she insisted she had not stolen the salver.

It was obvious that she was telling the truth.

When she finished her story there was an astounded silence in the room. The Laird was standing gripping the edge of a chair, his knuckles positively white with tension. I had never seen anyone look so angry.

"Such wickedness. Such depravity," he muttered. "To take advantage of a poor, simple girl who has only half her wits."

Mrs Aitken maintained her serenity.

"Why, Annie, you should have come to me, or to Mrs Robertson. We would have helped. We both know about herbs and healing. Instead you let that wicked woman trick you."

Then she carefully took Annie back through the whole story and showed her how she had been deceived.

The hens not laying and the cow's milk drying up. These things do happen unfortunately. As for the cat dying. Well it had been very old, hardly surprising. And her brother's broken leg, again accidents do happen. It was unfortunate that her mother took ill so soon afterwards, but again it was no proof of nonsense like the evil eye.

Then the Laird managed to speak at last. In a gruff voice he gave a reason for the dog howling. There had been a fox around after chickens. One of the lairdship workers had shot it a few days ago.

"But the switch against the shutters, and the deid licht?" stammered Annie.

Mrs Aitken spread out her hands.

"You ask that with all the strong winds and gales we have been having recently? Probably a branch blown against the wall. It could have been practically anything."

"But the licht? The DEID licht?"

The Laird looked even grimmer.

"There are trees behind your mother's cottage. It would be quite easy for Granny Simpson to get her rogue of a son to climb up and rig up some contraption of a lantern on a stick."

Even Mrs Aitken could hardly credit this.

"But that is really wicked. Do you think that ..."

"Yes I do and I am going to see that she pays for it."

The Laird forgave poor, foolish Annie. But she was severely warned that if she was ever in trouble again she was to go straight to either Mrs Aitken or Mrs Robertson. Annie thanked them both profusely.

"Oh I will. I will. Honest to God I will. Thank you kindly. God bless you both."

The Laird nodded to Mrs Robertson who quietly led her down to the kitchen.

I expected to be dismissed and sent back to my wagon, but not so. I still had a further part to play.

The Laird was waiting for his men to bring Granny Simpson to him. He was expecting them any time. As he waited he discussed Annie's story with his wife. I was asked for the occasional contribution.

It had all been so easy for the pretend witch. The hens not laying and the cows milk drying up — for centuries witchcraft had been believed to be the cause of these. And then the following run of bad luck of the family, coincidences which could be played upon quite simply by someone as fiendish as Granny Simpson.

But what really angered the Laird was the really sinister part of the old woman's work, where she had convinced Annie that her poor mother was getting a foretaste of the fires of Hell.

That was a shameful thing to tell Annie, but it was eminently believable, especially in Galloway, where the legends of the death of Grierson of Lagg are still fearfully told and retold. Grierson of Lagg, one of the most hated men in Galloway because of his actions in savagely hunting down the Covenanters. Everyone in Galloway knows the stories about his death. Before he died he suffered greatly from gout. His servants used to bring buckets of cold water for him and it is claimed that when he plunged his feet into the water he would cry out that the water was boiling and people present confirmed that it seethed and bubbled.

With such stories firmly embedded in the folklore of the region, small wonder that Annie was convinced her mother was suffering the pains of Hell.

The Laird paced up and down. He just could not keep still. He passed the window and caught sight of something outside.

"Good," he said, "Now we can go ahead with the precognition."

I soon found out what he meant. His friend, the neighbouring Justice of the Peace, had dropped everything and come to Longcrags in response to the urgent message. Now the two Justices could hold the precognition. In other words they would question Granny Simpson and decide if she should be brought to trial. They would also question any possible witnesses. In that case that meant myself and also Mrs Aitken and Mrs Robertson as they had heard Annie's story.

The Laird's friend was brought in and told the whole story. Almost as soon as he had been supplied with all the facts one of the Laird's men came to say that Granny Simpson had been arrested and was waiting in the hall. He further informed the Laird that the constables had also found the candlesticks in Granny Simpson's cottage.

"Bring her in at once. We are ready for her now," said the Laird grimly.

I held myself ready nervously. That was something which I had overlooked — that I could be called to give evidence.

Granny Simpson was brought in. She stood erect and spoke calmly and dispassionately. At first she tried to deny everything. Annie was a simple girl who had misunderstood her. She had just been trying to be a good neighbour and bring comfort and nourishment to Annie's mother.

Then I was called upon to give my evidence. I would never have believed it, but it turned out to be a proper ordeal.

Granny Simpson never tried to interrupt me, but all through my evidence she just stared at me steadily. Gradually this started to have an uncanny effect on me. There I was, in broad daylight, in the Laird's office, in the presence of two respected Justices, and yet I found myself actually afraid of the old woman. I found myself alternately shivering and then breaking out into a sweat. I even started to stammer. No wonder she had managed to terrorise Annie so easily.

Eventually I made an effort to be more sensible. I forced myself to look away from Granny Simpson and avoid her eyes. I looked out of the window instead. At long last my evidence was finished. I was thanked and dismissed.

Thankfully I left the room. All I wanted was to get back to the normality of the stables, my wagon and Lucy. But it was to be some time before I calmed down.

It was a bright autumn morning, with just a few clouds in the sky. As I left the house the sun suddenly, and quite unexpectedly, disappeared behind a dark cloud. At the same time two crows rose from a nearby bush and flew past me. It was as if Granny Simpson had a message for me — or rather a warning.

I resisted an impulse to run. I reminded myself of what my mother had told me again and again. "You have far too vivid an imagination." I had never thought that I would ever find these words comforting but at that time I did. Granny Simpson had deliberately cultivated a sinister manner and I was letting it affect me. But I knew what to do about that.

I walked resolutely to the stables and surprised the head groom by telling him that I wanted to help. I seized a broom and proceeded to brush all my vague and undefined fears away. The stable staff watched me in amazement but then they were joined by one of the men who had been sent to fetch Granny Simpson. All work came to a sudden stop as they huddled round the newcomer who told his story in a hushed voice with many dramatic gestures. Awe-struck glances were cast at me.

Eventually the head groom chased them all back to their work. Then he brought me a pile of bridles to be cleaned.

"Here you are," he said sympathetically, "Rub all your worries away."

Before he left he did his best to sound reassuring,

"She canna hurt you. But you're a brave lass, nae doot. There's few aroond here whae wad dare cross Granny Simpson."

The other grooms were looking at me as if I was a heroine. Granny Simpson certainly had a fearful reputation.

Later when I went back to my wagon I found that one of the grooms had tied, into Lucy's thick mane, a length of red wool — a well known protection against witchcraft. I really appreciated the little gesture. It made me feel that I had friends who would at least try to look after me.

That was the end of that particular episode — for the time being at least. Then, a few months later there was the trial. In the courtroom Granny Simpson looked exactly what she was — a nasty, conniving old woman with no special powers. I gave my evidence without difficulty. And so did Annie. The Laird had worried that she would be too afraid to speak up but Mrs Aitken assured him, "You just leave Annie to me. She'll be all right."

And she was. She gave her evidence in a quiet voice, a little more than a whisper, and she looked down at the floor all the time. But the Deputy Sheriff and jury were still able to hear her.

Granny Simpson was sentenced to a year in Kircudbright Jail with frequent appearances in the pillory.

But all that was in the future. The day after the pre-cognition I sat in the back of the wagon doing my knitting. My needles clicked mechanically. The progress of my work had no meaning for me. All I could think of was that I had failed. True, I had found the thief and recovered the candlesticks. But that did not matter. I had failed to find the salver and that was all that the Laird and Mrs Aitken cared about.

I had tried. I had done my best. Would that be enough to save my husband? Would the Laird still speak up for him?

I did not know and I was afraid to ask.

And then I had a stroke of luck.

Struan suddenly appeared with Patch in tow. He stood at the paddock railings. As was to be expected Lucy trotted up to him. I left my knitting and went over to them. Struan was giving Lucy an apple.

At the far side of the lawn a governess cart drove up to the door of the house. A groom got down and stood holding the horse.

"For the girls' dancing class, " Struan said carelessly. Then he added longingly,

"I wish they would let me drive the cart."

The girls came down the steps with their governess. Both were carrying small bags which, no doubt, held their dancing shoes.

Struan suddenly acted with all the impulsiveness of a ten-year-old. He slipped through the railings and into the paddock. He seized Lucy by the forelock and led her through the gate. For a boy as small as Struan Lucy stood quite high off the ground but Struan was very agile and somehow or other he managed to scramble onto her back. Before I fully realised what he was doing he had booted Lucy into a reluctant trot. By kicking Lucy's sides, and by slapping her neck, Struan still managed to guide her even although he had no saddle or bridle. He succeeded in turning Lucy onto the lawn in front of the house and was even able to urge her into a grudging canter.

I was annoyed with Struan. Lucy was my pony and he had no right to ride her without asking my permission first – even if I was just a lowly tinkler. I followed quickly. Patch came too. He gambolled around and then bounded ahead.

Struan reached the front steps. Because he was riding bareback with no bridle he may not have had full control of Lucy, or perhaps he did not really care. Anyway Lucy cantered too close to the governess cart and she startled the horse between the shafts. The horse stepped backwards and gave a half rear. The groom soon had it under control but at that very moment Charlotte had been in the act of stepping into the cart. She lost her balance and fell to the ground, dropping her bag. She was not hurt. I saw the governess help her to her feet.

Meanwhile Patch thought that he might be missing something. He pranced around and then, puppy-like, his tiny teeth seized Charlotte's bag. It was too big for him to lift but he ran off, dragging it along the ground.

He soon abandoned it but then ran back to it, seized it again and dragged it towards me. He dropped it once more and raced round in circles. Then he approached it again. He had now decided it was some kind of dangerous animal. He crouched down before it, front paws flat on the ground, hindquarters high in the air, tongue hanging out and eyes alert. He darted forwards boldly, made another snatch and then retreated. Time for another raid. He walked up to it and this time he took a firm grip. He tried to lift it, but dropped it at once. Then he started to drag it again before deserting it and running off.

There was something gnawing at the back of my mind. Patch was telling me something — but what was it? There was something about the way in which Patch had been dragging the bag. Desperately I forced myself to think. The bag should have been light. Charlotte's dancing slippers would not have weighed very much. But Patch was a very small dog. Would the bag have still been too heavy for Patch to lift? I tried to picture Patch hauling it along the ground. I was sure it looked heavier than it should have been. Patch should have been able to pull the bag and still run quite easily. Instead it looked as if he were being forced to make a real effort.

Suddenly it dawned on me. I now knew that the bag contained more than Charlotte's dancing shoes. I picked up my skirts and ran as I had never run before. I did not have much time. Charlotte was already making her way across the grass to retrieve her belongings. She saw what I was doing and increased her speed.

To make things easier for me Patch suddenly bounded back to the bag which he had now decided was his own very special toy. He took possession of it again and this time he started to drag it towards me. He reached me at the same time as Charlotte. He dropped the bag at my feet and stood there panting, his tongue hanging out, demanding praise for being a clever dog.

I picked up the bag. It was soft, made of fabric, embroidered and obviously made by Charlotte herself. I felt an oblong metal shape. Without opening it I knew exactly what was in the bag.

Charlotte stretched out her hand and said imperiously,

"My bag please, Mrs Marshall."

I ignored her completely, carried it to the governess and opened it. The governess glared at me but before she could speak I passed the open bag to her and said,

"I think this is what the Laird has been looking for."

Puzzled the governess looked in the bag. Slowly she drew out the silver salver. She turned to Charlotte and said tersely and coldly,

"An explanation, Charlotte. At once."

Charlotte scowled and said sulkily, "I did not mean any harm. I just wanted to show it to the girls at the dancing class."

The governess looked at the salver again and Charlotte took the opportunity to aim a savage kick at Patch. He dodged but still caught the toe of Charlotte's boot.

It was just a glancing blow with no power behind it and Patch was not hurt. Nevertheless, he let out a pitiful, heartrending little cry. The governess had seen what had happened out of the corner of her eye. She rounded on Charlotte.

"If you are in trouble it is because of your own misdeeds. How dare you try to blame your own wickedness on a poor, dumb animal. Go to your room at once."

\*      \*      \*

In due course all was explained. The day after the notable dinner party the house had been in disarray and the servants had had extra work putting all to rights. Charlotte had come upon the salver before anyone else and she had regarded it as a fine opportunity to show off to her friends. She was old enough to appreciate the significance of the verses but, with her usual selfishness, all she thought about was the chance for her to be the centre of attention.

I had been very lucky but I had actually solved my first case.

I returned to my wagon and waited apprehensively. In the evening the Laird came to see his horses. He took his time and then he came over to the wagon.

I stepped down and stood before him.

"You have done well," he said.

"You will speak for my husband?" I asked softly.

"Certainly. I always keep my word."

He looked at me thoughtfully and repeated what his wife had told me in the prison cell.

"If your husband is sent to Australia he will be all right. It will be a chance for him to make a new life for himself and later you can join him there if you wish. I could help you."

*Oh yes,* I thought to myself. *But not for a few years yet. The Laird will hold onto his little Solway Sleuth-Hound for as long as possible.*

"In the meantime, you are always welcome to camp here and whenever you need it you are sure of my protection."

That meant a lot. Tinklers were continually being hounded and harassed and the protection of a prominent Justice of the Peace was worth a great deal, and much sought after in travelling circles. Much of the success of the legendary Billy Marshall had been due to the fact that he had had the support of the family of the Earl of Selkirk. Now I myself had a powerful patron. Never again would I have to worry about being charged as a vagabond and never again would I have to worry about finding a place to camp at night.

Nevertheless I was still dubious. It sounded too good to be true. My first case had been easy, too easy. I could not expect such luck again.

The Laird had not finished.

"I trust that we will be able to work together again," he said.

This roused my suspicions once more.

"I'll not betray my kin. Or my friends."

"I should not expect you to

He sounded as if he meant it. He had always known that I had my own constraints, my own loyalties. That any help I could give him would always be limited. Even so there was still plenty I could do for him and deep down I knew I could also trust him. I relaxed and smiled.

"I'll be glad to help you, Laird."

I had given him my trust. Now it was up to him to seal the bargain.

"You have your pedlar's license and your wagon license but if you ever go beyond the area of their jurisdiction, perhaps to Cumberland, then I can give you letters to friends of mine who will help you there."

My eyes lit up.

"Thank you, Laird," I said simply.

Even as I spoke I wondered at his shrewdness. He had known exactly what I wanted. He had probably seen the rather wistful way in which I sometimes gazed across the Solway to Skiddaw. He understood my natural wanderlust. I could just imagine him saying to himself,

*Best not keep her on too tight a rein.*

He smiled at my delight. In the meantime he had something else for me. He turned and called to a groom who came with Patch on a lead.

"Unfortunately, my younger daughter is of a rather wilful disposition. She blames this little dog for the trouble she is in. Struan fears she may harm it in a fit of temper and he wants you to have it. I agree with my son. I know you will take good care of it."

He picked Patch up and placed him gently in my arms. Then he added in his soft voice which contained just the slightest hint of a lilt,

"Apart from that, both my wife and I would have been reminded of what could have happened every time we looked at him."

He took his leave.

"I think that is everything. Good night to you."

I cuddled the little dog and a rough, warm, little tongue licked my fingers. I did not like the name 'Patch.' Such a pretty little dog deserved a better name. Besides it was starting a new life. It should have a new name, a gypsy name.

I looked at the tiny animal lying in my arms. Why it was small enough to go into my basket. There was its new name.

'Rooskie.' The Galloway Tinkler-Gypsies' word for 'basket.'

"Rooskie," I said softly. "Would you like to be called Rooskie?"

A wag of the tail. "Yes."

I had a new friend and life seemed perfect.

I did, however, have one regret. It was that I would never know what Robin Burns had carved on the silver salver.

I had just solved my first case. All right, it may have been partly due to luck, but I had still solved it. Now I could relax for a while.

If only I had known! I was just about to be plunged into my second case, one which turned out to be far more difficult. And this time there was not only problem solving involved. There was also danger.

But, that evening, all that was ahead of me. Once more, with Rooskie snuggled up against me, I enjoyed another night of warmth and comfort.

I was awakened abruptly to the sounds of consternation and activity.

*Rooskie*

# CHAPTER 4

## CHARLOTTE

Only half-awake I lay on my bed of straw listening to the usual stable sounds; the voices of the grooms the jingle of bridles, the creaking of saddles, and the clip-clopping of hooves on the cobblestones. Then as my brain gradually returned to full consciousness there came the realisation that this was no normal morning stable routine. For a start, too many of the usual sounds were missing. There was no sloshing of water in buckets and no sound of horses busily champing on their oats. Also missing were the sounds of the brushes and pitchforks of the morning ritual of mucking out. Even more significant than the omissions were the sounds which *could* be heard – especially the notes of urgency and anxiety in the various voices. Curious to see what was going on I put Rooskie on the lead and stepped outside — and stared in amazement at the scene around me.

Nearly all the Laird's horses were in the stableyard being mounted by the lairdship workers. But this was obviously no gentle morning exercise. The Laird himself was present. From time to time he would approach a rider and give him his instructions. Then horse and rider would depart at a fast, purposeful trot. Suddenly the Laird caught sight of me and came over to me.

"Gretna, my wife would like to speak to you up at the house. Give me a few minutes and I shall accompany you."

I had no idea what was wrong but it was obvious that it was something very serious. I went back to the wagon and hastily tidied myself. I settled Rooskie, tied him up and then climbed down from the wagon to wait for the Laird. He was not long and we were soon walking up to the big house. After a few minutes silence he told me briefly what was wrong. Charlotte had run away. She had been severely beaten and then locked in her room but when her governess went to check on her in the morning her room was empty.

So I had been given my next assignment already. I was to help to find Charlotte. It was a daunting prospect. And what would happen if I failed? Would the Laird still keep his promise to help my husband?

We reached the house and I was taken up the steps and in at the front door. Then we went straight to the children's quarters on the top floor. I wondered what on earth the servants would think of a tinkler getting such unheard of treatment and then I saw that they hardly noticed. They had far more important things to worry about. Mrs Aitken was wondering just how Charlotte had managed to get out of a locked room.

"Someone must have helped her," she declared, her voice and face showing absolute fury. "And when I find out who unlocked her door ..."

All the servants were obviously terrified that suspicion would fall on them. Every single one of them had only one thought – how best to clear themselves.

Mrs Aitken showed me round the children's rooms herself. I saw the schoolroom and Charlotte's books, her bedroom with its pretty floral bedspread and curtains and the combined playroom and dayroom with toys, books and nursery screens. In a far corner of the room the nursery maid was dusting some books and trying to look as unobtrusive as possible. The books did not need dusting but the maid obviously thought that it would look better if she was doing something instead of just standing around looking useless. Mrs Aitken muttered to me out of the corner of her mouth,

"There's something sleekit about that girl. I never did trust her. I was going to dismiss her but I kept putting it off."

Then her eyes fell on Struan who was sitting very quietly looking at a book. His mother regarded him suspiciously and said to me,

"Struan may well know something about this, although he claims he does not."

She looked at her son sternly, "I hope you are not lying to me, Struan."

Without waiting for an answer, she turned to me,

"I hope you can help us, Gretna. Charlotte may well have run away to join the travelling people. I expect you to make enquiries among your husband's kinsmen. Of course we have sent the lairdship workers to ride round all the encampments in the neighbourhood, but I know from experience that travellers are more forthcoming with their own kind."

I thought it extremely unlikely that Charlotte would have run off to the tinklers. None of them would have dared harbour her. They were not going to risk incurring the wrath of the Laird of Longcrags. If by any chance Charlotte did turn up at one of their camps then the first thing they would do would be to take her straight back to Longcrags. But I kept silent. Mrs Aitken was in such a rage that I certainly was not going to contradict her.

Mrs Aitken then calmed down. She told me to look around. Perhaps my sharp eyes would spot something which would suggest where Charlotte had gone. And if there was anything I wanted to know, then I had only to ask.

I wondered what Mrs Aitken really expected me to achieve. Despite my travelling connections it seemed impossible. Nevertheless I set upon the task which had been forced upon me. The first thing was to try and find out more about Charlotte. A quick examination of her copybooks showed that her handwriting was surprisingly neat. Turning to her needlework I picked up a half-finished sampler. It was crumpled and grubby and it had obviously been unpicked several times. Mrs Aitken sighed and said,

"Actually Charlotte is, for a girl of her age, very skilled with her needle. But what she chooses to depict is so unsuitable. Of course she is made to take her stitches out and do her work over again but then she sews something even more outrageous. The wilful child."

I stared at the puckered, dirty piece of cloth for some time. My curiosity was aroused. What were the 'unsuitable' objects which Charlotte preferred to the conventional flowers and animals? But I dared not ask. I continued to look around but all the time there was something niggling at the back of my mind. There was something missing. What on earth was it? At last it dawned on me. I turned to Mrs Aitken and asked,

"Did Charlotte not have any dolls?"

Mrs Aitken shook her head wearily,

"No, Charlotte had no dolls." She paused before adding, "She did have dolls. Beautiful dolls. But we gave them all away to little girls who would appreciate them." She then gave me a full explanation.

Charlotte used to have some charming dolls. There was one in particular. She pretended it was a French Countess and spoke French to it.

Here Mrs Aitken broke off and explained that a young French girl came twice a week and gave the children lessons in French. The girl was from a French noble family. Many of her family had perished by the guillotine but she had managed to escape. She was now living in poverty and the Aitkens welcomed the chance to help her. In any case Mrs Aitken still believed that in spite of the war with France, a knowledge of French was still a useful accomplishment.

This digression over, Mrs Aitken returned to Charlotte. She had been pleased that while playing, her daughter had been practising her French. Then there had been a dreadful incident. Some other children were visiting. The dolls were produced and the children played with them happily. They seemed settled and the maid who was supposed to be supervising them left them alone for a short time. At least she claimed it was for only a few minutes but Mrs Aitken was sure that it was much longer. Anyway during that time the Countess was denounced to the Committee of Public Safety, arrested, tried and condemned to the guillotine. Struan then produced a makeshift guillotine. Somehow he had managed to get hold of a kitchen knife. The Countess was duly beheaded and, in the process, another child nearly had her finger cut off. Profuse apologies were made to the parents of the other children. The nursery maid was dismissed at once. The kitchen staff were driven frantic as Mrs Aitken conducted her own investigation as to how Struan could have obtained possession of a kitchen knife. Charlotte and Struan were both in disgrace and Charlotte's dolls were all given away to little girls who would treasure them and not be so ungrateful. Shortly after this the old governess left and was replaced with the present one. The old governess had no control over the children and they had become wild and undisciplined. She did not wait to be dismissed. She resigned first and married a wealthy widower. Here Mrs Aitken just told me the bare facts but her disapproval showed clearly in her face.

I listened to this carefully. I was gaining a different picture of Charlotte. Up till now I had thought of her as a prim and proper little miss preparing to grow up into a woman very sure of her social position.

My eyes fell upon a box filled with old clothes. I found out that this was the dressing up box. Old and discarded clothes were flung into this box. These clothes were often given to the poor but they were also used by the children for dressing up. Struan and Charlotte used to give readings of plays and poems. Charlotte in particular was very good at this. In fact she was a real little actress. Last Christmas she had given a reading of *Tam o' Shanter* before her parents and a few selected guests. Charlotte had held her little audience captivated with her rendering of Tam's flight from the witches. And how she managed to vary her accent and speak the Scots of Robin Burns. Why it was a marvel.

I considered this carefully. This was going to make finding Charlotte even harder. So she was an accomplished actress who could speak the old Scots of the lower classes perfectly. I looked at the dressing up box. Had she taken any of the clothes in the box? If she had then I did not even know whether I was looking for a girl or a boy.

I asked if any of the clothes in the box were missing and I received a most unsatisfactory answer. No one knew exactly what had been in the box.

I thought again about what was puzzling Mrs Aitken — and everyone else. Charlotte had been locked in her room. How did she get out? She must have had help. Who had helped her? The nursery maid? Charlotte would have been quite capable of threatening her with the knowledge of some misdeed which she had discovered. No doubt blackmail was yet another of Charlotte's dubious talents. But the maid had tearfully denied helping her. What about Struan? Up till now, whenever I had seen them together they had always been bickering. But Mrs Aitken obviously thought that Struan was not above suspicion. Why? I did not want to ask outright. I would nose out the answer in my own time – discreetly.

I picked up a large book with board covers and opened it. Mrs Aitken told me that it was Charlotte's common place book. I looked at it with interest. This was something which could tell me more about Charlotte. I thought rapidly about the common place books kept by many of the ladies of the time. They would copy into such books their favourite poems or stories and often include, as well, some of their own compositions. Charlotte had started early. I flicked through it and saw that she had been busy. Page after page was filled with her flowing copperplate. I asked Mrs Aitken if I could take it away with me and study it at leisure. She gave her consent at once.

Now that I had found out all I could for the time being, I wanted to go back to the wagon to think things over. As I left Mrs Aitken told me, once again, that if there was anything else I wanted to know about Charlotte, then I was just to ask.

I went back to my wagon, took Rooskie on my knee, stroked him and went over what I had learnt.

Firstly, Charlotte could be dressed as either a girl or a boy. Being a capable actress she could speak either the standard English of polite society or the Scots of the stable or kitchen.

Secondly, Mrs Aitken had offered to help but could she? The wealthy hand over the care and education of their children to others. And when in the presence of their parents children have to be polite and respectful. That is more important than being able to confide in a parent. Did the strict and distant Mrs Aitken really know anything about her own daughter? Often a servant might have more influence over a child than the parents. Who did Charlotte look up to? Who was her mentor? With Struan it, was obvious, one of the grooms in the stable. Why Struan even spoke the Scots of the grooms – although in his case it was strictly modified and toned down. But Charlotte? Who influenced her? Where could I begin?

I opened the commonplace book. I left the back flaps of the wagon open so that I could see all that was happening around me. This had the result that my study of the common place book had to be left until later because I suddenly caught sight of Struan.

Most of the horses were out of their stalls as the Laird's men were all riding round the countryside trying to find news of Charlotte. So the stables were deserted. But that did not matter to Struan. The stable block was his haven of refuge and he had somehow managed to slip away from the present commotion of the house. I watched him go into a room at the far end of the line of stables. Convinced that he was the one person who could help me in my search for Charlotte, I put Rooskie on a lead and walked him up to the little room which turned out to be the tack room. Struan was there alone busy cleaning his pony's bridle. He nodded when I entered but did not pause in his work. Rooskie tugged towards him and I dropped the lead. Rooskie rushed up to him and jumped up onto his knee. Struan put down the bridle and stroked him.

"Hullo, Patch. Good dog."

"He has a new name now, " I said. "Rooskie."

Struan looked up. "Rooskie. That's a strange name for a dog. Why do you call him basket?"

I answered at once without thinking. "Because he is small enough to go into a gypsy basket and I wanted to give him a gypsy name. Anyway it is easy to say and I like the sound of it."

Then the full significance of what Struan had said suddenly struck me. The gypsies and tinklers guard their cant, or secret language, very carefully. They had not even taught it to me. I had just picked it up gradually. I said sharply,

"How did you know that *Rooskie* is cant for basket?"

Struan obviously felt he had said too much. He answered casually, "I just did."

I knew that I would get no more out of him. If Struan did not want to tell something then absolutely no one could make him.

There was a large box beside him. He turned and rummaged in it and took out a cloth. I caught sight of some booklets, the cheap kind sold by chapmen. I picked one up and looked through it.

"That's Charlotte's." Struan sounded upset. I put it back. I had seen all I wanted. It was a book of Scots ballads. I said calmly, "I was only looking."

Struan seemed uncomfortable and he offered an explanation. "I let her keep some of her things down here. She thinks Mother would not approve of these books."

That simple statement spoke volumes. It was a sign that despite their continual sparring Struan and Charlotte were closer than appeared. But I could not press Struan. If I was not careful he would clam up completely. I decided to leave the matter and try something else. If I could find out when Charlotte had escaped then it would be a help. Had she escaped in the middle of the night or early in the morning? If in the morning then she could not be far away. She would not have had much of a start. I decided to take a risk and ask Struan right out.

"Do you think that Lizzie (the nursery maid) let Charlotte out?" Struan's reaction was most surprising. He let out a guffaw and shook his head. Chortling he told me that Charlotte did not need anyone to unlock the door. She could get out perfectly easily herself. All she needed was a hairpin.

"Keys are for gadgis."

I held my breath. Now I was really finding things out. Gadgis – the Galloway tinkler-gypsy word for house-dwellers. So a tinkler had taught Charlotte how to pick locks. But that was all I was going to find out. Struan had realised what he had just said and he determined to brazen it out. He said nothing but just stared at me relentlessly. I left him cleaning his pony's bridle and went back to the wagon. On the way I remembered that Mrs Aitken's first reaction was that Charlotte might have run away to the travelling people. I had privately dismissed that suggestion but now I was not so sure.

I climbed into the wagon again and opened Charlotte's common place book. I was sure it would contain some clues at least. I started to read the first entry. It was called:

# MAGGIE'S STORY

*The renowned poet Robert Burns wrote a story of how an Ayrshire farmer, Tam o' Shanter, escaped from witches. Riding home one night he passed a church, a haunted church. Although late the windows were blazing with lights. Curious, Tam rode up and peered in. He saw that many witches and warlocks were having a dance. Spotted by the witches Tam had to ride for his life. He knew that if he could just get over the bridge he would be safe because witches cannot cross running water. One of the witches caught up with him just as he was half way across. The witch caught the tail of his mare and hung on. Maggie made a supreme effort and sprung forward to safety. The witch was left holding her tail and poor Maggie now had just a stump.*

*There are those who try to belittle this account and say it is the ramblings of a drunk man but of course this is nonsense. How could it be when Maggie, his trusty steed, lost her tail? Here is Maggie's story told in her own words.*

*'I used to have a beautiful tail, long and luxuriant, the admiration of man and beast for miles around. As well as being so comely it was also useful. With it I could easily swat a fly even on my neck. But now, alas, I no longer have my lovely tail. Instead I have a short, ugly stump. I am so ashamed even although my master says I have no need to be. He says I am a heroine and my stump is the badge of my courage.*

*Certainly it could easily have been so much worse. It came about like this.'*

Then followed the story of Robert Burns' famous poem *Tam o' Shanter* as told by the horse Maggie. It was very well done. It also told me two things First, what I already knew. That Charlotte had a great admiration for Robert Burns and his work and that she, no doubt, could speak the Scots of Burns as easily as the language of the drawing room. It also reinforced my earlier opinion that Charlotte and Struan were closer than appeared. *Maggie's Story* was in Charlotte's neat handwriting but the name at the foot was Struan's. The story was Struan's and Charlotte had just copied it down. I turned to the second entry which was very definitely Charlotte's own work. It was a short story and it was entitled simply

## *JELLYFISH*

*Wind, wave and current had wafted it across the Atlantic from its spawning ground in the West Indies. And now it lay, spread out and helpless, on the sands of Satterness beach, on the shores of the Solway Firth.*

*The body of this monstrous creature consisted of a circular mass of grey jelly. There were two blue black circles in the centre — like eyes. Long tentacles stretched out on the sand in every direction. Truly it was a great chieftain of the jellyfish race.*

*Usually stranded jellyfish just lie helpless on the sand until they die. But not so with this one. The central mass pulsated furiously with a dull, throbbing sound. Then the monster made a strenuous effort and managed to push itself up on its tentacles. It staggered a few steps across the sand. Some people came along and it threw itself flat at once. Once again it lay stranded, forlorn and vulnerable on the Solway sands. But for anyone who would take a closer look there was menace and evil in those dreadful eyes.*

*Two ladies passed. They had a small dog with them, running to and fro. It lagged behind the ladies, investigating some particularly interesting seaweed. It approached the jellyfish and gave it a*

*tentative sniff. From then on the little messan was doomed. Suddenly the jellyfish heaved itself up and threw itself upon the dog. It pounded up and down furiously and then subsided. Once again it lay flat upon the sand.*

*The two ladies came back, calling the dog. They searched everywhere but could see no sign of it. Eventually they had to give up.*

*The jellyfish lay on the sand. It was now slightly bigger.*

*Then a nurse with three small, children came along. One little boy lagged behind, picking up shells. The jellyfish raised itself up on its tentacles again and forced itself towards the boy. It threw itself upon him. Again it shuddered up and down. Then it hurled itself flat on the sand again.*

*The nurse came back looking for the little boy but she could see no sign of him. She started calling frantically. She ran past the jellyfish.*

*When she had gone the jellyfish heaved itself up again and staggered on its tentacles towards the sea. But there was something wrong. It trembled. Then green and yellow liquid started to pour from it onto the sand.*

*The jellyfish was being sick.*

*It continued to retch violently. Then finally the small boy appeared covered in slime. He crawled away crying while the dying jellyfish flopped on the sand.*

*The nurse came back and seized the boy with a cry of relief. Then she looked at the mess he was in.*

*"However did you get in a state like that?"*

*She dared not take her charge back to her mistress covered in slime and so she looked around for a way to clean him up. Nearby was a large rock. Around this rock the tides had gouged out a pool in the sand and the nurse now washed the boy in this pool. The minute she was finished the boy rushed and picked up a smaller* rock. He ran to the jellyfish, raised the rock up high and hurled it down on the jellyfish. His brother and sister looked for other rocks and stones and followed his example before the nurse sternly told them that it was time for them all to go home.

Once they had gone away, other giant jellyfish which had been lying nearbye, pushed themselves up on their tentacles and struggled back to the safety of the sea.

Although he did not know it, the boy had removed a great threat from Satterness and made the beach safe for little children and small dogs.


I stared at this bemused. I did not see how this childish story could help but perhaps, on reflection, a deeper meaning would occur to me.

Just then I heard an ominous tearing, sound. Somehow Rooskie had managed to get hold of a piece of paper which had fluttered from the pages of the book. Alarmed I tried to snatch it from him. He darted away and, once safely out of my reach, lay down again and continued chewing. Trying to catch him would be impossible. As well try to catch a gust of Solway breeze. But could he be lured away from his new toy? I got a piece of cheese and tried to make my voice really exciting,

"Rooskie, what have I here?"

My stratagem worked. Rooskie dropped the paper and came for the titbit. I at once grabbed the paper and was relieved to see that it was not anything important. It was just some rough notes which Charlotte had made before copying the story into the common place book.

The paper was not of any significance but it easily might have been. But now I knew that Rooskie liked tearing paper it was up to me to see that he did not get his paws, and his little sharp teeth, on anything that really mattered. I was later to find that this was not just a puppy thing. Rooskie's liking for tearing paper was something which remained with him all his life.

I closed the common place book. I would come back to it later. In the meantime there was something which I had to do — visit my husband. He may have been in jail, but he still had access to his tinkler family and their wide reaching contacts.

The travellers' influence stretched far – rather like the tentacles of Charlotte's jellyfish.

I sought out the Laird to ask his permission.

*Rooskie*

# CHAPTER 5

## THE COMMON PLACE BOOK AGAIN

The Laird agreed at once. I was not surprised. Although my Danny was in a jail cell there was still plenty of assistance he could give – as the Laird knew well. But he voiced nothing of this to me. Instead he just said quietly,

"Of course, my dear. You must see him. But come right back here."

I decided to leave the wagon. I would get on quicker without it. I put Rooskie in his basket, mounted Lucy and took the road to Dumfries. Once there I stabled Lucy with one of the Laird's many friends and made my way to the jail.

My mind was in turmoil as I walked across the Old Bridge. My desire to see my dear Danny again was countered by an illogical dread of re-entering the jurisdiction of the magistrates of Dumfries. Memories of my own so recent imprisonment came flooding back to me and I began to panic. My imagination showed me men on horseback galloping towards me, leaping down and seizing me. I was under arrest again. My brain tried desperately to assure me that this picture was sheer nonsense but it was no use. Emotion won the struggle against logic.

This panic came to its height when I left the openness of the Whitesands and reached the Vennel – which in my state of mind seemed narrower than it really was. The houses were closing in on me. I was going to be trapped.

Fighting an impulse to turn and run back to safety I forced myself to continue up the hill to the plain stanes. Then things became worse. Danny was being held in the old jail which was near the Mid Steeple, the scene of my own imprisonment. Somehow I got past the Mid Steeple to the main door of the jail and was admitted. But as the solid, heavy door clanged shut behind me I shuddered and wondered if I would ever breathe the free outside air again.

I was taken to Danny and at once my foolish fears fell away at my joy at seeing my husband again.

Danny's own life was in danger but he was much more concerned about me. He took me in his arms and kissed me gently. Then came a flurry of questions and suggestions. How had I been managing on my own? If things were too difficult I did not need to stay with the travellers. I could always go back to my own family. Danny had so much to say that it took me some time to tell him my news – that I had found a powerful protector and that Danny's life was now safe, and that I would never, never go back to my own family. At this he gave a quiet little smile of relief,

"In that case my little gourie I will tell Michael to look out for you."

I knew that Danny was trying to reassure me but privately I had a few doubts about just how far Michael would concern himself about me. After all this was Michael, Danny's eldest brother and the head of the family who had never tried to hide his disapproval of me. To a certain extent, he would never forgive Danny for marrying outside his own kind. On the other hand he had a strong sense of duty. Like it or not I was now his young sister and he would always protect me.

And he had a large family of his own to help him. I suddenly knew why the Laird had agreed so readily to my seeing Danny. Prison cell or not, through his family Danny could still play his own part in the search for Charlotte. Although he did not know it, Michael was also a sleuth-hound and he already had his first task – to help me find Charlotte. The continued support of the Laird for both myself and Danny might well depend on it.

When I first saw Danny I had seen the strain and weariness in his face although he had done his best to hide them from me. But now he was beginning visibly to relax. No doubt, later that evening, reaction would set in and he would feel completely drained but for the meantime he was relatively calm. We both knew that the Laird was a fair and honourable man. He would keep his promise and speak up for my husband.

Danny picked up Rooskie and stroked him softly. Danny was one of the kindest people I had ever met. That was why I had married him. Other people might think that I was a silly, giddy girl carried away by some ridiculous romantic notion, but they would be quite wrong. It was not his charm that had attracted me to Danny. It was his gentle kindness.

Shortly before it was time to leave, Danny looked thoughtful.

"You know," he said slowly, "if I am sent to Australia, the Laird of Longcrags could be a great help to me there. He is bound to have contacts, contacts which reach to the other side of the world. He could make sure that I am assigned to a settler who will treat me fairly."

I drew in my breath. The influence of the rich can stretch across oceans. I had not thought of that but no doubt the Laird had. It meant that, even with my husband thousands of miles away, I would still be in Longcrags' power. I would still have to be careful not to go against him. For Danny's sake I desperately tried to suppress a shudder for his words had brought it home to me just how vital it was that I should succeed and find Charlotte.

All too soon it was time for me to go.

As we prepared to part Danny said,

"Michael will make sure you are all right gourie."

I could not help myself. I looked sceptical. Danny added gently,

"Michael has nothing against you, Gretna."

I looked disbelieving. Danny thought for a moment and sighed.

"I think it is time for you to learn more about our family history. Michael will never tell you that so I had better do so before I am sent away."

I listened carefully. Of course I knew the main facts but I had never been told all the details. All I really had was a brief outline. Now Danny told me the whole story. His grandfather had been a tenant farmer in Ireland. Then he had had a run of bad luck. His landlord had not given him a chance to mend his fortunes but had put him off his land at the first opportunity. He had gathered his family together, walked to the coast and taken a ship to Glasgow. From there they had walked south through Ayrshire pushing their few belongings on a hand cart. When they reached Galloway they joined up with some local tinklers. In the years to follow they prospered and did quite well — partly by such traditional methods as helping with the harvest and selling baskets but also by other more clandestine ways. The smuggling paid well. Michael could easily have afforded to buy a farm but he was used to the open road and did not want to give up the modicum of freedom it gave him.

Then came the explanation as to why Danny was telling me this.

"Don't you understand gourie? Michael has nothing against you. It is what you represent. He resents and despises the landowning classes and the gentry for what they did to our family. He feels more strongly about it than any of the rest of us. You must make him see you as an individual and not just as a symbol of the wealthy and privileged. Then he will come to respect you for what you are."

"As I do gourie, " he ended taking me in his arms for the last time.

Gourie. Danny's pet name for me. Gourie, tinkler-gypsy cant for girl or lassie. One of the few gypsy words I was allowed to know officially – although I had picked up many more myself.

As I jogged back to the Longcrags lairdship on Lucy I pondered over all that Danny had told me. He had certainly given me plenty to think about. But try as I might I could not accept his reassurances that the stern Michael would always look out for me. Why had Michael not come to see me in the Mid Steeple?

Then I switched my thoughts back to Charlotte. That was more important. Danny's words about the Laird's influence stretching as far as Australia had really frightened me. A strict master and one tiny mistake and Danny could be in danger of a brutal flogging which could even cause his death.

Somehow or other I *must* find Charlotte – if only to ensure that the Laird's influence resulted in Danny finding a fair master.

I could not get Charlotte's common place book out of my mind. I became increasingly convinced that there was a message for me in Charlotte's childish story of the jellyfish. But its true significance eluded me.

Then, suddenly like a flash it came to me, just as I was passing the New Abbey water mill.

Of course. I myself had seen these giant jellyfish on Satterness beach. It proved that Charlotte did not make things up. Imaginative she certainly was, but her imagination and creativity had their roots in hard fact.

So she knew Satterness beach. Was there any more about the Solway shore in the common place book? Suddenly I could not wait to get back to Longcrags. I urged Lucy into a faster trot.

Once arrived I put Lucy into the paddock, grabbed Rooskie's basket and hurried into the wagon. I took the common place book and settled down for a long session.

As I read on I became convinced that I was right. The next few entries were all about the Solway shore. Even more interesting, they began to show an increasing maturity.

The next entry revealed a fascination with the legend of the Barnhourie mermaid – a story which I knew well.

Just west of Satterness is the Barnhourie sandbank, a hazard to shipping. Many a ship has struck the Barhourie Bank and lain stranded there while the waves pounded it to pieces. But in the seas around this notorious sandbank lives a mermaid. She married a human and together they brought up a family of young merpeople. If they find any marooned sailors they swim before them through the many channels between the sandbanks and guide them to safety. But unfortunately the mermaid has evil sisters who will sing and lure sailors to their deaths.

If you were to hear the singing of the mermaids how would you know which it was? The good mermaid or the wicked sisters? How would a sailor know which one he had met? That was the legend but Charlotte had given it her own treatment. She had written another little story about an exciseman who stayed at an inn – the Barnhourie Mermaid. The exciseman was sure the Inn was a haunt of smugglers and he was determined to expose them. I read on.

## THE BARNHOURIE MERMAID AND THE EXCISEMAN

*Just above the sand dunes bordering the vast stretch of the Mersehead Sands there stands an inn known as the Barnhourie Mermaid. At one time this inn was the haunt of a band of smugglers. The supervisor of the customs in Dumfries was determined to expose the smugglers so he sent a young riding officer to stay at the Inn. The young officer rode along the shore daily but he did not discover anything.*

*One day he was feeling particularly depressed. He was cold and wet and completely disheartened. Even if he did find anyone what could he do? He passed an old man who was gathering driftwood for firewood. The old man looked up and said,*

*"The Barnhourie mermaid is singing her warning to-day."*

*The young man raised his eyebrows in question. The old man explained.*

*"The mermaid. Do you not hear her singing?"*

*The young man listened but all he could hear was the howling of the wind and, in the distance, the sound of the waves breaking on the sandbank.*

*The old man shook his head.*

*"She is singing a warning for those who will hear."*

He gave more details. Far across the sands lay the dreaded Barnhourie Bank. In the waters around it lived a family of merpeople who could often be heard singing. On fine days, a gentle happy melody but on days like this a frantic, sombre warning, telling of the storm to come and urging all to keep far away from the Barnhourie. But if any were so misguided as to disregard this warning, if any ship was so unfortunate as to find itself in trouble off the fearful bank, then the mermaid would lead them safely ashore.

Here the old man paused and then added that the mermaid and her family were good but that she had evil sisters. Their singing would lead sailors to their doom.

Interested despite himself the young exciseman asked how one would know the difference between the good and bad mermaids.

"We just know," was all the old man said.

He was silent and gazed out to sea then he said,

"She is giving a warning to-day. A fast tide, a great storm and fog and mist. If you are wise you will not ride your fine horse far across the sands to-day. Better get off the beach altogether."

So saying the old man turned and disappeared up a path.

The young exciseman gazed out to sea. The sky was dull and the wind was cold. But it was not strong. It did not look as if a storm was imminent.

He sat motionless and thoughtful on his horse. The Barnhourie mermaid. A fanciful tale, a good story. But that is all it was, a story. To believe that it was any more was just superstition.

But the old man had advised him not to ride across the sands to-day. Why? Because there was something there which he was not supposed to find?

Yes. That was one possibility. But there was another.

Perhaps he was supposed to ride out over the sands while the contraband and the smugglers were somewhere else.

Perhaps the old man's warning was a decoy.

Either explanation was possible.

After much thought the young man turned his horse towards the sea. He rode slowly. Even if he found contraband what was he supposed to do about it? Go and fetch the soldiers? By the time they got there the smuggled goods would have been spirited away.

Or even worse. What if he were actually to come across a band of smugglers? What could one man do?

Not for the first time the young riding officer thought about the utter futility of his job.

The tide was full out. In fact it was just on the turn.

He rode out to the Barnhourie Bank. Suddenly he saw something black. Strange, there were no rocks on this part of the coast. He shook his horse into a trot and found that what he had thought were rocks were actually lumps of coal — coal from Whitehaven on the Cumberland side of the Solway. Among the coal were some smaller weighted packages.

Now he knew the smugglers' secret.

They used to weight goods and throw them overboard. Then they would sail in with no contraband. He remembered the carts he had seen a few days ago. He had thought it was just harmless cockling but now he knew better. The smugglers would wait until low tide and then, under the pretence of collecting cockles and mussels, they would set out some in carts, and others on foot with creels. They would simply pick up the smuggled coal, conceal it under a layer of shellfish and take it back to the Inn where they would consign it to various hiding places.

The young riding officer had discovered the smugglers' secret.

He rode round the coals carefully. There was only one thing to do, ride back and get help. He looked towards the shore and got a shock. He could not see the land. It was hidden by a mist which had just arisen. He had a feeling of alarm which soon passed. He knew in which direction the shore lay. Even so he wanted to get back to land quickly.

The wind had strengthened and it was colder. He urged his horse into a canter. Suddenly he found his way blocked by water. The tide was coming in and the sandbank he was on was now surrounded.

Cautiously he urged his horse into the water. The tide had only just turned. Surely, soon he would strike dry sand again. But not so. The water was soon up to the horse's haunches. There was nothing for it. They would have to swim for it. The horse struck out strongly but the wind was rising and horse and man found themselves buffeted by ever bigger waves.

Suddenly the young man was washed off his horse by a huge wave.

The growing darkness combined with the mist meant that he could not see which way he had to go. All he could see was waves. Then his vision was further obscured by driving, pelting rain. He was trapped on the Barnhourie Sandbank.

Suddenly he heard a voice – and singing.

> "Follow me. Follow me.
> Follow me across the sea.
> Follow me and you soon safe shall be.
> Follow me across the sea.
> Mermaid of Barnhourie."

He saw the flash of a silver tail and had a glimpse of long fair tresses.

But was it the good mermaid? Or one of her evil sisters?

He decided to trust her. Surely such a sweet voice could not be bad. Anyway he had no choice. He was exhausted. Soon he would not have the strength to keep himself afloat.

He followed the mermaid and soon found himself in calmer water, obviously a channel between sandbanks. Then he found himself upon dry sand. A sandbank, a respite if only a temporary one. He heard the voice again.

"Rest here upon the sand.
Rest here until your strength you do find.
While you I do mind.
Rest and here do bide
Here upon the sand
Till the rising of the tide
Then follow me to land."

The young rider stretched out and fell into an exhausted sleep. It did not last long. He was soon awakened by the waves washing over his feet. Then he heard the voice again.

"Now it is time.
Hear my rhyme.
Now we must swim
Though the light is dim
The way is long
But listen to my song.
We must leave the sand
But I shall lead you to land.
Follow me across the sea.
Follow me and you soon safe shall be.
Follow me. Follow me.
Mermaid of Barnhourie."

Although his sleep had been short he felt refreshed. Night fell rapidly and all he could see was the silver tail in front of him. He could hear the wind howling all around him but the sea was much calmer than he would have expected. Soon, much sooner than he would have thought he found himself in shallow water. He heard the voice for a last time.

"To the land return again
Do not let these memories fade
If you feel a reward be paid
As you ashore do wade
As you to the land return again
As the beast to its den
Remember as I did you aid
So you aid your fellow men
Remember me. Remember me.
Mermaid of Barnhourie."

Then with a last flick of her tail the mermaid was gone.

The rider stood among the foam of the breakers and watched her leaping and plunging through the waves to her home under the waters which now covered the Barnhourie Bank. Then he finally struggled ashore.

He dragged himself up the beach then rose to his feet and stumbled through the increasing gloom. He found his horse eating grass as if nothing had happened. The horse turned and looked at him still chewing busily. The officer did not have the strength to mount but he managed to lead his horse to the Inn.

As his clothes dried and as he enjoyed a reviving bowl of soup he thought over the mermaid's last words.

Remember as I did you aid,
So you aid your fellow men."

*He looked around the room, bare of all except basic furnishings. If there were smugglers here, then what were they smuggling? Necessities like coal and salt, essentials which they could not afford if they were to pay the cruel government tax. Perhaps also a little tea. Surely they were entitled to some small luxuries. He looked at the woman serving him and noticed her well-worn, shabby clothes and there and then he came to a decision.*

*When refreshed he would ride away and leave these people alone. He would still do the job he was paid to do with the best of his ability but he would temper his work with compassion.*

*He would concentrate on hunting down the big smugglers who made healthy profits and leave the small fry well alone.*

That was the end of Charlotte's story, but she had copied out the poem again so that it stood alone, clear of the snippets of the story in between.

## *BARNHOURIE SONG*

*"Follow me. Follow me.*
*Follow me across the sea.*
*Follow me and you soon safe shall be.*
*Follow me across the sea.*
*Mermaid of Barnhourie."*

*"Rest here upon the sand.*
*Rest here until your strength you do find.*
*While you I do mind.*
*Rest and here do bide*
*Here upon the sand*
*Till the rising of the tide*
*Then follow me to land."*

*"Now it is time.*
*Hear my rhyme.*
*Now we must swim*
*Though the light is dim*
*The way is long*
*But listen to my song.*
*We must leave the sand*
*But I shall lead you safe to land.*

*Follow me across the sea.*
*Follow me and soon you safe shall be.*
*Follow me. Follow me.*
*Mermaid of Barnhourie."*

*"To the land return again*
*Do not let these memories fade*
*If you feel a reward be paid*
*As you ashore do wade*
*As you to the land return again*
*As the beast to its den*
*Remember as I did you aid*
*So you aid your fellow men*

*Remember me. Remember me.*
*Mermaid of Barnhourie."*

*"Remember as I did you aid,*
*So you aid your fellow men."*

Now I was really getting somewhere. This story and poem told me several things. First, as I had already suspected,

Charlotte knew and loved the Solway shore. And she obviously knew Satterness very well.

Secondly, it raised a question. Did Charlotte know any smugglers? Was she sympathetic towards them? The bit at the end was not what I would have expected from hard, selfish little Charlotte — that she would actually understand the plight of those who had to scrape a living as best they could.

I began to feel that my first impressions of Charlotte had been mistaken.

I read through the poem again and smiled to myself. So when most people would hear the howling of the winds and the sounds of the waves breaking against the shore, Charlotte would hear the singing of the Barnhourie mermaid. And after reading Charlotte's story I would myself – for ever afterwards.

I turned back to the common place book and found another legend. But this was one which Charlotte had created herself. The story of the Barnhourie mermaid was old and well known, but Charlotte's tale of the sleeping giant was entirely her own creation.

But once again it was not just pure imagination. On a clear day it is possible to look across the Solway and see, clearly etched against the sky, Skiddaw and the Cumberland fells. Just south of Skiddaw is a range which Charlotte had imagined was like a giant's head. I knew exactly what she meant because I had seen that particular formation myself many, many times.

Charlotte had written her own special legend in the form of a poem, a poem which she had written with great feeling, a poem into which she had poured her great love of Satterness. I read on.

# THE SLEEPING GIANT

*High above the Solway his watch he keeps,*
*When all is well he deeply sleeps.*
*But when those who love this northern realm*
*Face harm or danger,*
*Whether from neighbour or stranger*

*All of a sudden he awakes*
*And a great storm makes*
*Far below in the Solway Firth*
*His rage to a great storm gives birth*
*I tell no lies*
*Great waves arise*
*Huge, gigantic from across the Atlantic.*

*Flashes of lightening rend the skies asunder*
*And loud roars of thunder*
*Cast fear and dread into the hearts*
*Of those who come to plunder*
*Making them retreat.*

*So once his people are free from harm*
*And again all is calm.*
*The storm does cease*
*Now no need to watch over glen or ben*
*Well rid of the unwanted guest*
*The Giant again returns to his rest.*

When England was ruled by William the Proud,
Who determined that the people should be cowed
And all should be recorded in his Book
And none should escape – no cranny or nook
The Giant came to his people's aid,
And kept them safe from William's raid
And the story tells
How high in the northern fells
In a secret valley a band of Vikings dwelt.

But the Giant's help was not just for the people of old,
Or so it is told.
The Giant is for all who love the Solway
His influence does last
For those of present or past.

He comes from an age of ice and snow
When o'er this land mighty glaciers did flow.
Then with the passage of time,
Listen to my rhyme,
The ice slowly did retreat
Leaving behind a land of hills and dales,
For us to enjoy.

Oft when my spirits are low,
And my heart is full of dread
For whatever may lie ahead,
I go down to the Solway shore
And look across to the hills of Cumberland.
Listen and try to understand.

*On a day crisp and clear*
*The Cumberland fells seem very near*
*And there before my eyes*
*The Sleeping Giant lies*
*And my spirits rise*

*I have seen him from Satterness shore,*
*A place to me very dear,*
*Listen and you shall hear,*
*With the Sleeping Giant none shall fear.*

*Farewell to sadness*
*Farewell to sorrow*
*There is hope for the morrow.*


I read the poem again and then I closed the common place book. I looked across at Rooskie who was snoozing on a cushion.

"I know where she is Rooskie. Satterness."

It was late but I just had to find Mrs Aitken.

# CHAPTER 6

## SATTERNESS

I went round to back door and was taken into the kitchen. I told the cook that I wanted to see Mrs Aitken at once. I had been doubtful about how my demand would be received — a tinkler asking to see the Laird's wife! But the cook did not even raise her eyebrows. Charlotte's flight had obviously suspended all normal customs. A maidservant was told to take me to Mrs Aitken at once.

I was ushered into a small drawing room where the Laird and his wife were sitting looking solemnly at each other. Mrs Aitken rose to her feet at once,

"Well, Gretna, have you any news for us?"

She was outwardly controlled but I could hear the note of hope and almost pleading in her voice. I put the common place book down on a small table and said quietly,

"I hope so."

I explained how I had gone through the commonplace book and how I was now convinced that Satterness was the magnet which had drawn Charlotte. They both considered this thoughtfully.

"It's possible," pondered the Laird. "And she could have got there quite easily. She could have walked. It's less than ten miles." Then he added dolefully, "No she is not there. If she was someone would have told me."

Then Mrs Aitken took over. She threw aside her worries and became brisk and businesslike. She explained Charlotte's connection with the Solway coast.

A few years ago Charlotte had had a bad cough. The family physician had been in no doubt as to the cure. Send her to spend a few weeks beside the sea. The 'good Solway breezes' would soon blow her cough away. Most people were surprised at this as it was the middle of winter. And 'good Solway breezes?' again, surely 'icy, biting winds' would be a better description. But no one else had a better suggestion. Moreover Mrs Aitken had a great respect for the family physician and so Charlotte was sent to spend a few days with the Aitkens' great friend, Mr Craik of Arbigland and his family. And the physician was proved correct. It was cold but Charlotte was taken for daily walks along the beach. They were only short walks but they had a magical effect. After a few days Charlotte's cough was much better and after a week it had gone completely.

But Charlotte continued to be chesty. She could develop a cough very easily. So Mrs Aitken decided to ensure that she spent much of her time by the shores of the Solway. She would send both Charlotte and Struan away in the charge of their governess. At first they would stay, either at Arbigland House, or in a cottage on the Arbigland estate. Then Mrs Aitken found accommodation for them in Satterness.

Satterness is a small village built around a rocky point jutting out into the Solway. From the rocks and the lighthouse, it is possible, in each direction, to walk a short distance to a huge, sandy bay: in the east, Gillfoot Bay which leads to the Arbigland lairdship and, in the west, the Mersehead Sands which stretch for about seven miles.

The modern belief about how fresh sea air can benefit health had been turned to good advantage by the inhabitants of Satterness, many of whom had adapted their houses to accommodate convalescents. As a consequence some of the houses were bigger than the average country cottage of the time. They had to be, as more rooms were needed for those who came for the sea air and bathing. Mrs Aitken heard of one good woman who kept such a house, a Mrs Little who had a good reputation and who was very respectable.

Mrs Aitken had an arrangement with Mrs Little. She used to send Charlotte and Struan down to her for several weeks every summer – and for shorter periods at other times of the year. They would be sent with their governess, a maidservant, and a boy to look after the ponies.

I listened to all this carefully and then asked if I could go and speak to Mrs Little. They both agreed but the Laird was doubtful of any good coming from my visit.

"Charlotte is not at Satterness," he said sadly. "If she had turned up there, the first thing Mrs Little would have done would have been to send a messenger to me. And no one in Satterness would hide her."

That made sense. Anyone hiding Charlotte would incur the wrath of both the Laird of Longcrags and the Laird of Arbigland. Surely no one in Satterness would dare risking that?

But the Laird's remarks resulted in an exasperated and impatient outburst from Mrs Aitken. Of course I should go and see Mrs Little. I might still learn something. She might spark off some ideas. In any case did the Laird have any better ideas?

The Laird sighed wearily and said he would give me a letter to take to Mrs Little. He would also tell his friend Mr Craik of Arbigland to give me every assistance.

Letters to Mr Craik of Arbigland. I should be able to travel freely all over the Colvend coast.

In due course I would be provided with letters from Mr Craik too but in the meantime Longcrags gave me his own letters. I examined them eagerly. "The bearer of this letter, Mrs Gretna Marshall, is employed in my service. It would please me greatly if you would give her every assistance ..." Coming from an important laird and magistrate that would effectively give me the freedom of the area.

Early the next morning I hitched Lucy to the wagon and set out for the Solway coast. I arrived at Satterness in the early afternoon. But I did not go straight into the village. I stopped on the outskirts and went up to a small farm. I showed my letters from Mr Aitken. One look and the farmer was only too willing to let me set up camp in a corner of one of his fields. Later his wife actually came out with a few eggs, some bannocks and a jug of milk. A far cry from "Awa wi' you afore I set the dugs on you." The protection of the gentry is a wonderful thing.

I tethered Lucy and she settled down to graze while I made myself comfortable. I began to think over what I was going to say to Mrs Little. Would she speak freely to me? Or would she regard me as the Laird's representative and feel that she had to guard her tongue? I had no way of telling. I decided that I would wait until morning before going to see Mrs Little.

Then I had a disturbing experience. It happened when I was just settling down for the night. I had the back flaps of the wagon open and I could see Lucy. Suddenly I heard a whinny. I looked at her and saw her throw up her head. Then she pawed the ground furiously. This was quite unlike Lucy who was normally a very placid pony. I walked towards her, stroked her, spoke to her in a singsong voice and tried to calm her. I looked around wondering what had unsettled her. Had she sensed someone watching? Seeing nothing out of the ordinary I led her back to the wagon and gave her an apple. Rooskie was lying in his basket quite unperturbed. But that did not mean anything. He was just a pup, too young for guard dog instincts. I tried to shove the incident to the back of my mind but I still felt uneasy. But one thing was for sure. I was glad I had decided to camp near a farmhouse rather than down at the shore.

Lucy settled down and I knew that if anyone had been watching me they had now gone. Nevertheless, I spent a disturbed night with no proper sleep. I just dozed and kept waking up. But I felt better in the morning. It was bright and sunny and my mood cheered accordingly. I boiled two of the farmer's wife's eggs, had a hasty breakfast, then put Rooskie on the lead and set off to find Mrs Little.

I soon found her cottage and was about to approach and knock on the door when two ladies walked up the path and entered. There was an older one who looked rather frail, obviously convalescing from an illness. She was accompanied by a younger woman who was probably a paid companion. They had no doubt been returning from an early morning walk. I thought quickly. Mrs Little would now be busy giving them breakfast. It was definitely the wrong time for me to try and find out about Charlotte. I would go away and return in the afternoon when, hopefully, they would be lying down.

Instead of returning to my wagon I strolled down to the lighthouse and   settled myself on a rock. Some things had just occurred to me.

 Lines from Charlotte's poem about the sleeping giant kept running through my mind. Not from the beginning of the poem where she had created her own legend; not from the middle where she had mentioned the Ice Age and glaciation; or the historical part referring to William the Conqueror and the Domesday Book – (William the Proud). No, the lines which had caught my attention were all from the last part of the poem. Lines like:

> *Oft when my spirits are low,*
> *And my heart is full of dread*
> *For whatever may lie ahead,*

and again,
> *With the Sleeping Giant none shall fear.*

Why had Charlotte written this? Was it just because 'dread' rhymes with 'ahead?' Somehow I did not think so. The poem had the ring of truth about it. It was obviously written from the heart. Even more telling were the last three lines.

> *Farewell to sadness*
> *Farewell to sorrow*
> *There is hope for the morrow.*

For Charlotte Satterness was obviously a sanctuary, a place of refuge. But what could Charlotte the privileged daughter of a wealthy family have to be afraid of? It was puzzling. The more I thought about it the more convinced I became that the incident of the silver salver was only part of the story. That it was a culmination, not an isolated event. What had led up to it? Perhaps I should find out when I got a chance to speak to Mrs Little.

I looked across the Solway to the Cumberland fells. I found Skiddaw and then I looked for the ridge of Charlotte's imagination. With her poem fresh in my mind it did look very like a huge head. I gazed at it intently for a time. What troubles and fears had Charlotte been hiding? I gave up. I might get a clue when I was able to speak to Mrs Little but I would not puzzle it out myself.

I rose up from my rock and marched Rooskie back to the wagon where I prepared a simple meal. Then back to the village and Mrs Little's cottage.

I knocked at the door rather nervously. But the next moment I felt much better. The door was opened by a plump, cheerful woman who was wiping her floury hands on her apron. I handed her the Laird's letter and she read it quickly and shook her head.

"The poor Laird. And Mrs Aitken. They must be out of their minds with worry. She was always a wild one, Miss Charlotte, but I never thought she would ever do anything like this."

Then her attitude changed and she said sharply,

"The Laird seems to think that I can help. But how? I can assure you that Miss Charlotte has not been here. If she had I would have sent word to the Laird at once."

This was the one thing that I had been afraid of, that the Laird's letter would turn out to be a mixed blessing. On the one hand it gave me the opportunity to move freely around the area. But, on the other hand, it could make me a representative of officialdom, someone to be wary of — as now seemed to be the case with Mrs Little. I had noticed that she was speaking very carefully. I was sure that normally her Scots accent would be much broader. But some think it better to modify their accent when in the presence of the rich and influential.

I struggled to reassure her.

"Of course, Mrs Little. The Laird realises that. In fact he respects you and thinks most highly of you. He just thinks that if you chatted to me and told me how Charlotte spent her time when she was here – what she did, where she went, and who she met – that kind of thing. Then without actually realising it, you might give me some clues."

Mrs Little relaxed slightly, but only slightly,

"Well, if that is all it is about. And I would certainly like to help the Laird and his poor wife."

"It is," I assured her firmly. "Perhaps if I came in you could tell me over a dish of tea."

"Oh yes," said Mrs Little rather doubtfully. "Of course," and she showed me into the front room.

She left me while she went into the kitchen. Being in her natural environment had obviously helped because when she came with the tea, and plates of bannocks and oatcakes, she was looking much happier.

I started to drink the tea. It was good with no sign of any foreign bodies. Mrs Little pressed an oatcake on me and said,

"Now, how can I help you?"

"Well, for a start, how did Charlotte spend her time down here?"

Mrs Little started off. She was hesitant at first and obviously doubtful as to whether she was doing the right thing. But gradually her confidence increased and then she rattled on and on. I had come looking for information and now I had it in abundance. Mrs Little was a gossipy wee soul and I got all the details of Struan and Charlotte's Solway holidays with a few juicy bits of news about the governess thrown in for good measure.

The governess, a Miss Irving, had neglected her duties and the children had been allowed to run wild. It had begun quite innocently one afternoon when Miss Irving had taken them down to the beach for a nature walk. The tide was in and she was shocked to see an elderly gentleman struggling to the shore. She went at once to help him and got him safely to the beach where he stood blue and trembling. He had an attendant, a young man whom Miss Irving at once decided was worse than useless. She rounded on him and asked him what he was thinking of only to be told that he was carrying out the instructions of the elderly gentleman's physician. Miss Irving cut him short and ordered him to take his master back home at once, put him to bed and give him a hot drink. And she accompanied him to see that he did so.

That was the start of it. Mr Davison, the elderly gentleman, had been ill and his physician had recommended sea bathing. He had ordered Mr Davison to wade, up to his neck, in the sea every day. And Mr Davison had obeyed.

It sounds crazy but the physician was not alone in his beliefs. A few years later Robert Burns' physician was to advocate the same treatment. Robert Burns died shortly afterwards but Miss Irving saw to it that Mr Davison did not suffer the same fate. She told him firmly that the waters of the Solway were far too cold for bathing. If he wanted to bathe then he should go to the spa town of Moffat. The Solway had different benefits for invalids and convalescents. A brisk, bracing walk along the beach would do far more good. Miss Irving promptly worked out a routine for Mr Davison and saw that he followed it. There was much shaking of heads. What a presumptuous young lady she was to think that she knew better than the learned physician. In any case it was none of her business. Then opinion hardened. It was known that Mr Davison was a wealthy widower. So that was what was behind Miss Irving's apparent kindness. She was just a fortune hunter.

Miss Irving ignored the gossips. And so did Mr Davison. He followed her regime and gradually became much stronger. Then he married Miss Irving. Mrs Little was one of the few who took a charitable view.

"She may well have married him for his money," she said, "but at the same time she is good for him and she will make his last few years as happy as possible. Mind you I think he'll last a bit yet. He was a poor soul when she met him but he has improved no end. I wouldn't be surprised if he lives to a hundred."

Now Mrs Little had finished the story of Miss Irving I hoped she would get back to Charlotte. She did, although at first she told me more about Struan.

Because of Miss Irving's involvement with Mr Davison the children had been left to their own devices. Struan had spent most of his time with one of the local farmers. He would help around the farm by day and in the evenings he would pour over big books about sheep breeding and struggle with the pamphlets of various agricultural societies. Of course he was too young to understand them but in a few years' time he would. And he was thrilled when his hero, Mr Craik of Arbigland, came to see how they were getting on. Mrs Little was quite taken with the fact that Mr Craik did not treat Struan like a child but talked to him man to man. When he left he promised him a ewe lamb and for the rest of the stay Struan talked of little else. At ten years old Struan was already a farmer. It was a pity he was the younger son. The lairdship would have been safe with him. As for the elder son James ... well it was not Mrs Little's place to say.

Mrs Little talked and talked but she was not really able to tell me much about Charlotte. Charlotte had spent most of her time riding. She would gallop across the Mersehead Sands in the direction of Sandyhills. And she always rode astride. No side saddle for her. Sometimes she stayed away all day. She would put a couple of apples and some bread and cheese in the saddlebags and that would be enough for her. Of course Mrs Little had not been happy about this but what should she do? It was not her place to complain about the governess. Anyway Miss Charlotte came to no harm and she certainly enjoyed her freedom. And at her age she would not get much more of that. Mrs Aitken had been furious when she found out but she had not blamed Mrs Little. After all she had had no authority over the governess.

There was something else I wanted to learn. I asked it outright.

"How did Struan and Charlotte get on. Whenever I saw them they always seemed to be fighting."

"They were as thick as thieves. It is only in the last year that things have changed – and not always, I can tell you, for the better. It all started when that new governess arrived. She has tried to make Miss Charlotte into a young lady – and now see where that has led."

This was interesting. In the space of a few months Charlotte's whole life had been turned topsy-turvy. From being allowed to be a wild tomboy she was forced into the mould of a demure miss. Mrs Little had some surprisingly firm views about it and by now she felt she could trust me enough to express them.

"Of course Miss Charlotte could not continue the way she was going. She would have to grow up some time. But I still think Miss Elliot (the new governess) was wrong. There was no need to go to extremes. Miss Charlotte could have been shown how to conduct herself in the drawing room and still been allowed her gallops along the Mersehead Sands. Certainly nobody in Satterness would concern themselves about Longcrags' daughter riding astride – especially when plenty of other ladies do it anyway."

Mrs Little fell silent for a while and then came out with two interesting points.

"I think that Miss Elliot was mistaken about Mrs Aitken's wishes. I don't believe for one moment that she meant Miss Elliot to be so strict with her daughter."

*Why then*, I thought fiercely to myself, *did Mrs Aitken not make it her business to find out what was going on in the schoolroom? Why do the wealthy always turn the care of their children over to someone else?*

Mrs Little had one last observation.

"I think Miss Charlotte was only pretending to go along with Miss Elliott. Biding her time while working out how to get the better of the governess. She's a great wee actress, Miss Charlotte."

Shortly after this I left Mrs Little and went back to the wagon. I prepared a meal and thought over what I had learned. I had a lot to ponder over. That evening I sat late over my campfire with a dish of tea while the sky turned from a mass of saffron and flame to a pale, washed out blue and Criffel turned to a black silhouette. And still I sat and thought. Finally, with Rooskie snoozing on my knee, and with the sound of Lucy tearing at the grass, I came to the beginnings of some sort of understanding of Charlotte. With a sense of shock I suddenly realised that I had a lot in common with her. I myself had quarrelled with my own mother and run away from home – although my problems had been different from Charlotte's.

Charlotte had had a happy childhood running wild with Struan. And then, with the arrival of the new governess, changes had been forced upon her, sudden, abrupt changes. The new governess decided that it was time for Charlotte to begin to grow up. (Here, like Mrs Little, I am sure that the governess misinterpreted Mrs Aitken's wishes, but more about that later).

Charlotte did not like the picture of growing up which was presented to her. She envisaged a future where her body was imprisoned by stays and her sharp, active mind fettered by the constraints society placed on young ladies. Then one day she would be expected to marry and subject herself completely to the will of a man.

Thinking back to my first sight of Charlotte's copybooks I remembered how surprised I was to see how neatly Charlotte had kept them. But that too told its own story. Charlotte was obviously very intelligent and she would have valued the chance of a good education. But, as a girl, education would be denied her. Sawney, the humble clerk, would no doubt, go to Glasgow University one day and eventually become a lawyer. But despite her wealth and position Charlotte would never have that opportunity. And she was just at the age when she would be beginning to think about such matters.

Nevertheless, in her own way Charlotte had tried to conform and do what she believed was expected of her. It was her attempts to act the young lady which had led to the growing rift between her and Struan. Even her action in taking the silver salver was actually a perverted way of trying to please her governess and mother. It was her way of trying to gain acceptance by the girls in her dancing class.

But her attempt to gain approval had ended in failure. Even worse she had been severely punished for it. So now Charlotte was determined to go her own way.

But was Charlotte running away *from* or *to*? Thinking back over my own experiences I was convinced that Charlotte had convinced herself that the society in which she had grown up had rejected her. But did she know of another community which she could join? Where had she gone on those wild rides? Did she meet anyone? Had she made any friends, friends of whom her parents might well disapprove?

Why, oh why, do the wealthy hand over the upbringing and education of their children to others? It happens all the time. Often grooms and kennelmen are supervised more closely than nursemaids and governesses. Children need a guiding figure, someone to look up to, and when the parents are far and distant then other mentors are sought. In Struan's case no harm was done. At ten years of age Struan was already a gentleman farmer and his hero was William Craik of Arbigland. In a few years time Struan would be an enthusiastic member of all the local agricultural improvement societies. It was a pity that Struan was the second son as he would have made a perfect laird for Longcrags. But even if the feckless James were to inherit he would need an estate manager – or factor as it is known in Scotland – and his younger brother would be ideal for that job. So being given his freedom had worked out well for Struan.

But what about Charlotte? Her doings remained a mystery. Whom had she chosen to be her adviser?

I did not know but I was at least sure of where I would find the answer –westward along the beach where she had loved to ride. That was where the solution to the mystery would lie. There was only one thing to do. I would have to ride across the sands myself and see if I could discover where she might have gone.

The more I thought the more I felt that I understood Charlotte, and what had made her act in the way she had. Now I wanted to help her. At her age I had experienced similar problems and had worked out my own peculiar solution. But I certainly was not going to counsel Charlotte to run away with the travelling people. I had to find some more responsible advice for her.

I started to think what advice I could give to Charlotte if I ever caught up with her. For a start I was firmly convinced that a reconciliation with her mother would be much easier than it may have appeared at first. Knowing Mrs Aitken as I did I was sure that she had not been completely ignorant of the freedom Charlotte had enjoyed at Satterness. But the governess had gone too far when she had neglected her charges completely to go husband-hunting and this forced Mrs Aitken to take action. But I was certain that much of her anger was feigned for the sake of appearances. If it had not been so then she would surely have had more to say to Mrs Little.

No, where Mrs Aitken had slipped up was in not supervising the new governess closely enough and in not making her instructions clear.

Isabel Aitken was an intelligent and independent woman. She had far more in her mind than the latest fashions in hats.

She ran her household competently and probably helped her husband far more than most people realised. As for clothes, she was the kind of woman who almost constantly wore a riding habit. Obviously something which she found practical and comfortable, especially as she probably wore the short stays specially made for riding habits. It suited her to dress like that regardless of the fashion.

I refused to believe that such a woman would want her daughter's head filled solely with the trivialities of society. This present misunderstanding could be cleared up quite quickly if Charlotte and her mother could just *talk* to each other.

In this way I talked my way into making myself responsible for Charlotte. This may help to explain the dreadful mistake I was about to make.

My reverie was ended by Rooskie. He woke up and scrambled down from my lap. He opened his tiny mouth as wide as it would go and yawned. Then he stretched – first a paw and body stretch with his front paws flat on the ground and hindquarters high in the air, and, secondly, each hind leg in turn pushed stiffly out behind him.

I got up too. It was time to prepare for the next day when I would ride across the sands trying to trace Charlotte's route and solve a mystery.

# CHAPTER 7

## THE CATTLE DROVE

Next morning it was time to put my plan into action. Looking back and considering the later dramatic and disastrous events the day started off very quietly. I began by saddling Lucy. I can ride bareback as the tinklers often do but I was very glad that I had a saddle. It had been a present from Michael. It was an old one of his own and he threw it down before me one day with an expression of contempt. He was giving me a present but at the same time he was telling me that he did not really consider me one of his family.

(I have said that the gypsies and tinklers usually rode bareback but that did not apply to Michael. As head of the family he considered himself entitled to a saddle – and his new one was very fine indeed with tooling and silver facings. Almost as good as those of the Baillies who were renowned for their finery as befitted one of the leading gypsy tribes.)

I fastened Rooskie's basket to the pommel, put some apples and bread and cheese in the saddlebags and was ready.

I rode down to the lighthouse and then turned westwards. After about half a mile the path curved round to a large bay and the vast expanse of the Mersehead Sands. Reining in Lucy I looked at the scene in front of me thoughtfully. There were clues there, if I could only recognise them.

What I saw gave me a feeling of reassurance. I had been right to come to Satterness. Before my very eyes Charlotte's common place book sprang to life. It was a clear autumn day with that special sharpness and touch of frost in the air that is a warning of the winter to come. Visibility was perfect and I could see for miles. Across the Solway the mountains of Cumberland stood out etched clearly against the sky. They were so distinct that Charlotte's Sleeping Giant looked just like what it was, a mountain range. I could even make out the separate valleys sloping up to the top of the plateau. No for the Sleeping Giant of Charlotte's imagination a duller day would be needed. But it still showed how Charlotte had got the idea for her poem.

Likewise with the story of the Barnhourie mermaid. The tide was in and looking out to sea I could see little wavelets breaking over the notorious sandbank. White horses? No today they were more like white ponies. I heard the gentle lapping of the waves breaking on the shore at my feet. Today the mermaid was singing a gentle, happy song.

Smiling quietly I turned my attention to other things. I looked right across the bay to where the cliffs beyond Sandyhills rose up from the beach. The cliffs made me think. Cliffs and caves, smugglers' caves. Had Charlotte been friendly with any smugglers? I remembered her story about the smuggler and the Barnhourie mermaid. Had Charlotte ever been aboard a smuggler's boat? Unlikely. They would not want a girl aboard. But then if Charlotte had dressed herself as a boy?

Still on the subject of smugglers, I searched the bay with my eyes, trying to find the place where I knew the Isle of

Man would be. From Satterness it is not always possible to see the Isle of Man. Sometimes, if one knows where to look, the faint, blue shape of Snaefell, can just be seen. But that day the peaks of the Isle of Man were plain and recognisable. I thought again about smugglers. Their boats carried on a busy trade with the Isle of Man, also with Whitehaven just across the Solway. Could Charlotte have gone to the Isle of Man? Or worse, could she have slipped aboard a boat going to Whitehaven? That did not bear thinking about. From Whitehaven ships went all over — even to America.

I had a last look at the bay before setting off. The huge extent of it was going to make my task even more difficult. The bay stretched for about seven miles. It would have been possible to ride right to Sandyhills if it had not been for the Water of Urr which flowed into the Solway just at the end of Sandyhills Bay. There could be problems about getting across it. But perhaps I would not need to go as far as Sandyhills.

It was now time to begin. I rode Lucy at a slow walk along the edge of the beach keeping, all the time, a sharp lookout for the slightest hint or clue, although for what exactly I had no idea. After about a mile I came to a little burn and stopped so that Lucy could have a drink. A sandy path ran alongside the burn and up through the sand dunes and bent. I decided to follow it. It led through the rough, sharp dune grass, and gorse bushes to a clump of larches through which farm buildings could be glimpsed. I dismounted, led Lucy into the middle of the trees and tied her up. Then I wriggled along a little passage between the gorse bushes and found a place which gave a good view of the farm. In front of it was a field where a number of black, shaggy cattle were grazing. This was not very promising. There would not be much hope of finding any news of

Charlotte at this farm. It was far more likely that she had sought out a boat. Nevertheless I decided to stay for a while and watch. I was soon glad of that decision.

Some more cattle were driven into the field. The drovers consisted of three men, a boy and three dogs. Two were collies, the third looked like no dog I had ever seen before. It was short-haired, greyish black, slightly smaller than a collie but much more strongly built. It had a long pointed tail and terrier ears. I love dogs but this was the ugliest dog I had ever seen. It seemed to be attached to the boy and I heard him calling to it. I even heard its name – Tink.

That caught my attention. Tinkler is sometimes used as a name for a dog — a dog no one cares about very much... But Tink? Tink is a form of abuse. I know that well enough. There is the odd time someone has hissed at me, in a tone of venom so intense as to be positively frightening, 'You tink!'

And now I was hearing that insult used as a name for a dog.

Then something happened which jolted me out of my reflections. Tink did something wrong and the boy aimed a kick at him. Tink was obviously well used to this kind of treatment because he dodged neatly but the incident set me thinking. My mind went back to the scene outside Longcrags Hall just after I had found the silver salver in Charlotte's bag. Charlotte had blamed Rooskie and had aimed a kick at him in exactly the same way as the boy in the field. I looked at the boy carefully. Could this be Charlotte? It could be but the boy was too far away for me to be sure. There was one thing I could have done, something which I have always regretted not doing. I could have taken Lucy and ridden back to Satterness for help. And if I was mistaken and the boy was not Charlotte it would not really have mattered.

That would have been the sensible course of action. But fear of looking stupid held me back. I wanted to be perfectly sure that I had found Charlotte before telling anyone. So I lay among the gorse bushes and continued to watch. It was obvious that the cattle were being gathered together ready to be driven to market. But which market? The most likely one would be the weekly market at Dumfries. Cattle were sold there to dealers who then drove them to the south of England where they were grazed and fattened before going to the London markets. But some Galloway drovers bypassed the Dumfries market and took them down through England themselves.

I guessed that that was what was going to happen in this case. If they were going only as far as Dumfries there would not have been any point in Charlotte waiting for them. She could have got to Dumfries just as easily herself. She could even have walked. No I was quite sure that these cattle were going further afield.

But when were they leaving? Was the herd complete or were there more beasts to come? Or perhaps they would join up with other herds *en route*. Not wanting to lose them I decided to camp out and keep them under observation. One thing was for sure. They would not set off at night. So I had until the next morning at least. I decided to return to Satterness for my wagon, bring it back here and hide it among the larches. There was time to get it before dark. I quietly led Lucy back along the path to the beach, mounted and cantered back to Satterness.

Arriving back at my wagon I thought about Rooskie. Should I take him with me? Or would it be better to leave him in Satterness? I finally decided it would be better for both of us if he were to be left behind. And I knew who would take good care of him, Mrs Little. I was proved right.

"Certainly. In fact I used to look after his mother. My it's the grand lady I shall be when I take him for a walk."

Leaving him with her I drove off smiling to myself. Rooskie was very obviously the kind of dog usually owned by the rich and I was amused at the idea of Mrs Little parading him all over Satterness and pretending she was one of the gentry. It was a great relief to me to know that Rooskie would be well looked after.

Soon I was back at my clump of larches which proved to be a good campsite. The trees provided an easy hiding place for the wagon, and it was useful being so near the burn. Not wanting to risk making a fire my supper that evening was just oatmeal and water.

I wanted to make sure that I would wake early the next morning. It would not do to sleep late and wake up to find the field empty. So I slept with the back flaps of the wagon open knowing that the daylight streaming into the wagon would wake me at once. As it turned out this precaution was hardly necessary. Being worried about missing the beginning of the drove I slept fitfully, waking up at least every two hours, with the result that I was awake when the grey dawn stole over the dunes and the first birds started twittering.

Shortly afterwards the men and the boy arrived in the field and started to round up the cattle. A horse, saddled ready for departure, was tied to the fence. The drovers were also prepared for a long journey. They all (including the boy) wore narrow trousers and each had a plaid slung over his shoulders. With the help of the efficient dogs – Tink duly playing his part – the cattle were soon rounded up. Eventually they set off. Questions raced through my mind.

*Were they going to join up with some more cattle and form a bigger drove? Perhaps.* I followed cautiously – on foot. Lucy would have made it difficult for me to keep the drove under observation without being seen. I kept well back. There was no point in my risking discovery. A cattle drove moves very slowly and if I lost them for a while I would easily be able to catch up and find them again.

They moved northwards. It looked as if they were going to try to find a quiet place where they could ford the Nith without being seen and so avoid paying the tolls.

My first concern was to avoid being seen by the drovers. From time to time I had to let them get out of sight but this did not cause any tracking problems and all seemed to be going well. Nevertheless I was uneasy about something, although what exactly I could not explain to myself. Then my ideas became more definite. At one point I stopped and looked back the way I had come. At that very moment, with a loud, raucous squawk, a pheasant rose from the bushes, wings beating clumsily until it reached the safety of the upper air.

Had something – or someone – startled it? Was I being followed? A picture flashed before my eyes — Lucy the previous evening, my normally placid, calm Lucy pawing the ground like a flighty thoroughbred. Clearly something had upset her. A hidden watcher perhaps? Was that spy following me now?

From then on I did my best to keep a good look-out, keeping my eyes on the bushes at the side of the track as well as on the way ahead, and stopping every now and again to look back. Although I saw nothing to alarm me my nerves were still on edge and my fears were aroused again when I heard what sounded like the sharp crack of a twig.

What made things worse was that this part of the country was very lonely. Even under normal circumstances a desolate landscape can appear ominous and in my present sensitive state it seemed positively forbidding. There was a good reason for the wild, deserted countryside. The drove was not following the lawful, official track. It was obviously following its own route, carefully plotted so as to avoid the tolls and turnpikes. The bleak, barren terrain increased my sense of foreboding. Farms and cottages were widely scattered and we passed no riders or carts. There was complete silence apart from the sounds of the drove ahead – the occasional lowing of a beast, the voices of the drovers or the bark of a dog. All normal noises, nothing sinister. I told myself firmly that it was just my usual vivid imagination, exacerbated by the solitude of the countryside and I forced myself to concentrate on the drove.

Following them was not difficult. The trouble was that I could not get near enough to see whether or not the boy was Charlotte in disguise. I looked at the direction of the track. Would it be possible for me to get ahead of them, hide and get a closer look when they passed? Just as that thought occurred to me I had a stroke of luck. The track curved round a little wood and there was a narrow track through the trees. I decided to follow it. Once hidden by the trees I gathered up my skirts and ran. The path went right through the wood and came out on the droving road again. Convinced that I was now ahead of the drove I hid behind a clump of gorse bushes and waited. It was not long before I heard the sound of many hooves, the lowing of the cattle and the calling of the drovers. When they approached my hiding place I peered through the branches. Yes, there was no doubt about it. It was certainly Charlotte.

It was then I made my second mistake. I did something incredibly stupid. I should have waited and gone back to Longcrags but instead I stepped forward in front of Charlotte. Looking back I wonder how I could ever have thought I could persuade her to come home with me. I don't even know what I would have said to her, for she did not give me a chance to speak.

She looked at me and I saw the light of recognition in her eyes. Then her expression changed to one of utter scorn. She swished her stick and said,

"Oot o' the way, eejit. Or dae ye want to be trampled underfit?"

I tried to speak calmly.

"It's time for you to come home Charlotte. I am here to take you to your father."

Then something happened which I would never, ever, have expected. At the sound of my voice the leader had turned round. Now he suddenly drew his pistol. Even worse, the other drovers also went for their weapons — pistols, daggers and stout sticks. They looked a proper set of ruffians. I stared at them in horror and terror.

Why? Why? I was a solitary unarmed female. They had no cause to threaten me with pistols and daggers. Then I noticed that the drovers' leader was not looking at me. He was looking past me into the distance. I turned and followed his gaze and saw a small band of horsemen cantering towards us. I also noticed a man on foot standing on a low hill just to the side of the track. At once I worked out what had happened. It had not been my imagination. I really had been followed. The pheasant which had risen from the bushes, the crackle of a breaking twig – they had both been tell-tale signs, signs which I had ignored. The man on foot had followed me, keeping me in sight the whole time while the men on horseback kept further back. There was probably another man on foot acting as a messenger. But whatever their method of communication they had caught up with us.

The horsemen reached us and reined in their horses. The one who appeared to be their leader spoke quietly,

"The little lass is coming with us."

I looked at the horsemen carefully. At first I thought they might be friends of the Laird. They were all well dressed and riding thoroughbreds. But Charlotte soon put me right. It was quite clear that she had never seen them before. Eyes blazing furiously she rounded on me.

"Ye daft gowk, whaw hae ye brung tae me? They must have followed you. They would nivver hae fund me else."

The leader of the newcomers looked down on us from his chestnut gelding and smiled condescendingly.

"That's right my dear. We followed Mrs Marshall. It was quite easy. We guessed Longcrags' little sleuth-hound would be sent to look for you."

His voice changed and became businesslike. "Now we don't want any trouble but I warn you. We are armed and if necessary..."

He did not finish his sentence but he did not need to. We could see that three of the men carried pistols and the fourth had a blunderbuss.

"So Miss Aitken, if you just come with me. You can ride in front."

Charlotte was not having any of this. And she had her own way of dealing with the situation. She turned her back on the man, waved her hand and said firmly "Tink."

Tink darted swiftly among the cattle. He turned some of them so that they were now facing the horses. Charlotte gave another command and Tink started to drive the cattle towards the horses. The other drovers saw what she was doing and they turned the rest of the herd so that they faced the horsemen who soon started to have trouble with their mounts. The leader was riding a highly-strung animal which began to sweat profusely. Specks of foam appeared round its mouth and it started skittering about on its toes. Suddenly it reared right up but its rider managed to get it under control again. But he needed both hands for his horse. He dropped his pistol which fell to the ground.

The drovers' leader waved his own pistol.

"I just need to fire this into the air and the beasts will charge. Is that whit ye want?"

Stalemate. The horsemen could have tried the same tactic. The drovers and horsemen became still and just looked at each other. The leader of the horsemen was still having difficulty with his mount.

But the cattle were not prepared to keep still. The leading stirks were moving forward slowly. One of them jostled the leader's horse. This was too much for the flighty creature and it wheeled round on its haunches and set off back along the track at a wild gallop, its rider desperately clinging to its neck. Then Charlotte decided to send the rest after him. She gave another command and Tink flew at one of the other horses, barking furiously. One of the collies joined Tink. Two dogs snapping at its heels was too much for a horse which was already unsettled and it turned and galloped after the leader.

The other two horsemen had steadier animals but the cattle were still advancing on them and their leader had gone. They decided to follow him, but at least they rode off with their horses under control and they kept their dignity.

Once they were away a frenzied Charlotte turned on me in rage and scorn.

"Ye fule. Ye've ruined a'thing. I was doing 'a richt until you cam alang. But noo these men ken whaur I am. They'll be back. And they'll hae nae bother in finding me."

Then she frowned and spoke as if thinking out loud.

"Who were they onyway? Up tae nae guid withoot doot. Probably kidnappers."

She accompanied this with a look of complete contempt for me then she paused for a moment and when she spoke again it was in the polite tones of the drawing room.

"Mrs Marshall, I think that you should leave."

There was nothing for it. I had no choice but to comply. I walked back along the track slowly and thoughtfully. At first I had thought this was just about a defiant little girl running away from her parents. Then I had begun to wonder if there was not more to it than that, and now I had been proved correct. Charlotte obviously knew where she was going. It had been no impulsive action on her part. She was not just running *from* something, she was running away *to* something or somewhere. And who were the men on horseback? *Gretna, Gretna* I sighed wearily, *What are you getting yourself into?*

I also firmly berated myself for being such a fool. I should have reported to the Laird at once and let him check up on whether or not it was Charlotte with the drovers. What was I thinking of? Whatever was I hoping to achieve? How could I ever have thought that Charlotte would have listened to me meekly and accompanied me home? I must have been suffering from some kind of temporary insanity.

I can, however, put forward one excuse. People were already beginning to call me *Longcrags' little sleuth-hound.* It was not until later that it dawned on me that hounds run in packs. I was a member of the Laird's pack and not expected to do everything myself. All that was asked of me was that I was to play my part. That should have been obvious but it was some time before I realised it.

To add further mitigation, at that time the Solway Sleuth-Hounds were few in number. But even at that early stage there were still the Laird's estate workers and Michael and the tinklers. I should have understood that it was for me to call on them for help and not take stupid risks myself.

There was something else. I also realised that I had acted with a certain amount of arrogance. My duty to the Laird was one thing but there was also the special responsibility I had taken upon myself for Charlotte. That night, beside my campfire at Satterness, I had persuaded myself that I understood Charlotte's problems and vowed to help her. But my first efforts had ended in failure and Charlotte had made it quite clear that she did not want my help. This hurt my pride deeply. It was many years before I understood that there is often a very thin line between offering assistance and interfering.

I trudged on weary and despondent. My thoughts became even more depressing. Would the Laird be angry with me and go back on his promise to speak up for Danny? And what about Mrs Aitken? I was even more afraid of her wrath.

Eventually, absolutely exhausted, I reached the clump of larches and my wagon and climbed in thankfully. At least I would be able to lie down and rest.

But it was not to be. Suddenly a sack was thrown over my head and my arms seized and pulled behind my back. A voice said,

"Be sensible. We don't want to hurt you. Just do what you are told and you will not get hurt."

But these words failed to reassure me. I could not breathe properly and I panicked. I spluttered, wriggled and tried desperately to free my hands. I was sure that I was going to suffocate but my captor just held me all the more firmly. In despair I let myself go limp.

# CHAPTER 8

## THE MESSAGE

The pressure on my arms was relaxed slightly. My hands were tied behind my back and my legs were tied together. Then the sack was removed from my head and I was thrown down. I was lying face down on the floor of the wagon and I could not see my captor but I heard a man's voice say,

"We are not going to hurt you. You are going to be too useful for that. But just lie there and be quiet. I don't want to have to gag you but if you try to call out then I will."

The words were spoken calmly and quietly but with a kind of grim firmness. The man definitely meant what he said. I kept very still and did not answer.

The speaker did not leave the wagon. I could hear him settling himself and I knew where he was sitting. Various other little sounds and noises also conveyed their own stories to me. By straining my ears and from various clinks, the creaking of leather and the sound of hooves I deduced that Lucy was being harnessed to the wagon. Then the wagon swayed slightly and I could sense someone pulling himself up onto the driving seat. I even heard the slight flick of the reins as the wagon started to move. But Lucy's hoofbeats were not the only ones. At least two other horses were trotting behind. So I was important enough to have an escort.

I tried to work out where we were going but I could not. The various twists and turns were meaningless to me. Lying on the floor and without the use of my hands I was continually jolted and bumped but far worse than the discomfort this caused was the knowledge of my own folly. I lectured myself continually. Why, oh why, had I got myself into this mess? When I saw the boy in the field I should have sent word to Longcrags at once. I should have had more sense than to try to act on my own. If the Laird had come and found out that the boy was not Charlotte then no harm would have been done. Why had I tried to be clever? After a while my thoughts took a different direction. Who knew where I was? Nobody. When my disappearance was noted who would look for me? The Laird certainly because if he found me then he might also find his daughter. Anybody else? Yes. I was also Michael's responsibility. He would surely search for me. And he had all the resources of the travelling people at his disposal. But where would he look? There was a slight chance that Rooskie and Mrs Little would point him in the right direction. At least any seekers would know to begin their hunt around Satterness.

Reasoning like this helped me to control my feelings of terror and panic. Who were these men and what were they going to do to me? I tried to shut such thoughts out of my mind and instead conjure up a picture of Michael riding to the rescue. But try as I might I could not raise any faith in Michael.

Suddenly Lucy slowed to a walk and I felt the wagon swing round a sharp corner. Then we stopped. We had arrived – somewhere. My legs were untied and, stiff, bruised and aching, I was helped out of the wagon. Looking around quickly I at once recognised where I was – in the yard of a derelict farm. It had been up for sale for years but had not attracted a buyer. I knew it because tinklers had camped there in the past, before they were ordered off. The farm might be unoccupied but it still had an owner and he did not want any of the travelling people around.

I was hustled through the door of the farmhouse, and up the stairs and pushed into a room. My hands were untied, the door was locked and I was left alone. I sank onto a chair and rubbed my wrists. My legs were numb so I rubbed my ankles too. I tried to swing my legs gently to and fro to get them working again. The result was a sharp stabbing pain which I actually welcomed as it told me that things were gradually returning to normal.

I sat there and bit by bit the pain lessened. Holding onto the chair I rose carefully to my feet. I stood there for a few minutes and then took a few tentative steps. I was now ready to explore my surroundings, such as they were.

I was in a suite of rooms which had once been used as a nursery. That was obvious at once from the bars on the windows. No chance of any young children falling out – or of me trying to escape that way either. I was in a large room which had probably been a playroom or dayroom. Any nursery furniture had been taken out but there were comfortable chairs and a large table. Two doors led off this room into two bedrooms – also with barred windows. In a corner of one of the bedrooms there was a small table with a few books. I picked one up idly, and then I heard the door of the large room being unlocked.

I walked back slowly wondering uneasily what was going to happen now. A woman was putting a tray on the table while a man stood in the doorway making sure that I did not try to escape.

"I've brought a light refreshment. I'll bring a proper meal later."

The door was locked and I was left alone again. I looked at the tray. A dish of tea, bread and butter, and a piece of fruit cake. I had been so very uncomfortable, worried and frightened that I had not even thought of food, but now I suddenly realised that all this was very welcome. Being more thirsty than hungry I started on the tea at once before going on to the bread and butter. As I ate and drank I pondered over my circumstances. Whoever had kidnapped me had gone to some trouble to see that I was reasonably comfortable. My accommodation was spacious and quite pleasant and I was obviously going to be fed. I remembered the books in the bedroom. There had even been a slight attempt to entertain me. But I was still frightened. Why had I been brought here? I remembered the man's words in the wagon. "We are not going to hurt you. You are going to be too useful for that." Useful for what? What did that mean? And my kidnappers must know that both the Laird and Michael would be looking for me. How long could they afford to keep me here?

Nothing much happened for the next two days. My meals were brought to me and I was left to my own devices. I read the books and thought about my plight. What could I do? Surely there must be something.

On the morning of the third day I heard horse's hooves. I went to the window but I could not see what was happening. Then I heard footsteps on the stairs and a girl's voice shouting. The door was unlocked and there was Charlotte struggling fiercely in the grip of two men. When she saw me she shouted,

"Ye interfering bissom. This is a' your blame. If you ..."

I did not hear the rest. Charlotte was dragged away again and the door locked.

So the kidnappers had made another attempt and this time they had been successful. They had got Charlotte and she blamed me. I admitted ruefully to myself that she was probably right.

Shortly afterwards the door was unlocked again. One man stood in the doorway but another came into the room and sat down at the table. He waved his hand and indicated that I should sit opposite him. I did so and looked at him carefully. He was wearing a wig and spectacles. Obviously to try to make it difficult for me to recognise him afterwards, although he would probably make sure that there would not be much chance of that. When he spoke he came to the point at once.

"You see that we have Longcrags' daughter. We want you to take a message to him."

This had been sprung on me and I struggled to take it in. It seemed simple enough. There was no reason for me to refuse. By the time I had reached Longcrags, the kidnappers would have taken Charlotte to another hiding place far from this derelict farmhouse. In fact she was probably on her way right now.

"You will agree, of course."

I nodded dumbly and waited for further instructions – and was astounded when I received them.

"Nothing must be written down. You will learn your message off by heart – and you must be word perfect. I hope for all our sakes that you are a quick learner."

Then followed a period of intensive coaching. I had to repeat my lesson over and over again. At last my instructor seemed satisfied.

137

"You'll do," he said. Then he added sternly,

"Mind you tell that only to the Laird of Longcrags and to no one else. No one else. Do you hear?"

Again I nodded silently. There was nothing else to do.

The man was not finished. He had one last – and sinister – instruction for me.

"Make sure that you obey me implicitly. Take my message to Longcrags at once and do not think of running away. My men will be watching you and will find you wherever you are. If you do not do as you have been told you will be brought back to me instantly. And then you will find I can be very unpleasant. I trust I do not need to be more explicit."

He spoke quietly in a flat, expressionless voice, which made his words all the more ominous. He had not delivered an open threat. Instead he had left everything to my imagination, which, in my case, was probably worse.

He gave me only a few moments to consider his words before calling for his henchmen. I was hurried down the stairs to the yard to find Lucy harnessed to my wagon with one of the men already on the driving seat. I was helped up beside him. Obviously the men did not realise that I already knew where I was. I was driven away from the farm to the Dumfries road. Then the driver pulled up Lucy, handed the reins to me and jumped down.

I reached Longcrags in the late afternoon. As I drove towards the stables the first person who saw me was Michael's eldest son. Joe waved to me and ran off to get his father. A few minutes later I was sitting in Michael's wagon while Joe attended to Lucy. I had just found out that the Laird had allowed Michael and a few other travellers to camp in a field behind his stables. Michael ordered his brood outside and then made me tell him everything. I did so until I came to the message. Then I hesitated.

"I was told it was for the Laird and no one else," I said nervously.

Michael said nothing but he narrowed his eyes and looked at me steadily. I panicked. What was I to do? Then something else occurred to me? Who was I to trust? I looked again at Michael's stern face and knew there was only one thing for it. I would have to tell him. I tried to reassure myself. I had married into Michael's family. He disapproved of his brother's marriage and of me, but he had accepted me into his family even if on sufferance. I was now his little sister and he had a responsibility for me. At that moment I had more faith in Michael than in the Laird. I took a deep breath and delivered my message.

*"We have your daughter. If you want to see her again then you will do as we say. We will not harm her, but there are other things we can do. For example we could sell her as an indentured servant to the Caribbean. So listen to what your messenger has to say.*

*'We are friends of the Radcliffes, who were tricked out of Longcrags by your father and we want the lairdship returned to its rightful owners. We will be generous. We will give you the exact sum which your father paid for the estate. Have all the necessary papers signed and delivered to the Radcliffes' agent, Mr Taylor, Writer of Dumfries, together with the money. Then your daughter shall be set free.*

*'If you have any reply then send it by our messenger Gretna Marshall, to the house of William Young in the Bridgend of Dumfries as soon as possible. Do not wait too long if you want to see your daughter again.*

*'Pay particular attention to the following. Your messenger must be Gretna Marshall and nobody but Gretna. Nothing must be written down. Gretna must deliver her message by word of mouth only. If this instruction is not obeyed then we will not return your daughter to you."*

I finished and looked at Michael anxiously. I did not understand it all but I saw at once that he did. But he did not give me any explanations. He rubbed his chin thoughtfully.

"Sae that's whit it's a' aboot. Weel Longcrags has aye been a guid freend tae the travelling people. Awa wi' ye lass. Awa tae the Laird. Up tae the big hoose wi' ye."

In fact I did not have to go as far as the house. Word of my arrival had got around quickly and the Laird and Mrs Aitken were hurrying down the drive. I passed on my message there and then.

Even supposing that Mr Aitken agreed to the kidnappers' demands, selling an estate is a lengthy process. Lawyers have to be consulted, procedures followed and documents signed. But there was at least one spark of light. Mr Aitken's legal adviser and man of business, Mr Gordon, Writer to the Signet, was at that very moment in Mr Aitken's study. I was taken there at once where I found Mr Gordon together with a clerk. It was Sawney, the little boy clerk, Sawney, the bringer of good news, Sawney who had come to me in my cell in the Mid Steeple and had told me that I was to be released.

Remembering that I gave him a little smile and he inclined his head politely. Then I had to forget Sawney as the Laird and Mr Gordon were demanding my full attention. I repeated my message, word for word. Mr Gordon at once turned his legal mind to it.

"Verra clever, verra clever indeed," he said. There was actually a slight note of admiration in his voice.

"Abduction and threats. An almost certain death sentence for the culprits if they were ever caught. But nothing is to be written down. That means that there will be no evidence so we would not be able to bring a case in court. And that bit aboot the payment. Far less than the lairdship is worth of course. It has increased in value since auld Mr Aitken bought it, to say naething aboot the extra land which has been bought since. But even a nominal payment would be enough to stop any questions. It would be strange if the lairdship were to be just given away."

Mrs Aitken picked up on the 'no evidence' bit. She pointed out that I knew all the facts and could testify.

Mr Gordon shook his head slowly.

"For evidence at least twa witnesses are required. In this case we have only the uncorroborated evidence o' a tinkler. No it would not stand up in court. I wouldna even advise trying it."

He looked at me solemnly and then added,

"The insistence that the messenger should be Mrs Marshall and nae one else is also interesting. They have nae doot made their enquiries aboot her and they may weel hae found oot something compromising. Efter a' whaur was she afore she mairrit Danny Marshall?"

He looked at me sadly and shook his head.

"Naw. Naw. Here we have an unknown tinkler with, verra probably, a sinister past. Someone who could easily be discredited in ony court of law."

I sat and simmered silently. Why, he was talking about me as if I was not there. But at least Mrs Aitken realised I was human.

She was not going to give up so easily and this time she spoke directly to me.

"Would you recognise any of the men?"

I shook my head.

"The only one whom I really noticed was the one who taught me the message. And I suspect that his wig and spectacles were probably some sort of disguise."

The Laird cut me off impatiently.

"They were probably recruited from a distance. They'll be well clear of the district by now."

Mr Gordon repeated,

"It's still the word o' a tinkler against them."

Something else had occurred to Mrs Aitken's sharp mind. She looked directly at Mr Gordon.

"You say that even the payment of what is actually a nominal sum will stop people asking questions about the sale of Longcrags. But surely the suddenness of the sale will make people wonder and let us raise the matter of the kidnapping?"

Mr Gordon dismissed this at once.

"Naw. Naw. That argument wilna dae at a'. The sudden sale o' the lairdship will just be pit doon tae the gambling debts o' Mr James. I warned you aboot the rumours but ye didna listen."

Here the Laird started to say something but the Writer just ignored him and carried on. Mr Gordon was very sure of his position.

"And I would be dootful aboot the word 'kidnappers.' We could mak oot a case for threats and extortion – which both merit the death penalty – but no' kidnap. Efter a' Miss Charlotte left hame o' her ain free will. If pressed, these men could pit forrard the claim that they had fund her and were looking efter her for her ain protection. Of coorse, they would prefer to avoid any court case – and so would we."

He stopped at last and the Laird spoke quickly while he still had time.

"I paid James' debts. All of them."

Mr Gordon proceeded to cast doubt on this.

"Are ye siccar? There's talk in the toon that there's mair. I did try tae tell ye."

There was silence for a few moments. Personally I was amazed at the Writer's temerity. I could not imagine how anyone would dare to speak to the Laird and his wife like that. Then Mr Gordon spoke again and this time his words were slightly reassuring.

"At least we've time. The selling o' a lairdship is a lengthy business."

Then I was dismissed while they discussed what course of action they were to take next and what part I was to play in it.

I wandered back to the field behind the stables and the tinklers' wagons. Michael was holding some sort of conference in his wagon and no one else was admitted. I turned and slowly walked towards the stables. I found the stall where Joe had put Lucy, whose nose was now deep in a manger of hay. I went up to her and stroked her neck. Then I buried my face in her mane and drew what comfort I could from her placid presence. The Laird and Mrs Aitken, Michael and the tinklers – they were all deciding what I was to do in the next few hours and I had absolutely no say in the matter.

I don't know how long I stayed there but it was Joe who found me and summoned me to the Laird.

Back in the study I stood facing the Laird, Mrs Aitken and Mr Gordon who was still there. It was Mr Gordon who addressed me.

"We have decided tae play for time," he said speaking with a lawyer's deliberation. "You are tae gang tae the Bridgend as arranged. I shall draw up a message explaining the proper procedures involved in the sale o' a lairdship. It's nae' as easy as oor freends mak oot. It is too late for you to set oot the nicht and that is just as weel as it will give you time to learn your communication. I fear this may take you some time as it will be couched in precise legal language with many terms which will nae doot be unknown tae you."

He paused for a moment, then looked at the Laird and shook his head slowly.

"Of course, if the lairdship had been entailed, as I strongly advised, then this ploy could not have been tried. But you delayed the entail and this is the result."

*Pompous old fool,* I thought to myself. But at the same time I was desperately trying to think of a protest – one that would be listened to. I certainly did not want to enter the Bridgend of Dumfries – especially not alone. It is a village just across the River Nith from Dumfries and it has a very bad reputation. Eventually I managed to get out,

"Laird, I don't think I am the right person for this task. Surely it would be better if one of the tinkler men folk were to take the message to the Bridgend."

Mr Gordon shook his head.

"I think ony o' Michael's faimly would hae trouble learning my dispatch. You on the other hand, appear to have an excellent memory."

Mrs Aitken's face bore a condescending smile. Yes, she was actually smiling while her own daughter was in the hands of desperate kidnappers.

"Why, Gretna," she said, "you surely do not believe all the stories about the Bridgend. When all is said and done it is just an ordinary village with people going about their daily work, weavers, millers, brewers and the like."

That was certainly not what I had heard but before I could say anything she forestalled me.

"Of course it has an unfortunate reputation. And all because of that English magistrate Sir John Fielding who claimed that his constables could track a thief over the whole country except to the Gorbals of Glasgow or the Bridgend of Dumfries."

She broke off and gave a depreciating little laugh.

"Nonsense. What could an Englishman – and a Londoner at that – know about Dumfries?"

Mr Gordon continued ponderously,

"There is some foundation for his statement. It is true that the Dumfries magistrates hae nae authority oan the west side o' the river, and that this has resulted in several cases of thieves and felons taking refuge in the Bridgend. But, despite this, the village is far from the haven of vagabonds and scoundrels that it is often claimed to be."

"And it is not entirely true that the authorities cannot enter the village," put in the Laird sharply. "On the odd occasion they can."

*Yes* I thought to myself. *But they rarely catch anyone. Not with that rabbit warren of cellars.*

Mrs Aitken spoke again,

"Of course there are certain undesirable features. For example there are too many taverns. But drunkeness is not, alas, confined to the Bridgend."

Then she gave me a single crumb of comfort.

"There are also many gypsies and travellers there, gypsies who have tired of the open road and have settled down. So you should have friends there Gretna."

All these explanations failed to reassure me. I was firmly convinced of one thing. The Bridgend of Dumfries was certainly no place for me. But there was no point in my saying any more. It had been decided that I was to go to the Bridgend the next day and that was that. To clinch matters and make sure that I had no more doubts Mr Gordon made a last telling point,

"The abductors have insisted on you, lass. If onyone else takes the message they will not guarantee to return Charlotte."

His words also reminded me of something else, of my captor's vague, undefined threat – that if I did not do exactly what I had been told he would send his men after me. I had been trying desperately to tell myself that that applied only to delivering the message to the Laird, and not to anything else. But now, listening to Mr Gordon, I realised that I had been fooling myself. Delivering the message to Longcrags was only half the duty which had forced upon me.

I did not know what terrified me more – the thought of the threats of my former captor or of going alone into the Bridgend.

Thinking along these lines distracted me somewhat from the discussion but I was jolted back to attention when I heard my name again. I found out that I was to do more than just deliver Mr Gordon's message. I was to try to find out where

Charlotte was being kept prisoner. The Bridgend was the most likely place. If I kept my wits about me I might discover a clue to her whereabouts.

"Then we can make a rescue attempt," the Laird said simply.

To my surprise Mrs Aitken gave a grim little smile.

"I think we can be quite sure that Charlotte is being held prisoner in the Bridgend. In that case Mr Radcliffe and his friends have made a big mistake."

I looked at the Laird and his wife. Considering the circumstances they both looked surprisingly calm. A dreadful thought fluttered through my mind. Could it be that they did not really care about their daughter?

That was the end of the conference. I was given a light meal and then it was time for me to learn my message. I had taken it for granted that it would be Mr Gordon who would teach me but when I entered the study again it was Sawney I found sitting behind the Laird's big table.

He rose to his feet when I entered and said simply,

"I am to go over the message with you first and then Mr Gordon will hear you to see if you have learned it properly."

He sat down and I followed his example.

This was a new development, and one about which I had mixed feelings. Looking at the little boy across the table I was hard put to it to believe that he was actually fifteen. I also felt slighted. The messenger to the Bridgend was surely worthy of the attention of Mr Gordon himself.

On the other hand Sawney would probably be easier to work with. His next words bore that out.

He picked up a sheaf of papers and said without a trace of awkwardness,

"Would you like me to read the message to you or would you rather peruse it yourself?"

I said that I would like to read it myself and he passed the wad of papers over to me and said carelessly,

"Of course, once you have committed it all to memory then these notes will be destroyed. Remember, it was impressed on us that nothing is to be written down. Strictly speaking, this rough draft should not have been prepared. But both the Laird and Mr Gordon thought it necessary to facilitate your task."

I began to feel increasingly irritated. *Oh Sawney*, I thought, *Just for once stop talking as if you were in court. Surely this is one time when you can sound like a human being.*

I took the papers and glanced at them despondently. As was to be expected from Mr Gordon they were wordy and verbose. Learning the message off by heart would be a daunting task at the best of times, but to do it in one evening would be practically impossible. Nevertheless I settled down to study it.

The first part was not too bad. It was lengthy but at least it was in plain English and I could understand it. It was all about trust and the keeping of faith. Even if the Laird did carry out the instructions, how did he know that Charlotte's captors would keep their promise and set her free? Moreover, he was insisting on being given details as to how his daughter would be returned to him.

I read the passage through several times and then passed the page back to Sawney and repeated it to him. I got it right. Well near enough. And if I did not always remember Mr Gordon's exact words I was able to fill in myself with the sense. Sawney was satisfied anyway but I knew that Mr Gordon would be a harder taskmaster.

Then on to the rest, the legal bit. That was a very different story. It was full of specialised legal terms which I did not understand. There were even some Latin phrases. I struggled and did my best but, at the same time, I felt it was all rather futile. What would it matter if I made a few mistakes? No one, apart from a lawyer, would ever understand a single word. I didn't. And I certainly can't remember any of it now.

Then something suddenly occurred to be. This was not just Mr Gordon being pedantic. He was being deliberately obscure. He was playing for time and if he was going to force the Radcliffes to consult their own lawyer then so much the better.

Sawney was very patient with me. He took time to explain all the legalities but his consideration had the opposite effect from what he expected. I was beginning to resent Sawney and to take exception to being taught by someone three years younger than myself. At one point I threw down the papers and snapped,

"What does it matter. No one in the Bridgend will ever understand a word of this anyway?"

Sawney said gently.

"We cannot be sure of that. They may well have a legal adviser with them. Just try it again. You're actually doing very well. I know it is difficult for a young woman to understand the intricacies of the law."

That misplaced kindness was just too much for me. I stared at him, my eyes full of sullen anger. I could have understood as much about the law as any lawyer if I had been given Sawney's opportunities. But education is not for women. It happens all the time. Learning is forced on a boy who does not appreciate it and who truants whenever possible while his sister who would give anything for his chances has to content herself with sewing the letters of the alphabet on a sampler. Casting my mind back to my cell in the Mid Steeple I remembered how Sawney had told me proudly that he hoped that the Laird would pay for him to go to Glasgow University to study law. I was quite sure that he would be a lawyer one day, yes even an advocate.

Despite the fact that Sawney was just a poor writer's clerk he still had it in him to be anything he wanted to be. But that would never have applied to me – even if I had stayed in my former life of so called wealth and privilege. What privilege? I would never have been able to go to university and become a writer or advocate. And neither would Charlotte, despite her father's position.

No, neither of us would ever wear the red gown of an undergraduate.

Thinking along these lines I glared at the puny brat who sounded like a legal textbook and said coldly,

"If women were allowed the education they should be entitled to I think you would find that many would have no problems at all understanding the law. It's all right for you, the precious protégé of the Laird and Mr Gordon."

Sawney did not rise to this sneer. Instead he just looked at me intently and said very quietly,

"So you think that women should have the right to a university education? Tell me, do you think that they should also have the right to the press gang, to be virtually kidnapped and hauled aboard one of His Majesty's ships? Should women also have the right to be flogged, to have their arms and legs – and yes, their heads – shot off by French cannon?"

This certainly silenced me. It was worth thinking about. But while I was trying to think of a reply Sawney suddenly threw down his papers and said,

"Forgive me. That was uncalled for on my part. And my remark about it being difficult for a young woman to understand the law – I suppose that must have sounded rather condescending, although I did not mean it to be. You may find this difficult to believe, but I do understand how you feel."

He paused and then finished simply,

"I have sisters."

He added,

"And I do realise that our society does not always treat members of the fair sex with the consideration they deserve. I have copied out plenty of marriage contracts since I entered Mr Gordon's office."

Faced with this apology I felt almost guilty. Sawney seemed full of surprises. Very few of his elders would have been so understanding. Then Sawney broke into my thoughts and, almost with a sense of shock, I realised that he could speak plain English after all.

"Look, you're nearly there. Don't give up now, not after all your hard work. Run through it once more."

His next words showed that, in his own way, he could be just as persuasive as Isabel Aitken.

"After all it is in both our interests to please the Laird."

That statement was very true. Sawney had to please the Laird so that he could go to Glasgow University. I had to please him to save Danny from the hangman's rope. I stared straight ahead and repeated my lesson once more to Sawney. This time, to the delight of both of us, I got it right.

Now that I was able to relax a little I thought more deeply about the whole affair – and I thought out loud.

"I cannot really believe that this plan will ever work. How can the Radcliffes expect the Laird to hand over the estate just like that?"

Sawney considered.

"I do not believe they planned it. They are just being opportunist. They have been wanting to get Longcrags back into their possession for years. It was in the family for generations and then they fell into debt and the creditors forced them to sell the estate. They were able to keep one small corner with a farm, and that was all. But they gradually built up their finances again and it is well known that they would love to regain possession. Although they are still in no position to pay the price of its true value."

Here Sawney stopped for a moment to give me time to take this all in before continuing, "When they heard that Charlotte had run away they probably considered how best they could capitalise on her folly. And the news of Mr James' gambling debts also helped. His debts are worse than his father realises, and the Radcliffes can easily spread rumours to make them out to be even worse. Then it could be quite feasible that the estate would have to be sold."

Here he paused for breath before continuing, "As to whether the plan has any real chance of success – I don't think they are even thinking about that. There is a slight chance and they are trying to take advantage while, at the same time, ensuring that no blame or legal recrimination can ever fall on them. In other words they are really just trying to make things difficult for the Laird. If the plan succeeds great. If not then it does not matter all that much."

He fell silent and frowned thoughtfully. I did not interrupt him and waited until he was ready to go on.

"Even so, it is not what I would expect of William Radcliffe. I don't like him, or any of his family, and I certainly would not trust him. But working with these ruffians, and having you hauled off and illegally imprisoned – no it's certainly not his method of working. He prefers to conduct his affairs through the courts. He has a rather dubious agent, a Mr Taylor who will always try to bend and twist the law to his clients' benefit. But kidnapping, no that is definitely not William Radcliffe. The men who captured you, I would dearly like to know who they are. They could well be using William Radcliffe for their own ends, and he is too stupid to realise it."

The last part of this statement washed over me. I was more interested in what had come before.

"But Mr Gordon said that we could not claim that Charlotte was kidnapped because she had run away of her own free will."

With a quiet smile Sawney said,

"I was not thinking of Charlotte. What about yourself? You were kidnapped. And kidnapping a traveller is still kidnapping – and a very serious crime."

I drew in my breath. Here was something which Mr Gordon had missed. Why had that escaped his legal mind? No doubt because I was too insignificant to count. But Sawney had noticed. This meant that he regarded me as a normal human being. I looked at him, my eyes full of gratitude, then something occurred to me and I said despondently,

"But it would be difficult to prove. There is only my word for it."

"Difficult, yes," said Sawney. "But perhaps not impossible."

Then he returned to his other point.

"I still wish I knew who these scoundrels working for Radcliffe are. I am convinced that if we foil his wicked plot we will be saving him from himself, although he will never know and will certainly not thank us."

He gave his little smile again,

"Which is where you come in. Now, one final time, let me hear it again."

By this time I was actually beginning to feel more confident and I repeated the message with only one or two minor mistakes. We both thought that should be good enough for anyone.

But would I satisfy Mr Gordon, that was the question? And would I still remember it in the morning?

Bidding Sawney goodnight I went back to my wagon where I spent a sleepless night. I was dreading the next day. First of all I was to have my session with Mr Gordon and that would be bad enough. But not nearly as bad as what was to follow. I was to set off for the Bridgend in the wagon, which I was to leave, with Lucy, at a farm on the outskirts of Dumfries. Then I was to walk the rest of the way to the Bridgend. The Laird and Mr Gordon were both riding to Dumfries too. The Laird was going to stay at the Globe Inn and if I had a message for him I was to send it there.

I kept thinking of all I had heard about the Bridgend — a refuge for all the lawless elements of south west Scotland, a place where drunkeness and brawling were rife, a place which, even under normal circumstances I would never have dared enter. And now I was going there to take a message to a man who terrified me.

Then I stopped thinking of myself for a moment and thought of Danny. I could now forget the hangman. The Laird would keep his promise and speak for Danny and he would, no doubt, be transported to Australia. But I realised only too well that his fate there would partly depend on my actions. If my work satisified the Laird he would use his influence to have Danny assigned to a fair-minded settler. Otherwise Danny might find himself exposed to the harshness and brutal savagery of the new settlement. My imagination got to work again and I could visualise Danny strapped to a frame, his whole back a bloody mass of lacerations. I could even hear the sound of the whip as it crashed down on his helpless body. No, for Danny's sake, if for nothing else I would have to brave the terrors of the Bridgend.

Fear and anxiety kept me awake for most of the night, until morning brought a new set of worries.

# CHAPTER 9

## INSIDE THE BRIDGEND

Next morning I had company for breakfast. I was cooking my porridge when Sawney arrived at my campfire. Although he tried to hide it, he seemed tense and I realised that he was worried about my meeting with Mr Gordon. He was silently fretting that if I was not word perfect he would be blamed for not teaching me properly. He was all for having me repeat the message right then but I was certainly not having any of that.

"Breakfast first," I said firmly throwing another handful of oatmeal into the pot.

We had a good breakfast of porridge, boiled eggs, tea and bannocks. Then down to work. My fears that the message would have vanished with the last of the night's darkness were groundless. I remembered it very well – just a few mistakes which would not really matter. Even Sawney relaxed a little.

All too soon it was time for me to go up to the big house. As I left Sawney called, "Good luck."

Once in the study and facing Mr Gordon, I suddenly felt very nervous. I stammered and started to make silly mistakes. I had to repeat the message and this time I made different mistakes. He drilled me over and over again until he said at last,

"Ah weel, I suppose it will hae tae dae."

The result of all this relentless practice was that it was afternoon before I set off. This meant that it was evening before I reached Dumfries and so I decided to stay for the night at the farm where I was to leave Lucy and the wagon. Once again I spent the night in a waking nightmare. A rhyme about the Bridgend kept running through my mind.

> *Brigen', Brigen, a dirty place,*
> *A kirk without a steeple,*
> *A wee dunghill at every door,*
> *And full of Irish people."*

I thought of the last line resentfully. There was nothing wrong with Irish people. Why I had married one. And how I wished that my brother-in-law Michael was by my side at that very moment.

I rose early the next morning and dressed in my old clothes thinking that they would be more suitable for the Bridgend. How glad of my rags I was to be later! I was too churned up inside for breakfast but, making a supreme effort, I forced myself to swallow some porridge. I made up my mind to go and deliver the message early and get it over with.

That decided I set off, and soon found myself in sight of the Bridgend. I had passed it often before but I had never been actually inside, always preferring just to scuttle past as quickly as possible. Now I had to admit that, from the outside, it did not look too bad. I walked up the road to the bridge – the old narrow bridge built in the Middle Ages by the Lady Devorgilla. At the end of this bridge was the attractive red sandstone building which was now used as an inn. The main entrance to the village was just opposite the inn. I entered reluctantly and looked around.

The cottages of the village were of red sandstone. Most of the roofs were tiled in accordance with the fire regulations but here and there was still an occasional, older thatched roof. I was pleasantly surprised to find wide, spacious streets – an agreeable contrast to the crowded, back-to-back houses of the closes of Dumfries, those refuges of disease. True, there was, in the middle of the street, a huge midden sending forth its own pungent stench, to say nothing of a few private dungheaps. But then that would apply to many places and not just the Bridgend.

In fact, when everything was taken into consideration, the Bridgend did actually look like a respectable, relatively prosperous village. But, as I well knew, the dubious business of the Bridgend was all conducted underground – in the network of cellars and passages.

I paused for a moment and nerved myself to walk on. At first I saw nothing alarming and then I heard loud, angry voices and a number of men spilled out of a tavern. But I managed to slip to the other side of the street and scurry past. After that nothing untoward happened and I passed along streets filled with ordinary people following their everyday routine.

I soon found the house for which I was looking. It was near the end of the main street and it looked like a fine town house. It was one of the few two storey buildings in the Bridgend. I took a deep breath and rattled the tirling pin. The door opened at once, and a hand came out and hauled me inside. The hand belonged to a woman wrapped in a shawl. She led me upstairs and into a room and curtly told me to

"Bide a meenit" before leaving at once. She made sure that I obeyed her because I heard a key turn in the lock.

I looked around, as much as for something to do as for anything else. I was in a room which ran the whole breadth of the house. The furniture consisted of one large bed and two truckle beds, a few chairs and two large chests. There was one small window. It was not barred this time but it did not open. I stood at the window and looked out idly. A woman came to the door and knocked. Something about her aroused my interest, but what I could not say. She was muffled in a tartan screen and so I could not see her properly, but there was something familiar about her. She entered and I could hear footsteps going into the room directly below me.

Earlier I had noticed part of the floor where there was a slight gap between the floorboards. Moving as quietly as possible I made my way over to it. I lay down, put my ear to the gap and found I could hear every word spoken below quite plainly.

First, a woman's voice. "I cannae find it. I've looked but I cannae find it onywhere."

Then a man's angry voice. "Then look again. You must find it."

"It's no easy. I've tae watch fur a chance."

I had heard that voice before but I could not place it. I gave a cautious wriggle and got my eye to the space. Suddenly I could see right into the room below. I recognised the woman. She was the Laird's nursery maid, Lizzie. She spoke again.

"It micht no be at Longcrags. Miss Charlotte keeps some o' her things wi' Mrs Little at Satterness."

I heard the door open again and someone else enter. But I could not see who it was. The speaker continued. He was obviously trying to get himself under control. He knew he would not get anywhere by frightening the maid.

"Search her rooms at Longcrags again. It must be there. She can't have had time to take it down to Satterness."

Then a second voice broke in, a man's voice, sharp and decisive.

"No. We will do this properly. We will apply to a magistrate for a warrant to search both Longcrags and the rooms at Satterness. There must be no legal loophole. Let us not forget that we are talking about a possible charge of treason. And, if necessary, Lizzie can give evidence in court."

The maid left the room and the two men continued their conversation. As far as I can remember it went something like this.

First man, sounding frustrated, "We must find it. If it's proof of treason then the estate will be forfeited. And if we bring the proof to the authorities then we may be allowed to buy it."

Second man, thoughtfully. "Are you sure it would provide proof of treason?"

First man, impatiently. "No. Of course I can't be certain. The girl was too stupid to know what it was exactly. She said she could not read it. Probably because it was written in French. But there was a signature – which she could not make out, and a date."

Second man. "Are we sure it is in the girl's rooms at Longcrags?"

First man. "Where else can it be? She certainly did not have it on her."

Second man. "Could she not have taken it with her when she left and hidden it somewhere?"

First man thoughtfully. "The silly girl did say that Charlotte used to leave some of her things with Mrs Little at Satterness. I suppose she could have gone there when she ran away. She did go to the shore after all. But I still think her rooms at Longcrags are more likely."

I heard the men leaving the room. I waited for a few minutes and then got up, crossed the room and collapsed into a chair. This was getting worse and worse. Just what was I involved in? Treason? But how could the respectable Laird of Longcrags be mixed up in treason? Right then I wanted the reassurance of Michael. Yes, stern, forbidding Michael. Politics and treason would surely be beyond him.

My thoughts were sharply interrupted by a key turning in the lock. I jumped up, wondering what was before me now.

It was my old friend with the wig and spectacles, the one who had taught me what to say to Mr Aitken. He had come to hear the reply.

He sat down on one of the chairs and signalled to me to do likewise. I looked straight ahead and began to repeat Mr Gordon's lawyer's statement. I was concentrating so hard on the unfamiliar legal terms that I was only vaguely aware of the door being flung open and a man standing before us.

"She's escaped. The girl's got loose."

The man in the wig rose to his feet. I stopped speaking and looked at him curiously. He was furious. He spoke quietly which made his anger seem even worse.

"Do you realise just what you have done?"

A long pause and then,

"You have told Aitken's messenger. Now we cannot let her go back to Longcrags. If you had held your tongue a bit longer then she need not have known that our bird had flown and we could have sent her back to Longcrags with another message. Now what do we do with Aitken's little envoy?"

So saying he strode to the door, motioned to the other man to leave, went out himself and locked the door behind him.

Left alone again I tried to stifle a growing feeling of panic. I had been uneasy before but now I was terrified. Charlotte had escaped and I knew. If I did not know then the men could have continued to bluff the Laird. But now that I knew the truth and that there was no longer any need for him to agree to the kidnappers' demands. I could not be allowed to go back to Longcrags and tell him.

So what were the men going to do to me? How would they keep me quiet? There was one way but I tried not to think about it. Surely they would not kill me. Surely not. But I was not sure of anything any more.

My accursed imagination got to work again. My body could be concealed in one of the cellars for any length of time and then taken down the Nith and cast into the Solway.

Enough of this I told myself sternly. Instead of thinking about the two men I tried to think about myself and what I could do. The Bridgend was full of travelling people and no doubt most of them would be working for Michael.

I explored the room carefully, trying to find some way of escape. I was not really hopeful but it was one way of occupying my mind and it was better than dwelling on my fate.

First I tried the door, just in case it had not been locked properly. But it was. I looked at it. It was a heavy, solid door, more like an outside door than one you would expect to find inside a house I knelt down and examined the keyhole. If only the travellers had taught me some of their tricks – like how to pick locks. But they had only accepted me on sufferance.

I left the door and wandered over to the window. Small, made of glass and divided into  sections. It was not a case of being stuck. It did not seem to open at all. And even if I could have broken the glass it would not have helped. The panes were far too small for me to climb through.

Perhaps I could attract someone's attention? I took my handkerchief and waved it frantically. Nobody looked up. Any passers-bye kept their eyes on the road in front of them. Then a cart piled high with hay passed just under the window. There was a boy perched precariously on top of the hay. This time I rapped loudly on the window as well as fluttering my handkerchief. The boy heard me. He looked up, grinned and raised a hand in greeting. Then the cart moved out of sight. Demoralised I let my hands drop to my sides. The boy had just thought I was being friendly. He had no idea that I was being held prisoner.

But I was not going to give up so easily. Where were Michael's men? Surely they would be watching out for me. I peered out of the window trying to see if there was anyone lurking in a doorway. I waved my handkerchief again and this time I got a reply. A woman came to the door of the house opposite, looked up at my window and then shook a rug vigorously before retreating inside. I was sure that was a signal to me that friends were watching over me ready to mount a rescue attempt. Or was I just fooling myself? Was I imagining things? Was I just trying to make myself believe what I wanted to happen?

I turned away from the window and went over to the gap in the floorboards where I had been able to observe the false nurserymaid. Perhaps there was another gap, a bigger one,

one which I could slip through. I did find another gap. It was not big enough for me but it did give me a better view of the room below. The door opened and a girl came in with a broom. I watched her as she set to work. I could have called down to her quite easily. But should I? Was she friend or foe? Would she take a message to Michael or to my jailers? I decided not to risk it. Instead I looked up at the rafters. Could I manage to climb up there? And if so could I find a way of getting onto the roof? Reluctantly I decided that it was not possible.

Then suddenly, right before my eyes I saw my escape route.

There was a large fireplace and a chimney. Of course. I could climb up the chimney and get onto the roof. From there I would surely find a way of getting to the ground.

I went to the chimney and looked up. Darkness, but a square of light at the top of the tunnel. I felt around the sides of the chimney. They were rough with knobs and cracks, both of which could be used as handholds.

I have never been particularly agile and I found the prospect of scrambling up the chimney positively daunting. Then I thought of the two men again. I scolded myself severely.

*Don't be silly, my girl. There is nothing difficult about climbing up a chimney. Why small boys do it every day.*

But that remonstrance did not really help. However I took a deep breath and stepped into the fireplace. I found a handhold, pulled myself up and found a knob which acted as a footrest. Clouds of soot fell on my head and face but my ascent had begun. I managed to wedge myself relatively firmly in the chimney with my back against one wall and my feet against the opposite one. Gradually I managed to climb higher. Of course chimney boys are lightly clad in shirt and breeches but I found my long skirts both a help and a hindrance. They made climbing more difficult but they did protect me from scrapes and grazes. Most of the cuts and bruises I received were to my hands.

I was making good, if slow progress when I heard footsteps on the stairs, the door being unlocked and a volley of foul oaths. I knew that at least two men were in the room below me. I kept very still but it was no good. I had left an easy trail, the pile of soot in the fireplace.

Heavy footsteps crossed the room. I looked down and saw a face leering at me and heard a harsh laugh.

"Here's our little bird. This one did not get far."

# CHAPTER 10

## UNDERNEATH THE BRIDGEND

It had taken me a long time to get halfway up the chimney but the men had me down in a matter of seconds. Then I was gripped firmly by the arm and dragged downstairs. A trap door was flung open revealing a flight of steps. We descended into the depths. Down. Down until at last we reached the foot and a long passage. One of the men had a horn lantern and he led the way. Despite my terror I tried to make out as much as possible. At first we went along a stone passage. Then it changed and the walls seemed to be just earth, supported here and there by wooden props. Then back to stone walls. We turned into a side passage and came to a solid wooden door. It was opened. I was pushed inside and the door locked behind me.

It was pitch dark – and also deadly silent with no sounds at all. I had effectively been deprived of my senses and it was brought home to me sharply just exactly what this meant, what the alarming results of lack of sight and hearing were. For one thing this affected my balance, making me totter unsteadily on my feet. Fearing that I was going to go crashing to the ground I went down on my hands and knees. Sitting on the ground was safer than trying to stand.

The second result of sensual deprivation was complete disorientation. All around me was space. If I could only get my back against the wall I would feel some small modicum of security. It could not be far away. I stretched out my arms and groped around. Still nothing. Having lost my bearings completely I was afraid to move at all in case I went towards the middle of the cellar. Another attempt and this time my fingers brushed against the stone wall. I crawled in that direction, found myself at the wall, and sat up with my back firmly against it. That made me feel slightly better. It was an achievement after all, if only a minor one. But it was only a beginning. Now I had to find the door. I spread out my arms but there was still no feeling of wood. It was time to try something different, for example lying full length on the ground instead of sitting. I lay flat on the ground and pushed my arms forwards. Almost at once I felt the heavy planks. Now confident in my knowledge of the position of the door I edged nearer it. At least I now knew where I was in the cellar and this second small achievement gave me back a fraction of my self-confidence – even although it was not really of much practical value. I still knew absolutely nothing about my prison.

I thought over the little I did know. I was in one of the notorious subterranean cellars of the Bridgend. The cellars which had given the Bridgend its bad reputation: which acted as a haven for thieves and vagabonds: which played their part in the black economy of the Bridgend as they provided ideal sites for illegal whisky distilling.

I was in despair. After making one escape attempt which had resulted in failure I had no strength for another. No one would ever find me in this deep hole. The magistrates of Dumfries, as I had so often been told, had no authority on the west side of the Nith, but even if Mr Aitken did manage to get the authorities to enter the Bridgend they would never find me in this labyrinth.

I did not know what was worse, the complete darkness or the complete silence. I had no idea how long I had been there. Time had stopped.

Then my imagination got to work. I was far under the ground. I could picture tons of earth – and the stone buildings of the Bridgend – on top of me. What if the cellar was to collapse? I envisaged myself being buried under a mass of rubble.

Then I had other thoughts, but just as terrifying. The earthen floor was cold and damp. I had heard that there was a tunnel under the Nith. Surely I was not under the river? More feelings of irrational panic. What if the roof was to give way? Visions of torrents of water gushing through the roof and my helpless self being casually picked up and swept along with the rest of the jetsam.

I tried to shake some sense into myself. In desperation I looked for some glimmer of hope. There was absolutely nothing which I could do, but I was one of Longcrags' Sleuth-Hounds. And hounds work together in a pack. The rest of the pack should come to my aid. What about the many travelling people of the Bridgend? Surely they would find me. But how? How would they know where I was? How would anyone ever find me in this maze? *Oh Michael, where are you?* I muttered to myself?

I tried to find some crumbs of hope. What about the boy who had waved to me from the haycart? And the woman at the door of the house opposite?

Then panic began to take over again. What if I were to be left in this dreadful place? If no one ever came for me? If I were to be left to die of starvation?

I fought desperately to control my hysteria. Was there really nothing which I could do? How about trying to explore my surroundings? But I was not going to leave the security of the wall – or stand up... I proceeded to crawl round the cellar. What was I hoping to achieve? Perhaps to find another door? One which had been left unlocked? I did not really believe that but at least I was doing something instead of just waiting passively for what fate had in store for me. And that helped, it helped a great deal.

It was not long before I came to a corner. So I had learned something. The cellar was small. I dragged myself further along and then my hands brushed against something soft. It felt like rags – or clothing. I drew back my hands at once. Was there anything among the rags? Could I have stumbled upon a body? What unimaginable horrors were in this dreadful place? I kept very still for some time. I don't know how long as I had no way of measuring time. At last I forced myself to run my hands over the rags. It was all right. It was just a pile of old clothes – as well as I could tell in the darkness.

I slithered on round another three corners and arrived back at the door. But this time I was on the opposite side of the door from which I had started. I was now on the hinge side. A wild idea came to me. If I stayed where I was, then if my captors came back and opened the door, I would be hidden behind it. They would be puzzled by not seeing me. They might think that the travelling people had rescued me and they might go away and leave the door unlocked. I decided to stay where I was.

It was a crazy idea. I was not thinking rationally. But I had to give myself some hope.

Panic returned. How long was I going to be left alone? I became desperate for the sound of a human voice, any voice, even if it belonged to one of my captors. I could not bear this loneliness any longer.

Eventually I heard a key in the lock. But who was it? Friend or foe? A few moments ago I would have welcomed anybody, but now that I was actually faced with the arrival of someone I felt quite differently.

Who was outside the door? My captors returning to take me to my death or the tinklers to rescue me? I had no way of telling. The door opened. Light at last, light which dazzled my eyes which had been in darkness so long. I blinked furiously. Then I tried opening my eyes again and this time I managed to keep them open in dim lantern light which was still too bright for my eyes after their spell in pitch darkness. I cowered behind the door and heard an alarmed voice.

"Mrs Marshall. Gretna. Where are you? It's me. Alexander. Sawney."

Oh the relief! I struggled to speak and then I managed to gasp out,

"I'm here."

At the same time I crawled forward towards Sawney, the very last person I would have imagined as a rescuer.

Sawney saw me at last. He was horrified. He rushed forward and tried to help me to my feet but I stopped him.

"I'm all right. Just a bit disorientated after being in the dark. Give me a minute."

Then, when I was ready, he helped me up. I felt much better but I still wanted the steadying reassurance of his arm. Sawney proceeded to give me a hurried explanation. "We have been watching those felons and now I have come to lead you to safety."

I had thought of a list of potential rescuers, but I had never dreamt it would be Sawney.

He let a note of urgency creep into his voice.

"Come on. We are wasting time."

He led me back to the main passage.

"I'll explain everything later," he said. "But keep quiet just now. And try to walk silently."

That would not be difficult as my shoes were of soft leather. Looking at Sawney's feet I saw that his shoes were similar. I also noticed that although he had kept the exact speech of a lawyer, his appearance was more that of an urchin. His face was grubby, his hair tousled and his breeches old and crumpled.

Sawney allowed himself a brief further explanation. It was important for us to keep listening for anyone coming along the passage so that we could try to work out who they were. Most of the people of the Bridgend were good friends of Mr Aitken and would try to help us. They had no liking for the kidnappers in their midst – strangers or 'foreigners' as they called them. But down here the kidnappers would have us at their mercy so if we heard anyone coming we had better try to hide.

That was all very well but I wondered how.

Suddenly we heard footsteps in front of us. Fortunately there was a side passage just ahead and Sawney led me into it and covered the lantern with a thick cloth. But the footsteps never reached us. They turned off before our passage. We continued. Then footsteps again, and voices. I stiffened. I recognised those voices only too well, my two captors. Sawney dragged me down another side passage, and then down another two. The footsteps passed and we both began to relax. Sawney uncovered the lantern and I looked around.

We were in a kind of room. This time the walls had been covered with stone slabs. There were barrels, boxes and sacks lying around. Then I found that we had another problem.

Sawney was looking around and frowning.

"I am not sure where we are," he said slowly.

"You mean we are lost," I said bluntly.

Sawney was prepared to dispute that.

"No, no," he said. "We are not lost. Just that at the present time I am not sure of our exact position. But give me a few minutes and I will ascertain our whereabouts. I have a map."

I stood there astounded. Here we were deep below ground and in danger from desperate men and Sawney just stood there and spoke the clipped, precise words of a lawyer. Obviously he was trying to copy Mr Gordon's manner of speech. But to keep it up in such circumstances!

Sawney calmly pulled a map from his pocket and studied it carefully by the light of the lantern – as if it were a legal document and he was in Mr Gordon's office. After a while he looked up and said,

"I think I have our position but I want to make sure. If you will stay here for a short time, it will be safer. If the men find me they will just think I am helping with the malt."

He picked up a sack and threw it over his shoulders to give credence to his story.

It made sense but I did not know if I could bear to be left in the dark again. Sawney then had a suggestion, which made things even worse. He thought it would be better if I hid inside one of the barrels.

They were huge. I stood in front of one and it was all I could do to peer over the top. Even with Sawney's help however would I scramble inside? Moreover there was a strange smell coming from the barrel. I did not recognise it but it made me feel sick. I was about to make a definite refusal and then I thought of something. Surely I would be better hiding behind a barrel. Then if anyone did come I would be in a better position to escape. Sawney agreed reluctantly.

I wriggled behind a barrel. But my hiding place was not good enough for Sawney. He chose another barrel, one right in a corner. I was jammed tightly between the barrel and the wall in a narrow enclosed place with overpowering fumes coming from the barrel. But Sawney did not give me a chance to protest. As soon as he saw me settled he left me ignoring my belated and half-hearted objections.

Darkness again but at least it was not so frightening this time. I became more aware of the smell. My eyes closed and I swayed against the barrel. It had been a long day but surely I was not going to fall asleep, not with danger all around me. I sat up and forced my eyes open, but not for long. They soon closed again and I slumped down on the floor. Then, as if from a great distance I heard voices and men's laughter. I felt arms around me and a sensation of being lifted up. Then I knew no more.

When I came to I was lying on a grassy slope above the Nith. I heard a voice say,

"She's come roond at last."

I tried to sit up but fell back immediately. A man's face leaned over me, the face of a man used to hard work. Not necessarily a gypsy or tinkler, but like the people I had been living with the last year. An honest working man, definitely not one of the kidnappers.

"Dinnae try to sit up yet. You'll be a' richt in a few meenits."

Then another voice, laughing.

"You were drunk. Whusky fumes. Yon was the cellar where we store the whusky."

This was obviously a great joke. They had never heard of anyone getting drunk smelling whisky before. Drinking it yes, but smelling it no.

Actually I was not really drunk. I had just been overcome by the whisky fumes in the confined space. But the men still thought it a great joke.

I was given time to recover and then taken to a cottage where a woman had hot water ready for me. It was Helen my mother in law and she took charge at once. She shook her head and said,

"There's only wan place fur that soot – the river."

I was hustled down to a quiet part of the Nith which was sheltered by willows and dunked in the water. It was very cold, although not actually freezing but I knew that Helen was right and it was the only way to get rid of the soot from the chinmey. Fortunately the chilly experience did not last long. Helen threw a blanket over me and hurried me back to the cottage where the welcome hot water served both to warm me and complete the cleansing process. She then gave me a change of clothing.

Word had been sent to Michael and I was taken into a room to wait for him. I had not been there long before Sawney rushed in. He was looking frantic and – for the first time since I had known him – actually human.

"Oh thank God you're safe," he gasped. "When I went back to the cellar and found that you had gone I did not know what to think. And then I heard tell of a lass found drunk among the whisky barrels."

Sawney's arrival was followed by that of an equally relieved Michael. Now was the time for explanations and planning. The three of us had a kind of conference.

# CHAPTER 11

## EXPLANATIONS

First Sawney filled me in on the rescue attempt. Michael's travellers had kept me under close observation from the time I entered the Bridgend. I was right about the woman shaking a cloth at the door of the house opposite my window. She had, indeed, been one of Michael's watchers.

My guardians had been taken by surprise. They had not expected me to be taken prisoner and so did not have any contingency plans. Moreover the Laird had given strict instructions that they were to act 'discreetly.'

Even so they had still tried to cover all possibilities. They knew beforehand which house I was making for and they knew of the tunnel beneath it. A boy had been hidden at the foot of the stairs ready to take a message if necessary. Sawney had been with him and when the men dragged me along the tunnel he had followed me cautiously. When he set me free he had been sure that my two captors were going to be away for some time. It was just bad luck that something had made them change their minds and return.

Then it was my turn. I told of all that had happened in the house and Sawney and Michael listened intently. Sawney and I both wanted to know the same thing.

"How did Charlotte manage to escape?"

Michael was able to tell us. By this time, I at least should have known. Just as she had done at Longcrags, Charlotte had again picked the lock – although this time it had been more difficult. Michael was full of admiration. For once his grim features crinkled into an unaccustomed smile.

"Charlotte has nae need o' keys. She may be a gadji but she can pick a lock with the best o' the travellers."

Then his face took on an expression almost of admiration.

"Mind you, yon lock was a kittle 'un. It would have taken me a' ma time mysel. And to think of yon wee lassie."

He was speechless. As for me, it was still sinking in. Ability in lock-picking was, for Michael, something to be admired. Then something else occurred to me. How and where had Charlotte learned to pick locks?

Michael's face reverted to its normal stern expression. He wanted to know more about the conversation with the Laird's nursery maid about the proof of treason. But I could not tell him any more than I had already. In the end it was Michael himself who enlightened us.

"This is just a guess," he said slowly, "but I ken that the Laird has kin in France, kin whom the Government would not welcome over here. Recently the Laird had a veesitor who just stayed quietly at Longcrags and did not gang aboot the countryside."

"And you think this was a relative from France? And since we are now at war with France that visit would constitute treason?" I suggested.

Here Sawney thought I was taking too much upon myself. He was the one for legal matters.

"It certainly would be treason," he said definitely. He was about to launch into a full explanation of the law when Michael held up his hand and stopped him.

"I can assure the baith o' ye that Longcrags is certainly no a traitor, but he has a Highlander's belief in faimily, and, nae matter the circumstances, he would welcome a veesit from a relative. But I ken this for sure. No treasonable plot was ever discussed at Longcrags."

I puzzled over this. The Laird of Longcrags a Highlander? Surely not. Aitken is not a Highland name. Then I remembered something. I had noticed, and puzzled over, the Laird's accent. He spoke with something resembling a Highland lilt. But that mystery could wait. Michael had something of more immediate importance.

"The proof of treason? I can only guess. Perhaps this relative gave Charlotte some small memento and signed it. If found that could be taken as proof that this veesitor from France had been at Longcrags."

"And anyone harbouring ..." Sawney started. Michael ignored him.

"It's possible," I said, "but to be sure we will have to find Charlotte."

Michael sighed.

"The trouble that wee lassie's caused with a' her cantrips. We must find her. First she can tell us whit this proof of treason is and then we can decide whit tae dae aboot it."

Michael looked really fierce and then burst out,

"And if I am the first tae find her I shall gie her a guid skelping."

I looked at him carefully. Surely Michael, a humble tinkler, would not dare skelp the Laird's daughter. But one glance at his stern face gave me my answer. Yes, he would.

We tried to work out where Charlotte could be. Michael thought that she had probably crossed the Devorgilla Bridge. Then there would be a number of opportunities open to her. First there were the gypsy wagons camped on the Whitesands. She may have persuaded a gypsy to take her in, or she may even have slipped aboard a wagon secretly and hidden there. Another possibility, she may have tried the cattle markets on the Whitesands and have gone back to being a drover. A third likelihood was that she may have walked down the river to Kingholm Quay and gone aboard a boat.

Michael thought deeply for a few minutes and then made his decisions. He would cross the bridge into Dumfries himself. First he would go to the Globe Inn and try to contact the Laird. This was another case when messages could be conveyed by word of mouth only and nothing must be written down. Once he had reported to the Laird Michael would make enquiries among the gypsies at the Whitesands. As for Sawney and myself – Michael did not know what we could do. Finally he said to Sawney,

"Take Gretna out for some fresh air. She is still looking pale."

We all went outside and Michael strode away. Sawney turned to me and said.

"Come and I'll show you my pony, Ally."

Sawney led me through the grassland behind the village. We came to a field where several ponies were grazing. Sawney walked through the field calling quietly, "Ally, Ally." At once a black pony detached itself from the rest, trotted over to him and nuzzled his pockets. Sawney stroked its neck and fed it bits of apple. He was obviously very fond of it but, as I was later to learn, he preferred petting it, grooming it, feeding it – in fact anything to riding it.

Sawney told me all about the pony. He called her Ally – short for Alibi. Mr Gordon had bought her especially for him at last year's Kelton Horse Fair. As Sawney was probably the worst rider in the whole of Dumfriesshire Mr Gordon had chosen her very carefully. She was a Galloway — hardy and very sure-footed. Above all she was calm and placid. Mr Gordon even had a special saddle made for Sawney, a big one with a high pommel, one that would be actually difficult to fall out of.

She was all black except for a tiny star between her eyes.

The three of us walked along slowly, Sawney holding Ally's mane. We were walking past a clump of willows when we heard someone calling us. We looked around.

"I'm here, in the middle of the trees. Walk along that passage. I don't want anyone to see me."

It was Charlotte's voice. We followed her instructions and found that the path widened out into a kind of circle in the centre of the willows and provided a good hiding place for Charlotte. Once we were settled Charlotte said imperiously,

"I want to know what is going on and I know, Sawney, that you can explain everything."

I was about to say that it was Charlotte who owed us an explanation first and then I thought better of it. It was my duty to get Charlotte back to her father as soon as possible, but I would have to be careful. I could not force her. If Michael had been there it would have been different, but if I said the wrong thing then Charlotte would just run off again. No, I would let Sawney talk to her and then perhaps, just perhaps, I would be able to make her listen to reason.

"What do you want to know?" asked Sawney wearily.

"I heard some of what those awful men were saying. They seemed to think that they had a right to my father's lairdship. But that is nonsense. Longcrags belongs to us. How could they expect my father to sign it over to them?"

Sawney thought for a while before replying.

"The lairdship of Longcrags belonged to the Radcliffe family for generations. It only passed out of their hands fifty years ago when it was bought by your grandfather."

Charlotte seized on this.

"Bought. Yes," she said fiercely, "but they are claiming they were tricked. My grandfather would never trick anyone."

Sawney looked stubborn.

"I think you must ask your father that. It is not for me to tell you."

Charlotte used her spoilt little madam voice.

"Tell me. I have a right to know."

"Yes," I added with feeling. "And I have too after all I have gone through." I was now determined to find out all I could about the Aitken family. If I was going to continue to work for the Laird I wanted to make sure he did not have a dubious past.

Charlotte looked at me and I saw her lips curl in a sort of sneer. I knew exactly what she was about to say. That I was just a tinkler who was working for her father and there was no need for me to know the family business. Then her expression suddenly changed. She had just realised that it was in her own interests to go along with me. After all she wanted to find out too.

"Yes," she said. "Tell us. We both have a right to know."

She made it sound like an order, a command.

I was watching Sawney carefully and I saw a slight frown cross his face. Charlotte was making a dreadful mistake. Trying to bully Sawney would just make him obstinate. His next words proved me right.

"No," he said quietly and firmly, "neither of you have any right at all. It is not for me to divulge the private affairs of the

Laird of Longcrags. It is a matter of correct professional conduct."

Charlotte was about to make matters worse but I gripped her arm tightly and shook my head at her. By a wonder she heeded me and held her tongue.

Silence from Sawney as he sat and pondered. I could almost see his brain working. Then he gave in.

"Oh well. I suppose it will be all right in this case. Most of it is public knowledge after all. It is not as if I was breaking a confidence."

Then he took us back to the events of fifty years ago. He gave a very simple account of how the Radcliffes had lost Longcrags Estate, but he included all the main facts.

# CHAPTER 12

## THE AUCTION

*The lairdship of Longcrags was run down and neglected and the Laird was deeply in debt. This was due mainly to mismanagement exacerbated by gambling debts. But the Radcliffes had owned the estate for generations and they had many friends who rallied round and planned how to restore it. An efficient factor was found and the Laird's agent worked out a scheme by which the debts could gradually be paid off.*

*All this could well have succeeded if done earlier but these plans came too late. A number of the creditors were tired of waiting for their money and they formed a committee. They demanded that the lairdship should be sold so that the debts could be paid. Of course the estate was entailed and it would take an Act of Parliament to break the entail but the creditors got the Laird declared bankrupt. They went to the Court of Session and got an agreement that the estate should be sold at public roup.*

*Despite the decision of the Court of Session, the Radcliffe family were still determined to hang onto Longcrags and they worked out an ingenious plan. First they made sure that the asking price was set as low as possible. Everyone knew that the estate was suffering from neglect. Now the family tried to make it look even worse than it actually was. Weeds were allowed to grow around the house and a few tiles fall from the roof. One of the outbuildings had a door which had come off its hinges and several rusty agricultural implements were collected from the surrounding countryside. Indoors all the curtains were taken down and replaced with old, shabby ones.*

*The plan was that the estate would be bought cheaply by a friend of the family and then, a few years later, when the Radcliffes had repaired their fortunes, it would be quietly sold back to them. Steps were even taken to ensure that only friends of the family would be at the auction. Signposts were turned round so that strangers would go the wrong way and, by the time they realised their mistake, they would be too late for the bidding.*

*All this careful plotting could well have succeeded if it had not been for a certain young Mr Alastair Aitken.*

*The roup was held in the dining room. The sale started with the turning of an hourglass. When the sand had all run through the hourglass the roup was over and the last bid had to be accepted.*

*The bidding started slowly. Eventually the auctioneer's pleas were answered by a bid for the asking price. Despite all the efforts of the auctioneer there was no advance on this for some time and then someone responded with a slightly higher bid. Then there were a few more bids. The sand ran through the hourglass and the friends of the Laird began to relax. All was going to plan. Then there was a sudden bid from the back of the room. Startled everyone turned to see who this new bidder was. They saw a young stranger. At once a good friend of the Laird prepared to outbid him but he was too late. The sand had finally run through the hourglass.*

*The lairdship of Longcrags had been bought by Alastair Aitken.*

Sawney stopped. He had now explained why the Radcliffes resented the Aitkens and why they had taken such extreme measures to try to regain the Longcrags Estate. His account went a long way to explaining the actions of William

Radcliffe, the head of the family. Even so I still thought that he was acting irrationally and was probably mentally unbalanced.

But the account proved that Charlotte had been correct about one thing. Her grandfather had bought the estate fair and square. There was no question of the Radcliffes being tricked out of it.

Sawney was convinced he had told us everything. But not so as far as Charlotte was concerned.

"Where did my grandfather come from? How did he have enough money to buy Longcrags? Tell me." Sawney looked dubious.

"I think your father should tell you that," he said. "A lawyer must always respect a client's confidence." "It is not for me to tell you."

*Oh no,* I thought to myself. *Not again. We've been through all this already.*

Aloud I said quietly,

"Surely you can tell us. After all you have just told us about the auction."

Sawney stopped being the lawyer. Now he sounded thoughtful and doubtful. Even — and how out of character – unsure of himself.

"This is rather different. The roup is public knowledge. But the details of Alastair Aitken are private. If her father wanted Charlotte to know them, then I am sure he would have told her already. Perhaps her father wants to wait until she is older. Either way it is not for me to tell her."

Strictly speaking he was correct. But I had other considerations. I had agreed to serve the Laird because I believed that would bring me safety and security. Now my experiences in the Bridgend seemed to prove the opposite, that the Laird's wages were danger. For my own sake I wanted to learn all I could about the Aitken family. I wanted the same thing as Charlotte, if for different reasons.

Charlotte was obviously desperate to say something so I rushed to get in before her.

"Surely she deserves to know about her own family."

Sawney sighed, "Probably. But who has the best right to tell her?"

Now at last Charlotte seized her chance. She said vehemently,

"Another thing. When I was in that dreadful place that awful man said to me, 'This is where you belong?' What did he mean? How can I belong in the Bridgend? You must tell me. You must."

Sawney still looked undecided. How could I persuade him to tell us what he knew? But before I could think of anything there was a startling outburst from Charlotte.

"Lady Muck. That's what they call me. Lady Muck of the Bridgend."

Then in tones of real bitterness she quoted the old rhyme.

> 'Brigen', Brigen' a dirty place,
> A kirk without a steeple,
> A wee dunghill at every door,
> And full of Irish people.'

"Why do they call me 'Lady Muck of the Bridgend?' And also things like 'tinkler's brat.' I deserve to know why. I demand that you tell me."

We all stared at her in amazement. Charlotte calmed down slightly, only slightly, and gave us a full explanation.

From an early age Charlotte had always been very much aware of the fact that her parents were not fully accepted by society. It was something that Struan, interested only in his animals, never noticed but nothing escaped the sharp Charlotte. Her parents had a small number of very good friends, like the Craiks of Arbigland. Also, by a large section of the local community, Mr Aitken was respected for his wealth and for authority as a Justice of the Peace. But that was as far as it went. He was not respected for himself. The Aitkens were not invited out socially as much as would be expected for the owners of an estate like Longcrags. It did not worry Mr and Mrs Aitken. Mr Aitken was content with his few good friends and the running of the estate. His wife was kept busy with her charitable concerns. Besides she was in close contact with her own family on the other side of the Solway.

But it did worry their younger daughter. It was brought to her notice very forcibly when she was only eight. Mrs Aitken had just dismissed a housemaid whom she had found completely unsatisfactory. Struan was a great favourite of the cook. He knew she had been baking gingerbread and he persuaded Charlotte to go to the kitchen with him and beg some. Charlotte agreed. They found the kitchen empty except for the maid who was just about to leave. Struan and Charlotte stared at the bags at her feet. The maid gave them a look of pure venom and spat out,

"Weel whit are you staring at? Think you're better than me? Why you're naething but tinkler's brats, the baith o' ye."

She might have said more but at that moment Cook came into the kitchen and she got rid of Struan and Charlotte at once. She filled their hands with gingerbread and more or less shoved them out of the door. Struan enjoyed his gingerbread and promptly forgot all about the maid but Charlotte remembered and puzzled over the incident. She was old enough to understand what 'tinkler's brats' meant but why refer to her brother and herself like that?

It was not to be the only incident of its kind, as Charlotte soon found out. When she and Struan had a birthday Mrs Aitken would always invite the children of neighbouring estates to Longcrags. Charlotte gradually discovered that many of these invitations were declined. Moreover, she herself was not invited to as many birthday parties as she might have expected. She began to wonder why and then one day she got a clue. The children were always closely supervised but there were times when they managed to escape the eagle eyes of governesses and nursemaids. One year Charlotte had been given a new gown as a birthday present. It was a pretty leaf green and Charlotte was very proud of it. Another girl, a Barbara Morrison, had just arrived. A maid showed her to the room where she could leave her cloak and tidy her hair. The maid then took her governess to a room prepared for the governesses. Barbara completed her preparations and then went to join the other children. On the way she passed Charlotte in her new gown. For once there were no other adults present. Barbara smiled at Charlotte.

"What a beautiful gown. A birthday present?"

Charlotte was not quite sure how to react. The words were complimentary but they had been spoken with something of a sneer. However Charlotte decided to treat them as an honest compliment.

"Yes it is actually. Thank you."

Barbara then became more obvious. When she next spoke she was sarcastic and taunting.

"My, my. We are a fine lady today." Then she added spitefully, "Lady Muck. Lady Muck of the Bridgend."

She might have said more but both girls heard footsteps behind them and Barbara's governess saying, "So there you are. I've been looking for you everywhere."

From then on Charlotte was continually taunted with the title of 'Lady Muck.' Of course never when there were adults present. But despite their constant adult supervision there was always the odd occasion when they were left unattended for a short time and it was surprising just how often Barbara and her friends found an opportunity to jeer at Charlotte. It had been particularly noticeable when Charlotte started to attend the dancing class.

Charlotte finished and we all sat in stunned silence. I thought quickly. I said to Sawney,

"You must tell us what you know. This is something Charlotte has to come to terms with. She needs to understand what it is all about."

I paused and then, trying to sound really convincing, I added.

"You say that the details about Charlotte's grandfather are private, but the girls at the dancing class seem to know all about them. "

For a moment it seemed as if I had made things worse. Sawney looked stubborn again.

"They don't know about Alastair Aitken. They only think they do but actually they probably know very little. Just that he used to live with the gypsies in the Bridgend. But they don't know the full story."

For a moment Sawney had been on the verge of giving in but now he was back to his inflexible belief in doing the correct thing and respecting a client's confidentiality.

Somehow, I had to persuade him to tell Charlotte about her family. She needed to know the facts so that she could work out how to deal with the situation. It might be best to take her father's course of action, accept her true friends and ignore the rest. After all they could not do anything. But Charlotte had to be given the facts and then left to make her own decisions.

Suddenly something else occurred to me. I thought again about Charlotte's action in taking the silver salver. I now knew why she had done it. I had suspected before but now I was certain.

Charlotte had not chosen to learn dancing. That decision had been taken for her by her mother and her governess. Thinking back over what I had learned about Charlotte from Mrs Little I doubted very much if she was really interested. I considered it very unlikely that the girl of the wild rides along the Solway shore would find herself truly at home in the ballroom. But Charlotte was told that she was growing up and, as dancing is part of this, it was now time for her to learn to dance. Her mother, no doubt, impressed on her, that dancing was only part of the story. It was equally important to learn the social graces so that one day she could take her place in the society to which she should belong. So, as well as learning her dancing steps, she should also try to make friends with the other girls at the class.

I could imagine just what Charlotte's feelings would be. Of course I could! After all I had had to endure a similar experience when I was her age myself. First a feeling of slight resentment at being made to do something which did not interest her in the slightest, and then a feeling of trepidation at being plunged into an alien environment. It might well have been different if Mrs Aitken had waited a year or two before trying to turn Charlotte into a young lady. Then she might have been better able to cope. But children are expected to obey and not question.

Harking back to Mrs Little, I knew that Charlotte had been a completely different girl a year ago. Probably she was anxious to please both her parents and her governess. So she had gone along with their plan. She had worked at her dancing and practised her steps diligently. She had also tried to make friends with the other girls in the class.

And then things had gone terribly wrong. The girls not only rejected her friendly overtures but they also taunted her mercilessly. Now I knew just how very cruel they had been. No doubt Charlotte was telling us only half the story. They would also have called her much worse. This was the very first time that Charlotte had been able to tell anyone of her persecution and she had no doubt started with the mildest of the insults and gibes. What other horrors had she been subjected to? From what I had seen of Charlotte I thought it very possible that we would never know. She had her pride and once having let this slip she would very likely clam up again.

Charlotte was a girl of courage and spirit but the 'Lady Muck' week after week must have affected her deeply. How she must have dreaded the very thought of the weekly class and how miserable she must have been when she was there.

To make matters worse there was absolutely nothing she could do about it. The sensible thing would have been to have talked it over with someone. But with whom? Not the stern new governess. Mrs Aitken? But obviously Charlotte did not feel able to approach her mother. Her confidant and companion of a year ago, Struan? But Charlotte and Struan had drifted apart. There was no one.

So Charlotte was left to cope with the situation herself. Because she was forced to keep it all bottled up inside her, it preyed on her mind and every single incident took on an exaggerated importance. Charlotte was at a loss. Then a glorious opportunity to win her way into the girls' favour suddenly presented itself – the salver and its message. It would be something to show her classmates and interest them. In short, it was a desperate attempt to gain their acceptance.

That she even thought of it showed the depth of her despair. If she had been thinking straight she would have realised that it would not have worked. Instead it would have made things worse. The girls would have giggled and gossiped about the message and they would have laughed at Charlotte even more than before.

But the victims of bullying do not act in a rational manner.

And those in charge of children all too often do not realise how very easily their words can be misinterpreted.

Anyway, to sum up, Charlotte's action in stealing the silver salver had actually been a perverted way of trying to please her parents. The result had been severe punishment and Charlotte had reacted to that in her own way.

Her attempt to fall in with her parents' wishes and learn the ways of polite society had met with failure and rejection. As far as Charlotte was concerned that was that. She would seek out another society, one which she had learned about on her wild Solway rides.

Never again would Charlotte listen to her mother with blind, unquestioning obedience. From now on she was determined that she herself would have at least some say in her own life.

Having worked all this out I wanted to help Charlotte make the right decisions. She needed to know why she was being called 'Lady Muck of the Bridgend.' Only when she knew the full story behind that taunt would she be able to deal with it. And the one person who could tell her was Sawney. How could I convince him that telling Charlotte everything was the best way he could help her and her family?

I turned to him again. Despite all his legal knowledge he was just growing out of childhood. I tried desperately to make my adult authority count. I said,

"It is obvious that Charlotte is not going to let this rest. If you don't tell her about her family history then she will look for someone else to ask. It would be much better coming from you."

As I had expected Charlotte latched onto that.

"Gretna's right. If you don't tell us then I shall make sure that I find someone who will."

That was enough for Sawney. Nothing could be worse than Charlotte reminding the countryside of things her father wanted forgotten. He gave in at last and told us the remarkable story of how Alastair Aitken, Charlotte's grandfather, came to Dumfries.

"Mind you," he said. "It's a long story. A very long story."

"We've plenty of time, "I assured him."

"Yes," said Charlotte definitely. "And we want to hear the whole story. All of it."

She emphasised this by adding, "Nothing left out."

# CHAPTER 13

## GRANDFATHER'S STORY — THE JACOBITES IN DUMFRIES

### 1745

Alastair Murray was a cotter lad from a little clachan some miles to the north of Loch Lomond. He was only fifteen when Bonnie Prince Charlie landed at Moidart to raise an army to put his father on the throne instead of King George. Alastair did not really understand what it was all about. In any case, he did not see how it would make any difference to him, personally, who was on the throne. But the clan chief declared for Charlie and the chief's word was law. All the men in the clachan left to join the Jacobite army and Alastair went with them. They had to go. They were told their houses would be destroyed, their crops burnt and their beasts killed if they did not. In that case how would they live?

Alastair hated army life. But one thing helped to make it bearable. His two elder brothers, Callum and Donald, stuck by him for the whole of the following year and they did all they could to shield him from the worst of the campaign. Alastair had always been good with animals and somehow his brothers managed to get him assigned to the baggage and supplies and he found himself driving a cart. His brothers hoped that that would keep him away from the actual battles, and it certainly worked in the case of Prestonpans. That was one battle he missed.

His position with the baggage helped in other ways too. Daily marches were often up to an exhausting thirty miles. And winter was setting in just as the campaign began. Later the foot soldiers sometimes found themselves wading knee deep through snowdrifts. As a wagon driver Alastair was at least spared these hardships.

On the march south the three brothers were joined by one who was to prove himself a good friend. This was Steenie. He was not a Highlander. He was not even a Jacobite. He was an Edinburgh urchin living as best he could. When the Jacobite Army reached Edinburgh Steenie was trying to dodge the baillies. He had been caught pickpocketing but had managed to escape. If taken it could go hard with him as he had been in trouble before. In the words of the law he was a criminal by *habite and repute* and a simple act of theft could therefore be punished with the death penalty. Steenie was in hiding but, when the Jacobite Army entered Edinburgh, he saw his chance. He at once enlisted. Now he was safe from the Edinburgh baillies. He soon struck up a friendship with the Murray brothers and they stayed together. Steenie did not speak Gaelic but he soon picked up enough to get by.

It was this unlikely urchin, Steenie, who was to put himself forever in the debt of the Murray brothers. He probably saved Alastair's life. It came about like this.

Steenie had also managed to get himself assigned to the baggage carts. While in Edinburgh he had done his share of caddying and had often held a gentleman's horse for him. He had also helped out, on a casual basis, in various stables. Steenie made the most of this slight experience and led the

Jacobite officers to believe that he knew more about horses than he actually did. Because of this he eventually found himself among the baggage carts with Alastair. This saved both of them from the worst horrors of the Rebellion. In fact Alastair's life was in danger only once and that was not on a battlefield but somewhere quite unexpected. It happened when the Jacobite Army was advancing south towards the English border.

There was some trouble with the baggage carts. The Army was making good speed and advancing towards Carlisle and Brampton but the heavy, lumbering carts were having difficulty keeping up. They would have had difficulty in any case but the country they had to cross made matters much worse — no proper roads but just rough, narrow tracks pitted with large holes. If a cart did not get stuck in the mud it was liable to end up in a ditch.

Eventually at Ecclefechan, about sixteen miles from Dumfries, the Jacobite officers called a halt. They checked all the carts and chose some which they sent on after the Army. They decided to leave the rest, under guard, at Ecclefechan. Alastair thought he was going to be left behind but then the officers made a final check. Alastair's cart was one of the smaller, lighter ones and, at the last minute, Alastair was ordered to drive on and catch up with the rest of the baggage train.

He drove carefully and was making steady, if slow progress, when he heard a galloping horse behind him. A moment later a Jacobite officer reined in his horse.

"Try and speed up. Don't spare the horses."

He gave a hurried explanation. News of the baggage train had reached Dumfries and a group of youths had set out on a raid to capture the wagons. Alastair was to make haste and catch up with the rest.

Then the officer prepared to gallop off but first he tried to give some assurance.

"I'll try to send an escort for you."

When the officer was out of sight Steenie sniffed unbelievingly,

"Escort," he repeated. "Escort!"

Neither Steenie nor Alastair believed for one minute that they would get the promised escort. As for Alastair hurrying the horses, that was not only difficult, but on such rough ground, it was also dangerous. Even so they were making reasonable headway until they came to a short but steep hill. For a time it seemed as if they were never going to get up. They tried everything. Alastair stayed in the driving seat and urged on the horses with voice and whip while Steenie climbed down and took hold of the bridles and tried to pull the horses forwards. Then they looked for large stones to put behind the wheels to prevent them from slipping backwards. That helped a little and the cart progressed a few inches. At last, in response to a loud shout from Alastair, the horses made a special effort and the cart lurched forward. Then all of a sudden it was moving smoothly and easily. They had crested the hill at last.

Alastair at once stopped the cart. The horses were badly in need of a rest. Try and force them beyond their strength and they would just give up. Alastair was going to unhitch them from the cart but Steenie stopped him. If they did that then they would be in trouble if another officer came along. So Alastair had to be content with just letting the horses rest between the shafts.

Steenie and Alastair were practically as tired as the horses. Steenie found a large rock which was sheltered from the wind by a spreading gorse bush. He sat down thankfully. But Alastair's mind was still on the horses and he went to check them over. Steenie watched him as he bent down and ran his hands down their legs.

Intent on his beloved horses Alastair was aware of nothing else. But the alert Steenie thought he heard something. What exactly, he was not sure. A rustling in the bushes perhaps? A whispering voice at once shushed? He rose silently to his feet and stared in the direction of the sound, his hand on his pistol. Suddenly a boy emerged from the bushes and stole up behind Alastair. He raised an arm but before he could bring a heavy club down on Alastair's head Steenie rushed forward and struck the attacker a savage blow with the butt of his pistol.

What happened next was completely incredible.

Alastair's assailant slumped to the ground and lay there motionless while three of his friends burst from their hiding place. Steenie saw at once that they were boys in their teens. He at once worked out what had happened. He remembered what the Jacobite officer had said about the raiding party from Dumfries. These boys had tagged along and followed it. Steenie wondered where their horses were. They must have left them further back while they ventured forward to the attack on foot.

One of them knelt down beside the boy on the ground.

"Davie. Davie, speak to me."

He jumped up and shouted at Steenie.

"Ye've killed him. Ye've killed ma brither."

Steenie sighed to himself. Having had to fend for himself on the streets of Edinburgh from an early age had taught him a lot. Steenie well knew that war is about misery and suffering, about killing and being killed. But all too often young people are taught that it is a glorious adventure. In school they are given lessons and poems about Troy and Bannockburn, about Henry V and the Battle of Agincourt, and about tales of knights receiving their titles and lands for valour on the battlefield. Then these lessons are brought to life by modern methods of recruitment when boys are lured into the Army with the pageantry of bands and colourful uniforms.

Steenie looked at the boys before him and realised that to them this had been a prank or a lark with the chance of some cheap glory. They had not really thought about what was actually involved. The boy on the ground probably had no idea that he could easily have killed Alastair.

Steenie thought quickly. The situation could still become very ugly. And it was entirely up to him if further bloodshed was to be avoided. With his complete lack of English Alastair was only vaguely aware of what was happening and the naive Dumfries boys did not fully understand what they were involved in.

Steenie and Alastair were outnumbered, especially as Alastair did not really count. He would be absolutely useless in a fight. Also the Dumfries boys were older than Steenie. But he was more experienced and now he had to find some way of making his worldly knowledge tell.

He looked at the youth facing him and said scornfully,

"People get killed in wars. Dae ye no ken? Whit did ye think this is? A gem o' fitba'?"

As the youth stared at him speechless, Steenie knelt down and looked at Davie quickly and then he stood up again.

"Your brither's no deid. Yon wis some dunt an' he'll hae a sair heid but he's no deid."

Just then Davie gave a low moan and his brother was down at his side again at once. Steenie looked at the two other boys. He was alarmed to see that the elder had drawn an ancient pistol. Steenie struggled to sound calm and matter-of-fact.

"Whaur did ye dig that auld thing up? Ah shouldna use it if Ah wur ye. It'll blaw up in yer face."

The youth lowered it doubtfully and Steenie realised for the first time that he had at least a chance of getting through to these boys. He followed up this slight breakthrough.

"We're waiting for an escort. Proper soldiers no weans. They'll be here ony time. Tak yer chance and awa wi' ye."

But things were not going to be so easy for Steenie. The youth with the pistol hesitated and then said dubiously,

"Why should we believe ye?"

Steenie had an answer for that.

"Dae ye want tae bide and find oot?"

Silence. The youth just stared at Steenie.

Then Davie's brother jumped to his feet.

"We maun get Davie tae a doctor. We'll tak the cairt. Help me wi' him."

Here was a new development. If the youths used the cart for Davie then at least Steenie and Alastair would be safe. But Steenie still did not want to lose the cart. He was not sure what the attitude of the Jacobite officers would be. Military discipline is severe – in any army. But for the time being it looked as if there was nothing he could do. He could only stand and watch as Davie was hoisted onto the cart.

Steenie spoke quickly to Alastair in Gaelic and frowned at his reply.

Davie's brother climbed up on the cart and took up the reins. The other two stood at the horses' heads. It was obvious that they did not know about horses. They were probably apprentices.

The driver shook the reins and flicked the whip. Nothing happened. Then the boy with the ancient pistol walked slowly round the cart. Suddenly he gave an exclamation and he released the brake on the back wheel. Then the driver called to the horses and shook the reins again. The oldest boy pulled on the bridle of one of the horses – and jumped back quickly as it whipped its head round and snapped at him. Steenie strove to take advantage of this new development.

"Whit are ye? Soutars or weavers? Ye dinna ken aboot beasts onyway. An' the cuddies ken it fine."

He changed his tone and tried to sound conciliatory. He pointed back the way.

"There's a fairm just back yonder."

The eldest youth would not have given up so easily but that was enough for Davie's brother. He threw down the reins and jumped to the ground. Steenie helped him to get his brother off the cart. Then the oldest boy just gave up and helped to rig up a kind of stretcher with two rifles and a coat. Steenie watched them make their way back down the little hill with a sense of almost incredulous relief.

When they were safely out of sight Alastair picked up the reins and called to the horses and the cart moved off smoothly. Steenie wondered if it was true what Alastair had told him.

"These horses only understand the Gaelic."

They had not gone far when they heard the sound of hoofbeats. It was the escort. The Jacobite officer had been able to provide one after all.

Later in camp Callum and Donald had to be told all about the incident. At first Steenie was reticent and Callum heard the story first from Alastair. Gradually he pieced together exactly what had happened. He realised just what his family owed to Steenie.

Steenie had saved his brother from serious injury. More than that, he had probably saved Alastair's life. As a true Highlander, Callum strove to express his gratitude.

"You have saved my brother's life. My family owes you a debt which can never be repaid."

His gratitude went beyond Steenie. He went on to say that if Steenie, or any of his family, ever needed any aid or assistance, then Callum's family would provide it.

It was rather like the opposite of a family feud.

Steenie was rather taken aback by all this. He pointed out they had been dealing with a few witless youths, not a company of soldiers. Callum listened but was quite firm. The youths may have been foolish, ill equipped and untrained but they could still have done a great deal of damage and lives could easily have been lost. Steenie had acted with commendable courage and resourcefulness.

And Callum and his whole family would never forget it. The story would be handed down through the generations.

Even so, despite their gratitude, Alastair and his brothers did not expect the friendship to last. They were sure that Steenie would desert at the first opportunity. But Steenie stayed with the Jacobite Army both on the march south to Derby and also on the retreat north and was still with them when they crossed the Esk back into Scotland.

Then on the 20th December, 1745 the Jacobite Army entered Dumfries. While the Prince and his officers lodged in the Bluebell Inn and other buildings in the town the bulk of the Army camped out on the fields behind where the theatre is now. The three brothers were exhausted and only too glad of the chance of a rest but Steenie took himself off to explore the town. When he returned, late that night, he was looking very pleased with himself. He would not say where he had been but each of the brothers was asking himself the same question. Had Steenie at last found a place which he liked, a place where he would want to stay? They all felt that this time, when the Jacobite Army moved away, Steenie would not be with them.

Meanwhile the people of Dumfries watched with horror and dread the arrival of these wild Highlanders. They stared in awe at the invaders with their ferocious weapons – the huge swords they called claymores and the smaller but just as dangerous dirks or daggers – and gaped in amazement at their outlandish dress and their harsh, raucous, bagpipes. But far worse, the townsfolk knew that the Jacobites had good reason to seek retribution from the town. They remembered only too clearly the Jacobite advance south, the Jacobite wagons stranded at Ecclefechan and the Dumfries raiding party.

Now the Jacobites were in a position to exact compensation. The townspeople were soon to hear their fate.

Prince Charles demanded from the burgh two thousand pounds sterling and also, for the use of the Army, a thousand pairs of shoes together with all the arms in the town. If this was handed over then the citizens of Dumfries could rest assured that their houses would not be destroyed and their families would not be harmed.

But all this was to be delivered to the Prince before eight o'clock the next evening – an impossible task. However, the leading men of the town held a meeting and set about trying to borrow the money and buy the number of shoes.

Alastair was deeply involved in all this. He was ordered to take a cart and collect a consignment of shoes. He was about to harness a horse to the cart. It was a Dumfries horse, which had been requisitioned by the Jacobites. It was a young, flighty colt, an animal which was afraid of its own shadow. As Alastair led it to the cart, a Highlander walked right in front of it. The Highlander was carrying a set of bagpipes and, unbelievably stupid as it may seem, he raised the chanter to his lips. Suddenly there was a low drone followed by a high pitched screech.

It was the first time in its short life that the colt had ever heard bagpipes and it was terrified by the unearthly sound. It flattened its ears right back against its neck, rolled its eyes and tried to rear. Alastair somehow managed to keep a tight grip on the reins and forced it down. Callum went to help his brother but at that moment the colt managed to pull on the reins and gain a modicum of freedom. It lunged sideways and suddenly lashed out with one of its hind legs. The savage kick caught Alastair on the shin and he collapsed, writhing in pain. He was taken into a nearby building and an army doctor was rushed to him.

Alastair had a broken leg. The doctor set it and gave him a liberal dose of laudanum to kill the pain. From then on Alastair was barely aware of his surroundings and did not realise the problem he was causing his brothers.

The Duke of Cumberland and his Army were just behind the Jacobite Army. The Jacobites would be leaving Dumfries in a day or two and a retreating army was no place for a man with a broken leg. To make matters worse, the townspeople were loyal to King George. If Alastair were to stay in Dumfries he would be lodged in the jail and handed over to the Duke at the first opportunity. There were consultations among the officers. They hoped that they would find a local Jacobite supporter who would take Alastair and hide him.

Then Steenie came forward. He knew where Alastair would be safe, but he did not want to give details as the fewer people who knew the better. The Jacobite officers were doubtful but Callum knew he could trust Steenie. Moreover he remembered the exploration of the night before. Had Steenie discovered a place of safety? Callum decided to trust him. He had no other choice.

When the officers saw that the injured man's brother had faith in Steenie, they agreed to his unknown plan. It was one less problem for them to deal with. And so, later that day, a cart left Dumfries and trundled across the bridge over the River Nith.

Next day, when the effects of the laudanum had worn off, Alastair awoke to find himself lying on a straw palliasse in a cellar with Callum, Donald and Steenie watching over him. He was given soup and an explanation – the latter mainly from Steenie.

He was in a cellar in the Bridgend. This was a collection of cottages which formed a village on the Galloway side of the Nith. The Dumfries magistrates had no authority on the west side of the Nith and this had caused the Bridgend to become a haven for those fleeing the clutches of the law. Alastair would be safe virtually anywhere in the Bridgend. But, to make quite sure, until his leg was healed he could stay out of sight in the cellar. The cellar had a hidden entrance (Alastair was to find out the reason for this later) so that even if the forces of the government did succeed in entering the Bridgend – which would be both unlikely and unwise – they would not find him. So all he had to do was to lie low for a while. It was not as if he were a clan chief or a Jacobite leader. After the Rebellion was over the government authorities would not bother themselves about a lowly cotter lad.

Then, unusual for him, Steenie became very serious. It was obvious that the cause of Prince Charlie was doomed. If the Jacobites had pressed on from Derby they might have had a chance but now the Prince's Army was completely demoralised. Steenie was going to leave while he still could. He was going to stay in the Bridgend and look after Alastair. As far as Steenie was concerned the Bridgend was as good a place as any. Moreover, Alastair would need him. For one thing Alastair did not speak English and the inhabitants of the Bridgend did not speak Gaelic. But Steenie would soon rectify that. He would soon teach Alastair English.

Then Alastair had a visit from one of the leaders of the Bridgend community, a large man with long dark hair who looked like a gypsy. He made him welcome and Steenie interpreted.

"As long as you do not cause trouble you are welcome to stay as long as you like. King George or Prince Charlie, it is all one to us. We go by what it says in the Good Book. 'Put not your trust in princes.'"

He paused for a moment and then continued,

"If you stay with us we could do a lot for you. We could even learn you a trade."

Here he stopped, threw back his head and roared. Alastair was puzzled but Steenie obviously understood because he smiled.

The gypsy left soon after this and Callum told him he would have to go too. He agreed with Steenie when he said that the Jacobite cause was doomed but he had a wife and children and he wanted to see them.

"Afterwards," Callum shrugged, "I'll probably try to get to France or America. They'll be nothing for the likes of us in Scotland after this."

There was some discussion as to whether or not Donald was to stay in the Bridgend or go on with his brother. Eventually he decided to stay with Callum and the Jacobite Army.

They said their farewells, promising that they would find ways of exchanging messages. Then Callum and Donald left their young brother in Steenie's care.

# CHAPTER 14

## GRANDFATHER'S STORY – LIFE IN THE BRIDGEND

Alastair spent the next few weeks in the cellar. Steenie attended to him and brought him food. Steenie also brought him the news – and it was bad. On the last day of the year 1745 the Duke of Cumberland had retaken Carlisle Castle. Alastair worried about his brothers and how they were faring with the retreating army but, for the moment, there was nothing he could do. The pain in his leg lessened and gradually he became stronger. The Jacobite surgeon had done a good job in setting the leg and the time came when Alastair was able to get around with the help of a stick. But it would be too much for him to go up and down the cellar steps. Steenie tried to persuade him to move to the house above. His palliasse would be put in a ground floor room so it would be easy for him to get out and about. But Alastair refused. He was adamant. He felt safe in his cellar. Steenie tried to reason with him. The authorities were not going to come looking for him. He was too insignificant. His name was not on any list. It would be different if he were found just after a battle. But the authorities were not going to scour the countryside for the likes of him. They were after bigger fish. They were looking for salmon, not parr. But all to no avail. Alastair was sticking to his underground burrow.

Eventually the gypsy leader was brought to him. He assured Alastair that the authorities would not dare invade his territory. But, unlikely as it was, even if the Bridgend were to be searched, then he personally would see that Alastair was well hidden again. So saying the gypsy simply picked up the palliasse and carried it up the stairs. Without giving Alastair a chance to say anything, Steenie took his arm and hustled him after the gypsy.

So began Alastair's life in the Bridgend. Despite its bad reputation, the Bridgend was certainly not the poorest part of Dumfries. It had spacious, wide streets with comfortable houses. The buildings were mostly low, one-storey cottages but they had two or three rooms with an attic under the roof. Many of them were built of red sandstone and many had tiled roofs, not thatch. Because of fire regulations most houses in Dumfries were tiled. There were more thatched roofs in the Bridgend than in any other part of Dumfries, but even the Bridgend had its share of tiled roofs. And the Bridgend cottages had windows – not many but a few, which was more than many Dumfries dwellings had – as Steenie made sure Alastair knew. Steenie used to slip across the bridge from time to time and wander about Dumfries and he told Alastair how lucky he was to be in the Bridgend.

"The gentry have braw hooses in Irish Street with gran' gairdens stretching doon tae the river," he explained and there are lots of fine toon hooses up the High Street but ..." Then he would shake his head before going on to describe the closes between the High Street and Irish Street. These 'closes' consisted of a number of hovels all packed together, back to back with hardly any windows. Cramped and dark they were a natural breeding ground for diseases.

Alastair listened to all this but did not say anything. His palliasse was put on the floor of a room above the cellar and on the ground floor and Steenie had a palliasse next to him.

Alastair gradually became accustomed to his new surroundings. After the small round house in the Highlands the Bridgend house seemed huge to him. One of the first things he noticed was how clear the air was. This was because there was a fireplace at one side of the room. Alastair was used to a fire in the centre of the house, no chimney and the smoke going out through a hole in the roof. At least that was what it was supposed to do but instead it tended to drift all around the room. By contrast the clear air of the Bridgend cottage was a constant wonder to him.

Steenie continued to look after him. He helped him out into the street and steadied him while he walked up and down. Gradually his leg became stronger and he was able to discard the stick. He had also to get used to the feel of breeches. His kilt had been quietly taken away and a pair of breeches found for him. It was unlikely that anyone in the Bridgend would betray him. After all no one wanted to attract the attention of the authorities. Even so it was best to take no chances so the presence of a Highlander in the Bridgend was kept as quiet as possible. At first Alastair found his new breeches uncomfortable and restrictive. He had been much freer in his kilt. The rough cloth chafed and rubbed against his legs. But it was a severe winter and later he was thankful for the breeches as they were much warmer than his kilt.

Apart from his clothes Alastair had far more to get used to. After his little clachan the Bridgend was so big and crowded, and for him, positively claustrophobic. For a town the streets were actually quite broad but Alastair was used to the wide-open spaces of a Highland moor and the houses seemed to close in on him. There were so many people all bustling about. And the noise. Voices calling to one another to say nothing of the frequent brawling and drunken singing. Then from the chimneys poured smoke. But perhaps hardest of all after the fresh air of the Highlands was the stench, the smell of unwashed bodies combined with the rotting rubbish which had just been thrown into the street and was a source of joy for the few pigs which roamed up and down.

Gradually Alastair came to accept all this. By and large the inhabitants of the Bridgend left him to his own devices. He finally realised that what he had been told was true, that the more respectable citizens of Dumfries did not dare venture into the Bridgend. At long last he began to feel safe.

He did however have one frightening experience. He was passing a ruined cottage. The four walls were standing but the roof was off. On a sudden impulse he went inside. At the back of his mind was the glimmering of an idea. He knew how to thatch a roof. Could Steenie help him to thatch this cottage and would they then be allowed to have it to themselves?

As he entered he saw he was not alone. A man was kneeling in a corner. He seemed to be prising out some of the stones in the wall. Alastair had a sudden glimpse of a couple of watches on the floor beside him. On hearing footsteps the man whirled round and Alastair saw he had a knife in his hand. Alastair backed away as the man said something. Alastair's English was not yet good enough to understand but a knife talks the same in any language.

"Get oot o' here and keep your mooth shut or I'll slit you frae lug tae lug."

That night Steenie carefully explained things to him. The man was obviously a pickpocket and Alastair had surprised him at his secret hiding place. Alastair was to be more careful in the future. The Bridgend was a place where everyone's business was their own – and completely private. Alastair listened and learned the lesson and from then on he was even more careful to keep himself to himself.

A few days later Alastair wandered further along the banks of the Nith. He saw something strange in the water and went closer to investigate. He found it was a number of sacks which were full of something. The sacks were anchored in some way which meant that they remained under the surface. Alastair did not need anyone to tell him what he had found. He had seen similar sights often around his own clachan. The sacks contained barley which was being steeped, the very first stage in the distilling of whisky, in this case the illegal distilling of whisky. Alastair looked around quickly to make sure that no one had seen him. Once he had reassured himself on that account he hurried away, and he never breathed a word to anyone about the sacks in the Nith. He was learning how to survive in the Bridgend.

Steenie had made himself responsible for Alastair. He came and went and how he spent his time Alastair did not know. But Steenie found time to give Alastair a daily English lesson, or rather a lesson in what passed for English in the Edinburgh in which he had grown up. Apart from that Alastair was left alone for most of the day.

There was a family living in the cottage where he lodged with Steenie but Alastair did not really know them and his English was not yet good enough for him to converse with them. In any case Alastair would not have known what to say. He felt awkward in the cottage when Steenie was not around so, during the day, he got into the habit of wandering around the village.

One day he found a path, which led down to the banks of the River Nith. He sat down on the grass and looked across the river. He felt comfortable there. There was a feeling of space and he could at last see the sky. It was not like his native moorland but it was better than the streets of the Bridgend where all he could see would be the occasional pocket of blue.

Alastair got into the habit of going down there. He would sit for hours gazing across to the fields on the other side of the Nith. One day a girl came. She had two buckets suspended from a yoke across her shoulders. She slipped off the yoke, took one of the buckets and, in spite of the fact that blocks of ice were floating on the water, waded into the river and filled it. As she passed she gave Alastair a shy smile and he found he recognised her. It was Devorgilla, the eldest daughter of the family in his cottage. Alastair wondered what the bucket of water was for. Washing? Cooking? Drinking? Surely not. Used to the pure, clear water of Highland burns Alastair had been horrified when he saw the dark murky waters of the Nith. Little did he realise then that it was much worse in the summer when there was often green scum at the edges and the water was full of tiny insects. Alastair did not know then that he was actually seeing the river at its cleanest. To him it was bad enough. He looked at the girl again. On reflection he decided the girl's water would not be for drinking. Most people in the Bridgend seemed to drink ale or whisky. Given the state of the water in the river it was probably just as well.

Alastair was soon to see Devorgilla again but this time she was not alone. She was with a group of girls who had brought their washing down to the river. She called out a greeting to him and he waved shyly to her.

Alastair was now used to walking around the village but he stubbornly refused to set foot outside the Bridgend. To him it had become a kind of sanctuary. Steenie tried to persuade him he was being over cautious. If he would not cross the bridge into Dumfries then he could at least walk down the western side of the river. But Alastair was adamant.

To a certain extent he may have had a point. Small and quick and with a frequent perky grin on his face it was patently obvious that Steenie was not Highland. He could walk about Dumfries and no one would ever give him a second glance. It was different with Alastair. He was tall with the long, slow stride of a Highlander. Moreover he would give himself away every time he opened his mouth. If he were to run into someone who had been forced to contribute to the fund for Prince Charles' demands then he could be in trouble. So, no matter what Steenie thought, Alastair was probably right to lie low. But Steenie still meant to find some way of making him extend his horizons.

Alastair continued to spend his time wandering about the village. He often took the path leading to the riverbank and he would spend hours there just gazing across to the fields on the other side. He often saw Devorgilla – or Gilla as she was called for short – bringing her washing there too and they began to speak to each other. Alastair wondered at her unusual name and she told him that she had been named after the Lady Devorgilla who had built the bridge over the Nith and had also founded Sweetheart Abbey – away back at the time of the wars with England and Robert the Bruce.

One day he was in the cottage when she was gathering the washing together. Steenie was there too. He grabbed a large wicker basket and passed it to her. When it was full he took one side and told Alastair to take the other.

"Come oan. She's been feeding us for the last twa months. It's the least we can dae tae to help her noo."

It would never have occurred to Alastair to help carry a laundry basket. That was women's work, and not to be done by any man brought up in the Highlands. But the way Steenie put it he could not really refuse although he did wonder to himself, how did Gilla usually carry the basket when she was by herself? Would she not usually carry it on her back?

They set off. On leaving they did not turn and walk down the village as Alastair had expected. Instead they turned and walked up towards the bridge. They crossed the track and passed the inn at the end of the bridge and continued further down on the west side of the Nith until they came to an open part. There many women were doing their washing. Steenie made sure that Gilla's basket was taken right down to the water and then he left her with the other women, but not before he had given her a little sly smile. He then took Alastair back up the bank and found a log for them both to sit on. He did not say anything for a while but just let Alastair get used to his new surroundings. Then he put in a brief word of explanation about the various sights. He started off by reassuring Alastair that he was still safe. He may have been outside the confines of the village but he was still on the west side of the Nith – and he was still outside the jurisdiction of the Dumfries magistrates.

Alastair took small comfort from this. He was still very nervous. He was out in the open and he felt very vulnerable.

All he wanted was to get back to the safety of the Bridgend but, as time passed, he began to calm down. He was just a few hundred yards from the village and he was in full view of the bridge. In the unlikely event of a party of dragoons crossing it he would have plenty of time to get back to safety. So he relaxed slightly and started to look around.

He looked first at the women busy in front of him, scrubbing furiously on rubbing boards or beating their clothes in the icy water. They were just down from a little waterfall. Steenie saw him looking at it and explained. It was artificial. It acted as a mill-dam for the new grain mill further down the river. He then pointed out the large, rectangular red sandstone building at the foot of a hill. When Steenie saw that Alastair was relatively settled he quietly left him and slipped back to the Bridgend. He sought out the gypsy leader and told him that the plan had worked. Alastair would soon realise that he could not spend the rest of his life hiding like a rabbit down a hole.

Alastair continued to gaze around him. He looked across to the Dumfries side of the Nith. For a lad brought up in a remote Highland clachan there was plenty to look at. Alastair did not take it all in on that first visit but in the future he was to get to know it well and he never tired of watching the changing scenes. As he looked across the river to the Whitesands he became familiar with the tanneries, the sawmills and the rafts of timber being floated upstream. He became used to seeing the sheep and cattle being driven to the markets and he was fascinated by the occasional gypsy encampment. If he looked downstream he could sometimes see the mast of a ship.

He often saw Gilla and she told him that it was quite different in the summer. Then, if there had been a dry spell, the river would be shallow – especially at low tide – and there would be an island in the middle. The women used to wade out to the island and bleach their clothes on it.

In this way Alastair just drifted through his days in the Bridgend, until one day Steenie had a very serious talk with him.

## CHAPTER 15 – GRANDFATHER'S STORY

## WORK IN THE BRIDGEND

One day Steenie took Alastair aside and spoke to him very earnestly. Alastair was much better now and it was time he thought about making some contribution to the community. The gypsy leader had been very patient. He had given Alastair time to get his strength back and also get used to his new home – for that was what the Bridgend was. But now it was time for him to find some way of paying for his shelter. The gypsy had some ideas but could Alastair think of anything that he would like to do himself? Alastair thought and then shook his head. He was good with animals and back in the clachan he had looked after the cattle and acted as shepherd to the few sheep. He had also helped to drive the cattle to the great market at Falkirk. But there were not many animals in the Bridgend. Steenie looked thoughtful and said that there were a few.

Something had been puzzling Alastair for some time. Why had the people of the Bridgend been so kind to him and fed and sheltered him for nothing these past weeks? He looked at Steenie. Now might be his chance to find out. Did Steenie have anything to do with it? Had he asked them to look after him? He put this to Steenie who hesitated and then gave him a partial explanation. Yes, he had asked the gypsy who ran the little community if Alastair could stay and yes, the gypsy had agreed as a favour to Steenie. When pressed as to why, Steenie just said, "They found that I could be of service to them" and with that Alastair had to be content. But Alastair still had one last question. Why had Steenie put himself out for him?

Steenie answered almost fiercely.

"Because you're faimily. Or the nearest thing I've had to faimily since ma parents deed. I've been completely oan my ain since I wis ten years auld. But then you wouldn't ken onything aboot that. Oh I ken that your ain faither is deid but you've always had your mither and your brithers and sisters. And beyond them you hae the hale clan. And even here your clan members will be able to reach doon to you. But I've been on my ain, surviving best as I could, sleeping in cellars, begging a few bawbees, caddying whenever I could. But the last few months I hae felt as if I was pairt of a faimily again."

Steenie stopped suddenly. Alastair was looking rather startled at the intensity with which his friend had spoken. They were both silent while they tried to get back to normal. Then Steenie spoke again more quietly and told Alastair that he owed the people of the Bridgend something and to think what he could do.

The next day Alastair walked through the streets of the Bridgend thinking deeply. He looked at all the animals. A few pigs were rooting among the rubbish. They certainly did not need anyone to look after them. Likewise with the small number of scrawny hens. There were the cats and dogs, but the dogs all had owners and the cats had their own independent existence.

Then, from the shadows of his mind, Alastair suddenly dredged a picture of the day after he had first been brought to the Bridgend, a picture of a huge man laughing and saying, "We'll even learn you a trade."

The animals of the Bridgend did not need Alastair so it looked as if it would have to be the gypsy's trade – whatever it was.

The next morning the gypsy leader came for Alastair and took him down to the cellars. Although Alastair had spent so much time there before he had not really found out much about them. He had just been lying in the corner of one. But now he was taken from one cellar to another and through various tunnels. It was a veritable rabbit warren. Alastair now understood that even if the authorities decided to search the Bridgend they would never find anything – or anyone – if they were well hidden. Eventually they came to a large vault which was empty except for some dripping sacks in the centre. Another gypsy was standing over the sacks. This was Davie Aitken, Gilla's father. He was to be Alastair's new mentor and from now on Alastair was to answer to him.

From the moment he walked into the cellar Alastair felt a sense of familiarity. He recognised the dripping sacks at once. They were similar to those in his own clachan. The gypsy's 'trade' was illegal whisky distilling and smuggling. The sacks contained barley which had been submerged in water for a few days. Now Alastair had to take it out and spread it on the floor. He had to go into the adjoining cellars and examine the barley there and turn it carefully until it began to sprout. If he found any of the barley ready he had to put it in a kiln where it would be dried.

That was all Alastair was trusted to do that first day and he had plenty of time to think. He realised at once that he would not be much use. He could help with the menial tasks at the beginning but he knew well that the later stages of whisky distilling were a fine art – and one which he would never be able to master. He would have to find another way of making his own contribution to the Bridgend, but for the life of him he could not think what.

Late in the afternoon Alastair had a surprise. It was not Davie who came for him but Gilla. She led him swiftly through the labyrinth and up the stairs. Then she took him through the streets to a house on the edge of the Bridgend, near some open fields. They went inside and Alastair saw that the cottage had been turned into a stable. There was straw on the floor and a magnificent grey stallion was munching hay from a manger. Gilla walked quietly up to the horse, stroked its nose and gave it a carrot. Alastair saw at once that, although a stallion, the horse was a very gentle creature. He joined Gilla and patted it. That simple action had a great effect on him. At once he felt much calmer. This was where he belonged, in a stable, or anywhere with animals. Gilla was watching him carefully.

"Are ye no feart? Efter a' it wis a horse that broke your leg."

Alastair shook his head.

"No. It wisnae the horse. It was that fule o' a piper blawin' his pipes right under the beast's nose. Mind you, I'll be mair canny frae noo oan."

Gilla stroked the animal again.

"He's rather special. His name is Dominie. He is called that because he is wise and clever." Then seeing that Alastair did not understand she added,

"Dominie means schoolmaister."

Gilla produced a brush and held it out to him. Alistair took it and began to give the horse a good grooming. After a while Gilla said, "Would you like to ride him? He's quiet eneuch – even if he's a stallion."

"I canna ride."

Alastair was surprised at the question. How did she expect him to be able to ride? The clan chiefs rode and their gillies ran beside them. Even some of the tacksmen rode, but not cotter lads like himself.

Gilla checked the water trough. Alastair felt annoyed with himself. That was something he should have thought of. He seized a bucket which was in a corner and went down to the river.

When they had both seen that Dominie had all he needed and that he was settled they left him alone. Gilla was very careful to close – and lock – the door. Dominie must be a very special horse indeed.

The next few days followed a similar pattern. Alastair helped in the cellars and also helped to look after Dominie. But there was not really enough for him to do. He mentioned that to Steenie. He knew he would never be able to play a full part in whisky distilling.

Steenie listened carefully. The trouble was that that was where Alastair was needed. Apart from the whisky distilling and smuggling the Bridgend was just like any other village. There were three brewers, a number of millers, and then assorted tradesmen like weavers, bakers etc. What gave the Bridgend its bad reputation was that thieves, smugglers and vagabonds found it easy to hide and escape the authorities. But apart from that many of the villagers were just ordinary people. Steenie looked at Alastair and said,

"And you're guy auld for an apprenticeship."

Alastair latched onto something which Steenie had said. Weaving. Now that was something he had done before. Not much mind you, but he had sat at a loom before. Steenie looked at him and said nothing.

During the next few days Alastair noticed that a number of mares had been brought to the fields behind Dominie's stable. Every day there would be one or two more. Then one day Steenie spoke to him quietly and told him to be at the stable that night.

So after dark Alastair dutifully turned up. He found a number of men busily and quietly engaged in a number of activities. Davie came up to him and gave him his instructions. He thrust a bridle into his hands and told him he was to help to round up the mares. When they had all been caught and tied to a railing behind the stable some of the men took some rope slings and threw them over the animals' backs. Alastair was shown how to do this. He learnt quickly. He had witnessed scenes like this before. Finally a chain of men arrived carrying small kegs. These kegs were secured in the slings – two kegs to a mare. Then when all was ready Davie himself led Dominie out of the stable.

The little procession set off. The horses were led through the streets of the Bridgend. Alastair found himself leading one of the mares. Here he began to feel uneasy. This was obviously a smuggling trip. How far was he expected to go? They came to the end of the main street and were now at the foot of the bridge more or less opposite the inn. They stopped and the bridles were taken off. Then Davie led Dominie onto the bridge and released him. At once he broke into a canter and clattered over the bridge. All the mares followed their leader. Alastair watched in amazement. Davie came over to him.

"Worth his weight in gowd, that horse. He kens whaur to gae. An' his mares will follow him. All the Dumfries inns will hae their whusky by the morn. An' if ony o' the townsfolk hear the hooves they'll just pull the blankets o'er their lugs. That's if they're wise."

Next morning Alastair saw that the mares were back in the fields. He went to the cottage/stable and saw that Dominie was back too. The horses had a good rest for a few days and then there was another night run. Again they returned to fields and stable but, in the following days, Alastair noticed that each day there were fewer mares present until eventually the fields were empty again. Then the stallion was taken from his stable.

Alastair continued to help in the cellar but he kept thinking about the magnificent stallion and wondering at its uncanny ability. Would he ever see it again? He soon found out that he was to see it at regular intervals. Every few weeks Dominie would return with his mares and there would be another night run.

It was around this time that Alastair noticed that Steenie was much better dressed. Alastair did not know how Steenie spent his time or what he did every day but it was obvious that he was being paid for it, and paid well. Alastair did not know what he did to earn his money but he could easily guess. And having guessed he did not want to know any more. As for himself he was content to continue helping in the cellar. He was actually paid too, although in his case, not very much. But it was the very first time in his life that he had ever had any money at all.

Gradually he came to realise that no one was going to come searching for him in the Bridgend and he began to recover his confidence. He still would not walk across the bridge into Dumfries but he would often stroll down the west bank of the Nith with Gilla or Steenie.

Then there was a nasty little incident which, in a rather perverse way, Alastair found reassuring. One afternoon he was standing on the banks of the Nith looking across to Dumfries. Suddenly he was aware of great activity on the bridge. He was able to make out a cart with a crowd of people walking behind it. He also heard pipes and drums playing a lively march. His curiosity aroused he made his way to the main street. He arrived just as a cart was turning into it from the bridge. The cart had one occupant – a young man who had his arms pinioned to the side of the cart. The cart stopped and the driver jumped down. Then, with three laughing companions, he proceeded to untie the young man. That done they all jumped aboard the cart again and drove off. One of them turned to the crowd who had gathered in the main street of the Bridgend. He made a rude gesture and shouted behind him.

"He's your problem noo. You're walcome tae him."

Then the erstwhile prisoner was led away by one of the Aitkens.

Alastair found out later that the young man had been sentenced to be banished from the burgh of Dumfries. This news had the somewhat surprising result that Alastair suddenly felt much safer. To him it suggested that the respectable burghers of Dumfries regarded the Bridgend as a kind of human rubbish dump. And respectable people do not search among middens or dunghills. That is left to scavengers. Alastair felt much calmer. Now, at long last, he felt it unlikely that anyone from the outside world was going to come looking for him. He still did not accept Steenie's assurances that he was completely siccar, but now he was at least able to enjoy his daunders along the west bank of the Nith.

Then, suddenly, something happened to change all that.

# CHAPTER 16 – GRANDFATHER'S STORY

## CONDEMNED

The winter of 1746 was long and severe. But at the beginning of May there were welcome signs of spring. At long last the ice floes in the Nith began to melt – a very welcome sight for Gilla and the other washerwomen of the Bridgend – and buds began to appear on the trees. But all this was ruined for Alastair by the news which began to trickle through in the middle of the month – news of the Battle of Culloden and the rout of the Jacobite Army. Wounded Highlanders being slaughtered where they lay on Drummossie Moor, helpless women and children being butchered, their little houses burnt or torn down around them, their cattle killed, and, worst of all, members of the Jacobite Army who had survived the Battle ruthlessly hunted down. The Highlands had been turned into the Duke of Cumberland's private killing grounds.

Once again Alastair took refuge in the heart of the Bridgend and stayed there while spring merged into summer. His fear for his own safety had returned but even worse was his anxiety over the fate of Callum and Donald. He had heard no news of them for months.

Steenie did what he could. Every day he walked across the bridge into Dumfries to see if he could glean any crumb of news. He made a special point of hanging around the markets on the Whitesands and speaking to the cattle drovers. It was from one of them that he eventually found out what they had all been dreading. After Culloden Callum had escaped but Donald had been taken prisoner. That was all the drover was able to tell Steenie.

Steenie hurried back to the Bridgend with the sad news. Alastair was distraught but Davie Aitken was more practical and Steenie took his cue from him.

Of course it was possible that Donald had been summarily executed, or that he had died in prison. But there was no reason to imagine the worst. The government had decided that the trials of the Jacobite prisoners were to be held in England not Scotland. It would be easier to get convictions under English law, also English juries would prove more amenable – to say nothing of the danger of riots outside Scottish courthouses. This meant that all the Jacobite prisoners were being sent south. Davie looked thoughtful. The gypsies had their own news service and messengers. He was sure that he would soon be able to find out where Donald was being held. He would start immediately. Several Jacobite prisoners had been taken to Carlisle Castle and Davie knew just who could ferret out information there.

Steenie and Alastair never knew who Davie's informant was but he was certainly efficient. Within a few days they knew that Donald was indeed in Carlisle Castle.

So they at least knew where he was. But how could they help him? Should someone try to visit him? Could they find an agent to speak for him and perhaps have him released?

While they were still considering the best course of action, Davie's gypsy messenger brought some really bad news.

Donald had been chosen by lot to stand trial for his life. Alastair was shattered. Donald was seventeen, only a year older than Alastair himself. He was the brother to whom he had always been closest.

At first Alastair could not understand what was happening but Steenie and Gilla explained it all to him very carefully.

The vast numbers of Jacobite prisoners were causing problems for the government. Then the Privy Council devised a solution. It was that the prisoners should draw lots. One in every twenty would stand trial for his life. But His Majesty declared that he was willing to show mercy to the rest, if asked for it. He would pardon them on condition that they left His Kingdom never to return. In other words, this 'mercy' meant that they would be shackled, kept in filthy, disease-ridden conditions and shipped across the Atlantic where they would be sold as indentured servants to work in the plantations. In other words condemned to a life of slavery. But even this so-called 'mercy' was to be denied Donald as he had drawn the black paper.

Alastair was a mixture of emotions. Frightened, confused, devastated at the possible fate of his favourite brother, even guilty because he himself was safe while his brother was in such danger, but above all angry – very, very angry. He was determined to find out exactly what was happening at Carlisle Castle. To the amazement of everyone around him he suddenly announced,

"I'm going tae gang there mysel."

This was completely unlike Alastair. He just did what he was told. But now events had jolted him into making the very first decision of his life.

"Ye canna," said Steenie. "It wad be too dangerous."

"I'll gang," repeated Alastair.

"Naw," said Steenie firmly. "You might be recognised."

"I'll gang," said Gilla suddenly. "It will be much safer for me. They'll nae fash sae much aboot a woman."

There was some truth in that, especially as Gilla had not been involved in the Rebellion. But there was one stumbling block. Gilla did not speak Gaelic and Donald did not speak English. Long and furious arguments followed. Alastair pointed out that he had grown in the past year and that he looked quite different in his new clothes. But Steenie got really upset. He had lost his own family and he could not bear to lose his one good friend too. Then Gilla pointed out that she did know some Gaelic. Not much but enough to get by, especially if Alastair and Steenie gave her some intensive tuition. Always quiet Gilla now showed that she could be very determined. It was eventually agreed that she should go to Carlisle and find out what she could.

Preparations were made. In the next few days Alastair proceeded to cram into her as much Gaelic as possible. Meanwhile the Bridgend gypsies did what they could to help. They arranged for Gilla to be driven to Carlisle in a farm cart rather than walking the thirty-eight miles. Alastair watched her set off in a mixture of guilt and anxiety – guilt that he was not going himself and anxiety for her safety. But she returned safely within a fortnight and gave a very full account of all that was happening in Carlisle Castle. Her news was very bad.

Outwardly Gilla was calm and assured but inside she was in turmoil. She was very frightened but she managed to keep that to herself. Alastair had enough to worry about. It was years before he heard the whole story and discovered just what an effort Gilla had to make to carry out her plan.

Gilla had never been to Carlisle before and she gazed in amazement at the city walls and towers. She had a feeling of panic as she was driven through the Scotch Gate in the North Walls. She felt as if she was a prisoner herself. But she felt much worse when she had her first sight of the red sandstone mass of Carlisle Castle. She found the ditches, thick high walls, and solid towers both intimidating and awesome. She had to nerve herself to walk across the drawbridge over the old moat. Once inside the gatehouse she explained that she had come, on behalf of his family, to see the prisoner Donald Murray. To her surprise she was not questioned further but just led away to a yard where a number of prisoners were sitting on the grass. So she was spared the horrors of the dark, damp dungeon where the prisoners were kept chained to the walls. One of the prisoners was Donald. Even with her stumbling Gaelic Gilla managed to make him understand who she was and why she had come. Finally another prisoner, who spoke English, explained what had happened.

The prisoners had been sitting on the grass one afternoon – the way there were now – when a man arrived carrying an upturned hat. He shoved the hat in front of Donald and said something. Donald did not understand but a fellow prisoner said that he was to pull something from the hat. Donald did so and found out that he had pulled out a piece of paper – a black piece of paper. When all the prisoners had drawn papers from the hat the man went away but later returned with two officials who read out to them from a large paper. They went on for some time and Donald did not understand a word but the English-speaking prisoner explained it to him afterwards.

It was a petition to the King for mercy for the prisoners, and that the petition was to go off that night to London. When it came back they might be allowed home or they might be transported for the King's mercy was to hang only one in twenty and to let nineteen go for transportation.

But Donald had already drawn the black paper.

Gilla spent some time with him and assured him that Alastair and Steenie were thinking of him and that all was going well with both of them. Then she left him.

There was not much that Gilla could do but she could think of one thing, at least get Donald a good lawyer. This had also been discussed in the Bridgend and Gilla had been given the name of a Carlisle lawyer and she now went to him. He listened and said he would try and do what he could but he must warn her that there was not much hope. There was not any doubt about Donald's guilt. Moreover, there would be plenty of witnesses against him, fellow Jacobites who had turned King's Evidence to save their own skins, Jacobites who were prepared to give evidence against their own comrades in return for a pardon.

And, he continued gently, this was not all. Carlisle may have been just over the border from Scotland but Carlisle was very definitely part of England. The trial would be according to English law. And English law did not allow the accused to have a lawyer or agent to speak for him in court. That only applied to Scottish law. Nevertheless he would try to find some way of helping the young man – although it would be quite wrong of him to give her any false hopes. There was only one chance, to appeal for mercy on the grounds of Donald's age. He was, after all, just a young boy. Then the lawyer hesitated and mentioned his fee. Would she be able to pay him?

Gilla answered calmly that she had good friends who would easily be able to pay the legal fees. (She did not explain that the people of the Bridgend of Dumfries had their own ways of raising money).

The lawyer just accepted her assurances.

Gilla thanked him for his time and left him. She returned to the Bridgend. Alastair was shocked by her news. Horrified, frightened and desperate he was above all frustrated that there was nothing he could do to help his brother.

Gilla made further trips to Carlisle and she was sitting at the back of the court when Donald's case was heard at the end of August. Despite his age no mercy was shown. He was condemned to the barbarous traitor's death of being hanged, drawn and quartered. Gilla was allowed to see him in Carlisle Castle after the verdict. She did not want to. She did not know what to say to him and she found the idea of the meeting positively frightening. But she pitied the terrified boy from the bottom of her heart and she felt it her duty to show him that he still had friends and family. When she was finally brought to him she could find no words so, instead, she just flung herself into his arms. For his part, he was controlled and, outwardly at least, was calm. He gave her messages for Alastair and Steenie.

Then something horrible happened. An official came and told Donald that if he turned King's Evidence he would be pardoned. If he would identify other Jacobite prisoners and testify against them in court his life would be spared and he would be set free. He might even be given a small government pension. He spoke in English but there was another man with him who repeated his words in Gaelic.

Even Gilla with her limited Gaelic understood Donald's reply. He just said quietly,

"No. I will never betray my friends."

This was not enough for the official.

"We are not asking you to give evidence against your close friends and family. But there are many other prisoners with whom you are only slightly acquainted ..."

Donald did not give the other man a chance to translate this into Gaelic. As soon as the official started to speak again he just turned his back on him.

Gilla left him soon after that. While she had been with Donald she had forced herself to remain composed. But when she arrived back in the Bridgend it was a different story. She was tearful, overwrought, and distressed. She was also very angry. She collapsed into Alastair's arms and sobbed bitterly. When she had somewhat recovered she gave a full account of the trial. The offer of a pardon for Donald in exchange for him betraying his comrades particularly upset her, especially as it had been evidence from Jacobite turncoats which had finally convicted Donald himself. One of them had been a woman, one of the women followers of the Jacobite Army.

"That woman," Gilla spat out. "Ann Cameron. I'll remember that name until my dying day. And then they asked Donald to do likewise."

The little group listening to her were all horrified. Alone of them Steenie looked thoughtful.

"They had a guid reason for making that offer when you were present," he said. "They wad be hoping that you would try to persuade him to accept."

Although obvious this had never occurred to Gilla and she gasped in dismay.

Steenie's whole life had been a struggle for survival. Honour was all very well but it was not what he lived by. He was still trying to puzzle out a solution.

"Is there nae way in which he could accept the offer without daeing too much hairm?"

A shocked silence and then Alastair turned on him fiercely,

"Buy his ain life at the expense of some ither puir soul's? How could he live with himsel efterwards?"

Steenie ignored this outburst. For him, as always, practicality took precedence over emotion.

"There are ither things we can try, lawyers, an appeal perhaps if that is possible, a petition to the King begging for mercy. We can start by writing letters to onyone who may be able to help."

At that everyone's spirits lifted. It was not that they had any faith in the suggested actions, but the prospect of doing something was so much better than just accepting fate. And the gypsy leader of the Bridgend had a surprisingly wide influence.

So during the next few weeks important men were contacted, letters written and lawyers approached but all to no avail. The date of the barbarous execution drew nigh. Once again Gilla felt that she had to force herself to go and offer Donald what small comfort she could. So early one morning in mid October she was again driven to Carlisle. She made a supreme effort to control herself and Donald did the same. He remained calm and gave her messages for his brother and all his friends in the Bridgend. Then they had to part. Gilla left him saying,

"We are all praying for you."

Gilla had never planned on going to the execution site at Harraby Hill. She knew it would be too much for her. To see the boy she had befriended being hanged, and then cut down while he was still alive, his heart and intestines being torn from his body and being cast on a fire and, finally, his head being cut off and his body chopped into four parts. And all this amid a carnival atmosphere. No she could not bear to see that. But she would wait outside Carlisle Castle and see him being taken away. There she would say her private farewells and then she would return to the safety of the Bridgend.

And so she was standing among the crowds outside the Castle when the prisoners were brought out on their last journey. She had found herself a place on the grass next to the moat among a pathetic group of prisoners' relatives and friends. A pitiable, miserable gathering which was, nevertheless, ringed by masses of mounted soldiers. There was to be no chance of any rescue attempt or an attack on the guards. But the watchers were far too despondent and dispirited to try anything of the sort.

Gilla knew what to expect. The prisoners would be strapped to sleds pulled by mounted horses and dragged to the execution site.

Eventually the huge gates opened. Gilla was quite near the drawbridge and she had a perfect view of the first horse-drawn hurdle as it trundled across the bridge. As the slow procession passed Gilla looked carefully for Donald. She did not see him and she experienced a faint spark of hope. Then there he was, strapped to the very last sled – which he had all to himself, not shared with any other prisoner, unlike the others. He was leaning back and his eyes were closed – whether he was trying to hide from himself the last dreadful sights of the world he was so soon to leave, or whether someone had mercifully slipped him laudanum or some other drug, Gilla did not know.

Then she heard a sudden gasp and a woman's voice behind her.

"Why the last one is just a boy. It's a wicked sin."

Turning briefly Gilla saw an older woman who was very distressed and who was being supported by a younger one. It was the latter who had spoken. Gilla stretched out and gripped her arm. It was not a time for words.

The young woman suddenly stiffened and Gilla turned back to Donald. Something was happening. There, on the middle of the bridge, the rider reined in the horse and the hurdle stopped. Soldiers appeared and started to cut Donald free. Gilla was near enough to see their faces although she could not hear any words spoken. Donald opened his eyes and looked with a vacant, uncomprehending expression. One of the soldiers attending him was an older man who had obviously seen far too many of the world's horrors. Although she could not catch his words Gilla was sure he spoke to Donald in a kindly way. Donald still looked dazed but for a moment, for just an instant, Gilla thought she saw a sparkle of life light up his eyes. Then almost at once the former blank expression was back on his face. The elderly soldier helped him to his feet but shock was already taking over. Donald stood there unsteadily and it was clear that he could not walk. Two soldiers had to support him and help him back into the Castle. Gilla was in turmoil. What was happening? She was afraid to let herself believe that Donald had suddenly been reprieved, afraid in case it was not true. But the two women behind her had no doubts. She heard the younger one's voice again.

"See, Mother. God is merciful. He has melted the hearts of these wicked men and saved the boy. Perhaps there is hope for Ian yet."

Her mother had no such illusions.

"Nay, Margaret, dinna fool yersel. But give thanks that the boy has been spared at least."

Gilla looked at them and a gleam of understanding shone in Margaret's eyes.

"Your lad?"

Gilla nodded. She did not know what to say. Donald had been saved but these two women were about to lose their Ian. Gilla felt almost guilty. But Margaret made things easy for her.

"Then I am happy for you. Go to him and comfort him. And God bless you both."

Gilla said the only thing she could.

"I'll pray for you both. And for your Ian."

Then the crowd started to move and Gilla found herself separated from her new companions. She was desperate to rush to the Castle to find out what was happening but for the moment her hopes were dashed. Most of the crowd had turned and were walking to Harraby Hill. Gilla found herself forced to go with them. It was as if she was in the middle of a swiftly flowing river being carried along with the current. But she darted in and out among the crowd and managed to make her way to the edge. Then at last she was free of them. She gathered up her skirts and raced back to the Castle and across the moat. She was given permission to see Donald and taken to him at once.

He was in a state of shock. When he saw her he tried to speak but he could only gasp and it was left to a fellow prisoner to explain. Because of his age, His Majesty had been merciful and Donald's death sentence had finally been commuted to transportation to the colonies for life.

Then a mixture of fear and relief finally broke through the barrier of whatever drug Donald had been given and he sobbed and sobbed. Gilla could not speak either so she just took him in her arms and held him silently. Eventually Gilla left him with the other prisoners and returned to the Bridgend and to more tears. But this time they were tears of relief and joy.

Then the practical Steenie took over.

# CHAPTER 17 – GRANDFATHER'S STORY

## THE *VETERAN*

What could they do to help? What did Donald need? What would they be allowed to send to him in the Castle? When transported how could he send messages? And how could his friends send messages to him?

"I canna write," said Alastair, "and he canna read."

"Weel ye'll baith hae to learn," said Steenie. A great blanket of gloom had been lifted from the friends in the Bridgend, but they still felt horror and sadness as they received news of the wave of savage executions in Carlisle, York and London. Alastair retreated to the heart of the Bridgend and refused to leave the safety of the village. And this time Steenie followed his example.

Gilla managed to visit Donald a few more times. She made him repeat over and over again the name of Davie Aitken, and also Bridgend, Dumfries, Scotland. Letters sent to Davie would always find their way to Alastair. And if Donald could not write himself then he could always find someone to write for him.

Then the day came when Donald was moved from Carlisle. He was taken to Liverpool. He was obviously going to be put aboard a ship for America or the West Indies.

Donald had clearly taken Gilla's lessons to heart because, in due course, a letter arrived saying that he was on board the *Veteran* which was due to sail to Antigua and Jamaica.

Once they had the name of the ship the members of the little group in the Bridgend had their own ways of making the best use of that information. Steenie started walking over the bridge into Dumfries again. He would haunt the coffee shops. He would bring back newspapers which were then carefully searched for any news of the *Veteran*. Davie conferred with the gypsy leader of the Bridgend. What contacts did they have in the West Indies? Did they know anyone who could help Donald when he got there? Or even just send news of him?

Alastair was astounded that these seemingly lowly gypsies could have some influence in the faraway West Indies but Steenie said it was not really so surprising. Dumfries was a port which sent ships to the Americas and there were gypsies who sometimes had to leave their native town secretly and in a hurry.

From Steenie's newspapers they learned that the *Veteran* sailed from Liverpool on the 8th May, 1747. After this a period of silence and no news at all. Then summer arrived and suddenly the newspapers were full of news of the *Veteran*.

Not far from Martinique the *Veteran* was attacked by a French privateer, the *Diamant*. The French won and the *Veteran* was taken to Martinique. The British government wanted the Jacobite prisoners returned and letters were exchanged between the British Governor of the Leeward Islands and the French Governor of Martinique.

This news was eagerly devoured in the Bridgend, but there was no answer to the one important question. What had happened to the Scots prisoners? It was six weary months before they received their answer. In the spring of

1748 news came that the French had set the prisoners free and had already returned most of them to France.

So Donald was free. But where was he? Had he been sent to France or was he still in the West Indies? Or had he made his way to the American colonies? Long discussions in the Bridgend. Steenie said he hoped he had been sent to France. That would be safer than the American colonies where the word of King George was still law. Moreover there was a Scots-Jacobite community in France and they would help Donald to establish himself, find him work and a place to stay.

But Steenie did impress one thing on Alastair. Donald could never, never return to Scotland. A condition of accepting the King's mercy was that the banishment was to be for life. Any prisoner who returned without permission would be put to death as a felon.

In the absence of news all that Alastair and his friends could do was hope. It was not until nearly a year later that a letter arrived from France. Donald was safe and was working as a servant in the house of an exiled Scottish laird.

Alastair was only too glad that his brother was safe and had a roof over his head but Steenie frowned. When pressed he pointed out that this would almost certainly ensure that Donald could never return to Scotland. In addition to the conditions he had agreed to when accepting transportation was now the fact that he was working for an attainted chief – and one who was very friendly with the King of France.

But Alastair did not pay much attention to Steenie's concerns. He had heard from his brother and nothing could spoil his delight at that simple fact.

Now, with the worry about his brother behind him, he was free to get on with his own life in the Bridgend.

## CHAPTER 18 – GRANDFATHER'S STORY

## A WEDDING

But long before news of the capture of the *Veteran* by the French reached the Bridgend something very important happened. In July, 1747 a general amnesty was announced. As the names of both Alastair and Steenie were not on any list they were now free from the danger of arrest and trial.

This changed things completely. Their own safety was now assured and Donald was on his way to the West Indies. But Alastair was still reluctant to leave the sanctuary of the Bridgend. Still one day he at last yielded to Steenie's coaxing and allowed himself to be led across the bridge into Dumfries.

That first outing was very short but Steenie persuaded him to make several follow-up trips. Then Steenie skilfully and subtly handed over to Devorgilla and together Gilla and Alastair explored Dumfries. Of course many would have said that Gilla should have been chaperoned – but the people of the Bridgend made their own rules.

Since leaving his clachan nearly two years ago Alistair had had his horizons considerably and uncomfortably widened. First he had seen the Highlands merge into the Lowlands. Then came the great city of Edinburgh and, later, the towns and settled farmlands of England. But he had always had deeper concerns and worries at the back of his mind. Now, for the first time, he was free to relax and take in the new sights, and leisure to enjoy them.

First Gilla took him up the Friar's Vennel to the wide High Street. Alastair stared around at the red sandstone buildings and the little canopies of the many shops – something which was still a novelty to him as there had been no shops at all in the clachan in which he grew up. They walked up the High Street until they came to the Town Hall, which was placed right in the middle of the street. This building formed one of the town's main landmarks because it was adorned with a steeple and a spire. Alastair felt rather uncomfortable as it also contained the guardhouse. This was to be the first of many excursions into Dumfries – and Alastair continued to be fascinated by his first real insight into town life.

Despite the attractions of the High Street, Alastair preferred Irish Street with its fine town houses. It was not just the fronts of the houses he was interested in. He liked walking behind them and admiring their magnificent gardens. These gardens backed down towards the Nith and this walk took him to his main interest in Dumfries, the sheep and cattle markets. Alastair never tired of watching them. He also became friendly with several of the regular drovers – something which was to become useful later.

But Alastair's favourite walk was much nearer home. He was always content just to walk out of the village, past the inn at the beginning of the bridge and just walk southwards along the Nith. They would linger on the green sward below the inn and watch, as it was now summer and the Nith was much lower, the islands in the middle of the river with their white covering of bleaching linen. Then they would pass the large, and rather forbidding, grain mill and continue on under Corbelly Hill.

But Gilla did something for Alastair which was far more important than just showing him Dumfries. She taught him to ride. His lessons took place in a field behind the village and on a placid little gypsy pony. Alastair paid great attention and he was soon cantering round the field.

Then, in the autumn of 1748, Alastair asked Gilla to marry him, and was almost surprised when she said 'yes'. Her promise would have been enough for him. He did not expect that they would be allowed to marry for some time yet, not until he had established himself in some way which would allow him to support Gilla. But both Gilla and her father wanted the wedding to go ahead at once. Gilla had wanted to be married on the bridge built by her namesake but she thought it would be impracticable. They could not be expected to hold up all the bridge traffic. But her father did not agree.

"If my lass wants to be wed on the middle o' the bridge, then she shall be," he thundered.

And so, on the appointed day Alastair and Gilla, her father and all their friends from the Bridgend, crowded onto the bridge. Carts and cattle just had to wait. Any angry drivers were soon silenced. At one point two very officious gentlemen pushed their way into the crowd from the Dumfries end of the bridge.

"Now, now," one of them began, "you cannot block..."

He stopped suddenly when one large gypsy turned and took a step towards him. His companion took his arm and said quietly,

"It won't be for long. Best leave well alone."

The two men retreated under the stern looks of the gypsies leaving the wedding to go ahead.

Devorgilla and Alastair led their wedding procession to the very middle of the bridge. They came to a part where the wall bulged out slightly over the Nith. There they stopped and, looking down the river, they held hands and, in clear voices, exchanged their vows, not the vows of the marriage ceremony of any church, but their own promises, true and sincere. There was complete silence apart from their young voices. At the end the watchers sang the Twenty Third Psalm and the heartfelt simplicity of the massed voices drifted across to Dumfries and was heard in the middle of the High Street.

Officially it would be classed as a 'clandestine and irregular' marriage as no banns had ever been called in any church and no clergyman officiated, but, nevertheless, according to the laws of Scotland, it was still a real wedding. All that was needed was for Gilla and Alastair to declare their vows before two witnesses – and they had been heard by hundreds.

Afterwards they all walked back to the inn at the end of the bridge. As many as could get in entered. The rest went down to the grassy sward on the riverbank where trestle tables had been set up. The food was simple but there was plenty of it, salmon, mutton, potatoes. Also an abundance of bread, bannocks and apple tarts, the contribution of the women of the Bridgend who had been busy baking for a week. And the Bridgend brewers had supplied more than enough beer for everyone. The eating, drinking, speech making and toasting of the bride and groom continued into the late afternoon and then in the evening the feasting was followed by singing and dancing to the music of a group of fiddlers.

Half way through the celebrations Gilla and Alastair slipped away to their own house. It was in the middle of the Bridgend and had been empty for many years. It had no roof but Alastair had put that right himself. Thatching a roof was one thing he did know something about. Gilla's father organised parties to gather reeds, straw and heather – anything which could be used – and Alastair did the actual thatching himself. So they had their own house. And if it had a thatched roof when most of the other houses in the Bridgend had tiled roofs – well what did it matter?

Alastair took Gilla's name of Aitken. To him it made sense. After all his real name was MacGregor, not Murray. But he was not allowed to use the name of MacGregor, as the clan had been proscribed and the name made illegal. His family just used the name Murray to avoid the strictures of the law. His wife's name Aitken meant more to him than Murray. And so forever afterwards he was known as Alastair Aitken.

But there was still one problem. How was Alastair going to support himself? He himself was still wondering if it were not too late for him to become a weaver but Davie said to him,

"Take Gilla away from here. She deserves more. It is different for me but she deserves better than the brawls and taverns of the Bridgend."

At first Alastair was too stunned to answer. Then his first thought was that there were much worse places than the Bridgend. He thought of the glimpses he had seen of the lanes behind the High Street with their miserable little hovels packed closely together, built back to back with hardly a window between them. Why, in comparison, the Bridgend with its wide streets was Paradise.

Davie was continuing.

"You're guid wi' beasts. You could become a drover but ye would not earn much and ye would be awa frae Gilla for months at a time. Why don't ye become a fairmer?"

A farmer? Alastair gazed at him in silent amazement. At last he stammered out.

"A fairmer? But I've nae siller to buy a fairm."

Davie just looked thoughtful. Later he said to Alastair.

"There are ways to get siller, ye ken. The smuggling pays well."

Alastair replied at once.

"But I canna sail a boat."

"There is still much to be done on land," replied Davie.

Then he looked at Alastair and muttered,

"Ah weel, perhaps no."

No more was said on the matter and then they all found that there was indeed a way in which Alastair could earn money. And it was all due to his love of animals.

# CHAPTER 19 – GRANDFATHER'S STORY

## A MOST REMARKABLE HORSE

One market day two drovers walked over the bridge from Dumfries and into the Bridgend. They sought out Alastair who recognised one of the drovers at once. It was his elder brother Callum.

Callum was looking rather furtive. He said at once,

"I need your help," and then proceeded to give an explanation. His companion was a Highland chieftain who was not covered by the general amnesty. Callum was trying to get him to France. He was sure they had been followed by government agents and so it was imperative that the fugitive should be hidden immediately. Gilla at once went to fetch her father who took the runaway down to the cellars and the secret places known only to a few of the leaders of the Bridgend – hiding holes necessary for the illicit whisky-making equipment but also useful for concealing people.

The chieftain was soon where no one would ever find him.

Now there was time for Callum to tell his brother his news. There was no future for him in the Highlands any more and he planned to leave Scotland too.

"Things are hopeless," he said sadly. "There is nae work and we can barely scratch a living. Starvation is always just roond the corner. And to make matters waur we are noo expected to pay rent. The auld chief's no the man he was. He doesnae seem tae care aboot the clan noo. I've even heard tell that he is thinking of bringing in sheep frae the south."

He stopped and sat silently for a few moments. Alastair did not interrupt him. Then, as if all this was not bad enough, Callum found, for him, something even worse. Eyes flashing angrily he continued,

"They are trying to destroy us completely. Why we are not even allowed to wear kilt or tartan noo. Here, look at ma bonnie plaid."

So saying he thrust something at Alastair who took it and examined it wonderingly. It looked like a large, dirty blanket. It was mud coloured, although a kinder description might have been brown.

As Alastair turned it over in his hands Calum spat out bitterly,

"It's ma tartan plaid. Catriona dyed it. It doesna look verra bonnie the noo but at least it is still guid wool and it's warm and I can wrap my sel' in it the nicht."

Callum continued at length about the plight of the Highlands and then he became more practical. He was going to take his family to America.

"It's a new country and we will have a chance tae mak a fresh start."

He gave more details of his plans. He had got the idea from the tacksman, who was talking of going to America and taking his people, sub-tenants and cotters with him.

"But I am no gaeing to wait until he is ready. I am gaeing tae gang the noo," Calum declared firmly.

But he needed money for his fare and he had no idea of how he would earn it until he heard of the rebel chief's plight. He at once offered to smuggle him out of the country – as long as he was paid enough. It had been relatively easy to get him to Dumfries, disguised as a drover. He knew he could hide him in the Bridgend and surely someone would have some ideas as to how he could complete his journey.

"Normally it would be possible," said Davie slowly. "If we could get him to the Kingholm Quay and a ship which could sail to France. But ye say that ye think ye were followed?"

Callum agreed that they were almost sure of it. Davie pondered over the problem.

"There could be men in the inn. We must get o'er the bridge, but if they are watching frae the inn ..."

He tailed off and then he said,

"I dinna like it but I suppose we could go north and try to ford the river and then work back to the Kingholm."

He thought for a moment and pointed out an alternative. They could slip away through the fields at the back of the village and make their way south west to Carsehorne on the Solway where they could get a ship to almost anywhere. But there were still objections. It would be a journey of about ten miles – long enough to make it comparatively easy for any agent to pick up their trail. Moreover no doubt there were several agents already watching Carsehorne.

Then Alastair joined in. For once he spoke very decisively.

"There is a way across the bridge."

Everyone stared at him and he explained. Davie considered carefully.

"Aye. It could work."

Preparations were made, preparations which took a long time. Meantime the chieftain remained in his hiding hole.

As well as the preparations there was the question of payment. Davie was determined that his son-in-law should not be cheated. The chieftain had with him his family jewels but Davie preferred gold. The chieftain handed over a considerable amount and promised the rest later.

Meanwhile messengers went to and fro. A ship's captain was contacted and it was arranged that on a certain night, a ship should be moored at the Kingholm Quay at high tide and should be ready to cast off.

Shortly after this Dominie was back in his stable and the mares were in their fields. One night the whisky barrels were slung across their backs and they were led through the Bridgend. But this time there was something different. Two of the mares carried no barrels. Instead they had riders. And they were both right behind Dominie.

The little procession came to the end of the village. Dominie was turned in the direction of the bridge and his bridle slipped off. He broke into a canter at once. Just as he drew level with the inn some men darted out. One, more foolhardy than the rest, rushed to Dominie and managed to grab hold of him by the sling over his back. But Dominie was an old hand at this. He just swung himself round. The man bore the full brunt of the whisky barrels, lost his balance and disappeared beneath the galloping hooves of the mares. The other men had the sense to withdraw.

The horses clattered across the bridge. Alastair clung to his mount. He knew that all the people of Dumfries would know what the sound of the hooves meant and would take good care to keep well away but the government agents would no doubt soon be mounted and on their trail. But they could not overtake on the narrow bridge, so they should have a good enough start.

They came to the end of the bridge and turned and galloped south towards Kingholm Quay. Alastair cast a quick look sideways. Good. All was going to plan. The Highland chieftain was on the far edge of the herd, on the side nearest the river.

There was a three-quarter moon and Alastair knew exactly where he was going. Suddenly he saw masts black against the paler sky. He shouted, "Now."

The Highland chieftain slipped from his mare and rolled clear of the rest of the herd. It was difficult and dangerous but Alastair was sure he would be all right. In any case there was nothing he could do. He had done his bit. It was up to the chieftain now.

Later that night Alastair and the horses were safely back in the Bridgend. As to whether the venture had been successful, there was nothing they could do except wait. A month later they received the news they had been hoping for – together with more gold from the grateful chieftain who was now safe in France.

The gold was divided between the two brothers and Davie. Callum then said that this was only the first. He knew of others desperate to escape to France. In due course more fugitives arrived down his drovers' escape route. Callum had obviously learned some useful lessons the first time because none of the rest were ever followed by government agents. But despite this they still used Dominie and the mares to get the fugitives safely to their ships – although without the urgency and danger of the first flight.

Three more trips and Callum had enough not only for fares to America for himself and his family, but also enough to set himself up when he got there. And Alastair had enough to buy a farm.

Davie took charge of Alastair's money. He saved part of it and invested the rest, until he decided it was time to spend it.

The Longcrags roup and the rest you know.

\*\*\*\*\*\*\*\*\*\*\*\*\*\*\*\*

Sawney had finished at last. He had given a very full account and explained a lot, but certainly not everything. There was much that he could still tell us. And Charlotte too.

Particularly about the proof of the 'treason' which Radcliffe was so eager to get.

It was up to me to drag the last remaining facts from Sawney and Charlotte.

# CHAPTER 20

## THE LITTLE BOOK

I was so busy trying to work out all the implications of Sawney's story that it was a few moments before I noticed Charlotte. Then I got something of a shock. Selfish little Charlotte was overcome with emotion. There were actually tears in her eyes.

"If only I had known," she said. "Oh, I know that Grandfather was out in '45, but he never told me any details."

I latched onto something. "He told you," I said.

Sawney knew what I meant.

"Charlotte's grandparents are still alive," he explained. "They are living in a little cottage just behind the big house."

He frowned. "In fact I am not sure if Mr Aitken really *is* the Laird of Longcrags. He may just be called that and the old man may really be the Laird but, on the other hand, he may have signed the estate over to his son. I don't know the exact position."

This was something new — Sawney admitting that he did not know something!

Charlotte ignored his reflections. She had some more information for me.

"Steenie's still alive too," she said simply. "He often comes over to visit Grandfather and Grandmother."

Then she added something very significant,

"Steenie is Sawney's grandfather."

Here Sawney frowned slightly. For some reason it was obvious that he would rather I did not know this. After all, when telling us about the Bridgend, he had been very careful not to reveal Steenie's surname. I was watching him closely and I noticed that he looked relieved when he realised that Charlotte had said all she was going to about Steenie. She was more interested in her own grandmother.

With pride in her voice she continued,

"I never knew that Grandmother was such a heroine. Going to Carlisle Castle the way she did."

Then she sat up straight and announced defiantly,

"Next time anyone calls me 'Lady Muck o' the Bridgend' I shall tell them I am proud of that title."

I listened to this with interest. I had told Sawney that Charlotte needed to know her family history so that she could understand the taunts she was being subjected to and work out her own way of dealing with them. But I certainly had not expected Charlotte to come to terms with the situation so quickly.

She was not finished. She had another surprise for me, which she delivered with an almost fierce intensity,

"I used to think that when I grew up I would change my name back to MacGregor. After all, what right did anyone ever have to take my family's very name away from them. But now I know what a wonderful person my grandmother is I think I shall keep her name Aitken after all."

This statement made me realise just how little I really knew about Charlotte. I pondered over her emotion about the original family name MacGregor. I would not have expected her to feel so strongly about it. After all it was going back a long time. The clan had been proscribed away back in

1603 and the name had only been reallowed since 1774. So Charlotte was being remarkably passionate about what was actually a piece of ancient history.

Then the real meaning of all this dawned on me. Charlotte was showing the long memory of a Highlander – an attitude which she had no doubt acquired from her grandfather.

Sawney put an end to my thoughts. He had more for us.

"There is one other thing you should know. Ann Cameron – the woman who testified against your great uncle at Carlisle – she later married Robert Radcliffe, William Radcliffe's father."

So that was the real reason for the bitterness between the Aitkens and Radcliffes. The roots of the feud went away back to the '45.

Now everything was beginning to fall into place. At last I understood why Struan and Charlotte knew so much about the gypsies. They were the grandchildren of Devorgilla Aitken, a member of an important gypsy family. This in itself would have been enough for the two young Aitkens to be accepted by the travelling people but there was much more. The old Laird, Alastair Aitken, had kept up his early friendships and, no doubt, had a string of traveller visitors to his little cottage.

Struan and Charlotte were both closer to their grandparents than to their own parents. I could see it all so clearly – the two children escaping to their grandparents whenever possible. And once in the little cottage they would meet Alastair Aitken's old friends from the Bridgend – gypsies who would regard it as their duty to give the children their own particular brand of education. I had a slight, irrational feeling of resentment as I realised that as far as Michael was concerned, Struan and Charlotte were members of the travelling people in a way that I myself would never be. Michael had accepted them into his family while I was barely tolerated.

I considered these facts. Now there was no mystery as to why Charlotte had so many friends and helpers in the Bridgend. Then something else suddenly occurred to me. I forgot Charlotte for a moment and thought about her brother, Struan, and his passion for animals. I remembered how he cared for his pony and how the stables were a kind of refuge for him. Then I recalled my conversation with Mrs Little when she had told me how excited Struan had been when the Laird of Arbigland promised him a ewe lamb. Now I knew from whom Struan got his great love of animals – from his grandfather who, as a boy, had tended the horses of the Bridgend and whose devotion to the wise old horse Dominie had led to the foundation of the family's fortunes and the acquisition of Longcrags.

The murky glass had cleared at last. I had received explanations for so many of the things which had been puzzling me. I would have liked to reflect some more on these matters but there was something more immediate demanding attention – the question of treason.

I cast my mind back to when I was locked in the upper room of the house in the Bridgend, how I had put my ear to the gap in the floorboards and had listened to the conversation between the two men. I recalled the sudden sense of horror I experienced when I heard that they believed Charlotte had in her possession something which could convict her father of treason. My horror had turned to panic when they started talking about warrants to search

Longcrags. I could remember it as clearly as if it had happened moments ago.

I was no longer thinking of Charlotte or her father or any of the Aitken family. Now self-interest was paramount. If Gilbert Aitken was involved in treason then I could be implicated too and in danger of all the harsh penalties of the law. Now, before it was too late, I just had to find out what all this talk of 'treason' and 'warrants' meant. Charlotte probably knew. I was determined to force her to explain. I just came out with it without any warning and said bluntly,

"Charlotte, how do you come to have in your possession something which could convict your father of treason?"

Charlotte looked at me in astonishment. But there was rage and fury in her expression too.

"How dare you. Whatever do you mean? My father is not a traitor."

I held up my hands in a calming gesture and then I explained very quietly what I had overheard from the upstairs room in the Bridgend. Charlotte thought for a few moments and then said carefully,

"I think I know what it is all about."

She then proceeded to give us a detailed explanation.

A few days before she had been invited to her grandparents' cottage. They both wanted her to meet a very special visitor. It was her grandfather's brother, her great-uncle Donald. The same Donald who had been imprisoned in Carlisle Castle all those years ago: who had been condemned to death and then spared on condition that he accept transportation to the Colonies and would never return to Britain again: who had been rescued by the French from the *Veteran* and who had been taken to France where he had lived ever since.

But with a Highlander's belief in family ties, he had somehow managed to keep in touch with his brother and nephew and now he had made a rash attempt to see them in the flesh. He had particularly wanted to see Charlotte, of whom he had heard so much. He had brought her a little present, a book of French poetry, which he had signed for her.

When I heard this, I smiled to myself and shook my head. This kind of thing happens so often, a dangerous undertaking carefully planned down to the last detail and then jeopardised by a simple lapse. Donald had been so eager to give his great-niece something to remember him by that he had overlooked the fact that he was, at the same time, giving her vital evidence against himself and his nephew.

Charlotte had been charmed with his little gift. He was just handing it over when Lizzie came to ask if Miss Charlotte would be staying later or coming back to the nursery.

Even so, the scene should not have meant anything to Lizzie. But now we all knew that she had been employed by the Radcliffes as a spy – and she had been told to report back every detail. The Radcliffes must have been watching everything at Longcrags very carefully and had found out about the secret visitor. Knowing the family history they could have guessed Donald's identity.

Charlotte was not finished. She was able to tell us much, much more. The very next day Charlotte had found Lizzie in her bedroom. She had the poetry book in her hand and was scrutinising it closely. In one of her tempers Charlotte had seized it from her. Sounding hurt Lizzie had merely said that she was just dusting and that there was no need for Miss Charlotte to carry on so.

That little incident filled in quite a few gaps. Lizzie now had some definite information to take back to the Radcliffes. She could not read French but she had been able to recognise that there was a signature and a date. That would make it worth the Radcliffes' while to try to get hold of the book. If it proved to be Donald's signature, that might be enough evidence for a charge of treason against the Laird. Charlotte looked puzzled.

"Treason? I don't understand; an old man visiting his family. How can that be treason?"

Charlotte had yet to learn just how harsh and savage the law can be. We struggled to explain.

Sawney began. When Donald had accepted transportation to the colonies it was conditional on his staying out of Britain. If he ever returned it would be on pain of death. Charlotte looked incredulous.

"But it was all so long ago. And no one worries about the Jacobites these days. They surely would not put him to death now, would they?"

Silence for a moment and then, in his lawyer's voice, Sawney said,

"The original sentence still stands but, there would, of course, be the possibility of the King's mercy."

Charlotte seized on this,

"You mean that there is a chance that he could be pardoned, but that there is no guarantee and that he could still be put to death."

"In law there are no guarantees," I said quietly.

Charlotte was furious.

"In other words a harmless old man is going to be thrown into jail and left there to rot while you lawyers play your little games and decide whether he is to live or die."

I looked at Sawney to see how he was going to take this. But this time Charlotte's gibes about lawyers passed him by. He was looking thoughtful and rather distant.

"There is more to it," he said.

When he first went to France, Donald worked as a servant for a Highland chief who was not covered by the Act of Grace of 1747. After a few years, he found work on a farm on the Brittany coast, and eventually he became a farm manager. Then came the Storming of the Bastille and the formation of the Committees of Public Safety. In a desperate attempt to save his neck and ensure that he was not denounced, the owner of the farm had himself elected to the local Committee of Public Safety and declared that his farm was at the service of the Republic. By this time Donald was living in semi-retirement in a cottage and all this fortunately passed him by. But the fact that he had worked in the past for a prominent member of a Committee of Public Safety could go against him if he were found in Britain. It could be enough to convict him of being a spy for the French Revolutionary Government. Charlotte looked amazed.

"It couldn't. That's impossible."

"It's perfectly possible," I said grimly. "Especially now with all this anti war frenzy." And then I reminded her of the very first of the anti sedition trials.

"Remember the case of those printers. They just drank a toast to 'George the III and Last' and they were threatened with transportation even if they *were* eventually let off with sentences of imprisonment for nine months. And then there are the recent sedition trials of Thomas Muir and Thomas Palmer — Muir sentenced to fourteen years transportation and Palmer to seven years. Consider that and then just think what a court would make of a secret visit by a friend of a prominent member of a Committee of Public Safety."

Charlotte probably did not know what I was talking about. It was unlikely that her governess had discussed sedition with her but she saw my point.

"What should we do?" she asked.

"First, *find* that book," I said at once. "Where did you put it?

"It's in my kist at Mrs Little's." Charlotte then went on to explain more fully.

The little book meant a great deal to her and she had meant to take it with her. Then she began to wonder if she had better not find a safer place for it. She was nearing Satterness at the time and she saw Mrs Little leaving her cottage with a basket over her arm. Knowing Mrs Little's routines Charlotte guessed that she was on her way to a neighbouring farm to collect some eggs. Also aware that Mrs Little did not lock her door. Charlotte slipped in, hid the book in her box and then sneaked out again and made her way along the beach to the farm where she had joined up with the drovers.

It was quite obvious what we had to do. If only we still had time.

"We must recover the book and tear out that page," I said firmly. Charlotte gave a little gasp but I remained resolute.

"Yes. Tear out the page. It is the only safe thing to do. Without that signature and date a book of French poems will not mean a thing."

I added more gently,

"You will still have the book to remember your great-uncle by."

Charlotte nodded reluctantly and we started to plan how best to retrieve the book. She had finally made the right decision and Sawney did his best to point that out to her.

"Radcliffe's original plan of holding you hostage in return for Longcrags lairdship never really had any chance of success and I am sure that Radcliffe himself knew that all along. He just seized an opportunity to make things difficult for the Laird while making sure that no suspicion could fall on himself. And, distressing as your experience may have been, I don't think you were ever in any real danger, Gretna."

I had my doubts. I remembered the harsh cruel expressions of my captors and my terror in the underground cellar. But then, with his typical lawyer's calm, Sawney would undestimate any danger. However I remained silent and listened as he continued.

"But this is different. If they find the book and if it can be used to bring a charge of treason against the Laird then this could be the chance the Radcliffes have been waiting for for over fifty years. This could mean the downfall of the Aitkens."

Despite his usual understatement Sawney had managed to make us all realise the true seriousness of the situation.

# CHAPTER 21

## THE SEARCH

The one important question was, how long did we have?

When was William Radcliffe going to arrange to search Mrs Little's cottage? I guessed it would be as soon as possible. Charlotte filled me in on the ease with which he could obtain a warrant. He was friendly with a colleague of Mr Aitken's, a fellow Justice of the Peace. Charlotte put it very bluntly.

"Morrison's in Radcliffe's pocket," she said simply.

But would William Radcliffe and his men go straight to Satterness? Sawney suggested that they might go to the Longcrags Estate first but Charlotte and I were both adamant that they would not. Lizzie had already searched there. No, the best thing to do would be to get down to Satterness as soon as possible.

Charlotte took charge. She knew where to get horses for herself and for me. Sawney, of course, had Ally. She also said she would send a boy to Michael and tell him to follow us as quickly as possible. I suggested that Sawney could go and look for Michael. Charlotte considered this carefully and then shook her head.

"Sawney had better come with us. We might need him."

I could not see what difference Sawney would make but, as I later found out, I was underestimating him – as so many people did.

All my life I have been a natural ditherer and now I was rather overwhelmed by the speed with which Charlotte rushed us along. First she sent Sawney for Ally's saddle and bridle. Then she found a village urchin and hurried the pair of us to a field where some horses were grazing. The boy was sent to a nearby shed for bridles while Charlotte picked out a spirited bay gelding for herself and a quieter filly for me. The boy returned with the bridles and I experienced a sudden sense of shock as I realised that I was expected to ride gypsy-fashion – bareback. I could do so, but I was used to the saddle which Michael had given me, the gift which I welcomed and resented at the same time because I knew it was his way of saying that I was not really one of the travellers.

I was not going to let Charlotte see my misgivings about riding bareback. I threw the bridle over the filly's head and scrambled determinedly onto her back noting with relief that she had a long, thick mane, something to hold onto if necessary. I took a firm grip on the reins and sat up to find Charlotte already mounted and glaring at me impatiently. Then, in the authoritarian tones of her mother, she commanded the urchin to tell the owner of the horses that they had been borrowed, "for the business of the Laird of Longcrags." But he had to find Michael first. That had priority. The owner of the horses could wait. The lad ran off and Charlotte shook up her reins and kicked her mount into a trot.

She led me back the way we had come to a shed where Sawney was saddling Ally. He was such a dreadful rider that it was unthinkable that he could ever ride bareback. Charlotte fretted at the time he was taking but she restrained herself and did not urge him to hurry. No doubt she wanted to make sure that Ally was saddled properly. She was being unreasonable because Sawney was soon ready and in a remarkably short time we set off. Charlotte led the way and I followed with a grim looking Sawney.

We set off at a fast trot. Until we knew more about Radcliffe's plans, there was no sense in tiring the horses. But our chosen gait was rather too much for Sawney. Holding frantically onto mane and pommel he looked most insecure as he was jostled in the saddle. We made good progress and came to New Abbey where we passed a smithy. The smith was just beginning to shoe a horse while its impatient rider paced back and forth. Charlotte slowed her own mount.

"I know that horse," she said quietly.

It was William Radcliffe's own horse. We could guess what had happened. It had cast a shoe. Radcliffe had at once changed mounts with one of his men. So Radcliffe and his men were now in front of us, but probably not very far ahead as the smith was just beginning his work. Charlotte was still full of ideas. We would ride after them and, as soon as we saw them, we would slow down.

We soon saw a group of riders. They were going at a slow trot. We reined in our own horses and let Radcliffe get a safe distance from us. I did not see what we could do. We certainly could not pass them. But Charlotte had an answer. When we came to Kirkbean we would take the track leading to the Arbigland Estate. From there we could get down onto the beach. We could gallop along the shore to Satterness and we should easily get there before Radcliffe – always providing that something did not happen to make him increase his speed.

We walked our horses to Kirkbean and then turned off. Charlotte at once kicked her horse into a canter. We quickly threaded our way along the paths of Arbigland and were soon on the sands of Gillfoot Bay with Satterness Lighthouse gleaming in the distance indicating our destination. Knowing every inch of the beach Charlotte led us to the best ground. The sand in front of the dunes was dry, soft and powdery while lower down it was damp and squelchy, but in between there was a good firm stretch. This was where she guided us.

Charlotte at once put her horse into a gallop leaving us to follow as best as we could. I had ridden since early childhood and I had no difficulty keeping up with her but I wondered about Sawney. I snatched a quick glance at him. It was obvious that all he was doing was sticking on. He had abandoned all attempts to control Ally. He lay stretched out flat along her neck and I am sure his eyes were closed. As for Ally, she was no doubt just following the other horses. All things considered she was keeping up remarkably well. I forgot Sawney and concentrated on my own riding.

We just flew along. Charlotte certainly could ride. She did all she could to get the greatest speed possible from her horse – using her legs, shaking the reins and calling to it in a kind of gypsy shriek. She reminded me of the gypsy riders in their races. I wondered wherever Charlotte had learned to ride like that.

It was only about two miles and we covered it in a matter of minutes. When we reached Satterness we slowed down and walked our horses along the paths through the bent and then past the fields to the main road leading down into the village. Mrs Little's cottage was just above the lighthouse. As we reached it we both looked back up the hill. There was no sign of Radcliffe and his men. So far so good. But we knew they could not be far behind.

Charlotte rode her horse into a small paddock, jumped down and ran into the cottage. I checked that both horses were secure before following her. I heard her telling a startled Mrs Little that she had to get something from her kist. The cottage was much bigger than the usual Scottish cottage of the time. Many of the Satterness cottages were – they had to be. If the Satterness housewives were to offer accommodation for convalescents then they had to have somewhere reasonably comfortable to put them. Mrs Little's cottage had a kitchen and a room at the front, with a number of bedrooms at the back. I found her in one of the bedrooms watching in amazement as Charlotte rummaged in a large kist. I wondered what to say to Mrs Little. She certainly deserved some explanation, and it would certainly never occur to Charlotte to enlighten her in any way. This particular problem was solved for me by the arrival of a very dishevelled Sawney, for once looking quite unlike the neat lawyer's clerk. He burst in shouting,

"They're coming doon the hill."

I gathered he meant Radcliffe and his men. Charlotte calmly closed the kist and turned round. She looked at Sawney and said calmly, almost as if she was a lady giving her maid instructions about her clothes,

"Just give me time. I shall not need very long. But keep Ratcliffe busy for a few minutes."

Then as we both stared at her she added urgently,

"You know what to do Sawney. Now go."

She waved us out of the room and we obeyed. As we reached the front of the cottage we heard a thunderous pounding at the door, showing that Radcliffe was determined to do everything properly and leave no room for complaint. He was going to announce his presence to Mrs

Little in the approved manner. She went to the door and Radcliffe's harsh voice resounded through the cottage informing her that he had come to search the house as there was reason to believe that evidence of treason would be found. Before she could answer I heard another voice, loud and angry.

"Whit's ganging oan? Whau's trying tae force their way into ma hoose?"

This was Mrs Little's husband who had come to see what Radcliffe was doing at his home.

Radcliffe answered briefly and curtly. He had come to search the cottage for evidence of treason and he represented the forces of the law. He came into the room with one of his henchmen, a man whom I recognised as his grieve. He was also accompanied by a well-known constable. The Littles trailed doubtfully behind.

Then Sawney showed us all the reason why, despite his youth and lack of experience, Mr Gordon and Gilbert Aitken put so much trust in him and gave him so much responsibility. Outwardly he was still showing the effects of his rough ride, but apart from that, he had managed to calm himself. He was now the lawyer's clerk again.

"What authority do you have to search this good woman's house? I trust you have a correctly signed warrant. I must ask to see it."

Racliffe goggled at the little boy who had the temerity to address him like this.

"I do not have to show my authority to weans," he growled.

Sawney was not put out. He was well used to this kind of treatment. He replied quietly,

"Mr Gordon, Writer of Dumfries, is the agent, legal adviser and man of business of Gilbert Aitken, Laird of Longcrags and this good woman is in the employment of the Laird of Longcrags. As Mr Gordon's clerk I am, at present, Mr Gordon's representative. And so, I assure you, I have every right to ask to see your authority."

Mr Little then joined in. He nodded firmly.

"Aye, the lad speaks true. We a' ken him aroond here. He often acts as a messenger delivering court notices. He may look like a wee laddie but he is actually quite an important young gentleman." Then Mr Little added as an afterthought. "An' he'll grow soon enough."

Radcliffe was now looking less sure of himself. He was determined to do everything according to the due processes of the law and now it seemed that Sawney, no matter how unlikely it may appear, did actually have a right to see his authority. He held out a sheet of paper to Sawney.

"Here's my warrant. Drawn up and signed by John Morrison of Dumfries, Justice of the Peace."

Sawney said firmly,

"I shall have to peruse it at some length to see that it is in order."

Reluctantly Radcliffe handed it over. Sawney took it over to the window and stood there reading it. I was full of admiration but surely all Sawney could do was gain time. Would it be long enough for Charlotte?

Eventually Radcliffe snarled, "Well?"

Sawney had to admit defeat. "It appears to be in order," he said.

At that moment Charlotte slipped quietly into the room.

Radcliffe turned to Mrs Little. "We believe the evidence we are looking is to be found among the possessions of this wayward child." Here he indicated Charlotte. "Of course we have the authority to search the whole house but it would save time if you were to show us where the child keeps her things."

Before Mrs Little could reply, Charlotte stepped forward and once again I heard her mother speaking through her. How she did it I do not know. She spoke quietly but, nevertheless, her voice had a frigid undertone.

"You are wasting your time, but I shall take you to my kist."

We all followed her to one of the back rooms. And this time someone else came with us — Rooskie who had suddenly appeared.

Radcliffe, the grieve and the constable started to unpack the kist. They came upon some books and seized them eagerly. They tossed them on the floor, then picked them up one at a time and started to go through them carefully. I suddenly noticed that Charlotte was not looking at them. I followed her gaze and saw that she was watching Rooskie. Rooskie sniffed at a book on the fringes of the pile and Charlotte made to snatch it before he could grab it. *Charlotte, no*, I thought. I knew only too well what was going to happen next and I was proved correct. Rooskie grabbed the book and darted away. He lay down and the book fell open. He tore at the pages with his sharp little teeth. The three searchers suddenly realised what was happening. With curses they chased him but of course that was just silly because Rooskie was far quicker than any of them. Trying to catch Rooskie was like trying to catch a gust of Solway breeze. Rooskie picked up the book and tore round the room like a mad creature. Radcliffe and his henchmen started throwing books at him and eventually Rooskie dropped the book and retreated under the bed.

Radcliffe picked up the book and looked at it in disgust. "All that trouble for nothing."

He held out the book and we could all see what it was, a copy of Robert Burns' *Tam o' Shanter*.

Radcliffe and the others went back to examining the rest of the books. They did not find any French books but they did come across two other books with torn pages.

"That messan should be drowned," muttered the grieve.

"It might not have been the dog," Radcliffe said darkly. "The wilful girl could have destroyed her books herself, books which many a poor child would have treasured."

A moment later he gave a cry of satisfaction.

"Here we are. French poems."

He opened the little book and then threw it to the floor with a cry of rage. Sawney stepped forward and picked it up. I looked at it. All that remained of the title page was a ragged edge. The 'evidence' had been destroyed. The grieve looked at it.

"How did the dug ken which page tae destroy?"

"The dog didn't," Radcliffe said wearily. "It would not understand what it was doing. Just an unlucky chance."

This was not good enough for the grieve. "How can you be siccar the dug didna ken whit it was daeing? It's a gypsy dug noo."

"Don't let us make ourselves ridiculous, "said Radcliffe impatiently. He turned to Mrs Little, "We shall withdraw now and leave you in peace. We are sorry to have troubled you."

We all saw him to the door and found Michael and the gypsies just arriving. This diversion gave me a chance to take

Charlotte aside and ask her what had really happened. She told me that she had torn the pages herself and then shoved the books back in the kist again knowing that if they were found they would have no story to tell.

"But why?" I asked. "Why leave the book there to be found. Why did you not just take it?"

Charlotte's reply showed that for someone just turned thirteen she had a remarkably mature mind. She had wanted the book to be found. That was the one way of stopping Radcliffe from continuing his search. And if he were to find several torn books then he had fewer grounds for claiming that, in the case of the French book, evidence had been deliberately destroyed.

"I had meant him to think that I did the damage myself," she said simply and then I saw Rooskie and I knew how to make him pick up the book. He always snatches something if he thinks you are going to take it from him."

"I know," I said feelingly.

Rooskie had now appeared again. Charlotte picked him up and gave him a little cuddle. "You clever wee dog." She put him down again and Rooskie scuttled away. Charlotte may have decided to call a truce but Rooskie still did not trust her.

Charlotte picked up the savaged copy of *Tam o' Shanter* and looked sadly at the mutilated little book.

"We'll get you a new copy," I said gently. "And we'll get Robin Burns to sign it for you."

Then I caught a snatch of what Michael was saying.

"The Laird's just at oor back. He'll be along in a few meenits."

I went towards the front of the cottage. I looked back to tell Charlotte to follow me and then I realised that she had disappeared.

*Rooskie*

# CHAPTER 22

## CHARLOTTE'S PLAN

Charlotte had heard that her father was on his way and she had seized her chance to slip away again. But at least this time she had just gone and I had time to catch up with her. Which way had she gone? Not out the front. That would mean being seen by Michael. In any case most of the population of Satterness was now gathered outside the cottage. The back then? Was there a back door? I did not know but it would not matter. Charlotte could easily have got out of a window. I found that there was indeed a back door. I ran out and found that Ally and my filly were still where we had left them in the paddock but Charlotte's horse was missing. I scrambled onto my filly, looked around and was just in time to see Charlotte disappearing down the track leading to the lighthouse. I set off in pursuit.

Was this the right thing to do? My mind was filled with doubts, uncertainties and guilt. Surely Michael should have been informed at once what Charlotte was up to? With his band of travellers he would soon have caught her and dragged her back to her father. But deep down this logical argument failed to convince me. In the last few days I had learned a lot about Charlotte and gained a fuller understanding of her rather complex character. Persuasion would always be more successful with her than brute force. If she saw I was alone there was a good chance that she would stop and listen to me and at least give me an opportunity to reason with her. But I would have to catch her first.

Charlotte turned right at the lighthouse and followed the track leading to the Mersehead Sands. I trailed after her but made sure that she was always in sight. When she rounded the corner at the limekiln I speeded up a bit and, on turning into the bay, saw that she had let her horse out and was now galloping across the sands. Questions flashed through my mind. Where was she going? The sands stretched for about seven miles – right to Sandyhills barring the obstacle of Southwick Water. Was Charlotte going to the farm where she had previously joined up with the drovers? Or was she making for another refuge? Another farm or a smuggler's cottage?

It was vital that I did not lose her. Her mount was faster than mine but I was counting on the fact that once she saw that I was alone she would stop and listen to me. My filly was a game little girl with a good turn of speed. I coaxed her into a gallop and set off after Charlotte.

From time to time, Charlotte looked back over her shoulder to see if she was being followed. I waved and called to her and waited anxiously to see how she would react – whether she would see I was alone and wait for me or whether she would race away from me. To my relief she slowed down into a canter and I was soon alongside her. She pulled her horse up and I did the same.

"What do you want?" she asked sulkily.

"To try and talk some sense into you," I answered. "Where on earth do you think you're going?"

Charlotte did not answer right away. Instead she shook her reins and commanded her horse, "Walk on."

I kept pace with her and waited for her to answer in her own time. Eventually she did so.

"No one wants me at home. If you had not interfered in the first place I would, by now, have been with someone who would have made me welcome. I can still get to her."

"How?" I asked earnestly. "You cannot go with the drovers now. Is there someone else you can travel with?"

Charlotte shrugged her shoulders.

"There could be."

Did Charlotte have a plan which she was hiding from me or had she absolutely no idea what she was going to do next? I strongly suspected the latter. I persisted.

"Who is this friend who will welcome you."

We rode across the sands in complete silence for a while. Once again I waited for Charlotte's reply. Silence for a few moments and and then she mumbled,

"My aunt." Another lull before she expanded.

"My Aunt Emily. She is my mother's youngest sister. Rather like me in a way. The rest of the family feel she is a disgrace to them and so they have banished her. They have given her an allowance and sent her to live in a house miles from anywhere." She then qualified the last part.

"Just outside Skipton in fact."

That made sense. I knew Skipton well, a town on the North Yorkshire Moors. And, as the cattle droving trails went through Skipton, Charlotte's original plan had been a good one. At least the bit about getting there. But after that?

"Are you sure that your aunt will welcome you? When did you last see her?"

"About a year ago," Charlotte muttered. I felt that she was by now far less sure of herself, but was determined not to show it. In the last few hours Charlotte had been so strong, so mature, responsible and sensible. But now she had reverted to childhood and was behaving like a very silly little girl. I spoke firmly,

"Think girl. The very first thing your aunt will do when you arrive on her doorstep will be to send a message to your parents telling them where you are."

"She will still let me stay with her."

"Only if your parents agree. She will never keep you with her against their wishes. She couldn't. She would not be allowed to."

Utter silence from Charlotte. I left her to dwell on these facts, which she knew to be true but had so far refused to face. After a while, I said tentatively,

"Why not come back with me. We can suggest that you should go and spend some time with your aunt. If I put it carefully to your parents I am sure they will listen."

I shuddered to myself as I said the last words. How would I ever find the courage to suggest anything to Isabel Aitken? Charlotte turned my misgivings to certainty. She gave a harsh laugh,

"Mother would never listen to you. And you know it fine."

There was nothing I could say to that. It was quite true. Then I thought of something else.

"Things are different now," I said desperately. I continued doing my best to sound convincing.

"Your great-uncle. Your father will have to find a way of smuggling him to safety. If your parents are worrying about a possible charge of treason they will not want to have to deal with your problems too."

Much to my relief and rather to my surprise Charlotte reined in her horse. She looked at me thoughtfully and said slowly,

"You could have a point there."

Then she just sat mute and pensive. I did not interrupt her thoughts but just left her to come to her own decision. I only hoped it would be the right one. Finally she said,

"They may well want me out of the way now that I know all the details. It would be much safer if I were to be spirited away to the wilds of Yorkshire – and quickly before anyone can think of questioning me. Of course, I would never ever say anything that could cause trouble for any of my family but my parents could well think that I could let something slip by mistake."

I said nothing but I knew that that was exactly what her parents would think. And with good reason. It was inconceivable that a child like Charlotte could ever stand up to the relentless questioning of government agents. No, the best hope of the Aitkens would be to get Charlotte safely out of the way. Charlotte may well have realised that herself although she would never admit it.

Anyway, she agreed to come back with me and we turned our horses. I saw at once that it was going to take a long time, as Charlotte kept her horse at a steady walk. Suddenly I saw Michael and two of his sons galloping towards us. The search for Charlotte was under way.

This was what I had been trying to avoid. The sight of Michael might be enough to make Charlotte turn around and gallop away again. And now I had seen Charlotte ride I could not guarantee that Michael could catch her. When they got nearer I waved frantically to Michael. Charlotte ignored him completely and rode slowly past him. I signalled to

Michael to keep behind her and he did. I quickly filled him in on what Charlotte had told me. I was amazed at his reaction.

"That's a guid idea. Aye, the lassie would be better ganging tae her auntie for a wee whilie. I'll pit it to the Laird and see that she gets tae Skipton."

Was the world turning upside down? Since when, I asked myself did the Laird of Longcrags – or the Laird of anyhere else for that matter – take instructions from travellers?

Michael continued. "For that matter I could tak her there mysel'."

At that I remembered that Skipton and the North Yorkshire Moors are a favourite haunt of gypsies – to say nothing of the famous gypsy Horse Fair at Appleby. No doubt Michael had friends and kin near Skipton. Even so it did not entirely explain his enthusiasm for Charlotte's plan.

We reached Satterness and Mrs Little's cottage. By this time the Laird of Longcrags had arrived. He looked at Charlotte and just said quietly.

"So there you are Charlotte. I only hope you realise all the trouble you've caused."

Shortly afterwards we all set off for Longcrags, myself (with Rooskie in his little basket), Charlotte and her father, and Michael and the tinklers. Sawney tagged behind on Ally. Charlotte's fate would soon be decided.

It was late when we finally arrived back at Longcrags and night had fallen. Michael at once went to his wagon. The Laird left me at my own wagon which someone had brought back for me, together with Lucy. He paused before taking Charlotte up to the big house.

"If you want anything to eat – or if there is anything you need, such as eggs, bread or milk, then just go up to the kitchen. I'll tell Cook to expect you."

After that kindly remark, he left me and hustled Charlotte away.

# CHAPTER 23

## SAWNEY

I did not go to the kitchen. I was too tired. It had been a long day. In fact I found it hard to believe that so much could have happened in just one day. But it was true. It was only that morning, admittedly early in the morning, but still only that morning – that I had entered the Bridgend with Mr Gordon's message. Now all I wanted to do was sleep. But that had to wait for a while.

I was about to throw myself down on my bunk when someone rapped on the side of the wagon. Rousing myself I pulled aside the flaps at the front, looked out and saw Sawney. Being utterly exhausted conversation was really beyond me but we had been through so much together that I could not send him away. I had to make an effort to listen to him so I told him to come up and sit beside me on the driving seat. He clambered up and joined me with an agility which I would not have expected of the studious, sedentary Sawney.

Right from the start I noticed that he seemed awkward and uncomfortable. He carefully placed the horn lantern he was carrying on the seat between us taking longer to do so than was strictly necessary. This was obviously a delaying tactic to put off telling me the real reason for his visit. Then he was given another excuse for procrastination as a curious little nose thrust itself into his hand and a rough little tongue started to lick his fingers. Sawney took Rooskie on his knee and stroked him gently. When he at last began to talk to me his speech was jerky and hesitant and his manner was distant. By this time I knew Sawney well enough to realise that the best way of finding out the real purpose of his visit would be to let him ramble on and come round to it in his own time. Rather like Charlotte in a way.

"No doubt we shall work together again in the service of the Laird," he began, "but for the present our paths must diverge. I am being sent back to Mr Gordon's office but I could not leave you without saying farewell and giving you my best wishes for the future."

*Still the lawyer,* I thought to myself while saying aloud,

"And how do you feel about that after your adventures on the Solway."

Sawney suddenly abandoned his precise, legal speech and at last became more human. He even lapsed into Scots from time to time.

"I'm fair pleased. The office is my natural environment. It's dry, warm and comfortable. I can't wait to get back to my high stool, the sound of scratching pens, the cackling of the logs on the fire, the purring of Jury – he's the office cat – the smell of musty old ledgers, yes and even Wattie Beattie trying to jog my arm and spoil my copying. No you can keep your wet beaches and Solway gales."

*And kidnappers and ruffians,* I thought grimly to myself.

Sawney suddenly realised that I might need an explanation about something.

"Wattie Beattie. He's the apprentice who is always trying to make trouble for me. Remember, you saw him when you were released from the Mid Steeple"

"I remember," I said shortly while trying to think of something to say. All I could come up was the rather silly remark,

"So you are glad to be going back to the office then?"

A note of desperation crept into Sawney's voice."

"Aye. I am that. I want to get away from all this – and as quickly as possible.  I don't like what is happening right now."

A moment's silence and then with a rush,

"Gretna, I came to warn you. Watch out for yourself"

I stiffened. *Be careful girl,* I said to myself. *Let him take his time and all will come out in due course.*

Sawney explained in his own roundabout way.

"I am staying here tonight in one of the guest rooms and then I am being sent to Dumfries early tomorrow."

*Nothing surprising about that,* I thought. *It is too late for him to travel tonight.*

Sawney continued his voice becoming increasingly serious.

"But that is because of Mrs Aitken. The Laird was going to send me tonight in a carriage with Ally tied on behind. Then Isabel Aitken said that he was being ridiculous. Mr Gordon could surely do without the services of a junior clerk for a few more hours. It would be more sensible if I were to spend the night at Longcrags and ride to Dumfries in daylight. Oh Gretna, don't you see?" he ended frantically.

I had the glimmerings of an idea but I wanted him to put it into words himself.

"Go on," I said solemnly.

"There is something happening here tonight that they do not want me to find out about. The Laird was panicking. He was desperate to get me out of the way but Isabel Aitken realised that sending a humble clerk back to Dumfries in a carriage in the middle of the night would only make people curious and ask questions.

I thought this over carefully.

"But even if you saw something illegal you would never cause trouble for the Laird or any of his family," I said slowly.

"Normally no," said Sawney. "But in a case like this no one is to be trusted and the fewer people involved the better."

I had a good idea what Sawney meant but I sat silent waiting for him to give a fuller explanation. Sawney continued.

"Gretna, right now we are in the grounds of a house which is harbouring someone who could be accused of being a French spy. That means that anyone helping him is, in law, guilty of treason too. I am sure that the Laird is planning Donald's escape. I wish I was going to Dumfries tonight. I will not feel safe until I am miles away from here. But what about you? I fear that you are going to be part of the escape plot."

I drew in my breath and gripped the edge of the driving seat. This was what I had been afraid of. But it sounded much worse having my secret fears voiced by someone else. First of all, though, I wanted to know more about my own position in law.

"I am in the position of one of the Laird's servants. If the worst came to the worst and we were caught would it not be accepted that I was acting under the Laird's instructions?"

Sawney answered quickly.

"To a certain extent yes. But you would not evade responsibility completely. However, you would probably get a lesser penalty. For example if the Laird were to be sentenced to death and his estates forfeited then you might get off with being transported for life."

I could hardly get the words out but I managed to whisper,

"Could I still be sentenced to death myself?"

I waited for some time but Sawney did not answer so I asked,

"What should I do?"

Sawney sighed,

"I don't know but I felt I had to try to warn you."

Silence for a moment and then Sawney suddenly gave an anguished cry.

"It reminds me of what happened to my own father."

He buried his head in his hands and I watched his heaving shoulders. Then he got control of his emotions and sat up and said in something like his usual voice,

"Forgive me. I did not mean to mention that but now I suppose I had better tell you the whole story."

He took time to compose himself and then I learnt of the struggle which had been Sawney's life.

His father had been hanged when Sawney was only four. Sawney did not remember much about it. His memory retained only random pictures. There was the time when he was taken to a bare room in a large building to see his father who took him on his knee. At the time his mother seemed quite calm but on leaving the building she started sobbing violently. A woman put her arms around her while another woman took the young Sawney away. Then, in the weeks which followed, Sawney often wondered where his father was but no one would tell him. His mother was alternately cross and affectionate with him. She would scold him and shout at him and then she would seize him and hug and kiss him.

It was not until Sawney was a few years older that his grandfather – the Steenie of the Bridgend – told him that his father had been hanged. But he did not give Sawney any details or tell him why. He said that Sawney would have to wait until he was older for the full facts. Sawney's natural curiosity was increased by his grandfather's continual mutterings about 'betrayal' and 'murder even if it was judicial murder.'

Sawney may not have known why his father was hanged but he did know the efforts Steenie had made to save his son. Because of the mysterious work he did in the Bridgend Steenie eventually became quite well off. Then he beggared himself spending his money on lawyer's fees trying to save his son. All to no avail. His son was still hanged. Steenie was now an embittered old man who had to suffer the sight of his family living in poverty and who was continually railing about 'lawyers, the worst criminals in the country.'

Here I just had to interrupt.

"Then how does he feel about you becoming a lawyer yourself?"

"Fine," said Sawney surprisingly. "It appeals to his own particular sense of humour – that I should learn all the legal tricks and use them for my family instead of against it, that I should acquire the weapons of the law and employ them for my own benefit."

I pondered over this. I could understand the Steenie of the Bridgend, Steenie the survivor, thinking like this. And I could quite see his grandson Sawney turning into an astute and wily lawyer and using the forces of the law for his own ends. Years ago Steenie was always prepared to break the law if he could profit by it but his grandson would always keep to the letter of the law but make it his servant.

Once again, as in the case of old Alastair Aitken and his grandson Struan, family traits and characteristics seemed to have skipped a generation. Struan had inherited his grandfather's love of animals while Sawney had inherited Steenie's smeddum – smeddum, that old Scots word meaning courage, resourcefulness and determination all rolled into one.

Sawney fell silent for a moment and frowned thoughtfully.

"Even so," he eventually continued, "I am rather puzzled by the way in which both my mother and grandfather encourage me to become a lawyer. At times they actually seem keener on the idea than I am myself. My mother has even suggested that I should go to Glasgow University now whether or not the Laird will pay for me. She says I should just do what plenty of other lads do – take a bag of meal and live on it for a term. She says she will manage without my wages somehow."

His voice became more determined.

"But I'll not do that. Not for a time anyway. I'll not put my own ambition before the welfare of my mother and sisters."

Then he became more thoughtful and returned to his original question.

"Even so I wish I knew why my mother and grandfather are both so keen that I should pursue my legal studies."

It may have been puzzling Sawney for years but the answer came to me in a flash. I remembered something which he had said earlier."

"You said that your grandfather is always muttering about 'betrayal' and 'murder, judicial murder.' Perhaps they fear that if you knew exactly what happened you would want to take revenge on someone or other, and fall foul of the law yourself. If you become a lawyer you will still be able to seek vengeance but you will know how to do it within the law – and so you will be all right."

Sawney looked at me appreciatively and nodded approvingly.

"You could well be right. Now why didn't I think of that?"

He was still wondering about his father. It was obvious that his mother had told all his relatives and family friends not to tell him why his father had been hanged and Sawney himself did not want to ask anyone outside the family.

"But I shall find out somehow," he said. "It must be in a law book somewhere. When I learn more about the law then I shall know where to look for the records of the trial."

Here something else occurred to me. The fact that he did not know where to find the relevant records was also significant. Obviously Mr Gordon was deliberately withholding that part of Sawney's legal education for as long as as possible. But Sawney was now fifteen. The mystery of his father's death could not be kept from him much longer.

Sawney then quietened down and told me about his family's circumstances. Steenie was living in the Bridgend but he still visited Alastair and Devorgilla Aitken. His mother and sisters were living in a cottage on the Longcrags Estate – a cottage which the Laird let them have for a nominal rent. Most of the pittance Sawney earned in Mr Gordon's office went to help his mother and sisters. He hoped he would not be a mere clerk much longer. The Laird would pay for him to study law at Glasgow University because of the debt the Aitken family owed to Steenie. But the Laird would do so when it suited him and not before.

"Yes," I said. "If tonight's plotting works out all right."

In the last few minutes Sawney had become more relaxed but now he became serious again.

"Oh Gretna, I shall be all right but I fear you are going to be part of the plan. I wish I could think of some way of helping you. If you can think of anything at all then let me know."

I thought quickly. Sawney was obviously sincere and he had offered to help. I was sure I could trust him. Perhaps there was something he could do.

"If anything goes wrong tonight then you could always take a message to my own family."

I told him. He nodded and said that was the least he could do. He added,

"And I shall not reveal your secret unless it is absolutely necessary."

I could not see his face in the darkness but I sensed a smile in his voice. He scrambled down from the wagon and picked up his lantern.

"I must be getting back to the big house now. I said I was just checking on Ally. Take care, Gretna."

He set off but then turned and came back.

"There's always Michael. After all you are his family too. You married into it. I would always trust Michael. He has his own code of honour. The Laird will always put his kin first regardless, but Michael takes his position as head of his own family very seriously and realises he is responsible for you. And I can assure you that Michael will never die at the end of a hangman's rope."

These last words were spoken with firm conviction.

I was sceptical. Was this really Michael the lockpicker he was talking about? I voiced my doubts but Sawney had a ready answer.

"Michael will make sure he is never caught but, even if he were to be apprehended, he would find an agent to say it was a first offence and claim benefit of clergy. He would also find some powerful friends to speak up for him."

Sawney had spoken almost lightly then he became more serious again. He paused before adding with a rush,

"You can always trust Michael, but watch the Laird. Under normal circumstances he will always do what he can for you, but if it is a case of saving his own then he would not hesitate to throw you to the wolves. Or me either."

He then proceeded to emphasise and back up what he had just said.

"With Michael you have the best of both worlds – the protection of the wily head of a travellers' clan who also has the patronage of the gentry, but who knows well how to wriggle out of any trouble the said gentry might find themselves in."

He was going to give a fuller explanation but the butler suddenly appeared.

"Mr MacBean, your room is ready for you."

This was very significant. The Laird had discovered that Sawney was missing and had sent the butler to look for him – the butler not a humble servant. There was obviously something afoot which Sawney was not to learn about.

I went back into the wagon, threw myself down on the bunk and pulled some blankets over myself. Despite my exhaustion I could not sleep. My mind was racing and I kept thinking of the penalties for treason. I threshed about wildly alternatively kicking off the covers and pulling them over myself again. Eventually I dozed off but I was soon wakened by Michael. He had been sent to tell me that I had been summoned to a conference in the house.    Bleary eyed I followed Michael. I was feeling slightly sick and there was a throbbing ache over one eye. I do not know how long I had slept but it was now the middle of the night. There was a full moon and it was easy finding our way. We reached the house and Michael led me into the library. Present were the Laird and Mrs Aitken and Charlotte. Michael sat down so he was obviously to be included in the proceedings.

Rather surprisingly it was not the Laird who took charge. It was his wife. When we were all settled she said,

"We have decided that it would be a good idea for Charlotte to go and stay for a time with my sister. For one thing, it will give everyone around here a chance to forget the recent unfortunate events. And then Charlotte might very well settle down with Emily. There will be many opportunities for her. She could even attend a school in Harrogate as a weekly boarder and return to Emily at the weekends."

I could see that Charlotte was doubtful about that last remark and so could her mother because she added,

"It's only an idea."

Then Mrs Aitken produced a letter and passed it to me.

"I have written to my sister explaining everything and requesting that she will have the goodness to allow Charlotte to stay with her. I am entrusting this letter to your care. You are to give it into my sister's hands yourself. I stress, you are to give it to her yourself. You are to hand it to nobody else, absolutely nobody. I hope I make myself clear."

"Perfectly, Madam," I said quietly.

So Charlotte was being given her way, but her mother was not giving her her trust. There was to be no chance of this letter going astray – or of Charlotte intercepting it. No doubt Mrs Aitken would have her own way of checking that I really did deliver the letter. She would probably send a duplicate by another messenger anyway.

There was more, much more. Charlotte was to travel with me in my wagon. We would not be entirely on our own. Michael and the travellers would be keeping a discreet watch over us just in case Radcliffe made another attempt on Charlotte. Then Mrs Aitken handed over to her husband and matters suddenly became more serious. There was still the question of the old man. He could not remain at Longcrags any longer. True, Radcliffe had failed to find the evidence he had been looking for, but he could still tell the authorities of his suspicions and a search could be made of Longcrags. No. Donald had to be smuggled away to safety as soon as possible.

The Laird had a plan and I was part of it. True, I was to play only a very small part, but I wished with all my heart that I was not involved – not in treason!

Sooner than I had expected, I had found out that Sawney's vague fears were indeed justified.

# CHAPTER 24

## INVOLVED IN TREASON

After that events moved swiftly. The Laird lost no time in putting his plans in motion. Charlotte and I were to leave early in the morning, very early, practically at dawn. Preparations were made, Charlotte's boxes were stowed in the wagon and there was much activity among Michael's tinklers. Despite my utter exhaustion I did not get any rest at all. Finally, when the trees and hedges were standing up stark and black against a sky which was steadily growing lighter, I drove Lucy through the front gates of Longcrags.

Thank goodness Lucy was such a steady, sure-footed pony because I was too worn out to guide her properly. There was, however, one good thing about this. I was also too tired to worry any more about my involvement in treason.

Gradually the black trees and hedges turned to a pale green and I was able to distinguish the separate fields—and nothing happened. The dawn continued its slow advance and then it was as if someone had suddenly lit a gigantic lantern. Golden sunlight chased away the last of the grey dawn and daylight gave back to the landscape its normal appearance. And still nothing happened – until we had passed through Annan.

Then I heard the sound I had been waiting for—hoof beats behind me. Suddenly, the wagon was surrounded by dragoons. Their officer was young, and, considering his mission, polite. He explained that his orders were to search my wagon for a suspect person. I said nothing but I tightened my grip on the reins. I told myself fiercely that I had nothing to fear and that the soldiers would not find anything—or anybody—incriminating, but it was no good. My heart still pounded frantically.

I sat petrified as two of the dragoons climbed into the back of the wagon. Almost at once I heard a cry of, "Who do we have here?" The next moment a boy of twelve or thirteen was standing before me held firmly by two of the dragoons. It was Michael's eldest son, Joseph.

I looked at the officer. "It is my nephew, Joseph."

The dragoons had been told to search for an old man and instead they had found a young boy. But the officer was still going to investigate further.

"Why was he travelling in the back of the wagon? Why was he not sitting at the front?"

I had my answer ready. "He has been ill with a fever. He is recovering but he is still weak."

That was enough for the young officer. "On your way and good journey to you." With this he cantered off, his men following him.

In the presence of the dragoons fear and tension had held my exhaustion at bay but the moment they were away fatigue swept over me again. I felt weak and drained but I had to stay in the driving seat. Lucy followed the road with little help from me. Somehow we got through Carlisle and came to the farm where we were to spend the night. I showed the Laird's letter to the farmer who led me to a place where I could camp.

I was so weary that I just lay down in the back of the wagon. Joseph made himself useful. He pitched a rough tent or gellie as he called it, while Charlotte organised some food and roused me and coaxed me to eat something, after which I lay down again.

I slept soundly and woke to find the sun already high in the sky. But that did not matter because we had no reason to hurry now. Physically I felt much better, but I was also uneasy. I had allowed myself to be made a decoy. All the activity at Longcrags Estate the night before had been for the benefit of any watchers. If the tinklers had wanted, they could have gone about their business quietly and unobtrusively and slipped away with no one seeing them. I had a horrible suspicion that anyone who really knew and understood the travelling people would have guessed at once what they had really been doing – setting a false trail with Joseph instead of Donald.

That was the Laird's plan, to smuggle Joseph aboard my wagon in 'secret.' But it was a secret that was to be easily discovered. While the authorities were following us, Donald would have been spirited away somewhere else. I did not know where. The Laird thought that the less I knew the better.

"You can't tell what you don't know."

The full realisation of the enormity of what I had done now struck me. I had allowed myself to be made part of a plot to aid the escape of a possible traitor. In the next few days that uncomfortable thought was to recur again and again but for the present I shoved it aside. After all, provided Donald got clean away, as I was sure he would, I had nothing really to worry about. The period of high drama was now over. I no longer feared for my life.

But I had other worries which were more mundane but still important, namely the future course and direction of my life – and of Charlotte's. We had both similar decisions to make. Were we going to go back to our respective families or were we going to branch out on our own?

There was something else niggling at the back of my mind. I had a feeling that my true identity was not going to be a secret for much longer.

# CHAPTER 25

## DOUBTS AND FEARS

Charlotte, seemed to have put herself in charge of the food for, despite the lateness of the hour, she now prepared a simple breakfast. She was still dressed as a boy having persuaded her parents that that would make her look more like a tinkler. Looking at her, I had to agree. In fact she actually looked more like a tinkler lad than many tinklers. But then Charlotte was a superb actress and she was revelling in living this particular part.

We were not in any hurry to proceed with our journey. I, in particular, wanted longer to recover from the efforts and stresses of the last few days. We lingered over Charlotte's meal before finally setting off. That day we covered only a few miles but the next day we got as far as Appleby and camped on a farm just south of it. The day after we found ourselves travelling across the North Yorkshire Moors and I started to relax. We were now in gypsy country and Joseph knew all the friendly farmers who would let us camp on their land and we were able to buy bread, eggs and milk from their wives. We supplemented this diet with the occasional rabbit caught by Tink, for Charlotte and Tink had been mysteriously reunited at Longcrags before we left. Charlotte had insisted on taking him along. In fact she now referred to him as 'My dog.' I had some misgivings. I wondered how Aunt Emily would welcome Tink. Surely it would be bad enough having to accept Charlotte without being landed with a disreputable hound as well. From time to time I caught sight of Michael or another of the tinklers and I found their presence comforting and reassuring. Usually I could not see them but I knew they were not far away and that made me feel safe. My shattered nerves started to mend at last.

Then Michael made a sudden visit. He had actually come with a couple of ponies for Charlotte and Joseph but he had some very important news for me.

"The fish slipped through the net," he said quietly.

I cannot describe the feeling of relief which swept over me. I had convinced myself that Donald would escape and shoved aside all thoughts of his possible capture. Even so worry about it had still been gnawing at my mind. But now at last I was free of that anxiety.

Michael handed over the ponies and rode away as quickly as he had come. Charlotte and Joseph were both delighted. Now they could ride beside the wagon, an arrangement which suited both of them. It also suited me. I had some hard thinking to do. There were some things I had to get straight in my head. I had to decide the future course of my life.

Did I really want to remain as one of Longcrag's Sleuth-Hounds? Or should I grovel and go back to my own family? A short time ago I would have stated vehemently that I would never, never do that. But the events of the last few days had made me think differently.

When my husband had been put in jail I had suddenly been given my freedom. For the first time in my life I was answerable to no one but myself and I relished the experience. When I was living at home I had to do what my father wanted. Then, with my marriage, I exchanged one form of obedience for another. I loved my Danny but I did not love the fact that, as his wife, I was expected to obey him. I cast my mind back to the days of my childhood and I thought about my mother. Most people thought of her as a wealthy lady, a very fortunate woman indeed. But I was a very shrewd little girl and I knew only too well that she was certainly not free. She had to do exactly what my father wanted. She accepted the situation and seemed not displeased with it, but I was beginning to question what I saw around me. And then I began to make other discoveries. If I were to marry, as was no doubt expected of me, then I would effectively have no money of my own as it would all be controlled by my husband. Of course neither my mother nor my governess told me anything of this but I had other sources of information – visiting cousins, girls I met at the various classes I attended. I could not discuss any of this with anyone but I thought about it, and worried.

Oh why, why can it not be realised that women are intelligent creatures who are entitled to their freedom? Why do they not have more rights instead of being legally under the complete domination of their husbands? A wife is little better off than a dog except in one respect. Her husband is not allowed to drown her.

Then, when my husband was put in jail, I suddenly found myself free. I could have gone to his family, or to my own family, but I did not. I stayed on my own, and learned to cope. Freedom is a very precious and fragile commodity, but too many people do not know what to do with it. They need a structure or framework to be imposed on their lives. They may grumble about that framework, but, once it is removed, they are lost and uneasy. But I had shown that I could make my own framework.

I had shown that I could handle freedom.

Then I began to realise the disadvantages. I was alone and vulnerable with no one to look after me. But even that problem solved itself when the Laird of Longcrags made me the first of his Sleuth-Hounds. Now I had the best of both worlds. I still had my freedom but I had a wealthy protector too, someone who was also a respected member of the community, a Justice of the Peace and a heritor of the parish. I was safe at last.

I considered the irony of that last thought. Safe? I had been seized and imprisoned in one of the Bridgend cellars. Even worse, I had been involved in helping the escape of a suspected traitor. The Laird was not the respectable member of the community I had thought he was and the Aitken family had some dark secrets. For my own safety, would I not be better to sever all my connections with Longcrags? I remembered Sawney's warning that the Laird would always put the Aitken family first.

I kept churning these thoughts over and over in my mind. I would go back to my own family. No I would stay with the Laird. Finally I decided to let the matter rest. I would enjoy the remainder of the journey. In the long run events would probably make my decision for me.

Having once made that decision it was not difficult to stick to it. We were passing through some beautiful countryside. I was in charge of my own wagon and I had the company of my two faithful four-footed friends—Lucy in front of me and Rooskie just behind me. (Rooskie was sitting where he could look out of the front of the wagon but he was tethered securely so that he would not fall out). I decided to make the most of the present and let the future take care of itself.

We took our time. The weather was perfect for early autumn, warm and sunny but with that sharp undertone which heralds the frosty days of winter. We went through little valleys and then climbed to the top of the Moors where sheep tugged at the rough grass. Every so often we would come across a little moorland stream which gurgled and tumbled over its rocky bed down the hillside. Here and there we passed isolated farms or cottages, and sometimes a little village.

I was relaxed and content. This represented the best side of being a traveller. I had pushed my immediate problems aside—for the time being at any rate—but Charlotte could not do so easily. She had her own private worries and, every now and again, she showed signs of wanting to confide in me. Without realising what I was doing at the time, I made myself responsible for her. I felt obliged to listen to her and help her.

# CHAPTER 26

## ADVICE FOR CHARLOTTE

Charlotte preferred to ride but sometimes she would tie her pony to the back of the wagon and sit beside me on the driving seat. She would chat to me about her aunt. I listened to her ramblings and felt that she really wanted to ask me something but was finding it difficult to come out with it directly. I did not press her. No doubt she would work her way round to it in time.

As she prattled on I learned a great deal about Charlotte and I found that we had much in common. I also found that I had been quite correct in the conclusions I had drawn after my conversation with Mrs Little at Satterness. I had understood Charlotte perfectly.

Charlotte had enjoyed a happy childhood running wild with Struan. Then, with the arrival of the new governess, changes had been forced upon her. It was decided it was time for her to begin to grow up. Charlotte did not like the picture of growing up which was presented to her. She envisaged a future where her body was imprisoned by stays and her sharp, active mind was imprisoned by the constraints society placed on young ladies. Then one day she would be expected to marry and subject herself completely to the will of a man. Charlotte often came back to this and then she eventually let out a deep-seated fear. Once married she would be expected to have children—many of them. And Charlotte knew exactly what that meant. She had had a favourite cousin, a girl a few years older than herself. She had married and had had two children. She had been very ill after the birth of the first. She had died shortly after the birth of the second.

There was not much I could say to that, only that many women do bear healthy children without any trouble. As for the rest, I thought desperately how best I could help Charlotte. At her age I had experienced similar problems and I had worked out my own peculiar solution. But I certainly was not going to counsel Charlotte to run away with the travelling people. I had to find some more responsible advice for her.

Part of the trouble was that in her own way Charlotte had actually tried to conform and do what was expected of her. Taking the silver salver was her way of trying to gain acceptance by the girls in her dancing class – and she had been punished for it. So now Charlotte was determined to go her own way. I struggled to help her.

"Decide what you really want to do and then try to find an acceptable reason," I said at last.

Charlotte looked at me enquiringly. I tried again.

"You do not like the idea of wearing fashionable clothes. Then you could always become religious"

I took a deep breath and intoned solemnly,

"Vanity is a sin. Far too many people think that when the good Lord created woman he did not do it very well. Too many commit the sin of trying to improve on His good work and try to mould the female form to their own image."

Charlotte's eyes widened in amazement and she laughed, an honest carefree laugh the like of which I had never heard from her before.

"I like that she said." She repeated,

"Far too many people think that when the good Lord created woman he did not do a very good job."

"That's dreadful but I like it."

I had more for her.

"What do you like doing—really like doing?" I asked.

Charlotte answered at once.

"Riding. But I don't like side-saddle so much."

"Well," I continued thoughtfully, "you could always ride about the countryside doing good works. Visiting the sick, bringing them gifts and delivering Bibles. Or you could find a worthy cause to work for like the abolition of the slave trade. If you were riding long distances in the course of carrying out all these charitable works I don't think there would be too much objection to your riding astride."

A mischievous grin spread over Charlotte's face.

"You are awful," she said.

"Not really," I retorted. "Think of all the medieval pilgrimages. They were only partly religious. Often they were just an excuse to travel. Travelling for pleasure was not acceptable then so people had to find some other reason."

Charlotte looked very thoughtful and we sat in silence for some time. But I had more for her.

"You could also compromise. Like your aunt."

An uncomprehending look from Charlotte. I continued, striving to make my meaning clear.

"She has her own establishment in the middle of nowhere. She is free to ride over the moors all day. And I don't really think the sheep will mind whether she rides side-saddle or astride. But from time to time she also rejoins the civilised world for a while. You told me that she visits Harrogate from time to time and spends a week or two there."

Charlotte gave an enlightened nod.

"Yes. She stays at a very respectable inn which caters for people wanting to take the waters."

"A way of getting the best of both worlds," I added.

I had given Charlotte plenty to think about. But there was one last thing  and it was probably the most important of all.

"You are a superb actress," I said. "Then be an actress."

A spark of sudden longing flashed into Charlotte's eyes and then, almost at once, it vanished.

"I couldn't. My father would never allow me to go on the stage."

"I did not mean that, not the stage. Act your way through life. Act the part which society expects of you but compromise and find a way of being yourself at other times."

Charlotte considered this carefully. Then she said slowly,

"Like Aunt Emily living out in the wilds but still going into Harrogate and acting the lady."

"Exactly," I replied.

"Meaning that I could do what Mother suggested. Attend a boarding school in Harrogate during the week and come back to Aunt Emily at the weekends and ride among the sheep."

"It's a possibility," I said. "And we could look for a school which will let you have long holidays."

I was relieved to hear Charlotte saying this. I had been wondering grimly, what if Aunt Emily did not want to have Charlotte to stay with her. No doubt her family had a hold over her since they paid her an allowance. Nevertheless there could still be a difficult situation if she really did not want Charlotte but felt that she had to take her. The prospect of Charlotte being away at school all week would certainly make circumstances much easier. As for the long holidays, it should be simple enough to find a schoolmistress who would be agreeable to that arrangement if she was eager to get Charlotte's fees. It might even be better if a private arrangement could be reached, that Charlotte could stay in the house of an ex-schoolmistress who would instruct her and also initiate her into Harrogate society.

Then something else struck me. When I had told Charlotte she should be an actress she had at once replied that her father would not allow it. So even when running away, Charlotte had never intended cutting herself off entirely from her family. She had never meant to run far. Perhaps her running away had been, in itself, an act.

In later years this conversation was to come back to me again and again.

"Act your way through life."

I little realised then just how seriously Charlotte was to take my advice, or how she was, in her turn, to become the most remarkable of the Solway Sleuth-Hounds.

This was the last of our serious conversations. But from then on Charlotte seemed much calmer and she was certainly friendlier towards me. We had reached an understanding at last and she had decided that I was someone in whom she could confide.

During the next few days Charlotte would talk to me endlessly about her aunt. I listened silently but with increasing misgivings.

I had been suspicious before. At the back of my mind was a sneaking feeling that I knew her aunt—and that she was a lady whom I certainly did not want to meet. But before there had always been doubt. I could have been wrong. Now, as Charlotte continued to prattle on, I could fool myself no longer. I knew her Aunt Emily and I was about to meet her,

the one thing I had hoped to avoid. And it was all Isabel
Aitken's fault.

# CHAPTER 27

## MY SECRET

Oh why had Mrs Aitken been so insistent that I should deliver her letter to her sister myself? That I was to entrust it to no one else? If it had not been for that I could have seen Charlotte to her aunt's house and then just slipped away quietly.

Then I fell to thinking about Mrs Aitken, of how she had come into my prison cell and made me the first recruit of the Solway Sleuth-Hounds. I had always taken it for granted that it was just by a lucky chance that she had chosen me. I was in trouble and she could help me—if I helped her. But now I was convinced that there was more to it than that. I had since learned of the long and close connections between the travelling people and the Aitkens. The more I thought about it the more I became convinced that Mrs Aitken had picked me out specially—and she had a good reason for making sure that I would meet Aunt Emily in person. I did not like the idea but there was little I could do about it.

We were now nearing our journey's end. We descended from the top of the Moors, passed through the market town of Settle and reached the bottom of a wide valley. Ahead was a range of low, rounded hills and, to our right, was the canal. I looked at a brightly coloured narrow boat being towed by a huge shire horse while Charlotte told me that Aunt Emily owned a canal boat. At the time her words just washed over me but I was later to find that that apparently innocent piece of information hid a piece of very real significance.

Aunt Emily's house was on the outskirts of Skipton. It stood on its own among a few fields. Emily was actually the owner of a small farm. A single field separated the house from the canal where there was a small landing stage.

Now for it. I turned Lucy into the farm road and drove up to the house but stopped before I got there. Charlotte was now looking exceedingly nervous. Incredible as it may be, it seemed it had just occurred to her that Aunt Emily might not welcome her presence as a permanent addition to her household. A guest for a week or two certainly, but an indefinite stay—that was a different matter. Charlotte looked at me,

"I'll stay here and wait. You go and take Mother's letter."

I did not like that arrangement but how could I persuade Charlotte to go with me? Then, once again, Michael came to the rescue. He cantered up to the wagon with some news. Aunt Emily was away from home. She was spending a few days in Harrogate. But that should not cause any problems. Michael knew the housekeeper. He would take us to her and she would let us camp in one of the fields and wait for Miss Fletcher's return. No sooner said than done. We paid our respects to the housekeeper who assured Michael that we could camp in 'the usual place.' So, before long, we were settled in a new camp in a field behind some trees. It was a good site as there was a pump in the field. This was for watering stock but it came in very useful for us too.

Once he had satisfied himself that he had done his duty by safely delivering us to our destination Michael rode off taking Joseph with him.

For the next few days we spent a pleasant time lazing about. At least it would have been pleasant if I had not had some worries gnawing at the back of my mind. Charlotte passed the time by repeating what she had already told me about her aunt and constantly adding new facts. I now knew I was correct about Aunt Emily's identity.

She was the black sheep of the Fletchers. She came from a wealthy and well established Cumberland family but they considered her a disgrace to their good name. She had been a wild child but it had always been accepted that she would grow up and mature into a respectable young lady. This had not happened. Emily had stubbornly refused to accept the conventions society expected of her. Eventually her relations worked out their own solution. They decided to banish her. They gave her a meagre allowance, bought her a small farm and installed a manager. The farm was far from their estates in Cumberland—far enough away so that she would not shame her family more than necessary.

One afternoon we were lying at the top of a slope overlooking the house and Charlotte was just telling me this yet again when we heard hoofbeats. Four horses were approaching the house. One was a packhorse; two others carried servants – a groom and a woman servant – while the fourth was ridden by a woman in a smart, green riding habit who was, no doubt, Aunt Emily.

I strained my eyes. Was this really the shadowy figure I had heard my parents discussing before I was noticed and the subject abruptly changed? I had met her briefly at Christmas at a family gathering three years ago — before my governess had hurried me away. I could not be sure it was the same person. She was too far away. But if all my fears were to be proved correct she would certainly recognise me. There was no doubt about that.

Charlotte drew in her breath and then muttered something about going back to the wagon to tidy herself. I made to follow her but something held me back. Charlotte said that that her family had given her aunt a 'small allowance.' Just what did they mean by 'small?' Despite the distance I could see that Aunt Emily's riding habit was of good quality material and well tailored. I turned my attention to her horse, which was beautifully mannered and carefully groomed. It was obviously an animal of careful breeding, and, I estimated, expensive.

I made my way back to the wagon thoughtfully. Here was another puzzle, another one which I did not like. Aunt Emily was supposed to have a 'small' allowance but she was obviously living in comfort. How? I passed a few sheep and glanced at them. No they were just ordinary sheep – no sign of a golden fleece. Then I told myself firmly not to create a mystery where none existed. Aunt Emily's family obviously gave her more than they had let out. No doubt they hoped she would return to the fold some day and they were not going to jeopardise that by antagonising her.

I reached my wagon and stared at Charlotte in amazement. What a transformation in such a short time. Charlotte had been busy at the pump and had washed her face. She had changed from her boy's trousers into a pale green gown. She had even done wonders with her shoulder-length hair. She had brushed it and tied it back neatly with a green band. Charlotte now looked the very model of propriety.

Then I remembered our earlier conversation when I had told her, "Act your way through life." She had now begun.

313

Charlotte was in no hurry so I had plenty of time to tidy myself too. At the very last moment I took my tartan screen and flung it over my head. If I was muffled in it there was just the slight chance that Aunt Emily would not recognise me, although I did not really believe that.

As we could not put off any longer we walked up to the front door. The housekeeper let us in, took us to the library, and told us to be seated and wait, while she fetched Miss Fletcher.

We did not have long to wait. Still wearing her riding habit Aunt Emily swept into the room and, at first, it seemed as if all our careful preparations had been wasted.

We both rose to our feet when she entered but she waved us back into our seats. She sat down herself at a desk. Silence and then, to Charlotte,

"Goodness, child, whatever have you done to yourself? Am I to consider myself honoured that you have got yourself up fit to grace the best drawing room in the country?"

The very same acerbic tones which I remembered only too well from our brief meeting. I produced Mrs Aitken's letter and handed it to her. She took it and her shrewd eyes seemed to go right through me."

"Ah yes," she said absentmindedly, "A letter by the tinkler messenger." Then sharply, "Take that ridiculous blanket thing off your head, Elizabeth. Did you think that I would not recognise you? Surely, you did not believe that for one minute that you could fool me."

I blushed scarlet and threw off my screen. Confused, flustered but at the same time angry. My Aunt Emily—for yes, Emily was my own aunt as well as Charlotte's—was always to have that effect on me. But despite all my conflicting feelings I had noticed one thing. Charlotte had

314

shown no sign of surprise. For how long had she known my identity?

Another silence and then Emily murmured to me, "It has been a long time, Miss Fletcher."

I bristled at this, "I am Mrs Marshall now," I said defiantly.

A condescending wave of the hand. "A Gretna Green marriage. It should not be too difficult getting that annulled."

"I don't want it annulled," I said stubbornly.

Emily just sat there and then, with that infuriating smile which, in the years to come, I was to know only too well, she said,

"What on earth have we Fletchers and Christians done to rear such a younger generation? You, yourself, running away with the tinklers and your cousin Fletcher, leading a mutiny on the high seas and the whole of the Royal Navy desperate to track him down. You are two fine examples of a noble family."

I was speechless. How could she compare me to my cousin Fletcher Christian, leader of the most famous mutiny in the history of the British Navy? Fletcher Christian who had put his captain, William Bligh aboard a small boat and then, with his own supporters, had sailed the *Bounty* across the South Seas and had vanished.

How could she compare us? My marriage to Daniel had been unconventional but it was not illegal, nothing like mutiny against the Royal Navy. And I had never liked Fletcher anyway.

Then something else struck me. It was not Fletcher the mutineer, who had disgraced the family name. It was Emily herself with her unconventional behaviour, with her flouting of the code of polite society. Wearing breeches and riding astride among the sheep is a far worse crime than mutiny aboard a ship of the King's Navy.

Emily's manner suddenly changed. She stopped taunting us and became more practical. She read her letter again.

"So, Charlotte, you think that you would like to come and stay with me? You may change your mind about that."

"I don't think so," said Charlotte firmly.

"We can but try the arrangement at any rate. Now, as for you, Gretna, as you prefer to be called." Here she paused. "Gretna. I like that. It suits you. Elizabeth is such a colourless name. Since you are not ready to rejoin society yet, you may camp in my field as long as you like. You could always return to Dumfriesshire with Michael. I believe he is going to travel around the neighbourhood for a while. And if you are ever passing this way again you will always be welcome."

I stammered out my thanks. I was always to find it more difficult dealing  with Emily's generosity than with her barbs.

Emily then rang for her housekeeper and gave instructions for a room to be prepared for Charlotte. She also ordered food for the three of us.

After a light meal I went back to my wagon. I had a lot of thinking to do. I had to make my final decision – whether to remain a Sleuth-Hound or whether to go back to my own family.

# CHAPTER 28

## MY DECISION

Before meeting Emily again I had worried that I could be in danger from the dark secrets of the Aitken family. But were the Aitkens any worse than my own family? With Fletcher Christian, mutineer? Make no mistake about it, if his present haven were ever to be discovered then the Fletchers and Christians would join together and do everything they could to protect him. Certainly everything legal, but would they be prepared to break the law? I did not even want to try to answer that question.

No. There was really nothing to choose between the Aitkens, Fletchers and Christians.

I cast my mind back to my last meeting with Sawney. He had told me straight that I would be better putting my trust in Michael than in the Laird of Longcrags. Now I began to wonder if that did not also apply to my own family. The Aitkens had allowed themselves to be involved in treason. But what if my own relations ever found themselves helping the leader of a naval mutiny?

I rejected that possibility at once. Fletcher Christian was almost certainly dead by this time. And if he had managed to survive he would be virtually marooned on some lonely island with no possibility of returning to England. No I had nothing to worry about there.

This was the common sense view. But at the back of my mind were some little doubts. Why should it be assumed that if not dead, Fletcher was stranded somewhere? The South Sea islanders thought nothing of setting out across the Pacific in their primitive canoes. They would sail thousands of miles without the benefits of modern science and navigation. On his noted voyage Bligh at least had a sextant but how did the islanders find their way? I did not know and I doubt if anyone else did at that time. But there was one thing I was quite sure about. If the natives of the South Seas could find their way across the ocean then Fletcher probably could too.

It was highly unlikely, but just possible, that Fletcher could find his way home. I shuddered to myself as a series of pictures from the last week flashed before my eyes – myself in my prison in the Mid Steeple, imprisoned in the cellar in the Bridgend, and finally Sawney coming to my wagon with his dreadful warning. After all these experiences I was not going to risk anything which would expose me to the harshest penalties of the law. Especially as my arrogant, pompous cousin was just not worth it.

I puzzled over these questions. Everything was topsy-turvey. Michael and his tinkler clan were the law-abiding members of society and not the members of two of the best known families of the Solway – the Aitkens and Christians.

Sawney had told me to place my trust in Michael. I was beginning to think that he was right. Michael knew how to use the protection of the gentry but, in the event of anything going wrong, he had the advantages of the tinklers' escape routes. If he could not defend himself then he could always disappear.

A few days ago I would not have thought like that but I had changed a great deal in a week.

Rooskie was lying snuggled up against me. I stroked him gently, "What do you think, Rooskie?" He roused himself and pawed me, asking me to cuddle him.

Rooskie clinched my decision. I would stay with the Sleuth-Hounds. I would keep my much-valued freedom and the company of my two best friends, Rooskie and Lucy.

Next day I found that Charlotte had also made a decision. She rode up to me, still on the tinkler pony, with Tink at her heels. (So Emily had accepted Tink too). Charlotte was once again dressed in her boy's clothes. Her cheeks were flushed and she was obviously just back from an exhilarating ride.

"It's all right," she told me. "I am going to stay with Aunt Emily. She does not mind me riding across the Moors dressed like this—as long as I make myself look respectable from time to time. She is going to find a governess for me but we are going to think about a school in Harrogate later." Then, with a wave of her hand, Charlotte galloped off again.

Later in the day I had another visitor, Michael. I saw at once that something had changed. Gone was his previous stern disapproval. He actually greeted me as "Gourie," not lass, but the tinkler-gypsy gourie – a  sign that he was accepting me at last. He told me what Emily had told me the day before, that he was going to spend some time travelling round the neighbourhood and, if I liked, I could travel back to Dumfriesshire with him and his family in a month's time. I agreed at once. I did not really want to make that journey back on my own.

Then he asked me where I was going to spend the winter. I thought it over and then I realised I had a choice, either in the Laird's stable at Longcrags or with my mother-in-law in her cottage in the Bridgend. I would probably divide my time

319

between them. Michael nodded. He thought this a good idea. Then he took his farewell with the parting words.

"My you've some smeddum gourie."

Yes he had certainly accepted me as his sister-in-law at last and my worries vanished like the ebbing tide on a Solway beach. I was so relieved. I had believed Sawney when he said that I could trust Michael. But I knew he disapproved of me. He would do his duty by me and fulfil his obligations but that would be all.

Now all that had changed. Michael had actually smiled at me and called me 'gourie.' I had been welcomed into his clan. Now I knew he would always do all he could for me.

Michael had finally clinched my decision.

Then something else occurred to me. Someone as shrewd and astute as Michael would not expect me to deny my background and upbringing completely, especially when the support of the gentry is so important to the travelling people. No he would want me to keep in touch with my own family to a certain extent. I would have the best of both worlds.

But after the terrifying events of the last week I was now sure of one thing. It was Michael I wanted as my protector far more than the Laird of Longcrags or even my own relatives.

That night, with Lucy tugging at the grass and Rooskie watching my every move I brewed tea over my camp fire and thought of the day when Mrs Aitken came into my prison cell. Now I realised that she had known right from the start who I really was. It was not surprising that I had not recognised her. I had been very young when she married and moved away from Cumberland and, after that, I had seen her only briefly at the occasional family gathering.

But no doubt she knew all about me. Letter writing is one of my mother's passions and no doubt she corresponded constantly with Isabel. She had probably asked her sister to look out for me. Isabel Aitken had picked me out deliberately – partly to please my mother but more for her own ends.

Suddenly another thought ocurred to me. Did the Laird know that I was actually his niece by marriage? After a few minutes reflection I decided that his wife had not told him. That was going to be her secret. It obviously suited her to let him regard me as a simple tinkler. Although why I did not know. But if the Laird knew the truth he would be horrified at the idea of his own niece coming to Longcrags and sleeping in a stall in the stables.

My Aunt Isabel (I was already beginning to think of her in this way) always knew how to get her own way. She had been the first to think of the Solway Sleuth-Hounds but she had very cleverly managed to make the Laird think that it was his own idea.

The real leader of the pack was not the Laird of Longcrags. It was Isabel Aitken.

# SOLWAY SLEUTH-HOUNDS

## THE FACTS BEHIND THE STORY

# Map of the UK showing position of the Solway Firth

# Map of the Solway Firth

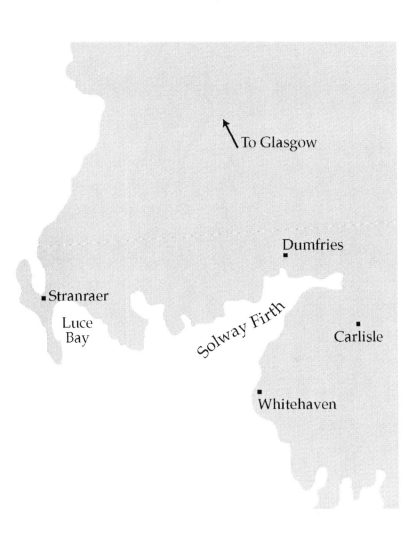

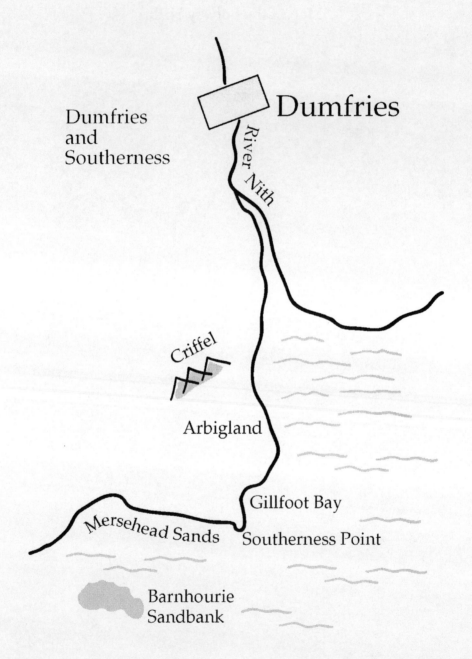

Dumfries and Southerness

Dumfries

River Nith

Criffel

Arbigland

Gillfoot Bay

Mersehead Sands

Southerness Point

Barnhourie Sandbank

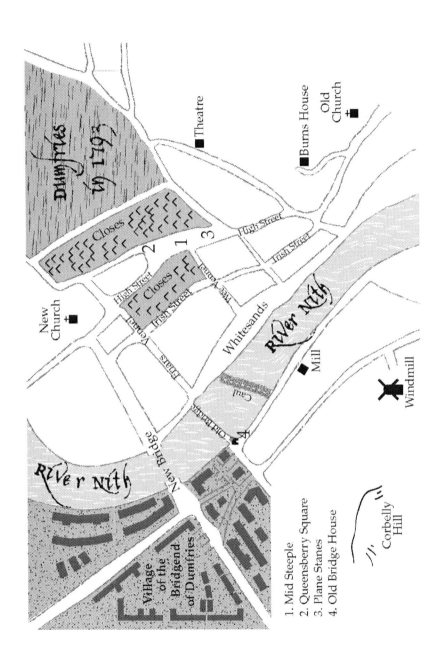

Dumfries in 1793

New Church

Theatre

Burns House

Old Church

Closes

High Street

Irish Street

High Street

Irish Street

The Vennel

Vennel

Friars Vennel

Whitesands

River Nith

Caul

Mill

Old Bridge

New Bridge

River Nith

Windmill

Village of the Bridgend of Dumfries

Corbelly Hill

1. Mid Steeple
2. Queensberry Square
3. Plane Stanes
4. Old Bridge House

# DUMFRIES IN 1793

## Explanation of sketch map on page 327

## See also Dumfries Notes and Photographs and Historical Notes

**The town centre**.

The **High Street** ran for about a mile from the **New Church** to the **Old Church**. With its town houses and shops this was the main street in Dumfries. Half way along the High Street was the **Mid Steeple** — 1 — which is where Gretna was imprisoned in Chapter 1. It is still a prominent landmark in Dumfries. Behind and to the side of the Mid Steeple was **Queensberry Square** — 2 — where there was a statue to the Duke of Queensberry. At one side of the Square was a public well. The statue is still there but the well is now marked by a plaque. In front of the Mid Steeple was an open space which was sometimes used for market stalls. This space was known as the **plane stanes** — 3.

Near the Old Church was the house where Robert Burns spent the last few years of his life. It is now a museum. Just up from the **Burns House** was the **Theatre Royal** which was completed in 1792 and had many connections with Burns. It is now used by an amateur theatrical company. Running down from the High Street to the River Nith were the two lanes — **Friars Vennel** and the **Wee Vennel**. They both crossed **Irish Street** which ran parallel to the High Street and contained many fine town houses with large gardens which ran down to the river.

**The closes.** Between the large houses of the High Street and Irish Street were the closes which consisted of many cramped hovels built back to back. These were breeding grounds for disease and were partly responsible for the cholera epidemics of the nineteenth century. There were closes like this in other parts of Dumfries too.

**The River Nith.**

Alongside the river was an open space known as the **Whitesands** with timber yards and tanneries. Cattle markets were also held here. From time to time gypsies also camped on the Whitesands. The River Nith could be crossed by the **Old Bridge** or **Devorgilla Bridge.** This dated from the Middle Ages. By the end of the eighteenth century it was proving rather narrow for modern carriages and so the **New Bridge** was built. But the New Bridge was not completed until 1794 so at the time of *Sleuth-Hounds* it was still only half built.

**The west bank of the Nith.**

At the western end of the Old Bridge and built right into the bridge itself was the **Old Bridge House** — 4 — This was built in the seventeenth century and is now the oldest house in Dumfries. It is mentioned several times in *Sleuth-Hounds*. It is now a museum. Opposite the Old Bridge House was the entrance to the village of the **Bridgend.** The magistrates of

Dumfries had no authority here so it became a safe refuge for felons.

In the opposite direction from the Bridgend was a large **grain mill** which is now the Robert Burns Centre. Opposite the mill was the **caul.** This was a kind of artificial waterfall. It was originally constructed to prevent the Nith from encroaching on Dumfries but it later supplied the power for the grain mill. Above the mill, on top of **Corbelly Hill**, was a **windmill,** which now houses a museum and camera obscura.

*******

The centre of modern Dumfries still follows this basic layout. The High Street, Irish Street and Friars Vennel and the Wee Vennel (now Bank Street) are all still in existence although many of the buildings have been rebuilt. But thankfully the closes are no more. The statue is still in the middle of Queensberry Square but the old well is now marked by a plaque. The Mid Steeple still dominates the High Street and the plane stanes are still there. Corbelly Hill still dominates the western side of the river but the name was changed in Victorian times to the present Corberry Hill. And the caul is still a feature of the River Nith and appears on many postcards of the town.

# DUMFRIES NOTES AND PHOTOGRAPHS

## See also *Historical Notes*

### DUMFRIES MID STEEPLE

Built at the beginning of the eighteenth century, the MidSteeple is still a prominent landmark in Dumfries.

In the photograph the door at the first floor level can be clearly see, along with the balcony and the outside staircase.

**The Milage chart on the front of the Mid Steeple**

This metal plaque was placed on the wall in 1828 so it would not have been there at the time of *Solway Sleuth-Hounds.*

The presence of the name of the town of Huntington shows the importance of cattle droving to Dumfries as that was the destination of many of the droves

## The Mid Steeple from the back and the Side

Here is a different view of the Mid Steeple from the back and the side.

The part which is jutting out from the main building and is now occupied by a shoe repair shop would have housed prison cells in the eighteenth century. It is thought that there were also extra cells on the second floor.

# BURNS HOUSE

This red sandstone house is where Burns spent the last three years of his life. It is now a museum.

Burns became an excise officer in 1789. At first he had a wide ranging Excise area and he stayed at Ellisland Farm six miles from Dumfries. Then in 1790 he was appointed to a new area in Dumfries. He gave up the farm and moved to Dumfries in November 1791.

At first he lived in a house at the foot of the Wee Vennel (now Bank Street) where he and his family occupied three rooms and a kitchen on the second floor. This is now marked by a plaque on the outside wall.

This was rather cramped for the Burns family and in May 1793 they moved to this substantial house in the Mill Vennel – later called Mill Street and now called Burns Street. The rent was £8 a year.

His son later described the house. The rooms on the ground floor, together with the two bedrooms upstairs were carpeted and well furnished.

Burns also had a small study off the main bedroom where he could work on his Excise records. The family even had a maid servant.

Burns lived here until his death in July 1796.

# THE ROBERT BURNS CENTRE

The Centre is in an old grain mill which was built at the beginning of the eighteenth century. It was rebuilt in 1781 after being damaged by fire the previous year. It stands on the banks of the Nith just down from the Old Bridge House.

The Centre houses a restaurant, a gift shop, and a cinema. It has displays about the life and work of Robert Burns and two videos about Burns can also be seen.

One of the most interesting exhibits is the three dimensional map in the display area upstairs. It shows Dumfries at the time of Burns.

# THE THEATRE ROYAL, DUMFRIES

The Theatre Royal was completed while Burns lived in Dumfries and he had many connections with it. The Theatre opened in September 1792. It is now used by an amateur dramatic society.

Burns was on the free list of patrons and attended regularly. He wrote prologues and addresses for the Theatre. He wrote the poem *The Rights of Women* especially for the company's leading lady Louisa Fontenelle.

Politically these were turbulent times. Abroad there was the French Revolution and the Reign of Terror. At home in Britain the Society of Friends of the People was urging reforms and the panic stricken government felt that Britain was on the verge of revolt. Anyone expressing sympathy with the French was branded a traitor.

Seen against this background several of Burns' actions were indiscreet and unwise.

Burns was once involved in a controversial incident in the Theatre Royal. At the end of a performance of *As You Like It* someone called for *God save the King* to be played. The audience all stood up and sung and the gentlemen took their hats off. But not everyone joined in the singing, as there were counter calls for the French revolutionary song *Ca Ira*. This demand was drowned by the singing of the national anthem. Here it should be mentioned that the national anthem was specially requested. It was not sung at the end of performances as a matter of course.

Unfortunately Burns happened to be sitting in the pit right in the middle of those who were calling for *Ca Ira*. In an attempt to remain neutral Burns remained sitting with his hat on — an action which later brought him much criticism.

It was shortly after this that Burns wrote *The Rights of Women.* Although this had nothing at all to do with politics it also laid Burns open to criticism as the title was a parody of *The Rights of Man* by Thomas Paine, one of the leading radicals of the time.

A few weeks later Burns was informed by Mitchell, his Collector, that he had received an order from the Excise Board to enquire into his political conduct and to examine the charge that he was 'a person disaffected to the Government.' Burns could easily have lost his job with the Excise but his explanations were accepted and he was able to continue as an exciseman.

## DEVORGILLA BRIDGE

Here two canoeists paddle towards the arches of the Devorgilla Bridge, or the Old Bridge.

This is the oldest bridge in Dumfries. Its construction is commonly attributed to the Lady Devorgilla. It is built of red sandstone and is the oldest surviving multiple-arched stone bridge in Scotland. It had originally nine arches but now it has only six.

This bridge was perfectly adequate for medieval wheeled traffic but by the end of the eighteenth century it was proving rather narrow and a new and bigger bridge was clearly needed – especially as the old toll-gate had been removed in 1769. So the New Bridge was built and completed in 1794. This is one year after the time of *Solway Sleuth-Hounds* so Gretna still had to drive her wagon across the Old Bridge.

The New Bridge is now called Buccleuch Bridge as it is at the foot of Buccleuch Street.

# THE OLD BRIDGE — PASSING PLACES?

This is a close-up of one of the bulges in the middle of the Old Bridge. I am guessing but I think this may have been a kind of passing place. If two carts wanted to pass then one could have driven in to one of these passing places and waited there for the other to pass. Rather like the passing places on narrow roads in some country districts today. After all it was because the Old Bridge was becoming too narrow for modern wagons that the New Bridge (now the Buccleuch Bridge) was built in the 1790s.

# THE OLD BRIDGE HOUSE

This red sandstone building is the oldest house in Dumfries. Dating from the seventeenth century, it is built right at the end of the Devorgilla Bridge. It has had various uses and is now a museum. In the eighteenth century it was an inn.

It is mentioned several times in *Solway Sleuth-Hounds* as it stood at the entrance to the village of the Bridgend. Gilla and Alastair held their wedding reception at the Old Bridge House – although most of the festivities took place on the grassy shore of the Nith behind it.

# THE CAUL

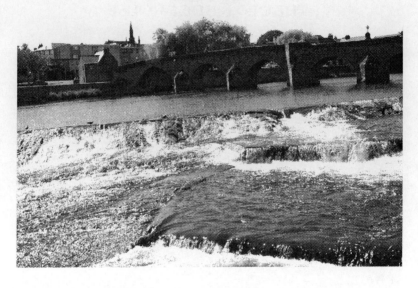

This is a kind of artificial waterfall which originally supplied power for the grain mill. (Actually it was built before the grain mill when a small cutting was made in the bank of the Nith on the Galloway side. This was to stop the river encroaching on the Dumfries side).

There were objections to the construction of the caul on the grounds that it would prevent salmon running up the river as formerly. But these objections just delayed the construction of the caul. They did not stop it.

Once built the caul made that part of the river look more interesting and picturesque.

At low tide there can be seen islands in the Nith just down from the caul. Women used to bleach their linen on these islands.

In his *History of Dumfries* McDowall speaks affectionately of the caul and says how it is remembered by exiles of the town. He mentions one such woman in a small town outside London. She said that she never sat down herself but,

*that I hear the sough o' the Caul as plain in my ears as when I was bleachin' claes on the island.*

# THE VIEW FROM DEVORGILLA BRIDGE

This view from the Devorgilla Bridge clearly shows the Caul and the islands in the middle of the Nith.

In *Solway Sleuth-Hounds* this is what Gretna and Alastair would have seen when they held hands, looked down the river and exchanged their marriage vows — minus the modern buildings and vehicles on the Whitesands of course.

# SOUTHERNESS NOTES AND PHOTOGRAPHS

## SOUTHERNESS LIGHTHOUSE AND COTTAGES

The village of Southerness lies on the Scottish shore of the Solway Firth about fifteen miles south west of Dumfries. It was planned by Richard Oswald of Cavens in the eighteenth century.

Coal was sometimes found on the beach and Oswald had plans for mining. He had cottages for miners built near Southerness Point. And these cottages are still standing — as the above photograph shows.

But these cottages were never used by miners. Trial shafts were sunk but the surveyor's report was unfavourable. So the cottages ended up being used by people who came for sea bathing. The hey day of sea bathing was later than this – in the nineteenth century – but it was popular in Southerness earlier than this as the *Statistical Account of Scotland* (the 1790s one) says

*A trial for coal was made in its neighbourhood but without success. It is now chiefly inhabited by persons who keep furnished rooms, to accomodate such as, during the season, come to it for sea bathing.*

# SOUTHERNESS LIGHTHOUSE

## SOUTHERNESS LIGHTHOUSE AT LOW TIDE

Southerness Lighthouse is one of the oldest in Scotland. Nowadays the Solway Firth is almost empty. A few yachts and pleasure boats and even fewer fishing boats. That is all. But in the eighteenth century the Solway was a busy shipping thoroughfare.

# SOUTHERNHOUSE LIGHTHOUSE AT HIGH TIDE

Southerness was a dangerous part of the coast for shipping. At Southerness Point treacherous rocks stretched out into the Firth while to the east was the other hazard to shipping — the Barnhourie Sandbank.

In 1748 the Merchants of Dumfries, together with the Town council, decided to erect a tower at Southerness. It was completed the following year although it was made taller later. At first it was probably just a tower which acted as a landmark for ships because it says in the *Statistical Account of Scotland,*

*This tower, at present, is of great advantage to the navigation of the coast, and would still be of greater advantage, were lights placed in it.*

But in the 1790s light was probably introduced as Dumfries records refer to the salary of a lightkeeper and oil for his lamp.

It was built of rubble masonry covered with lime. The upper part is built of red sandstone but this part, along with the room for the light, was added in the 1890s.

At the time of *Solway Sleuth-Hounds* Southerness Lighthouse would have been half its present height.

## SOUTHERNESS LIGHTHOUSE SHOWING ROCKS

Tis photograph shows the reason for the existence of Southerness Lighthouse — the treacherous rocks on which it is built.

Behind the Lighthouse Criffel can be seen clearly.

# SOUTHERNESS BEACHES

## GILLFOOT BAY LOOKING TOWARDS ARBIGLAND

Gillfoot Bay lies to the east of the Lighthouse.

Charlotte, Gretna and Sawney galloped along this beach when they were trying to get to Southerness in time to save the incriminating little book. Of course, in the eighteenth century, the caravans would not have been there.

The sands at the Southerness end of Gillfoot Bay at low tide.

# THE MERSEHEAD SANDS

The Mersehead Sands lie to the other side of Southerness Lighthouse — to the west. They stretch for a distance of about seven miles and this photograph shows the wide sweep of the bay.

This was where Gretna rode when she was trying to find out where Charlotte had gone.

This photograph was taken looking across the wide expanse of sand at low tide. The cliffs in the distance are at Sandyhills — a distance of seven miles.

Having fun on the Mersehead Sands

# CRIFFEL

Criffel is the highest hill at the western end of the Scottish side of the Solway. This photograph was taken from the Southerness end of Gillfoot Bay.

The name *Criffel* is Scandinavian. It means *Crow's Hill* or *Raven's Hill.*

# HISTORICAL NOTES AND SOURCES

## SLEUTH-HOUND

 The word *sleuth-hound* meaning bloodhound has been used from the Middle Ages. It was also used by Sir Walter Scott. But *sleuth* meaning a detective dates only from the last part of the 19th century.

## THE SOLWAY FIRTH

The Solway Firth is a long, wide arm of the sea which divides Scotland from England in the west.

On the Scottish side the western part of the Solway is dominated by the hill Criffel which looks down on a wide and diverse range of scenery. There are level plains which border a wide expanse of sand which stretches for miles. The coastal scenery varies between beaches, little rocky coves and bays, islands, majestic cliffs with stacks, arches and caves. Away from the coastline there are cliff top footpaths, woods and forests and low but steep hills giving, on a clear day, a view of the Lake District fells, distant but distinct, on the far side of the Solway. And everywhere in the spring there is the gleam of gold from the countless gorse bushes while, in late August, there is the deep purple of the heather.

What is rather remarkable is that all this variety of scenery is found within a few miles. The same variety also applies to towns and villages and buildings. Busy little country towns contrast with holiday and yachting villages. And the houses consist of large villas, modern bungalows, traditional farmhouses, farm cottages and fisherman's cottages. There is also a very wide range of holiday accommodation consisting of hotels, bed and breakfast establishments, Scandinavian wooden chalets and innumerable caravan sites and tents.

## SOLWAY FIRTH — THE MEANING OF THE NAME

About one thousand years ago many Scandinavians settled on both sides of the Solway — Danes on the southern shores and Norse on the northern shores. And it is these Scandinavians who have given the name *Solway Firth*.

The name *Solway* means *muddy ford* from *sul* for *muddy* and *vath* for *ford*. It is thought that at one time there was a ford across the Solway at the eastern end. Eventually the name came to refer to the whole of the Solway and not just one part of it.

The word *Firth* is also Scandinavian. It is directly related to *Fiord* meaning an *inlet*.

## THE GALLOWAY TINKLER-GIPSIES

There are two main sources for the tinkler-gypsies of Galloway.

The first, and the most recent, is *The Tinkler-Gypsies* by Andrew McCormick. Published 1907. Republished EP Publishing Ltd 1973.

This book involves both primary and secondary sources. The author visited gypsy encampments and spoke to the gypsies. He also researched the tinkler-gypsies of earlier years. This is a very detailed account. McCormick was particularly interested in the Tinkler-Gypsies secret language or cant and he gives a glossary of all the words which he managed to collect.

The second source is found in the writings of Joseph Train. Joseph Train was an excise officer and a friend of Sir Walter Scott. He corresponded with Scott and gave him much material about smugglers and gypsies – material which Scott subsequently used in his books, notably in *Guy Mannering*. Much of Train's information about the Galloway gypsies is contained in *Memoir of Joseph Train* 1857.

Strictly speaking the gypsies came originally from India or eastern Europe and they had their own culture and customs. The Scottish and Irish travelling people were tinklers. But the terms are often used loosely and both the tinklers and gypsies would meet at various fairs where the native tinklers would absorb some of the gypsy language and customs.

Also the travelling people were a disparate group and the tinklers could also include those who had fallen on hard times.

## TINKLER HORSES

The gypsies and tinklers often used **cobs** – which are strong and have a very placid temperament. They are often black and white or brown and white and, if this is the case, they are known as **coloured cobs**.

A cob could be defined as a smallish workhorse bred for pulling tinkler carts. Sometimes loosely referred to as a pony.

They can be seen at the modern gypsy horse fairs such as the Appelby Horse Fair.

As well as cobs native **Galloway** ponies were often used. They were small — about thirteen or fourteen hands — sturdy, sure-footed and very tractable. They were good all-rounders and could be ridden or could carry packs or pull wagons. Often dark in colour they were often used by smugglers. Sadly the Galloway pony is now extinct but the nearest equivalent is the fell pony.

The gypsies often rode bareback but both McCormick and William McDowall (see below) mention some of the gypsy tribes, such as the Baillies, having very ornate saddles.

The word **powny** was used in Scotland in the early eighteenth century and Dr Johnstone refers to it to the word **pony** in his Dictionary of 1755.

## GRETNA GREEN

Gretna Green is a village in Scotland just over the border from England. In 1754 Lord Hardwick's Marriage Act tightened up the laws regarding getting married. But this Act applied only to England. It did not apply to Scotland where the only legal requirement was a simple declaration to be made by both parties before two witnesses. Moreover, the English Act also stated that the marriage of a person under twenty-one was not valid unless the parents had given their consent.

After the passing of the 1754 Act many young people in England defied their parents and fled to Scotland to be married there. And Gretna Green became a favourite centre because of its proximity to the English border.

This is a very brief summary, but the legal requirements, and the often very colourful details of the various marriages are given in the following little excellent book. *Gretna Green. Scotland's Gift to Lovers,* by Olga Sinclair. Dove House, 1997.

In *The Statistical Account of Scotland* published in the 1790s, Gretna is spelled *Graitney* but Jane Austen spells it *Gretna* and I have followed her example.

## ROBERT BURNS AND THE FRENCH REVOLUTION

Robert Burns (1759-1796) is Scotland's national poet. He spent the last few years of his life in Dumfries, where he worked as an exciseman. His last house is now a museum.

Burns wrote mainly in Scots, but a few of his poems, including *The Cotter's Saturday Night,* are written partly in standard English. Unfortunately the rich language of his poems is now all but lost and understood only by scholars and linguists but all really good collections of his poems are accompanied by glossaries. But comprehension apart, Burns had such a good sense of rhythm that his poems have a music of their own.

Burns was often indiscreet and he was warned that this could endanger his official position with the Excise.

One of his more ill-considered actions was to carve some verses about the royal family (the house of Hanover) on the windows of an inn at Stirling. The verses end as follows. *An idiot race, to honour lost – Who know them best, despise them most.* Not the best way to advancement in the 18th century.

Burns' lack of judgement was to lead to some serious allegations in the early 1790s. Abroad there was the French

357

Revolution and at home there was the Society of the Friends of the People pressing for reforms. The Government panicked and thought that Britain was on the verge of a revolution similar to the one in France. There was a series of sedition trials and sentences of transportation to Australia.

As a Government servant it was unwise for Burns to make political statements or show any sympathy for the Jacobins. But there were further reckless acts from Burns and he was accused of joining a crowd in the Dumfries Theatre in singing *Ca ira*, the song of the French Revolutionaries. Shortly after this Burns was informed by his superior officer that he had received an order from the Excise Board to enquire into Burns' political conduct and to examine the charge that he was 'a person disaffected to the Government.' Burns managed to clear himself but the incident showed him just how careful he had to be.

Robert Burns was an animal lover. Cruelty to animals always incensed him and when a hare, which had been shot, limped past him, he vented his anger in the poem *The Wounded Hare*. Another poem which shows his concern for the animal kingdom is *To a Mouse*.

Robert Burns and his diamond stylus are well documented. Details are found in almost any biography of Burns. The Stirling window verses are in every complete collection of Burns' poems.

Before moving to Dumfries Burns lived at Ellisland, a village a few miles away. Sometimes he would not be able to get back to Ellisland at night and in that case he would stay at the *Globe Inn* Dumfries. The bedroom where he used to stay has been kept as it was in his day. On the window are some verses which he carved.

Burns' birthday, the 25th January, is celebrated and Burns suppers are held all over Scotland. Traditional food is eaten including the haggis which is piped in and *Address to the Haggis* recited. Burns refers to it as the *great chieftain o' the pudding race*. Charlotte parodies this famous line in her story about the jellyfish when she refers to *truly a great chieftain of the jellyfish race.*

The poem *Tam o' Shanter,* which Charlotte so admires, is one of Burns' best known works. It is a long dramatic and humorous narrative telling how an Ayrshire farmer escaped from witches when returning home late one night.

The Dumfries theatre was built while Burns was living in Dumfries and Burns was a frequent attender. The theatre is still standing and is now the headquarters of an amateur dramatic society.

## DUMFRIES IN THE 18th CENTURY

There is an excellent if rather brief description of Dumfries in the *Statistical Account of Scotland* – the First Account published in the 1790s. The Statistical Account was the idea of Sir John Sinclair. Ministers all over Scotland were asked to write accounts of their parishes. The entry for Dumfries was written by the Reverend William Burnside.

The *Statistical Account of Scotland* can be downloaded and accessed free of charge from the website of Edinburgh University. The address is **http://www.edina.ac.uk/**

More detail is given in *A History of Dumfries* by William McDowall, first published in 1867.

A quick visual reference is provided by the three dimensional map upstairs in the Robert Burns Centre.

## THE MID STEEPLE OF DUMFRIES

In 1703 the magistrates of Dumfries decided to build a new town house. This was to act as a repository for the burgh records and the town's arms and ammunition, a prison, and a council chamber. (The council eventually decided to meet elsewhere).

At the end of the 18<sup>th</sup> century, the ground floor housed the weigh house and the town guard house. On the first floor were the meeting rooms and council offices. This was also the part used as the court house.

The Mid Steeple was also used as a prison and there may have been prison cells on the second floor. There could have been more cells on the ground floor – in the part which juts out on the northern side and which is now occupied by a shoe repairer's shop.

The Mid Steeple is a prominent feature of present day Dumfries. It is a sandstone building with a spire and steeple. The main entrance is at first floor level, reached by an external staircase.


## THE BRIDGEND OF DUMFRIES

The Bridgend was a village on the western side of the River Nith. Although just on the other side of the river the magistrates of Dumfries had no authority there as it was beyond the burgh boundaries and in another county. This fact resulted in many Dumfries criminals fleeing across the river and taking refuge in the Bridgend, which was sometimes compared with the London Alsatia – that no go area and haunt of criminals mentioned by Sir Walter Scott in the *Fortunes of Nigel*.

This view was given credence by an oft quoted statement by the London magistrate Sir John Fielding who stated that his constables could pursue a criminal the length and breadth of Britain unless he found refuge in the Gorbals of Glasgow or the Bridgend of Dumfries.

But the Dumfries citizens found a way of turning the Bridgend to their advantage. They often used it as a dumping ground for their own incorrigible criminals, who would be tied to a cart, driven over Devorgilla Bridge, and released in the Bridgend.

In his *The History of Dumfries* (first published 1867) William McDowall describes the position regarding the position of the Bridgend. He considered Fielding's statement to be exaggerated as there were times when the authorities could enter and search the Bridgend. But once there, they experienced other difficulties. Under the Bridgend was a labyrinth of cellars and tunnels, a perfect hiding place for any refugee. There are even rumours that there was a tunnel under the Nith.

These cellars were useful in another way too. Illicit whisky distilling was one of the industries of the Bridgend, and the network of underground cellars provided an ideal place for it.

But apart from these illegal activities, the Bridgend was in many ways, just an ordinary village with many people living there and working at perfectly normal occupations. And living conditions in the Bridgend were better than many in the more respectable Dumfries just over the river. Dumfries had wide streets such as the High Street and Irish Street with their fine town houses. But in between these streets were the closes with their windowless hovels built back to back. The cramped closes were a magnet for germs and disease. By contrast the Bridgend had wide streets backing onto green fields. True there were perhaps too many inns, taverns and dung-heaps. But then the latter applied to many places in Scotland in the 18th century – and not just the Bridgend of Dumfries.

Many retired smugglers took up residence in the Bridgend, also many gypsies who were tired of the open road and who wanted to settle down. McDowall mentions one gypsy in particular – a Ryes Aitken who, at one time, more or less ruled the Bridgend. Unfortunately I have not been able to find a reference to him anywhere else.

McDowall also mentions a little pamphlet by a Mr Forsyth, *Reminiscences of Maxwellton.* This booklet is at present in the Ewart Libray, Dumfries and gives a useful picture.

The three dimensional map of Dumfries at the time of Burns in the Burns Centre gives a good impression of the Bridgend at the end of the eighteenth century.

## DEVORGILLA BRIDGE AND THE OLD BRIDGE HOUSE

This is the oldest bridge over the River Nith. It was built in the 13th century by the Lady Devorgilla and it is still standing. It is a substantial red sandstone bridge with six arches, although originally it probably had at least nine. In the 18th century tolls were levied on cattle being driven across.

(Devorgilla was the mother of John Balliol who reigned as King of Scotland for a short time after Edward I of England said that he had the best claim to the Scottish throne.) Devorgilla also founded the Cistercian monastery at New Abbey. Also Greyfriars Abbey, Dumfries and Balliol College, Oxford).

At the western side of the Bridge is the oldest house in Dumfries – the *Old Bridge House* – a red sandstone building which dates from the 17th century. It has had various occupants and uses but in the 18th century it was an inn. It is now a museum.

## THE CAUL

This is a small artificial waterfall just below Devorgilla Bridge. It was built to give power to the grain mill. In the eighteenth century, especially in the summer and at low tide, there would be islands in the Nith just opposite the mill and McDowall describes how the local washerwomen used to spread their clothes over them and leave them to dry.

## THE NEW BRIDGE

At the end of the eighteenth century it was felt that Devorgilla's bridge was too narrow for the increased amount of traffic and so a new, wider bridge was built just up the river from the old bridge. This bridge was completed in the autumn of 1794. Then it was just referred to as *the new bridge* but now it is called the *Buccleuch Bridge* as it is at the foot of Buccleuch Street.

## THE ROBERT BURNS CENTRE

This is a large building just down the Nith from the Devorgilla Bridge. It was originally a grain mill but is now a kind of small museum devoted to Robert Burns. It also contains a cinema and restaurant.

Upstairs is the main Burns display area. It has, as a centrepiece, a three dimensional map – what I personally call a 'map-model' — of Dumfries at the end of the 18th century. There are tiny boats and lumber rafts on the Nith, and miniscule cattle and sheep at the markets on the Whitesands.

It shows, as no written text can do, the cramped conditions of the Dumfries closes. And thereby gives its own explanation for the cholerea epidemics of the nineteenth century.

I have long been fascinated by this 'map-model' in the Burns Centre.

## SMUGGLING

I have already said that many retired smugglers made the Bridgend their home. In his *The History of Dumfries* William McDowall mentions that the smugglers had a group of horses which took the contraband goods to their ultimate destinations – unaccompanied. These horses had an intrepid leader who was well able to deal with anyone unwise enough to try to stop it.

McDowall got this story by word of mouth. It has been repeated in countless later accounts of Solway smuggling. I have used it in *Solway Sleuth-Hounds* but I have embroidered it a little. I have made the leader a stallion who was being followed by his mares.

By the 1790s smuggling was past its heyday. This was partly because of the actions of the prime minister Pitt the Younger who reduced the duty on a wide range of articles thereby making smuggling much less profitable.

# CATTLE DROVING

Large numbers of the distinctive black cattle were bred and reared in Galloway. They were then sold and driven to southeast England, where they were fattened for the London markets. A great deal has been written about cattle markets and cattle droving. There are both contemporary accounts and modern versions.

To start with two examples from classical fiction. Firstly a short story by Sir Walter Scott *The Two Drovers*. Here Scott tells a story about a cattle drove from the Highlands to the Borders. Secondly, Robert Louis Stevenson started to write a novel about a French prisoner of war who escaped from Edinburgh Castle. *St Ives.* (Stevenson died before the novel was finished). In his flight to England St Ives travels part of the way with two drovers.

Now for contemporary factual accounts. As has already been mentioned, in the 1790s *The Statistical Account of Scotland* was first compiled. It was done by asking the minister of every parish to answer a questionnaire and write an account of his parish. Edinburgh University has now put the Statistical Account on the internet. The url is **http://www.edina.ac.uk/** In the account for the Burgh of Dumfries, mention is made of the weekly markets and the three annual fairs. Cattle were sold in Dumfries and then driven south.

In the various accounts for the Galloway parishes details are frequently given of the numbers and quality of the cattle. There is an interesting note at the end of the entry for Colvend and Southwick where the minister claims that sometimes farmers entrust their cattle to drovers who then fail to return with the money.

Another very useful contemporary account is *General View of Agriculture, State of Property and Improvements in the County of Dumfries* by Dr Singer. Published 1812.

A later description of the Dumfries cattle markets is given in *A History of Dumfries*, by William McDowall, first published in 1867.

Evidence of the cattle droves can still be seen in Dumfries. On the Mid Steeple, in the town centre, there is a metal plate giving the distance from Dumfries to various towns and cities in England. The distance is given to Huntington, 272 miles. Huntington was one of the destinations of the cattle droves. This chart was added to the Mid Steeple in 1827.

To move on to modern accounts. One very detailed and carefully researched study is *The Drove Roads of Scotland* by A.R.B. Haldane, published by Birlinn in 1997.

The above book covers the wide general picture, but for details of the trade in Dumfries and Galloway there is a particularly interesting chapter in *History of Annan and Dumfries, Volume II* by John A. Thompson, 1999. The chapter in question is *Chapter XVIII Cattle Droving and Farming'*

## WILLIAM CRAIK, PROPRIETOR OF ARBIGLAND

The Arbigland Estate lies on the shores of the Solway Firth, just down from Kirkbean village, which is approximately eleven miles south west of Dumfries.

For much of the 18th century, its proprietor was William Craik, a friend of Benjamin Franklin and one of the great agricultural 'improvers.' He introduced crop rotation and the use of fertilisers such as lime and marl.

He also developed a plough and a seed drill. Regarding livestock, he brought in Bakewell cattle to improve stock, and grazed Cheviot ewes on the hill pastures of Criffel.

(An old lime kiln is still in existence at Southerness. It looks like a large grassy mound but a little of the stonework can still be seen underneath the grass. It overlooks the thirteenth tee of Southerness Golf Course. But it was probably built by Richard Oswald, see below, and not Craik.)

William Craik lived to be over ninety.

John Paul Jones, who later became the founder of the American Navy, was the son of William Craik's gardener and was born on a cottage on the Arbigland Estate.

A natural son of William Craik became personal physician to George Washington.

## SALTERNESS OR SATTERNESS

Salterness is the original name of Southerness. The present name of the village is due to a mistake. The name Salterness refers to the fact that salt was once panned there.

A planned village was built in the 18th century by Richard Oswald, who hoped to mine coal. One of the mine shafts which was sunk can still be seen. It is beside the twelfth green of Southerness Golf Course. It has been flooded and now forms a deep pool. There is a willow bush growing beside it. It is marked by a notice saying *Danger. Deep water.*

(Richard Oswald was a personal friend of Benjamin Franklin who suggested to the British Government that he should be sent as an emissary to help to draw up a peace treaty to end the American War of Independence.)

The plan for a mine fell through and Salterness became a retreat for those wanting to enjoy the benefits of sea bathing which doctors were beginning to advocate for invalids and convalescents. The heyday of sea bathing at Salterness came later in the 19th century, but in the 1790s *Statistical Account of Scotland* it says

*It is now chiefly inhabited by persons who keep furnished rooms, to accommodate such as, during the season, come to it for the benefit of sea bathing.*

At Southerness there is a rocky point which juts out into the Solway. This divides the shore into two large bays. In the days when the Solway was a busy shipping thoroughfare, ships had to negotiate the twin hazards of the Barnhourie Sandbank and the Salterness rocks. In 1749 Salterness Lighthouse was built – the second oldest lighthouse in Scotland. At first it was just a tall tower without a light but in the 1790s a light was provided. At first this would probably just consist of a fire in an iron basket.

The entry in the first *Statistical Account* says that *This tower, at present, is of great advantage to the navigation of this coast, and would still be of greater advantage, were lights placed in it.*

Today Southerness Lighthouse still stands. And on the shore opposite it are some of the original white washed eighteenth century cottages. Just up from these cottages is a large hotel on the site of the house for the manager of the mine.

Apart from a few bungalows the rest of modern Southerness is dominated by caravans and chalets and there is a championship golf course.

A short history of Southerness was published in 1999 for Southerness Community Council. The details are, *Reflections on the Solway. Southerness, the Holiday Village with an Historic Background,* compiled by Richard F. Bickford.

## BARNHOURIE

The Barnhourie Sandbank lies south west of Southerness and, in the days when the Solway was a busy shipping thoroughfare, it was a hazard to sailors. Ships could be driven onto it and lie there helpless while the waves pounded them to destruction.

The legend of the Barnhourie mermaid is a well known piece of Solway folklore. A mermaid and her family lived in the seas around the Barnhourie Sandbank and they used to lead marooned sailors to safety along the channels between the many sandbanks.

But the mermaid had evil sisters and their singing would lure shipwrecked sailors to their doom.

## SAWNEY BEAN

According to legend, at the time of James I, Sawney Bean was the head of a family of cannibals who lived in caves in South Ayrshire and preyed on lonely travellers. But they were eventually discovered, captured and executed. Although a well known story there is some doubt as to its authenticity.

## THE JACOBITE REBELLION OF 1745

The Jacobite Rebellion of 1745 was the last attempt of the Stewarts to reclaim the throne from the reigning Hanoverians.

Prince Charles Edward Stewart landed on the west coast of Scotland with only seven men. He was hoping to win back the throne for his father. A few of the Highland clans joined him. At first Prince Charles had a modicum of success. He marched to Edinburgh and occupied it for six weeks and then he marched through England and got as far as Derby. But his expected support in England did not materialise and his army turned and marched back to Scotland to eventual defeat at the Battle of Culloden, 1746.

The Battle of Culloden has sometimes been portrayed, quite falsely, as a battle between the Scots and English. This is just wrong. Many Scots lowlanders fought on the government side. The support of Prince Charles was confined to a section of the Highlanders.

Nevertheless the government was alarmed and severe measures were taken to see that such a rebellion could never take place again. In brief this meant the destruction of the clan system and the traditional way of life of the Highlands. The Highlanders were disarmed and the clan chiefs lost most of their powers. The Highlanders were even forbidden to wear tartan. Which is why Callum's wife had to dye his plaid in Chapter 19.

In actual fact, the end of the power of the clan chieftains would probably have come about in any case. But the government Acts after 1745 certainly hurried things along.

One excellent book about the Jacobite Rebellion of 1745 is *Culloden* by John Prebble. Penguin 1967. It is well researched and much use is made of contemporary accounts.

As far as the actual campaign is concerned, John Prebble deals with only the latter part. But he also gives a comprehensive picture of the Highlands at the time with details of how the clan system worked. Then, after the Battle of Culloden, he uses primary sources to show the brutality with which the Duke of Cumberland's forces hunted down the Highlanders. Later Prebble gives details of the Jacobite trials, executions and transportations.

A more specialised book, but just as useful about the'45 is' *Damn Rebel Bitches* by Maggie Craig. Mainstream, 1997. This is, as the title suggests, an account of the part played by women in the Jacobite Rebellion. It is well researched and use has been made of both primary and secondary sources. A welcome addition to the many books on the '45.

Both John Prebble and Maggie Smith give details of the drawing of lots and the trials and executions of the Jacobite prisoners. And they both also give details of the ship, the *Veteran* which was captured by the French while transporting Jacobite prisoners to the American colonies.

In his *The History of Dumfries* William McDowall gives a very full account of the occupation of Dumfries by the retreating Jacobite Army.

## CLAN MACGREGOR

During the Middle Ages, in the Highlands of Scotland there were many disputes over land ownership and much fighting among the clans. The Clan Macgregor incurred the enmity of the powerful Clan Campbell, to whom they were forced to sell many of their lands. The Macgregors often plundered their neighbours' property and the Campbells had enough influence with the King to have laws passed against the unfortunate clan.

Things came to a head in 1588 when the Macgregors murdered one of the royal foresters. There were more reprisals against them and then in 1603, by an act of the Privy

Council, the clan was proscribed. All of the name of Macgregor were compelled, on pain of death, to adopt another surname. They were also forbidden to carry weapons and to meet in greater numbers than four at a time.

But the Macgregors survived and adopted various names from neighbouring clans. They supported the Stewarts in the Civil War and, after the Restoration, the various enactments against them were annulled, only to be renewed again under William III. It was not until 1774 that the laws against the Macgregors were finally abolished although in the years before this they had gradually been falling into disuse.

One of the best known members of the Clan MacGregor was the outlaw Roy Roy, who was immortalised in Sir Walter Scott's book of the same name.

## FLETCHER CHRISTIAN AND THE MUTINY OF THE BOUNTY

Fletcher Christian was born in what was then known as Cumberland. He attended Cockermouth Grammar School. He came from a wealthy and well-established Cumberland family. There was another branch of the Christian family in the Isle of Man.

Fletcher Christian became the leader of what is probably the best known mutiny in British history.

In 1787 the HMS *Bounty* set sail for Tahiti under the command of Captain William Bligh. His mission was to collect samples of the breadfruit plant. It was hoped that breadfruit could be used as food for the slaves in the West Indies.

Two years later in 1789, after collecting the breadfruit, and after leaving Tahiti, some of the crew mutinied under the leadership of the first mate, Fletcher Christian. Bligh, with some of the crew who had remained loyal to him, was put aboard a small boat and set adrift. Bligh was a magnificent sailor and he managed to get his men to safety to Timor – a distance of over three thousand miles.

Meanwhile Christian took the *Bounty* and sailed, first back to Tahiti where he took on board some of the islanders, and then to the isolated Pitcairn Island where he had the *Bounty* burned. Christian then set up a little community on Pitcairn Island.

It is not quite certain what happened after that. Probably Christian and most of his men died a few years afterwards. But there is a story that Christian actually managed to get back to Britain. Coleridge is believed to have got the inspiration for his narrative poem *The Ancient Mariner* from the plight of Fletcher Christian.

One of Fletcher Christian's descendants has written an account of the Mutiny from Fletcher's point of view. His book is particularly interesting for the first section. Here he goes back to the family's roots in Cumberland and gives the family tree. Later he gives a detailed picture of Tahiti and the lives of the islanders. In the last section he dismisses the theory that Fletcher could ever have returned to Britain.

This book is *Fragile Paradise* by Glynn Christian.

Many, many books have been written about the Mutiny of the Bounty, both fact and fiction. There is also an excellent web site – the *Lareau Web Parlour* with a sub site devoted to the *Bounty*. This can be found at

http://www.lareau.org/bounty.html

## SCOTTISH LAW

I was fortunate in finding an excellent primary source for the law of Scotland in the 18th century – a commentary written by one of the leading lawyers of the day. *Commentary on the Laws of Scotland regarding Crime* by Baron David Hume, first published in 1797.

An excellent secondary source is *Braxfield the Hanging Judge? The Life and Times of Lord Justice-Clerk Robert McQueen of Braxfield* by Brian D Osborne. Published in 1997 by Argyll Publishing.

## THE POSITION OF JUSTICE OF THE PEACE

A first rate description of the history of the position of Justice of the Peace is given in *All Manner of People. The history of the Justices of the Peace in Scotland* by Johan Findlay. Published by the Saltire Society, 2000.

## SMALL DOGS IN THE 18th CENTURY

Thomas Bewick, the Newcastle printer and engraver, has an engraving of a small dog. His picture is called *The Comforter*. It is a perfect reproduction of an 18th century papillon. Or a modern papillon, the only difference being that most modern papillons (except for a few known as phalenes) have erect ears while 18th century ones had drop spaniel ears. A touch of genius from Thomas Bewick. He included an inkstand and quill pen in the picture to give an indication of the dog's size.

In the 18th century such dogs were usually owned by the rich.

Marie Antoinette had papillons. She had one in her arms when she went to the guillotine and, just before her execution, she handed it to someone to look after.

# GLOSSARY

agent – a solicitor acting on a person's behalf

bannock – a round, flat cake of oats or barley

bawbee –  A small coin. Originally worth six Scots pennies it later came to mean a halfpenny

bent – rough, coarse seaside grass

bide – stay, wait

biggin – a building

caddy, caddying– A caddy was a servant. In Edinburgh in particular there were men and boys who hung around the streets to see if any visitors to the city needed assistance. They would help them with their luggage, hold their horses and help them to find accommodation. Acting in this way was known as caddying.

clachan – a small village in the Highlands of Scotland

cob — a smallish workhorse bred for pulling tinkler carts. Sometimes loosely referred to as a pony. If a cob is black and white or brown and white it is referred to as a coloured cob.

daunder – a stroll

deid – dead

dominie – a schoolmaster

factor – the manager of an estate

fashed – vexed, worried, troubled

gadgi – the Galloway tinkler-gypsy word for house dweller

Galloway pony – the native breed of pony. Small — about thirteen or fourteen hands — sturdy, sure-footed and tractable, Galloways were often used by tinklers and gypsies. And, because they were usually dark in colour, by smugglers. The Galloway pony is now extinct but the nearest modern equivalent is the fell pony.

gang – go

gars – makes

grue – shiver or shudder from fear

gars me grue – makes me shudder

gellie – a gypsy word for a kind of rough tent

gourie – a gypsy word for girl or lass

grieve – a foreman or supervisor on a farm A grieve was a farm manager whereas a factor was an estate manager.

grue – shudder,

(gars me grue – makes me shiver)

havers – nonsense

kist – chest

kittle – tricky, difficult

laird – a landowner

lairdship – estate

licht – light

Luce Bay – a large bay at the western end of the Solway Firth. It is bordered by the western shore of the southern part of the Mull of Galloway.

lug -- ear

messan – a small dog

rooskie – the gypsy word for basket

screen – a kind of small plaid worn by women. It could be worn either over the shoulders as a shawl or pulled over the head like a scarf.

siccar – sure, certain

sleekit – sly, cunning

smeddum – a combination of courage, determination, resourcefulness and commonsense

siller — money, silver

skelp – spank

spae – foretell, tell the future

Steenie – an old Scots contraction for Stephen

stirk – bullock, steer

soutar – shoemaker

tacksman – a leaseholder, a tenant farmer. A clansman who leased land from the chief and who was a man of importance in the clan

tirling pin – door latch

waur – worse

wheest – Be quiet. Hush

# ABOUT THE AUTHOR
## Mary S Moffat

**http://www.marysmoffat.co.uk**

*Mary writes*

The above photograph shows me with Rooskie when he was nine months old.

I have an M.A. degree with second class honours in history from Glasgow University and I have worked both as a teacher and a schools librarian.

Now I am putting my experience to good use in acting as Children's Review Editor to the Historical Novel Society. I have also compiled a Bibliography of Historical Fiction for Children which I have put on my own personal website where it can be accessed and downloaded free of charge. It is not just a list of books. There are detailed and comprehensive notes on all the books mentioned. These notes are not reviews in the usual sense. Rather than passing judgement I aim to give an idea of the style and content of the books so that potential readers can make up their own minds about what they want to read.

Regarding my own writing, I enjoy doing the historical research for the background of my stories. Wherever possible I like to use primary or original sources. For example, for *Solway Sleuth-Hounds*, I have been fortunate in getting commentaries on the laws of Scotland regarding crime written by one of the leading lawyers in the country — in 1797. I have also been using the newspapers of the time.

As well as being interested in history I am also interested in dog training and, with my papillons Moff and Dusty, have competed in both Obedience and Working Trials. Moff and Dusty both gained the coveted Kennel Club award of CDEx. (Companion Dog Excellent). I am now competing in the new dog sport of Heelwork to Music with Rooskie — who is called after the little dog in *Solway Sleuth-Hounds*.

In all my writing the actual geographical setting is very important. I was born and brought up in Glasgow. I did not like living in Glasgow and I still do not like big cities (I now live in a small country town.) As a child I read widely. I did not realise it then but I read to escape from Glasgow's grey streets. I read all Arthur Ransome's books and revelled in his descriptions of the Lake District and the Norfolk Broads.

Other favourites of mine were pony stories – little girls riding about the countryside. I also liked historical adventure stories and another of my favourite authors was Geoffrey Trease. Later I read the Waverley novels of Sir Walter Scott.

Another form of escape was found in going to the pictures. I liked historical films in technicolour, also westerns. I think I liked the latter for the scenery of the American west just as much as for the actual stories.

All this gave me a fascination for the mystery of windswept moorlands, rough mountains and wild coastlines. Not for me a tamed and civilised beach. I wanted somewhere where I could imagine smugglers landing in a deserted cove.

I am now able to spend much of my time in such places and they form the basis of much of my writing. But I like to think that I am more realistic about them now than when I was a child growing up in the big city of Glasgow.

My fascination with wild places was increased when I started to compete in Working Trials with my little dogs. While competing I travelled all over Britain — from Aberdeen in the north to Tunbridge Wells and Tewkesbury in the south. I was not seeing the big cities or usual tourist resorts. Instead I found myself in the forests or on the moors. As well as going for the actual competitions I also tried to find out about the part of the country I was in — both in the present and in the past. This was to have an influence on my writing.

My dogs also helped me in other ways. When I was working on *The Canine Cavalier* I explored Newmarket with my little Papillon Moff. We walked along the mysterious Devil's Dyke, tramped all over Newmarket Heath and climbed Warren Hill. Then, when I was writing *Ghost Dog of the Solway*, Moff and my older dog Dusty, took me for endless walks along the Solway shore. On these walks I would soak in the atmosphere and carefully plan out the details of the stories and wrestle with any problems with the plots.

I call my dogs my 'research assistants.'

Moff and Dusty both had long and happy lives but, sadly, they are no longer with us. But I now have Rooskie who has the Kennel Club Good Citizen Club certificates Bronze and Silver.

Rooskie is competing in the relatively new sport of Heelwork to Music. He has been taking the tests for the Progress Awards of the Paws and Music Association. He has also been competing in Events (in Heelwork to Music they are called Events and not shows) under Kennel Club regulations.

We both thoroughly enjoy Heelwork to Music. Instead of the older, more dominant methods of training, HTM trainers often use the newer methods of clicker training — which is much pleasanter for the dog as well as having an extra benefit for myself. It offers an insight into how dogs' minds work. And as the mystery of learning how to communicate with another species is a theme I am interested in, clicker training, as well as its successor bridge and target, is also helping my writing. That is not all. Personally I find HTM an excellent method of keeping fit. In particular it is helping my balance.

Dogs apart I am also interested in swimming, digital photography and machine knitting. I also tried step aerobics but that has rather fallen by the wayside since I started training Rooskie. Still I can use what I learned there in my HTM.

# Rooskie

*Take a Bow, Rooskie*

*Mary Writes*

Rooskie — who has given his name to the *Rooskie Press* — does Heelwork to Music and in the above photograph he is demonstrating the HTM pose, the bow. Sometimes known as the play bow as puppies do it naturally when playing.

This photograph was used as the basis of the logo of the Rooskie Press.

Rooskie was born in 1998. He is a little papillon. He has proved himself a wonderful friend and companion and he helps to keep me fit by taking me for long walks.

He has the Kennel Club Good Citizen Dog certificates bronze and silver. But more important, he has introduced me to the new canine sport of Heelwork to Music and we have travelled widely competing in Events. We both enjoy the training and I have also met many wonderful people in HTM. As well as competing we have also taken part in a concert.

I have concrete memories as many HTM Events are filmed and put on video or DVD — and I have Rooskie's routines saved on CDs which are kept and treasured.

Rooskie is called after the little dog in *Solway Sleuth-Hounds.* And the Rooskie in the book is modelled on my own little Rooskie.

Rooskie has made another contribution to *Sleuth-Hounds.* His full Kennel Club name is *Longcrags Rooskie* and I have used his prefix Longcrags for the name of the Laird's estate.

### Note on Rooskie's name

Rooskie is the Galloway Tinkler-Gypsy word for 'basket' and he is called that because he is small enough to go into a gypsy basket. The Rooskie in *Solway Sleuth-Hounds* is quite an important character in his own right. For more photographs of Rooskie, his own online diary, and much more go to my website at

**http://www.marysmoffat.co.uk/**

# ABOUT THE ARTISTS

**Evelyn
McKinnell**

Evelyn contributed the cover illustration and also the frontpiece — the picture of the Mid Steeple in 1790.

She spent five years training as a scientific illustrator and graphic designer at Hornsey Art College and Middlesex University in London where she obtained a B.A. Honours degree.

After twelve years studying and working in London Evelyn spent a further twelve years in Balloch by Loch Lomond with her husband John, a species adviser for Scottish Natural Heritage, and her son James.

Evelyn has had several solo exhibitions. She enjoys painting flowers, animals, birds and insects, and welcomes commissions for her work. She also likes to do portrait work. Her greeting cards are very popular too.

Among Evelyn's favourite artists are Fantin-Latour, Redoute, Durer, Waterhouse, Edward Lear and George Stubbs. She is very interested in children's book illustration and Edmund Dulac, Honor Appleton, Ernest Shepard and Quentin Blake are illustrators whose work she admires.

# Halla Whittier Valentine - DeLeon

Halla contributed the internal drawings of Lucy, Rooskie and Gretna's camp.

Halla Whittier Valentine-DeLeon is a model and an artist as well as a costumer. She received awards for her drawings as well as for mural work while still in school.

Born into a military family and a relative to the American poet John Greenleaf Whittier, Halla decided to pursue art at an early age. She received private lessons in oil painting and also attended the American College of Applied Arts in Westwood (Los Angeles ), California.

Her current expertise is designing and creating Renaissance as well as theatrical costuming. Halla and her husband, Durmel, live just south of Pasadena, California, with their Staffordshire bull dog Chai.